THE HILLS WERE JOYFUL TOGETHER

Roger Mais

HEINEMANN

Heinemann International Literature and Textbooks
a division of Heinemann Educational Books Ltd
Halley Court, Jordan Hill, Oxford OX2 8EJ

Heinemann Educational Books (Nigeria) Ltd
PMB 5205, Ibadan
Heinemann Educational Boleswa
PO Box 10103, Village Post Office, Gaborone, Botswana
Heinemann Educational Books Inc
361 Hanover Street, Portsmouth, New Hampshire, 03801, USA

LONDON   EDINBURGH   MELBOURNE   SYDNEY
AUCKLAND   SINGAPORE   MADRID
PARIS   ATHENS   BOLOGNA   TOKYO

First published 1953
First published in the African Writers Series 1981

ISBN 0–435–98586–8

Set in 10pt Baskerville
Printed in Great Britain by
Cox & Wyman Ltd, Reading, Berkshire

92 93 94 10 9 8 7 6 5 4 3

Further Reading

SOME PUBLISHED WORKS BY ROGER MAIS

The Three Novels of Roger Mais (London: Jonathan Cape, 1970).

Brother Man (London: Heinemann, Caribbean Writers Series, 1974).

The Hills Were Joyful Together, Introduction by Daphne Morris (London: Heinemann, Caribbean Writers Series, 1981).

'The White-Wing', short-story in *Focus* (Jamaica, 1943).

'The House of the Pomegranate', long short-story in *Focus* (Jamaica, 1948).

'World's End', short-story in *Focus* (Jamaica, 1948).

'Men of Ideas', poem in *Focus* (Jamaica, 1948).

'The First Sacrifice', a play in *Focus* (Jamaica, 1956).

Face and Other Stories, May 1942 (Mais Collection, UWI Library, Mona).

And Most Of All Man, December 1942 (Mais Collection, UWI Library, Mona).

SELECTED CRITICAL READINGS ON MAIS

Brathwaite, Edward, Introduction to *Brother Man* (London: Heinemann, Caribbean Writers Series, repr. 1974).

Carr, W. I., 'Roger Mais – design from a legend', *Caribbean Quarterly*, XIII, 1 March 1967.

Creary, Jean, 'A prophet armed: the novels of Roger Mais', in *The Islands in Between*, ed. Louis James (London: Oxford University Press, 1968).

D'Costa, Jean, *Roger Mais: a critical study of The Hills Were Joyful Together and Brother Man* (London: Longman, Critical Studies of Caribbean Writers, 1978).

Grandison, Winnifred, 'The Prose styles of Roger Mais', *Jamaica Journal*, VIII, 1.

Hearne, John, 'Roger Mais: a personal memoir', BIM, VI, 1955.

Lacovia, R. M., 'Roger Mais and the problem of freedom', *Black Academy Review*, Fall 1970.

'Roger Mais: an approach to suffering and freedom', *Black Images*, I, 2, Summer, 1972.

Moore, Gerald, *The Chosen Tongue* (London: Longman, 1969).

Ramchand, Kenneth, 'The achievement of Roger Mais', in *The West Indian Novel and its Background* (London: Faber, 1970).

An Introduction to the Study of West Indian Literature, Nelson Caribbean, 1974, ch. 2.

Williamson, Karina, 'Roger Mais: West Indian novelist', *Journal of Commonwealth Literature*, December 1966, no. 2.

THE HILLS WERE JOYFUL TOGETHER

The floods clapped their hands, Alleluya!
And the hills were joyful together . . .

(*Words for a revival song, based upon a
passage from the psalms.*)

The scene is a yard in Kingston, Jamaica.
Time: Today.

CHARACTERS IN THE STORY

DITTY JOHNSON   Daughter of GOODIE and PUSS-JOOK JOHNSON. This one is a tart.

RAS   He is tall, angular and bearded. He lives with CASSIE, in the yard; he pushes a handcart for a living, and is learning to read and write.

CASSIE   She is along with RAS. She has an idiot son, PATTOO, and scarcely ever grumbles at life.

ZEPHYR   A prostitute. She is continually being embarrassed by the bigness of her heart.

EUPHEMIA   She is SHAG's woman, a seductive creature, and the cause of much trouble in the yard.

BAJUN MAN   He is EUPHEMIA's lover, and everybody in the yard knows it but SHAG.

SHAG   He is EUPHEMIA's man. A quiet, unobtrusive fellow, until he turned the tiger loose.

BEDOSA   CHARLOTTA's husband, and father of MANNY and TANSY. He was scared of his own shadow, and compensated by bullying his wife.

MASS MOSE   An old cobbler who played on the clarinet.

TANSY   Daughter of BEDOSA and CHARLOTTA, aged thirteen. She wanted to go back to school.

MANNY   Son of BEDOSA and CHARLOTTA. He was always getting into trouble, until he found out why. When he did, he was up to his neck in the worst mess of all.

WILFIE   Another boy in the yard, about MANNY's age; seventeen. They have plenty in common, including DITTY's affection.

CHARLOTTA   The wife of BEDOSA, and mother of MANNY and TANSY. She has plenty of patience and courage and needs it all.

SURJUE   He is REMA's man. He plays the horses and rolls his own. He is impatient with life, he wants to get on.

FLITTERS   His protuberant lips earned him this nickname. He is a slick one, and REMA doesn't trust him, but SURJUE doesn't let her meddle in his affairs.

REMA   She is SURJUE's woman; a pretty sambo girl.

BUJU ⎫ These are a couple of SURJUE's friends. They belong to the
CRAWFISH ⎭ underworld.

THE THREE SISTERS OF CHARITY   They belong to a religious cult.

CUBANO   Another character from the underworld.

LENNIE   He is in love with ZEPHYR, who thinks him a real nice boy.

NANINE   A girl about nineteen who lives in the yard.

PATTOO   CASSIE's idiot son. He is quiet and inoffensive until he is aroused.

7

BOOK ONE

1　　THE YARD COUNTED among its ramshackle
structures an old shaking-down concrete nog
building with the termite-ridden wood frame
eating away until only a crustacean shell under the dirty white
cracked and blistering paint remained.

This building stood on the south side. A row of barrack-like
shacks at back and another row of barrack-like shacks to the
north, with the crazily-leaning fence out front, enclosed what was
once a brick-paved courtyard in the middle of which there was
an ancient circular cement cistern and above it a standpipe with
a cock leaning all to one side and leaking continually with a weary
trickle of water that was sometimes stronger than at others,
depending on the pressure from the main outside.

In the middle of the crazy front fence, on top of a dilapidated
brick step that had belonged to the premises before the great
earthquake, was a little paint-blistered, wry-hinged, buck-toothed,
obscenely grinning, tin-patched, green-and-white gate.

Near the cistern in the yard a gnarled ackee tree reached up
scraggy, scarred, almost naked-branched to the anaemic-looking
sky. A thrifty black-mango tree leaned over the southern half of
the front fence, its branches lopped back every so often to keep
it from overhanging the narrow sidewalk. A prickly lime tree
struggled up from among the earthed-in, seamy, rotting bricks in
the yard; it stood against the northern row of wooden shacks right
outside the room where the three Sisters of Charity lived, and
crooned and gossiped and cooked and sing-sang sad hymns of
wailing the livelong day.

Immediately across the street from the yard was a row of little,
dowdy, huddled-together shops shut in on one side by a two-
storey building that was a bar with rooms above, and on the other
by an ironmongery-drygoods-and-provision store that carried a
small notions department and a soft drink counter.

The sign-painter who had one of these small shops had worked
on the walls of all of them, so that from a fast-moving car they looked

like a row of playing card single-storey houses that a child had put together. He painted these signs at a special cut-rate, figuring it would be good advertising.

There were five of these small shops in the row. One of them flew a dirty little triangular red flag which indicated nothing more sinister than the fact that ice was sold here. It also sold newspapers as the tin sign said, and sweepstake tickets according to the amateur lettering on a piece of cardboard tacked on the wall. On the other side of the cardboard was a voluptuous Coco-Cola girl, but you couldn't know that because she had been tacked flat against the rough unfinished boards, right below one of the cross-eyed wooden windows that latched from inside.

The other three shops in the row were occupied by a cobbler, a tin smith, and a tailor, but the tailor-shop had lately given place to a fry-fish shop, and if you stood on the top tread of the brick step to the yard facing you, you could see the scaled, gutted and brined sprats hanging on a string to sun in the bit of space behind this shop. The sun made the bones of the little fish so brittle and crisp that when they were fried you ate them bones and all. Nobody bothered about the flies that buzzed them on the line, and the dust off the street and the dirt-yard that settled on them, for that was the way sprats had been handled from the morning of time.

Ditty Johnson, sitting on that top step now, slapped dingie flies on her bare legs, scratched the lumps that they raised with her finger nails to ease the itching, sometimes pulling her dress up her thighs, erased the white scratch marks against the smooth black skin with a spit-wet finger, and waited for the ice-shop to put out its flag.

Inside his room the bearded man, Ras, was stirring among the bundle of rags on the floor that was his bed. Cassie, his woman, had been up with the sun; she was roasting his breakfast now on a borrowed coal pot outside the door. Breakfast consisted of five fingers of plantain, peeled, and laid on the glowing charcoal embers around a chipped enamel pot of galloping bush tea; the pot had carried a hinged cover in the days of its glory when it had come off the ironmonger's shelf from among a row of prim-looking blue-banded enamelware; that was before the war.

Ras rolled over on his back, scratched himself all over, broke wind, made a face, getting the first taste of his mouth for the morning, hawked and spat in an earthenware yabba set beside him for the purpose, and knuckled his eyes coming out of sleep.

He sat up, grunted, eased himself over on one cheek of his bottom to make the wind come free, sighed, feeling better, stood up, tall, rangy, stretched his arms ending in knotted fists above his head, tidied his clothes about him, and stroked the tips of his fingers gently, thoughtfully, through his matted beard.

The sun had rolled high up in the sky already, for Ras, having no job to go to, could afford to lie abed late. The day's scuffling would start properly when the steam whistles screamed the noon hour above the steady roar of the city, drowning out the sounding automobile horns, the steady drag of tyres wearing at the asphalt, the hoarse gabble of gossip, the Sisters of Charity's sing-song crooning, the shout of voices going down the street.

Zephyr, who lived in one of the rooms in the concrete nog house, because she could manage to pay the higher rent, also lay abed late, for the reason that she did most of her business at night, although occasionally she had men in during the day.

There was a ring attached to a string attached to the blue-black spring curtain over the window right beside her bed. She clutched the ring between her great toe and the one next to it, getting it firmly with the third try, gave it a sharp tug and released it; the curtain rattled up the spring rod and let light into the room.

She sat up, felt with her feet for her slippers, looked at her fingers, saw that the purple nail-enamel was flaking off in patches, stood up in her thin lace-top nightie with the strap coming down the left shoulder, one big firm breast looking out; saw Lennie Risden through the open window grinning at her.

He whistled and said, 'Oh baby!'

She turned away from the window and went across to the wash basin to brush her teeth. She squeezed the tube of toothpaste in the middle so that it bulged at both ends, ejecting an inch of toothpaste on to the brush.

She had no time for Lennie, although he was always plaguing her. Funny she didn't want to sleep with Lennie . . . just couldn't see herself doing it . . . she had never stopped to figure it out. One time he had brought her his whole pay envelope . . .

he worked at the printery down the street . . . she had handed him back the pay envelope, smiling as though she didn't believe he meant it. . . .

'You fool around with that, some gal will take it off you.'

'Sure, that's what I mean, an' she's you.'

'No,' shaking her head, smiling so as not to make him take it hard.

'Go on. What's the matter now?'

'Don't you know?' giving him a look.

'You mean it — ? Awe, you're just kidding me.'

'It's true. Now don't be a sap, Lennie.'

The corner of his mouth puckered up, giving him a downright mean look.

'I guess there's something about me that just don't click with you.'

Why the hell did she go on holding out on him like that . . . something about Lennie, she wouldn't take him on . . . and Lennie knew . . . it burnt him up because she was — what she was, and she gave him the air . . . nice, clean-looking boy, good job, everything . . . but it was there, just the same . . . she had never stopped to figure it out.

She finished brushing her teeth, stuck the cap back on the toothpaste without screwing it on, slipped into a bright dressing gown that drooped like a thirsty flower and was slightly soiled at the neck line and the cuffs, and went out into the passage and down towards the bathroom.

But she found that Euphemia, who had two rooms across the passage with Shag, had got there first. Euphemia sang softly as she lathered herself in the tub.

Euphemia was a big, stolid girl, firm-fleshed and magnificently statuesque, but she acted a bit torpid with Shag. In the last few weeks, however, a subtle change had come over the girl. She had blossomed out like one of those big juicy mallow flowers that only opened fully when they had the full sun on them, as though the sun warmed their juices and brought them awake, and flaming and lusty with life. And it had happened only a comparatively short while back, since Bajun Man had started stealing looks at her.

Zephyr, who was alive to all that was going on around her,

though she kept what she knew strictly to herself, and never talked people behind their backs, noticed the warm glances that Bajun Man sent in Euphemia's direction from time to time, as they sat out under the shade of the mango tree in the yard and played dominoes — Bajun Man, Shag, Bedosa and Mass Mose. She saw these glances and knew that something was stirring in that big, frigid, statuesque body that had never come awake under the caresses of the patient, adoring, stupid, generous-hearted Shag.

And that was curious, too, because Bajun Man was short and squat with long hairy arms and a broad flat face, and he looked slow and dull. Not the sort of man you would think would arouse Euphemia, and make her turn and sigh into her pillow when she ought to be asleep. But there it was.

And it had been going on for weeks . . . showing all sorts of little signs . . . and everybody saw it, that is to say everybody except Shag.

She leaned against the bathroom door and whistled so that Euphemia would know she was there . . . and heard Euphemia stop singing to herself in the tub, and the splash of water swishing around as she stood up and let it run off her . . . and thought, wonder what'll happen when Shag finds out?

The singing started again, and Zephyr leaning against the bathroom door winced with the effort to contain herself, drawing up one foot behind her and holding on to the ankle, holding it tight against her buttocks as she did when she was a child in such cases of extremity, and said loud enough for the other woman to hear, and no mistake about it, 'Euphemia, I want to get in there.'

2   THE SUN HAD ROLLED up high and hot in the cloudless metallic sky that was the colour of new corrugated iron roofing; the light seemed to split up into a thousand flaky fragments as it flowed over the oily leaves of the lime tree; past that, and the shadow of the shacks, it lay like a starched white sheet across the rectangular yard.

The wind made a shushing sound going through the mango

tree, lifted the loose dust that covered the worn bricks and scattered sharp grit on the iron roofs of the shacks like dropping rain.

Dust blew on the clothes hanging to sun on the line, sprinkling them all over powdery grey like mildew, lifted them wetly flapping against each other, and let them fall again like loose sails luffing in the wind.

Tansy was out in the yard by the cistern under the standpipe washing clothes, and she ought to have been at school, only her mother, Charlotta, was always making her stop home to help her, and it turned out that almost every week Tansy, thirteen, and making the third grade already, had to wash for a family of four — Daddy Bedosa, Manny, going on seventeen, Charlotta, and Tansy herself.

Manny loafed into the yard now, his hands in his pockets, his bare toes deliberately scuffing up more dust, a leering ugly look on his face, coming from the gully behind the shacks at back of the yard, with Wilfie, a boy of about his own age, tagging along.

'. . . I found it down the gully by a stone, and you mind your own business now,' said Manny, looking mean.

'It's Pattoo's though,' said Wilfie, not wanting to rile the other, but getting his conscience into the open.

'He got his name on it? I'd like to see him try to get it from me even if it is his, that's all.'

'I know that knife, it's got a chip out of the handle where it fell and broke against a stone when he was practising throwing it to stick in a tree stump, and I always seen Pattoo carrying it around.'

'Oh, kiss-ass, man, I'm tired to hear you call the name of that pulp-eye son-of-a-bitch.'

'Well, what we going to do now? I tell you what, let's get our slingshots and go through the cemetery after birds.'

'Awe, them little nightingales ain't worth a big man's time, you bring back a passel of them they don't even make up into a stew.'

'Huh! You a big man now!'

'Yes. You know what I'm going to do? I'm going by myself alone down the gully, see, to meet that half-Chinese gal, Squiz-Eye, I was tellin' you 'bout, under the bridge. You want to know if I'm a man, you should be around. Only you won't be, 'cos I'm goin' alone. Get me?'

'Boy, you can go chasin' half-Chinese gals all over the place, I don't care. I guess I'll wait here for Pattoo, he won't be long now, an' I'll just ask him if he's lost his knife.'

'Good. An' then just let him come an' try to get it from me, the pulp-eye son-of-a-bitch with his ass out of doors.'

'Why you hate him like that, Manny, what he done you?'

'He don't done me nothing, he wouldn't miss his pass to done me somep'n boy, but I just can't stand the sight of him around.'

'I seen him give you half a sugar-bun the other day, though.'

'Yes. So what?'

'An' I seen you took it an' et it, that's all.'

'Why shouldn't I take it, ain't he give it to me?'

'I wouldn't take nothing from a guy I hated that bad — enough to talk about him the way you do. Why you always pickin' on him, I'd like to know.'

'Man, I don't even hate the guy — Awe, I'm gonna walk follow the gully down to the bridge — '

'An' stone Miss Angie's jew-plum tree, I know.'

'So you figure I'm not a man, eh? Well, I could show you somep'n would make you change your tune.'

'Awe, I didn't mean anything, Manny, just giving you a tease. Jeeze, I just seen a scorpion run under that stone.'

'Let's get him.'

'You could pry that brick loose with the knife. . . .'

'Hold everything now.'

'The biggest scorpion I ever seen . . . Go easy there, Manny . . . if he get you you'd be sorry the day.'

'Hold everything now . . . No ole scorpion is goin' get me, boy.'

'Biggest scorpion you ever seen.'

'I got it loosened up now. You take hold of it an' yank it out . . . I'll get him with the knife . . . Ready? . . . Go!'

'Look out! . . . Gee, what a bugger . . . watch that tail. . . .'

'Got him, all right . . . Look, Tansy, want to see a scorpion we killed under that brick?'

Manny balanced the scorpion on the blade of the knife and went towards Tansy with it, with a leer on his face. Tansy took one look over her shoulder, screamed, seeing him coming toward her with the scorpion and that look on his face, dropped the clothes she had been wringing between her hands, and ran toward the room.

Charlotta came out to the door and screamed louder than Tansy, 'What is it?' And Tansy clutched her and wriggled round behind her with Charlotta trying to shake her off. Manny came on grinning, with that mean look on his face.

'What's that you got there, Manny? Drop it! Drop it this minute, you hear?'

'It's only a dead scorpion, Ma, it wouldn't hurt anyone, Tansy's a little fool.'

'You take that thing an' throw it down the gully, dead scorpion or no dead scorpion I'm scared of them ugly things too ... *E-e-e-k!* You throw that scorpion on me, Manny,' she bent down, picked up a chunk of firewood from the pile by the door, 'I'll break your dam head open, so help me God!'

'Awe Ma, I was only jokin'. Imagine anybody scared of an ole dead scorpion.'

'Go throw it down the gully now. Do like I say this minute an' don't stand there grinning at me.'

Tansy came from behind Charlotta as Manny turned sulkily away, Wilfie going after him, looking down at his toes.

'Last week he put a lizard down my back, Ma,' said Tansy.

'Don't mind him honey, it's only his little joke.'

'Joke!' said Tansy. 'It was a big green lizard, and it was live.'

'That's a shame now. It coulda bit you.'

'I screamed and tried to run and he held on to me.'

'Manny mustn't do these things ... but he don't mean no harm, honey, he's just full of life.'

'An' Pattoo hit him with a stone to make him let go.'

'What did Manny do?'

'He knocked down Pattoo, an' kicked him in his belly, that's what he do.'

'I don't want him to start no fighting with the people in the yard now.'

'You ought to talk to him good, Ma. He don't listen to no one, 'ceptin' you.'

'I don't want him to get the people in the yard up against us. Fighting the people you have to live with is a fool thing to do.'

16

'It woulda ended bad maybe, but Zephyr grabbed him by the arm an' pitched him away.'

'Zephyr shouldn't do that. She shouldn't try to fight with Manny.'

'Oh, Zephyr can handle him, don't worry.'

'Not if he has got a knife on him. He don't stop at anything, that Manny, when he gets real mad. But he don't mean it, an' he's like to be sorry afterwards.'

'Sorry afterwards don't mend anything, Ma.'

'I know, me child. Sometimes I'm scared what's goin' to happen to Manny, an' your father don't say nothin' to him at all.'

'He hates Pattoo. It's his knife he's got. Says he found it down the gully, but I know better, an' Wilfie too.'

'I'll make him give it back. I don't want him to have no knife.'

'You talk to him good, Ma.'

'All right, Tansy. You get back to washin' them clothes now. You leave it to me.'

'You not careful he get us all into bad blood with the people in the yard.'

'He's not really wicked, he don't mean any harm.'

'Hm!'

'Don't talk like that, honey, your own brother, too.'

'He ain't no brother of mine, Ma, an' I wish I didn't have to stay home from school.'

'I've got to have somebody help me. You don't start grumbling now. I make these patties an' take them out to sell, an' it helps to buy you clothes.'

'I wish people didn't have to work so hard.'

'Hush you' mouth, child, you don't know what you talkin' 'bout.'

'I don't want to stop away from school.'

'You lazy, that's what. Talkin' all that foolishness, people shouldn't work.'

'I didn't say . . .'

'You hush you' mouth now, an' do what you have to do.'

Manny and Wilfie sat on a big stone by the side of the gully behind the shacks. It was dry now, but when it rained it was a roaring torrent carrying down chicken coops and latrines and dead pigs and even people's houses with it clear out to sea. Scrub and wiry grass and even trees grew on either side, but the bottom was dry sand and silt.

They were always finding things down the gully; you could find almost anything there. People were throwing things away down the gully all the time, people who lived on the gully banks for miles and miles where it twisted and writhed and took its tortuous course through the heart of the city, starting in the wash of the foothills, in the basins that caught the water that drained away from the part-denuded hills when it rained, and went clear out to sea.

When you came by something that people didn't know how you came by it you could always say you found it down the gully. One day Ras even found a goat dragging a chewed-off piece of rope down there. And it was night, and he butchered it and sold the unstamped hunks of meat to the people in the yard, and to people who lived in other yards like this down the street, who came secretly and bought some of the meat and carried it away wrapped in old newspaper at the bottoms of their baskets, with other things piled on top of it, because it was a prison charge to sell illicitly slaughtered meat in the city these days. They would fine you, that is, but the fine was so high that you just went to jail.

Sunlight lay along the scalded limbs of the trees and set the coppery dropping leaves blazing with colour that was warm like the upward licking flames of a wood fire in the open yard.

The breeze whished and whished through the trees and scrub and dry seeding wiry grass, and a heap of old tin cans caught the light that licked and flecked them where they hadn't rusted yet, and a flung pebble among them would make a sound like the clink of coins.

A nightingale warbled from the blazed limb of a copper-berried lignum vitae tree, and a broken plate caught in a lipped crock of shaling limestone rock looked like a letter somebody had read and ripped up fine as confetti and left to lie among the close-cropped sun-scorched grass.

Wilfie flicked another pebble and it clinked among the tin cans with a brash metallic sound, and sifted quick new glints of sunlight over them that lit on a thousand facets an instant and went out as the shifting pile of tin cans settled down.

Manny eased into a new position on the rock, hitched one leg up, put his arms around it, hugging it to him, and let his chin rest upon his knee.

'Squiz-Eye gimme the sign to meet her; came to the side door of the shop as I was goin' down the lane.'

'Cho, all you think about is chasin' gals these days.'

'Boy, they chase me.'

'There's john-twits an' ground doves feedin' on the grass seeds over by the cemetery, I seen them.'

'You got nothin' on your mind but chasin' after little birds with a slingshot, you gimme a gripe.'

'You make a pass at Squiz-Eye, the Chinaman ketch you, he mess you up fine with his meat chopper, I tell you.'

'Grabbed a-hold of her comin' across the bridge one night an' backed her up against the pillar, she was crazy for me.'

'You like 'em half-Chinese.'

'You bet I do. They is — silky like a cat.'

'An' the thing turned cross-ways, they say. . . .'

'You crazy with the heat.'

'If Ras was to ketch you knockin' Pattoo around he'd lick the hell outa you.'

'Ras a no-good, hulkin', small-time scuffler, I'm not scared of him. If you can keep it quiet, I'll tell you something, though.'

'What?'

'You gonna squeal?'

'No.'

'You think I'm not a man, no?'

'Awe, forget it, you back on that again?'

'I can prove it to you.'

'How?'

'Plenty.'

'You got some hair comin', that's nothin', I got it too.'

'Hair on my ass, you lissen to me. . . .'

'Well? How you gonna prove it?'

'I got a dose.'

'You got what?'

'A dose boy, a real mansize dose.'

'Wha — you think that's something? You think that makes a man outa you?'

'Sure it does. It's the real man-sick I got, I'm tellin' you.'

'Jesus God, I thought you knew better than that. You better tell your pappy. . . .'

'What for?'

'He'll tell you what to do.'

'Don't need nobody tell me what to do.'

'You goin' to keep it?'

'Sure. Why not? It's the sickness men get, didn't you know?'

'I thought you knew better than that, Manny, didn't anybody ever tell you?'

'Don't want nobody tell me nothing. I know what I know. Tell you somep'n, the girls don't figure you nothin' until you got it.'

'They tell you so?'

'You don't talk about it with them. They just kinda know.'

'Jesus God, Manny, you don't know nothin' at all. Man, that's 'cos you never went to school.'

'I did go to school, too, but I quit.'

'You quit so far back you don't know a thing.'

'What's schoolin' got to do with this? You gimme the gripes. Want me to show it to you?'

'Look, I'm goin' up to the yard now, see you later. Somep'n I iust remember.'

'What's the matter, you feelin' sick?'

'Guess I'll be all right, must be somep'n I et.'

'You look sick like you want to puke. I wonder . . . you're a pukin' little pickney, that's what you are.'

Manny's laughter shamed him, did something to his sprouting manhood, made him hot and angry like he wanted to fight. But he moved away up toward the shacks, said over his shoulder:

'Guess it must be something I et, that's all.'

Up at the yard Tansy was wringing out clothes and hanging them on the line to sun. She took the pieces of clothes one by one between her hands, all the muscles of her face shut tight with the effort of wringing as much water as she could out of them until her arms hurt at the shoulders, sighed: 'Oh God, oh God, wish people didn't have to work so hard.'

Charlotta was singing as she worked away at making her

pastries. The patty tin was scrubbed clean inside and outside an sunning on the step.

To rest her arms a bit from the wringing, Tansy unknotted the handkerchief that tied her head, shook it out, folded it afresh, flipped it up and about her head, tied it securely again, sat down on the side of the cistern, drew up her toes and stretched them out until she felt the flex of the muscles way up her calves.

She stood up, stretched herself a little, and bent over the wash tub again.

Got to get these clothes wrung out and pinned on the line . . . scared of scorpions and green lizards and things, no foolin' . . . Ma ought to talk to that Manny real hard . . . that was her now, singing over the bake-sheets she was puttin' in an' takin' out the oven . . . hot patties . . . plenty of pepper an' high seasonin' to make your mouth-water come . . . an' curry with the wet rolled oats to make 'em stretch. . . .

> Lo, when the day of rest was past
> The Lord, the Christ, was seen again;
> Unknown at first, he grew to sight:
> 'Mary' he said — she knew him then:
> *Alleluya.* . . .

Singing it soft and sweet . . . Charlotta used to sing in a choir when she was a country girl . . . always led the singing when they had revival in the yard . . . better than them three ole crows Miss Katie, Miss Evangie, Miss Mattie, the White Sisters of Charity . . . John Crows, that's what they were, just three dressed-up John Crows.

> And dimly in the evening light
> He joined two friends who walked alone —
> A stranger, till he stayed to sup;
> He brake the bread, and he was known:
> *Alleluya.* . . .

Lizards crawling down her back made her screaming mad and Manny knew it . . . he was just cruel mean . . . ought to speak to him real hard, Ma . . . Oh God, would she ever be finished with washin' clothes . . . wish people didn't have to work so hard. . . .

The sun had rolled higher up in the sky . . . and it seemed to stand still now as it beat down on the back of her neck where she had a mole, and the shadows cast by the shacks on this side seemed to shrink as though the sunlight was drinking them up . . . so that you could almost see them shrinking before your eyes . . . and the leaves of the lime tree had lost their oily look now and turned a darker green.

'. . . if it's a sin let it pass Jesus, but I wish it just the same.'

3   SURJUE SAT ON the edge of the bed and studied the race card that was open on his knee. He had a bland, large, good-looking face, with the lips turning up slightly at the corners, giving him a good-natured, easy-going appearance. He was generously built, his frame was plumped out a bit, but not fat, he was healthy-looking, and abundant with life.

Flitters . . . it was Manny who gave him the nickname . . . 'Gwan! you' mout'-lip favour flitters' . . . he meant fritters . . . ducking the long swing the man took at him, ran out through the gate into the street, but it was so apt it raised a laugh . . . the name had stuck and Spencer had grown reconciled to it, everybody called him Flitters now, and it didn't matter any more . . . Flitters chewed gum now and studied Surjue's face as he bent over the open race card on his knee, tracing out the lines of fine print with his finger as he read.

'In the first race it should be a close thing between Rock Water and Bendigo,' said Surjue.

'Rock Water is carrying four pounds more weight than Bendigo, though,' Flitters said.

'You forget,' said Surjue, looking at him, 'that Rock Water is out of Maud Mahal by Rockstone. 'Member the horse Rockstone? He was a sprinter.'

'He wasn't no sprinter in the six furlong more'n Roxita as a two-yers old, though.'

'Who's talkin' about Roxita?'

'I'm sayin' she's the dam of Battle Song, man.'

'An' who's Battle Song?'

22

'Colt out of Roxita by Bonamis, another flyer . . . an' a stayer, too, Bonamis.'

'Who's ever heard of Battle Song? You put your money on Rock Water an' leave it to Gordon, don't you take your eye off that jockey, man.'

'Mm-hm.'

'What you mean, mm-hm?'

'Just that.'

'You sound like you was doubtful about the tip I give you. Well, do as you dam well please, it's your money you'll be throwin' away.'

'Keep you' shirt on, man, I'm listenin' to you.'

'I been sellin' racin' tips for years. Look at me. You think I'd be out on top if I didn't know what I was sayin'? An' I'm *givin'* you Rock Water for nothin', you gotta nerve.'

'Okay. I didn't say I wasn't goin' to buy Rock Water, did I say that now?'

'That's better talk. Light one of them cigarettes for me.'

Flitters took his hand away from stroking the side of his face with his long fingers to light another cigarette from the business end of the one he was smoking.

'You know I'll do anything you say, Surjue. Cigarette?' holding it out to him.

'Light it for me,' said Surjue, without looking up from studying the race book on his knee.

'I done lit it.'

'Like Shag, I been rollin' me own lately, but I'm clean out of the makin's now.'

He laid aside the race programme, and took a long drag at the cigarette, closing his eyes as he sucked the smoke in, opening them again with a look of infinite satisfaction as he let it out.

'Talkin' about Shag,' said Flitters, shaking ash off his cigarette on to the floor, and painstakingly brushing the least evidence of it from his new brown tweed drape trousers, 'if he don't look out sharp he'll be wearin' a jacket for somebody one of these days.'

'You mean about Euphemia an' Bajun Man?'

'That's who I'm talkin' about. Ain't you seen it you'self?'

'Who hasn't?'

'Not Shag.'

'Well, it's right under his nose, he could smell it if he was blind.'

Flitters giggled. 'That's good, 'bout he could smell it if he was blind.'

'The sucker.' Surjue spat through the open window.

'It makes me sick like that to see a man made a sucker by a woman,' he said.

'Yes. I get what you mean.'

'Anyway it's his dose of salts, he can take it an' like it.'

'He won't like it, but he'll take it just the same.'

'Now take me an' Rema. I make her do the worryin' see?'

'That's the way it should be, I reckon, Surjue. It's the man wears the cojones, like they say.'

'It's me has the cojones in this here set-up, anyway. She's scared to death I might walk out on her some day. Yes, sir. An' I want it should be that way.'

'You got the right idea, Surjue.'

'You dam right, I have. The other way about you'll be wearin' another man's jacket sure as God made little apples.' Surjue carefully broke off the ash with his fingers, dropped it through the window, considered the end of his cigarette a minute, and shook his head.

'You're born lucky, Surjue, things just naturally come your way.'

Surjue looked at him quickly.

'What you mean?'

Flitters beat a drum on his knee with his long blue-nailed fingers, his bottom shifting and fretting in the chair, threw a quick glance out the window, down at his hand against his knee, caught his fingers back from their quick nervous drumming, cracked his knuckles loudly, looked an instant like an anxious hen that was getting ready to lay an egg.

'What you mean by that crack?' said Surjue again.

'Wasn't a crack, Surjue . . . well, take Rema for instance . . . she's a woman in a thousand, I'd say.'

'You bet she's a woman in a thousand, else you think I'd be living with her so long?'

'That's what I mean. You're just natural-born lucky, that's what. Look at the kinda money she makes doing piece-work in that cigar factory.'

'What you know 'bout that, anyway?'

'Well, I just figured it, like. They pay them good money for that kind of work. Cigars, the expensive ones, got to be hand-made.'

'You figure too much, that's what I don't like about you. You figure like Anancy, that's what I mean.'

'I didn't mean to say anything out of the way, Surjue. . . .'

'Well, it's me who runs my family, see? It's me who earns the money, 'cos my racin' tips are good. I got a string of customers, see? I don't even know what kind of money Rema makes. I never bother myself to ask her. I just give her money, an' keep givin' it to her, hell man, money don't mean nothin' to me.'

'I didn't mean to say anything, Surjue. . . .'

'I didn't say you did. I'm just tellin' you. You want me to stop talkin'?'

'Didn't mean that neither, man.'

'I'm glad to hear. This dam cigarette is gone out . . . light another one for me.'

'Sure, sure, Surjue.'

Flitters lit the cigarette, passed it to Surjue, deftly took one for himself from the packet, nursing the flame of the match in the cup he made of his big bony hand, brought it up to the cigarette that hung loosely from his lips, sucked the flame toward him with his big thick protuberant lips and threw the matchstick to the floor.

'Buju and Crawfish are coming here,' said Surjue.

'What you want to keep company with them crooks for, Surjue?'

'They're not crooks, an' I got business with them, what's the matter with you?'

'I didn't mean anything, Surjue. . . .'

One side of the hinged window suddenly slammed shut with a gust of wind that rattled the panes in the cracked discoloured putty that held them loosely in place against the wooden frame. Surjue got up and hooked the window, came back and sat down on the bed. His bootlace dragged along the floor.

'Sometimes you make me so mad I don't know why the hell I bother with you,' he said.

'I didn't mean . . .'

25

'So Crawfish and Buju are crooks, eh? Well let me tell you somep'n, they ain't no more crooks than — anyone else. They both been to jail, yes. Plenty of times, but it's only because the police is riled with them. You know what it is with them police.'

'Yes, I know. They is an interferin' set of bastards, won't leave a man alone.'

'I don't mess with them, they leave me alone,' said Surjue.

'I guess that's the way.'

'I go into a bar, I see one come in for a drink, I wipe my mouth an' leave right away, don't mess with them nohow.'

'Coupla them ain't so bad. . . .'

'I wouldn't even know. Every police is a police, I don't mess with them, an' they don't mess with me.'

'It's mutual.'

'Eh?'

'Cuts both ways, mean to say.'

'It's the way I want it should be.'

'I guess you know what you're doin', Surjue. . . . I guess things just come your way.'

'What you mean?'

'Mean to say you're lucky, that's all. Things just naturally come to you.'

'I work dam hard for what I get, an' I use my brains, if that's what you mean.'

He took another drag at his cigarette and a cracked teapot on a shelf against the opposite wall caught his eye where the sunlight winked on it, tricked him, so that he winked back at it without knowing that he did.

'Yes, of course,' said Flitters, cracking the knuckles of both hands, 'that too. But what you want, Surjue, is to pick up a big piece of money one of these days. I mean a big piece of cash you'll be sittin' pretty for the rest of your life, not messin' around with no smalltime racket like, somep'n you can reach back an' put your feet up in front of you an' take it easy the rest of your life, you get what I mean?'

'Yes, I get you. You mean a real big piece of cash, that's what you mean.'

'Yes man, that's it.'

'Well I mean to say that kind of thing don't happen every day.'

26

'That's right, too.'

'But like you said yourself just now, things just naturally come to me. I wouldn't be surprised I could see the way to gettin' my hands on a big piece of cash like that some day.'

'Me neither. It's like I said, things just naturally come to you.'

Surjue looked at him speculatively, squinting a bit. Flitters sat with his big hands folded on the table before him, and waited.

'You know,' said Surjue presently, 'there's something about you, Flitters, that makes me kinda take a fancy to you, spite of everything I hate about you.'

Flitters smiled understandingly.

'You're like Anancy, you just sit an' wait. But there's something about you . . . you want a drink? I got a half-bottle in the cupboard there.'

'You know I don't take plenty of that stuff,' said Flitters, licking his big lips.

'Just as well. I said a half-bottle. Good rum too. Stuff that doesn't get into bond, an' isn't aged with chemicals an' things. Buju's got a whole demijohn of it. He brought a coupla bottles for me. They is glasses there behind you.'

'I could run an' get some ice across the way, Surjue.'

'You sit down, I'll get the ice.'

'I could nip across as easy as you.'

'I'll get the ice.'

He went to the door, opened it, looked out into the yard, called: 'Hi, Ditty. Come here, me child.'

Ditty looked up from sitting on a box in the yard, her dress drawn way up, elbows planted on her knees, staring down at the ground in front of her in a day-dream; gave him a warm smile, got up, walked slowly across the yard, something in her face, the shape of her mouth, her eyes, the way she carried herself, exuding sex like a warm pungent odour, like some over-scented flower, every time she looked at a man she was just asking to be laid.

She came toward him now, smiling like that, a little sullen, a little saucy, wetting her lips slightly with the red tip of her tongue, her eyes dewy, the tight tits jerking under her dress, the tight flesh on her hips jerking the same under her short dress, making him think of a bitch-dog in heat.

'Yes, Surjue?'

27

A look of annoyance flitted across his face. He was sorry he had called to her, but now it was too late.

'Do me a favour?'

'Yes, Surjue.'

'Run to the ice shop across the street, get some ice an' a bottle of Pepsi Cola.'

'Yes, Surjue.'

She walked slowly toward the gate, glancing over her shoulder saw him watching her . . . made her hips twitch, or perhaps they just naturally twitched of themselves with a subconscious urge that possessed them, scuffed her bare feet a little through the dust that lay thick in the yard, giggled once going through the gate.

'Ass a-fire.'

'What's that, Surjue?'

'That Ditty, she's crazy for a man.'

'Well? How's about it?' Flitters giggled.

'Not for me . . . I hate a woman that starts chucking it in my face.'

'I know what you mean.'

'Funny thing, it gimme the creeps.'

'She goes at it too hard, I get you.'

'Lay her once, just to help her out of her trouble, you got her round your neck the rest of your life. A gal like that wouldn't care if the world was to know you was stroppin' her. No sir, not for me.'

Flitters said after a bit, thoughtfully: 'What you think of Beaverbrook in that six-furlong trip?'

'Well, Beaverbrook is a good colt, but not in the class of Beccaquimec his sire, if that's what you have on your mind. I give you Rock Water, and first you want Battle Song, an' next you want Beaverbrook. If you don't like the tip I give you suit yourself.'

'Man, I didn't mean it that way,' said Flitters apologetically, and he said Surjue should know better than to think he would doubt or question his tips, and what the hell kind of a friend did he think he was, anyway.

All the same he went out and bought four win-tickets on Battle Song, at four shillings a ticket, later that day, and Battle Song came in first and paid fourteen shillings on the win-ticket, and Rock Water didn't even place.

4 REMA JUST COME home from the cigar factory where she worked, pulled off her outdoor clothes to change into a house frock. Surjue lay in his undershirt and drawers on the bed, studied the race programme wetting the point of a pencil at his lips from time to time as he made cabalistic signs in the margin.

Rema, a pretty sambo girl, stood in the middle of the room in panties and brassière and decided it was too hot to put on any more clothes; she sat down on the side of the big wooden bed, kicked off her shoes, and wriggled in beside Surjue who sprawled in the middle.

'What's the matter with you?' he said, without taking his eyes off the race programme.

'Move over a bit honey, can't you? How's the tips coming?'

'I didn't know you were getting to bed, how late is it?'

'Honey, I'm tired, I'm just home from work.'

'You got any money for cigarettes?'

'I got a pack of cigarettes in my bag for you.'

'Get 'em, I'm just dyin' for a smoke.'

She got out of bed, fetched the cigarettes out of her handbag and a box of matches, figured she might as well slip on her house dress for all the difference it would make to Surjue, and sit and rock herself in the rocker over by the window where she could look out the back at the trees that rimmed the gully and listen to the talk they made in the wind, for something to do.

'I notice you never bring any of that shag home again, you know I like to roll my own.'

'I thought I'd save you the trouble. It's the same tobacco goes into the cigarettes.'

'Can't be the same, the shag tastes better, kinda moist like.'

'I'll get you some tomorrow. How's the tips coming along?'

'If I'd had some money I'd have laid a bet on Rock Water in the six-furlong race for two-year olds this aft'noon. I give Flitters the tip, just give it to him for nothing, the dope.'

'If he wins he'll give you something, I bet.'

'Sure he will, that's why I give it to him, see? He's bound to win. You have any change in your purse could lend me a dollar?'

'I got the change, yes, an' you can have it, you aimin' to go out?'

'A little ways — later.'

'Oh. I don't ever aim to meddle in your business honey, but I'd be careful of that bosom friend of yours, Flitters, if I was you.'

'What you mean?' He was looking at her now.

'Nothing, I don't like him I guess. He gives me a kind of feelin', I can't explain.'

'You don't have to worry about Flitters, see, I can take care of a dope like that without turning on my side.'

'I don't aim to meddle none with your business honey, I guess you know that Anancy-man better than I do.'

'You always callin' him that Anancy-man . . . you just don't like Flitters, I guess.'

'That's right. He's smooth an' trickified, that number.'

'You leave him to me, you said you didn't aim to meddle in my business, an' that's the way I want it should be. This dam cigarette just taste like trash.'

'I'll bring you home some of that shag tomorrow. I've got some change in my purse, we could go to a movie tonight, what you say?'

'Not for me, I got some business down the street a-ways, later. You keep some of that change, honey, I might need it. . . .'

'I don't mind so long as you're not going to give it to some woman. . . .'

'Awe, honey, you know me better'n that.'

Papa Bedosa watched Charlotta as she went busily about the room fixing him something to eat. He had come home early from the Slaughter House saying that he wasn't feeling so good and almost in the same breath that he was hungry. He said he hadn't eaten scarcely any lunch that day and that he must have took up wind on his stomach from keeping it empty so long.

His irritability showed not so much in what he said as in the nagging quality of his voice because his irritation with Charlotta was deep down and subconscious, and his way of getting back at everyone and everything in the world for his lack of manliness was to take it out of Charlotta. For Papa Bedosa was a timid man and he made up for it in two ways: bullying Charlotta and making life miserable for her was one; the other was the sneaking underhand way he went about poisoning anybody's mind he could about everybody else. He was an incorrigible gossip with a mean tongue and the ferocity of a rat who would run away every time rather than stand and fight, but was without kindness or mercy when he had the advantage, such as when he was talking behind the other fellow's back.

In self-defence Charlotta turned to religion and became bigoted and narrow-minded, the springs of her being that had flowed with love dried up, so that she was unjust and shrewish with everyone but Papa Bedosa whom she feared and Manny whom she spoiled outrageously, shutting out his faults from her mind and painstakingly glossing them over.

Charlotta wasn't really cruel and greedy as she appeared, but she suffered from a terrible deep-down insecurity that left a void inside her, and she filled this void with a narrow religion, seeking to cover up her insufficiencies and escape her gnawing fears in that way.

Her fear of Papa Bedosa and her cringing before him hid from her something that she could not bear to admit to herself, the fact that she despised him for his cowardice and treachery, which she pretended not to see, not even when it became so glaringly obvious in relation to Manny, their son; for Papa Bedosa was afraid of Manny, who flouted his authority and, knowing himself the stronger, despised him and laughed at him to his face.

Papa Bedosa watched Charlotta burning her fingers at the fire; she was now getting ready something to set before him.

'Can't come with something yet, God woman, I'm hungry.'

'Coming, Papa, stove is smoking I don't know why, must be that chimney wants cleaning again, or mebbe the wood the man selling to us is green, an' the price you have to pay for it, it is a scandal.'

'Always grumbling about something; must be think you livin' in heaven already; other women manage without complainin'; comes from fillin' your mind with all that dam religion, I guess.'

'Coming right this minute, Papa, an' I got something you like special, some of that cow-heel you brought me yesterday, with rice-an'-peas, an' a nice cornpone.'

'Cornpone fo' feedin' dawg wid, woman. What! yuh waan' puff me up wid cornpone?'

'You used to like it, so I thought I'd make it special to please you. Never mind, me an' Tansy will have it for supper. You want to try two of them Indian Root pills I got from the doctor-shop the other day? Maybe a clearin'-out would help you, all that wind on you' stomach.'

'Wind I got on my stomach, Mama, is on account I don't get my grub reg'lar, I reckon.'

'Coupla them Indian Root pills would set you right just the same, take them before you eat, best thing.'

'Take them now I would vomit the way I feel. Can't you get here with that cow-heel yet? That Euphemia just sets under the mango tree all day pickin' them up as fast as they drop, nobody else in the yard can get one, must be think she did put it there, gettin' herself plumped-up for Bajun Man's stroppin', I reckon. Christ a-mighty, what's matter Tansy not here helpin' you?'

'I sent her to the shop.'

'What you want from the shop now? Seems you never tired of givin' a man shop food to eat, no wonder I got wind in me guts.'

'I wanted some oil for the lamp an' a half-bar of brown soap to finish the clothes washin', an' some matches an' some sugar. Clean run out of sugar.'

'Always clean run out of something around here, would think I didn't give you money enough to manage you' house business, an' more.'

'Here you are, Papa, that cow-heel stew nice an' hot, you want the pickles too? That country pepper is plenty hot, I warn you.'

'Pass the pickles, woman, guess I know how hot I want a thing to be without anybody tellin' me. You goin' to eat some of this?'

'Not now, Papa, you eat first an' what you don't want you can leave. I think you should try talkin' to Manny, he's into some bad mischief or other the live-long day.'

'Past time for Manny to get a job. He's just foolin' his time at home, an' you encourage him.'

'I wish you could get him a job, yes.'

'Me must look a job for him? I wouldn't do it, Mama. Let the bwoy go out an' look work for himself.'

'He's gettin' man-ways, chasin' gals an' that, an' I can't say nothin' to him, he won't lissen to me.'

'If I start talkin' to Manny sure as anything I'll lose my temper an' then I don't know what I might do, you wouldn't want that, I expect.'

'There he is grinning at Euphemia now . . . I just thought I'd tell you. He should get him a job.'

'That's what I said. But you tell him. Mebbe he'll lissen to you.'

Tansy came in with a basket on her head. She went in to the next room and set it down.

'You got all the things I sent you for?'

'Yes Ma, but the Chinaman would sell me only one box of matches, said if I didn't hear they was goin' to call another strike at the match factory soon. He read it in the papers, he said, but I think he was lying, he has them under the counter, hid.'

'What he hidin' them under the counter for? Mama, you think she is lyin'? I should take my belt to her, mebbe.'

'No, Papa, they do that all the time, an' Tansy's been a good girl, helpin' me with the washin'. I guess they hope there's goin' to be another strike at the factory any day an' the price will go up. That's it.'

'You dam right, too. I 'member the other day I went into a shop an' bought a pack of cigarettes an' when I asked for a box of matches the Chinaman just looked at me an' grinned an' said, no habbe, the son-of-a-bitch.'

'I guess they don't make much profit on matches, the Government takin' so much for taxes, that's what.'

'I'd like to no habbe him with a meat knife in his guts, the son of a Chinie-whore.'

'Watch you' language, Papa, the child will hear you an' be usin' words like them, next.'

'I'd take the skin off her back with me belt if she was to miss an' use one of them in my hearin', she know better than that, Mama, don't worry.'

Euphemia walking in the yard saw a mango lying under the tree where it had fallen, picked it up and was eating it when Manny came up grinning at her in his over-bold force-ripe way, like he was hot in the pants and didn't care the hell who knew it, as Zephyr said.

33

'Hi, Euphemia, gimme a piece?'

'You want the mango seed to suck, you can have it when I'm through.'

'Don't want no mango seed when you done suck it.'

'Well, that's all you would get.'

'You mean that, you mean you wouldn't give a man a little piece when he beg you for it?'

'Yuh better gwan 'bout yuh business, bwoy, Ah don't feel to chop mout' wid yuh today.'

'We could chop something else, though. How's about it?'

'You know somep'n, yuh pappy should drop yuh pants an' flog yuh bottom to teach you manners, if Ah fire a box in yuh face today yuh Mammy belly woulda hot her, Ah tell you.'

She left him standing there and went over to the standpipe to wash her hands and mouth from the mango. He followed her, grinning impudently all the while.

'You woulda fire box eena fe-who face, gal? Talk again mek me hear you?'

She cupped one hand under the standpipe cock, turned on the water, took some of it in her mouth, swished it around, spat it out again.

'Talk yuh talk again mek me hear you.'

He came nearer, grinning as before.

She paused with her mouth halfway to her cupped hand again to say: 'Ah don't want hold no argument with you, you is a bwoy.'

'Hm! Bwoy, no? Ah could show you something now would mek you change you talk, gal. Ah got something here fo' you,' he was right up against her now, insinuating his grinning lips close to her ear, 'would mek you fo'get dat Bajun Man—'

And then she hit him with the flat of her hand across the side of his face so that he staggered under the blow, followed him up and hit him again; he pitched, taking a few quick steps, short, trying to catch himself up, fell sprawling in the yard, his mouth hitting the dust.

Euphemia was a big girl, a heavyweight among women, with the limbs of a black Juno; stung to anger she didn't know the strength she packed in that big firm-fleshed, lazy-seeming body.

Manny sat up, the taste of earth and blood in his mouth, his

34

teeth grinding upon sharp grit, spat, came up on his hands and feet, stood up, and went for her with his fists. He hit her hard in the belly, low, and she caught him by the front of his shirt, splitting it straight down as she jerked him toward her, hit him with the flat of her heavy hand across the side of his head again to make light gash behind his eyeballs and send him reeling. He held himself up from falling on his face again by putting out his hands, and scrambled up, game with the hot blood rising in him, rushing her this time with his fists and his feet.

She fell and he kicked her in the belly, but she made no sound; her face set with her purpose frightened him as she rolled over, stood up, squeezing the pain in her belly holding it in with both hands, staggered toward him, that set look on her face; he tried to dodge her but this time her hand came away with the rest of the shirt off his back, some skin off the side of his belly with it where her big blunt nails scrabbed him. Two long weals lumped-up and reddened at his side. Her other hand with the heavy gold ring she wore for Shag cut his top lip so that the two axe-teeth in front shoved out through it, pinning the lip stiff against his face. He put his hand up to pull the split top lip from over his buck teeth, and she caught him, with his guard down like that, a heavy whack with her right hand in the back of his neck. Again Manny bit the dust.

The neighbours came out into the yard. First Bedosa and Charlotta. They stood on the doorstep, ineffective, not knowing how to proceed, with Tansy hopping behind them, screaming.

Mass Mose and Zephyr came out to the door of Mass Mose' room, and looked on, and he was holding the clarinet halfway to his lips as though he had half a mind to play a jaunty tune. Zephyr stood at his elbow, her fingers plucking at his sleeve, and then she put her hand up to her forehead and a little wrinkle came between her eyes as though she was remembering something.

Wilfie and Ditty stood with them; one side of Wilfie's mouth was jerking and he started as though he was going toward them, but Ditty who was watching him more than the fight, put out her hand and stopped him; she drew closer to him, holding on to his arm, and she stood like that with one of her tight phallic breasts pressing hard against his side, shifting her weight from one foot to the other, as though she couldn't stand still.

Surjue came from his room right out into the yard in his undershirt and drawers, his fleshy good-looking face wearing a grin; he folded his arms across his chest and followed the blow-by-blow progress of the fight with his eyes. He spat out a matchstick he had been using as a toothpick and didn't relax his spectator's stance until Manny got up from the ground the second time and he was holding a sharp-pointed long-blade knife in his hand.

Rema standing behind Surjue and a little to one side screamed, but Surjue was right up to Manny already. He didn't make a grab for the knife but he just pushed his left hand palm outward into Manny's face, and brought down his right fist sharply against Manny's wrist. Manny yelped and the knife clattered to the ground, and Surjue, still smiling, put his foot on it.

He took up the knife now, looked at it, saw it was one of those with a catch that held the blade rigid, released the catch, clicked the blade shut, and smiling like that, handed it back to Manny.

'Put it away in your pocket,' he said, 'and don't go for it another time, somebody could get hurt bad with a thing like that.'

'You give it back to him, take it away,' Bedosa screamed. He came down the yard a few steps as though he was going to take the knife back from Manny, but Manny just looked at him, spat blood, put his hands in his pockets, turned sullenly and walked out through the gate.

Surjue laughed, watching Bedosa fume.

Zephyr left Mass Mose' side, went across to Euphemia, who was sitting on the side of the cistern, squeezing her hands into her belly and sobbing with anger and pain.

'You feelin' bad, honey, come let me help you inside.'

'The bastard,' Euphemia sobbed, 'the little buck-teeth monkey.'

'Hush, honey, never mind, you give it to him good.'

'I could kill him, though.'

'Don't worry, you give him the first good wallopin' he had in his life. He'll respect you after this. You hurt bad? Let me help you inside.'

Mass Mose blew his nose loudly, taking it between his thumb and forefinger, drew his shirtsleeve across his face, and went back inside. He sat down on the side of the iron bed again and fingered his clarinet thoughtfully a while, then he grunted, shook his head, and put the instrument away inside the black case, unscrewing it in the middle.

Ditty, still clutching Wilfie to her, said against his ear, 'Lawd, she blood him up, though. You seed it, she brung blood.'

Wilfie, as though suddenly conscious of her, wrenched away. He walked stiffly over to the standpipe and stood looking down at Euphemia; there was a strange dark look in his eyes. 'He kick her in her belly,' he said.

'Come on, honey, you're not hurt so bad, let me help you inside.'

'The little monkey, the ugly little cow-son. . . .'

'It's Pattoo's knife he's got,' said Wilfie, grubbing at the dust with his bare toes.

'Where is Pattoo?' said Euphemia suddenly.

'I give him money to buy something for me in town,' Zephyr said.

'You get that knife away from him,' said Euphemia, hysterically. She put her hands up to her head and started to scream.

'Hush, honey, don't let it get you, I'll tell Pattoo get that knife from him, you bet.'

Rema sat in the steam-bent rocker, rocked herself, looked across at Surjue, grinning to himself, squatting on the side of the bed. He smoked a cigarette, looking back at her through eyes half-closed to keep the smoke out of them.

'You bring me home some of that shag they make at the factory, I'll roll my own,' he said, 'this stuff tastes like trash.'

'I was so scared I couldn't catch my breath.'

'Eh?'

'Him with that knife. . . .'

'Cha, he just a kid, don't have the knowhow.'

'He's 'most as big as you, Surjue, an' he had that knife in his han'. . . .'

'I know, that's why I took it away from him. Anything might happen with a kid like that with a knife, he could even cut himself.'

Surjue laughed, and Rema thought of the thin scar, almost

37

faded now, that ran from his shoulder down his left breast. Seeing it in her mind's eye, she shuddered. She'd never asked him about it, and never would.

Her eyes blurred suddenly with a hot rush, and she went down on her knees before him and laid her face against his thighs.

Her shoulders shook a little with something more than breathing. Late sunlight came in through the window and lay in a patch like a handkerchief on the floor. A gust of wind thrust at the hinged window so that it rattled on the hook.

'What's the matter with you, Rema, honey . . .' patting her head . . . 'you not aimin' to start cryin' on me now, are you? . . .' his hand lightly stroking her neck, her shoulder . . . suddenly jerking the half-smoked cigarette through the window . . . 'Shit, this stuff tastes like trash.'

5   THAT EVENING IT was very hot and everybody came out into the yard and sat on chairs and stools and boxes and gossiped and cracked jokes and sang songs. And there was a big fish-fry, and it happened this way. Ras went out with his handcart as usual, and that day a great quantity of fish was mysteriously washed up on the beaches. People went out in trucks and cars, and even on bicycles and walking, and came home with more fish than they knew what to do with.

An officer of the Fisheries Department later reported that the fish had died of a lack of oxygen because of the decomposition of microscopic life in the water, one of the functions of these micro-organisms being to dissolve oxygen into the water. The recent heavy flood rains seemed to have been responsible for the condition, previous occurrences appeared to be related to such heavy rains and the consequent entry into the harbour of a large body of fresh water and the absence of wind currents to distribute it, the Fisheries expert reported.

But today throngs of people shouted, 'Ha! ha! we got fish fo' nothin'! . . .' 'Fus' time I ever seed anything like it in me life' . . . 'Mus' be de Lawd send them' . . . 'Fo' sure it's de hand of de Lawd!' . . . 'Is like de quail birds he sen' de children of Israel in de wilderness' . . . 'Ha! ha! ha! Ah tell yuh sah!' . . . picking them up off the shore and out of the shallow water and throwing them into their baskets that were already brimming with the evidence of this miracle.

The water in the harbour was still as a pond all that day and the next, with scarcely any breeze at all. And more and more fish swam into the shallow water just off shore and gaped as though they had been brought in by invisible nets, and died and were thankfully piled high in baskets and taken away to the town.

And that was how Ras came to have the bottom of his handcart lined with silver king fish and snapper and jack and mullet and piper and cutlass fish and grunt. He sold what he could and not having any means of keeping the fish fresh until the next day, and prodigal with the sense of miracle that invested this phenomenon, he decided he would take the rest of the fish up to the yard and everybody would have one hell of a feed.

It had been a good day's scuffling, and although he was not a religious man he never doubted that the Lord had somehow had a hand in his affairs that day, and many another scuffler felt the same . . . 'Bwoy, Big Massa tek pity 'pon we poor, him don' let we go outa him han' altogether, Ah tell yuh' . . . 'Yes, bwoy' . . . 'Lawd sah, look we live to see a day like this' . . . 'Is suttinly de Lawd!'

That evening they built a big fire and set big stones about it in the middle of the yard, and they sat around on chairs and benches and stools and upturned boxes and anything they could sit on, and the women fried fish and johnny-cakes, and the big fire lit up the darkness and sent up showers of sparks, and they sang songs and told stories and cracked jokes and forgot their worries and their fears and their jealousies and their suspicions and the occasion took on all the aspects of a picnic, and they were like children again.

When they had eaten their fill they let the big fire die down to a bed of glowing coals among the white-hot stones, until Surjue said, 'Hell, let's have a blaze,' and got up and chucked some sticks of firewood on to the bed of coals, and the flames came up with hot quick licks like yellow tongues and split where a piece of wood overlaid them and twisted in the least suspicion of wind and were forked, some, and hissing, like the tongues of snakes.

Glow from the flames folded the shadows back against the walls of the shacks two sides of the yard, flickered, swept up from the ground, made grotesque dusky shapes dance a dip-an'-fall-back curtseying against the cracked rough plaster that faced the weathered boards.

Feet scraped the dirt floor beneath them as they pushed back a piece from the too hot fire, coming to rest again in a larger circle, their dark faces shiny with grease, but grinning their enjoyment, belching with gusto, making cracks about this or that, laughter always near to their lips, their bellies full.

'Wha's matter, Fats, gotta fishbone in yuh craw?'

'Lemme yuh lap, Rema, a feed like that an' I just gotta flop, how yuh feelin', child?'

'With yuh shirt-front undone an' yuh flies open, what you figure now, you puttin' up for repairs?'

'Bwoy, you see how my gal can back-chat me an' get away with it? You should keep it in the family, though.'

'*Go-long gal, I like yuh sister better, the reason why she gotta better figure . . .*' Lennie sang.

'Is like Christmas,' said Pattoo, his eyes popping out of his head, sitting almost at Zephyr's feet, taking confidence from the glow of her smile. She reached out and laid a hand on his head an instant and he grinned all over his cretinous face wriggling his toes in the dust and looking down shyly at them.

Bajun Man squatting like an ape before the fire took a long sliver of wood that had splintered away under the axe and employed it as a toothpick, sucking air between his teeth noisily and making gross sounds that told of his deep-down, animal, naive belly-satisfaction.

'Jus' let this settle a bit I guess I'll drag meself across to the bar an' put down top of it a big gill of white rum; a pity the night is so hot, plenty-plenty time befo' we all get to sleep accounta it, I bet.'

He threw a warm glance at Euphemia across the glowing coals, saw she sat braced back in her chair, her hands clasped about her belly, sullen, not saying anything, or taking notice, and tried to guess what she was thinking about.

Manny sulked behind Charlotta sitting a little behind the circle on a box that creaked every time she shifted her weight on it. Charlotta folded her arms across her thin bosom and brooded, staring at the back of Bedosa's head, and Manny his lips swollen, lending his face a pouting mean look, glowered around him, his gaze coming to rest with a perversity on Euphemia's face that showed no emotion at all.

Bedosa, sitting on a large flat stone he had fetched from the gully brink, leaned a little toward Nanine, a girl who lived in a room in the north row of shacks beside the Sisters of Charity and made a kind of living selling socks and ties, and chances on a pushboard on the side, slyly stroked her legs in the semi-darkness, first making sure that sitting where he was Charlotta couldn't see what his left hand was doing. He had contrived that the first tentative contact should wear the innocent aspect of a fortuitous accident, noted that the girl did not draw away, let his hand come out again slyly and touch her bare leg another time; she pretended not to notice; then bit by bit he was slowly stroking the smooth tight skin of her near leg from the ankle up to the under-knee and back down again to the ankle, and all the while she just leaned forward with her lips parted upon a little smile as though she was taking a lively interest in the general conversation.

Ras was fast asleep in his handcart; he had filled his belly, taken a few turns up and down the yard to settle the food, he said, scratching away at his crotch all the while; had gone to lie down in the up-tilted cart under the open sky, retorted to Cassie's 'H'm, him goin' drop asleep now,' with a 'Hush yuh mout' gal, when Ah settle this feed proper goin' be *"belly-lick Uncle Joe what a hell tonight,"* watch yuh pudd'n!' Which raised a hearty round of laughter, and Bajun Man said, 'Mout' talk him talk, belly say him no want no mo'.' And Lennie raised the singing and they swung their bodies and clapped their hands and sang together a song that went: *'Draw down gal, me belly full, me no want no mo'* . . .' until they came to the end, and before the singing was done Ras lay on his back in the handcart, his feet on the ground, his head pillowed in his hands, his mouth open, snoring up a storm.

'Lissen him, no!'

41

'What Ah did tell yuh?'

'Ole time folks say cock mout' kill cock, is a true talk.'

After a bit Zephyr went across to the standpipe, drank some water out of her cupped hand, dried her hands by rubbing them together and swinging them briskly in the air; she bent over Euphemia's shoulder in passing and asked her in a whisper how she was feeling.

'All right now, it's nothing,' said Euphemia, unclasping her hands from before her belly.

She said: 'A little while back I was feelin' sick, but it passed.'

'You take a dose of salts tonight before you go to bed, you feel better in the morning. I got some in my room if you want it.'

'You notice anything?'

'No. Like what?'

'I don't know. Just a kinda feelin' I've got.'

'I don't feel anything — different.'

'All right.'

'You sure you not hurt anywhere?'

'I feel okay.'

'A dose of salts will fix everything, I bet.'

'Yes. I got some in my room, I'll take it before I go to bed. You notice how Shag is quiet? I seen Bedosa whisperin' to him this evenin in the yard. . . .'

'That sneakin' liar. . . .'

'I know. That's what I'm afraid of.'

'Walk with me to the gate.'

'Okay.'

Euphemia got up and she and Zephyr walked toward the gate, as though they were going for a little stroll.

'I don't trust that Bedosa.'

'He'd try to poison anybody's mind, yes. Don't trust him neither, he's a sneak.'

'I think he hates me, I don't know why, unless it's because he's just that mean . . . or on account of Manny.'

'He don't care a dam about Manny. Manny's nothing more'n a dose of poison to him.'

'Why he hates me would do me a harm then I don't know. I never done him nothing in my life.'

'It's his nature.'

'I could kill him like a cockroach, an' laff.'

'Hush, Euphemia!'

'Is true, though, I hate him like that.'

'Don't say it make anyone hear you. It'd get back to him for sure.'

'I wouldn't bother my head about that.'

'It'd make him hate you more. He'd plot something against you, you don't know him, he's a mean sneakin' devil, that's what he is.'

'Sorry's the day I ever set eyes on him. God, I hate this place; I'm scared. . . .'

Zephyr looked at her a moment without saying anything, then: 'What you goin' to do about it?'

'I don't know.'

'Ever think about it?'

'What could I do?'

'Send Bajun Man packing.'

'You don't understand about that, he wouldn't lissen to me if I did.'

'He'd do what you ask him, if he loved you.'

'You think so? I guess you should know.'

'Yes,' said Zephyr, with a tight little smile, looking straight at the other. 'I know what I'm talkin' about,' she said, slowly.

'I couldn't do it,' said Euphemia.

'That's what I wanted to know, honey. You love him, that means.'

'I don't even understand it good meself — but something has happened — I can't explain.'

'Well, you both got to go away —'

'I can't do that, either. You see, he hasn't got a job — he's looking one, but he hasn't got it yet.'

'I see.' Zephyr's face made a hard little smile, thinking: 'He should keep himself inside his pants then,' but she said out aloud, 'That's tough now, honey.'

And she watched Euphemia put her handkerchief between her teeth and rip it clear across with a sudden twist of her hand.

Presently: 'Shag is sick too, I know it. I wouldn't want to leave him just yet on account of that,' she said.

'How sick?'

'I don't know. He hasn't told me nothing yet, but I know he been to see a doctor.'

'If it was anything bad he would tell you.'

'He pick up a lot of dust on his chest down at that tile factory.'

'If anything was wrong with him he'd tell you.'

'Might do, yes.'

'He would, I know.'

'I gotta watch an' see . . . I gotta bide my time an' wait . . . I'm scared, that's what, an' I wish I knew what to do.'

'Let's go back now. An' just be yourself.'

'Yes.'

'Go drink some water at the pipe first, I'll come with you.'

'Yes. I gotta watch my step, that's what. But sometimes I feel — I don't know how to say it.'

'Sometimes you feel you don't give a dam, let things rip, I know.'

'Yes. I want to come out with it into the open, an' don't give a good God dam.'

'You got to hold on to yourself, until you make up your mind.'

'It's inside me here. Like it'll bust out any minute. An' I'm scared with it . . . don't know what to do.'

'Come, drink some water, an' let's go back, don't let them think we're talkin' private.'

'Yes. Come.'

Ditty sat on the same box with Wilfie a little apart from the rest, and in the darkness out beyond the glow of the fire she took his hand in hers and held it and the palm of her hand was hot and damp, and he didn't take his hand away. He felt like things crawling around inside his belly bottom and in his crotch and down his thighs. It was not an unpleasant sensation, he found, if he let go to it and let it go sliding and snaking through his flesh.

And seeing he did not pull away, Ditty presently took his hand between both of hers, clasping it warmly, and carried it to her bosom, and knowing that it gave her pleasure, and him too, he let her do what she would with it. And so they sat for a long time in the semi-darkness outside the circle around the fire, close together on the same box, and they were nearest to the kitchen end of the shacks overlooking the gully. And the others around the fire talked and laughed and sang songs, but Ditty and Wilfie sharing the hard box-bottom between them never spoke a word.

Tansy said to Rema, shyly, 'Let me rest me head in yuh lap?'

'Go ahead, honey, you feelin' sleepy, no?'

She let her arm rest across the girl's shoulder and stroked her cheek lightly, scarcely thinking about it, with her fingers, and Tansy's heart glowed with the warmth of love under that touch. Nobody had ever made her feel like that before. She was shy of Rema on account of this. She had come to regard such a thing as warmth between people as something suspect. In her home the meaning of love was never apparent. She knew such things as the need for security in the terms of a bed to sleep on, a roof over your head, a full belly, and knew that you had to do what you were told in order to secure these things, but there was always that underlying fear that at any time these things may be withdrawn, almost without notice. And with it came the meaning and knowledge of fear.

She had grown with this deep-down understanding of fear, but not of love, and feeling this attachment to Rema, this sense of being drawn to her like that, she was afraid of it too, without knowing why or in what way precisely.

Rema touched Surjue on the shoulder and said, 'Lemme your back to lean on.'

'You want me cotch you up? Okay,' he said, and moved over so she could lean against him.

Charlotta got up and went into her room to fetch something, and Bedosa let his head down on Nanine's knee. She drew down her dress.

'Wha's matter, yuh 'fraid something run up you?'

And she giggled and said: 'You better lif-up before Charlotta come back.'

Mack, the renovator, was telling a long and tedious story about an experience he had had in foreign parts. He had never left the island. He was one of those eternally discontented men who wanted something to fill their lives but didn't know what.

45

A completely negative type, he read the newspapers, denouncing everything or praising it according to the latest secondhand opinions he gathered from the editorials and special articles he read. Today he would agree with one writer that something was scandalous, and tomorrow he would turn around and laud it to the skies in accordance with the opinion expressed by the last spurious pedlar of half-truths plugging it out at so much per column inch.

He worked at home at his trade of renovator, collecting and delivering clothes on his bicycle. He had a few customers who patronized him regularly because he saved them some trouble rather than because of the quality of his work. He was Wilfie's father, but it was almost as though at times he didn't remember it. His wife had died many years ago, and he was like a man adrift in a world of day dreams.

He was always planning something, but nothing ever turned out for him the way he planned. He lived from day to day in the sustaining hope of winning a lump sum of money. He bought sweepstake tickets and the Chinese lottery on that account. He was always relating the most fantastic travellers' tales, which he picked up from time to time, amplifying them as he passed them on.

' . . . this Cooga is a funny animal he lives in trees . . . he gotta horn in the middle of his face. . . .'

'What for?' said Surjue.

'Well, I guess you would find out soon enough if you was to come up with one of them beasts in the jungle, bwoy.'

'I know, you been readin' up about it in a book, ever heard about the Walla-walla bird?'

'Cho man, Ah brush you off . . . as Ah was sayin' Ah was two months in that town without a job. . . .'

'I been out of a job too, Mack. Down in Belize it was. I used to wear a snake round me waist for a belt.'

'Is all right, Surjue, I don't tickla 'bout you' jokin'. . . .'

'Had a pair of suspenders too, but I couldn't afford to feed 'em.'

'You comfy, honey?' said Rema, bending over the girl to see if she was asleep. And Tansy whispered back, 'Yes,' and closed

46

her eyes again, and she was still without movement except for her breathing.

Charlotta returning from the shacks dragged her slack house-shoes across the gravel; Nanine quickly pushed Bedosa's head off her knees and pulled her dress down primly; realizing that Charlotta must have seen, she suddenly said out loud in a sharp tone, 'But is what dis man want wid me, eh?'

'Yuh knee so soothin' he went to sleep on them, an' the funniest thing you didn't even know, *tsk*, you see that now!' said Surjue.

Nanine looked at him fiercely, but he only smiled back at her and shut one eye tight so everybody could see, and Nanine looked as if she were getting ready to spring across and hit him, and he said, teasing her because she was angry, 'Hi baby, 'member leave yuh room door open for me tonight, soon as Rema drop asleep I'll be comin' over, look out for me.'

'You fancy you'self to think somebody would want you.'

'Stop gal, you don't want somebody, is what you want then?'

Rema said, 'Don't tease her, Surjue, she's tired. Scratch me back for me . . . not there, more over to the other side . . . the *other* side . . . Ah, that feels so good. . . .'

'Hush, don't tell them, honey, already I have me hands full fightin' 'em off.' He looked across at Nanine again and shut one eye tight, and put the tip of his tongue out at her, and laughed.

'Tansy, go to you' bed,' said Charlotta, sharply, and Tansy got up immediately and went toward the shacks, without a word or a look, or anything.

Bajun Man came in through the gate from the street, wiping his mouth with the back of his hand.

'Hm, had a selfish one, eh?' said Surjue.

'Ah, bwoy,' Bajun grinned.

'You mighta ast me tek a walk. I could buy you a likker, maybe.'

'Come den, no?'

'Too late now. Changed me mind.'

'Let us go down the gully a little ways,' Ditty whispered quickly in Wilfie's ear.

She got up and stood before him, shuffling impatiently. He made no move to follow her.

'Come, no?'

He stood up, and looked down at his toes.

'Come on, come on before somebody see us,' Ditty hissed at him from out of the gloom by the side of the shacks.

'All right,' he whispered back, 'I'm coming.'

Behind the shacks she suddenly put out her hands and drew him to her, and bore him to the ground and fell on top of him, rolling over. Her hot hands burned against his flesh, and suddenly he wanted to break away from her and run. There was something about her panting intensity that frightened him, so that he didn't heed the things crawling around inside his belly bottom and up and down the insides of his thighs now so much as his panic. He struggled to get up but she rolled over on top of him again, almost suffocating him. He realized that she was stronger than he, and he relaxed, and his excitement quickened within him again, and suddenly she rolled over on her side, and then over on her back, and threw her arms and legs wide, and lay still, still, like someone dead.

The wind freshened and snaked up the gully bottom, and shook the leaves of the trees and set up suddenly a great rustling, and two limber guinep branches chafed together in a high crotch and made a sound like an old grandfather rocking chair.

The deep shadows under the trees drew together, and spread again, as the wind looped a tightening silken sash around the trees, and loosed them from that smooth sleasy noose and flashed away in a jaunty pirouette and wound the sash about itself, and unwound it, and came back with a sudden sprint up the gully, straight, and twisted, and caught the trees in a running noose again, and tossed away.

The darkness laid on and thickened and the guinep tree stood up still and tall and its cast shadow was a thick brush dipped in wash and laid upon the lesser greyness in deft splotches squeegeed around the clumped trees.

The guttered tin roof on the shacks and the weathered boards shrank and warped in the dry heat and cracked and eased themselves and settled, and the only other sound was the quick crisp rustle of ground lizards among the dropped leaves.

When things began getting a little dull in the circle around the fire Lennie it was who thought up something to put life into them. He left the stool where he was sitting beside Zephyr and went up to the fence and pulled out a loose wooden paling, and came back with it grinning.

'Yuh breakin' down the front fence now,' said Bajun.

'I'll tack it back proper when I'm through,' Lennie said. He laid the plank on the ground. 'You all know this song. It's "Ribber Ben Come Down". I will sing the words, an' you all clap han's an' sing the chorus.' He put his two feet on the plank, teetering a bit, on purpose, the others taking part faced him in a semi-circle.

> The ribber ben come down,
> The ribber ben come down,
> The ribber ben come down,
> A-how me come over? . . . .

Lennie rocked and teetered on the plank as he sang, giving a realistic imitation of a man trying to cross a river on a piece of board. And the chorus clapped their hands and swayed their bodies in rhythm and sang the responses:

> Woy-oh, a-how you come over,
> Woy-oh, a-how you come over? . . . .

The wooden fence looked like a ragged picket line with so many of the paint-blistered palings knocked out and others leaning awry. Some people passing on the sidewalk stopped, hearing the singing, looked in through the broken fence, grinning to see the people inside merrying-up themselves, and some even clapped their hands too and joined in the responses.

> Me t'row piece-a deal board,
> Me t'row piece-a deal board,
> Me t'row piece-a deal board
> 'Pon de broad dutty water. . . .

The bodies swaying rhythmically all the while, the hands clapping to keep time . . . Pattoo beat a drum with two sticks on the side of a packing case . . . Mass Mose stroking the back of his bent head with one hand, nimbly buck-stepped with a realistic show of anxiety on the opposite bank, added mime, as well as his voice to the chorus.

49

> Woy-oh, a-how you come over,
> Woy-oh, a-how you come over? . . . .

Ras broke off in the middle of a snore, on the intake, sat up, blinked his eyes, stretched his long arms above his head, came buck-stepping up to join them, rocking on his knees, his bearded face split in a grin.

> Me see green gran-gra,
> Me see green gran-gra,
> Me see green gran-gra
> 'Pon de broad dutty water. . . .

Zephyr broke away to come across to Euphemia, grabbed her by the arm, 'Come on, Euphemia, shake up you'self, gal.'
Euphemia started to shake her head, changed her mind half-way through the first motion, stood up, smiling, and went across with Zephyr in time to join in with the responses:

> Woy-oh, a-how you come over,
> Woy-oh, a-how you come over? . . . .

Shag smiled a little turned-in smile, rolled himself a cigarette, brushed the crumbs off his pants leg, lit up, and smoked silently looking on.

> Me 'tep-so, me 'tep-so,
> Me 'tep-so, me 'tep-so,
> Me 'tep-so, me 'tep-so,
> Me 'tep-so come over. . . .

Lennie shuffled' the board forward with his feet, teetering perilously, on purpose; the others, acting the spirit of the adventure, teetered with him in a dance movement, patterned, rhythmic, explicit.

> Woy-oh, a-so you come over,
> Woy-oh, a-so you come over. . . .

The teetering became even more exaggerated now, it was impossible to tell how he managed to keep his balance on that narrow plank, jumping it forward with his feet all the while.

> Me rock-so, me rock-so,
> Me rock-so, me rock-so,
> Me rock-so, me rock-so,
> Me rock-so come over. . . .

Pattoo's eyes gleamed with excitement as he beat his tattoo faster, faster. . . .

> Woy-oh, a-so you come over,
> Woy-oh, a-so you come over! . . .

Cassie teetered too far over to one side, lost her balance, fell to the ground clutching at Rema's skirt to save herself, dragging it away . . . Rema stepped out of the skirt quickly to avoid falling on top of Cassie, let out a shriek of laughter . . . Lennie now started to jump the board along with both feet, bending low at the knees like a man ski-ing . . . his face glowing with perspiration. . . .

> Me jump-so, me jump-so,
> Me jump-so, me jump-so,
> Me jump-so, me jump-so,
> Me jump-so, come over. . . .

The chorus went into the jumping motions of the dance with him, and it was here that some more of them fell out, the deep knee-bend and forward jump, together, too much for them. . . .

> Woy-oh, a-so you come over,
> Woy-oh, a-so you come over! . . .

Nanine stumbled away from the group and went and sat down beside Pattoo, panting to catch her breath, and wiping her face with a damp, balled-up handkerchief she took from her bosom, fixing her brassière strap at the same time.

> De ribber ben come down,
> De ribber ben come down,
> De ribber ben come down,
> An' a-so me come over.

Now everybody stood up and pressed around the leader, Lennie, who stood grinning with real triumph and mopping his streaming face . . .

51

> Woy-oh, Ah glad you come over,
> Woy-oooh, Ah glad you come o-o-over!

And Zephyr in the simulated and real excitement of the moment, put her arms up around Lennie's neck and let her face down against his chest, as though she wanted to tell him before them all how glad she was he had come across the swollen river safely.

And they all laughed, and bright tears stood in the eyes of some, to witness that they still understood the meaning of miracles.

They gathered around the fire again and Shag told a story about something that happened when he was with a bunch of other Jamaicans working on a construction job on the Canal Zone. One of his friends — there were five of them, and this one was called Wallacy — had a girl with a funny Spanish name, but they all called her by a pet name Wallacy gave her, Susu.

She was a good-looking high-yaller, figured-up like one of them gals on the Coco Cola signs you see around town but a bit more on the hips. Boy, she had hips, that gal! She used to do a sort of dance in a cheap night club where she wore only a stiff little red organdie pleated skirt like a flower that came down just below her buttocks and two patches of green cloth cut out to look like leaves coming up under her pointed breasts. It was the kind of get-up that you wouldn't have looked at her so hard if she had come on with nothing on at all. She used to get right up on a big table set in the centre of the room and sing and dance.

She made a big hit, and when Wallacy fell for her he had to fight off the night club boss with a chair, he come at him with a knife, this guy, because Wallacy made up with Susu she should leave the little shrivelled-up night club owner who had picked her up off the street, and come and live with him, Wallacy, who had a way with women he held up his finger at them they just flopped in his lap.

Well to cut a long story short she was living with Wallacy about six months and he found out there was a spiv used to get money off her regular. Well the rest of the Jamaicans moved from that place and went to work on a factory construction job another part of the town, all of them except Wallacy.

The next news they had of him he had gone across the border and clear away to Guatamala City from where he wrote them a letter without giving them any address, only said he was trying to push on into Mexico and he had changed his name. Well of course they had read all about it in the papers and it had gone bad with them because even before that it was getting tougher and tougher for Jamaicans to get jobs in Panama. Jamaicans had got a bad name on the Isthmus, and the Panamanians didn't want them in their country at all.

It happened that Wallacy caught Susu in bed with her spiv, a little rat of a man with his belly and chest and hips all run into one like a snake and he went through the window in only his underpants, and Wallacy reached under the mattress where he kept his machette, sharp, and chopped up Susu like cuts of meat. First he chopped her head off and then the rest of her he chunked up, and he did it so quick and businesslike nobody in the apartment house even heard a sound.

When Shag finished telling the story nobody said anything, because Shag was always one for laughing and cracking jokes and merrying-up himself, and this story was not at all the kind of story they had ever heard him tell. So nobody said anything, and you could almost hear them drawing their breath and a couple of the women shuffled their feet a bit in the gravel, and nobody looked at Euphemia although everybody wanted to see how she was taking it.

And Shag sat and rolled a cigarette and lit it from a stick he took out of the fire and when he put it back a shower of sparks broke with a puff and shot up into the air. And Sister Mattie, one of the White Sisters of Charity, sitting to themselves, screamed, and said a spark fell on her foot, that was why.

And Shag leaning over a bit and staring into the fire laughed and said: 'Now I wonder why I had to tell that story tonight?'

And nobody said anything, and Bajun Man who was squatting on his heels the other side of the fire from Shag shifted his position to ease himself a bit and took a long wood splinter he had been chewing on from his mouth and made a big X in the dust in front of him.

'I know what,' said Shag, 'I dreamed about Wallacy last night. I saw him standing in the doorway with the machette in his

53

hand, saw him plain as I can see anyone of you around the fire here.'

A wood knot went *phee* and then *phut* in the fire, shooting up another big shower of sparks, and a piece of green mango wood chirruped like a cricket in the lick of a split tongue of blue and yellow flame, and that was the only sound in the yard until Shag said again:

'Dam funniest thing about that dream, the first person run into my mind this morning was Susu. . . .'

And Surjue said: 'Dam funny things altogether, dreams.'

'It's God talkin' to us,' said Miss Evangie, and Miss Mattie and Miss Katie nodded their heads, and there they were the White Sisters of Charity — they were called that because of the white ceremonial head dress and robes they wore — sitting side by side on the wooden bench they had brought out from their room, nodding their heads together like they were impelled by the same piece of hidden mechanism.

'De Lawd moves in a mysterious way,' said Miss Katie, and Miss Mattie capped it with, 'Ay, Sister Katie . . . his wonders to perform.'

Surjue said, irreverently, 'I caught a 6-mark on a peakapeow ticket last month, an' it was a dream I had, ask Rema if you think I'm lyin'.'

'You told me the dream in the morning while I was puttin' on me clothes, sure enough Surjue,' Rema said, 'and it was about you' cousin Emma who married now in America, an' you bought belly-woman an' big-water mark.'

'De Lawd don't send that dream, though,' said Miss Evangie, fanning herself primly with the back of an exercise book.

And Zephyr said, slapping her thigh and laughing, 'You hear that now?'

'De Lawd don't send a gamblin' man dreams, is de debbil, an' destruction an' tribulation is at de end of it, you mark me word.'

'Then is the devil lookin' after me all this time an Ah didn't even know so Ah could kneel down an' say, thank you Mass D, *tsk!* now just look at that!' said Surjue.

And Zephyr laughed again, rocking back, and Lennie's arm was there to keep her from falling off the stool. He looked down into her eyes, his arm still about her, and said, 'Some day you'll

want me to want you, when I'm strong for somebody new . . .'
crooning it like, softly, and it made her feel suddenly kind or
queer inside.

Shag, still staring into the fire and private with his own
thoughts in the midst of all the give and take of conversation
going on around, said out loud, 'Funny though, my mind never
run on Wallacy once these five years. . . .'

And then he seemed to collect himself and said, looking at
the faces around him, smiling, happy, carefree, himself again,
hearty, generous to the bone: 'This party's getting dry, anybody
want a wet, I got a demijohn of pimento dram inside.' He
looked across at Euphemia now, half-teasingly, 'Unless Euphemia
done use it up all in her pudd'n. Boy,' he winked at Surjue,
'she been feedin' me up on pudd'n so hard can scasely sleep from
proppin' up a tent all night.'

And now everybody laughed, except the White Sisters of
Charity shifting on their bony fannies on the hard board bench.
Bajun Man laughed loudest of all; he had a big bull voice, and
when he put his head back and laughed the muscles on his neck
stood out so you could see them, and you could hear him from
across the street.

'He just love it, you hear,' said Euphemia, like someone waking
out of a dream, laughing, getting up now, going across to Shag,
taking hold of him by the hair, playfully thumping him in the
back.

'Hey, go easy on me kidneys, gal, you knock 'em loose an' have
'em floatin' around inside me, you'll be goin' off with another
man next.'

He laughed, started to cough, real hard, trying to catch his
breath and laugh between bouts of coughing, until Euphemia's
face lost its laugh now and she helped him up to his feet and
went with him as he staggered, coughing, across the yard and
inside.

After that things sobered down a bit, but not for long, because
Lennie trying to kiss Zephyr caused the two stools to upset and
they ended up on the ground. She had to act like she was real
mad with him to get him quiet, his face had flushed to a deeper
chocolate colour and his eyes were very bright.

Mass Mose said: 'Shame!' because he thought Zephyr was so

55

mad she was going to cry, and Lennie said, in a different voice, 'Sorry, Zephyr, you hurt you'self?'

'It's nothing,' said Zephyr. 'Some skin off my elbow, 'bout all.'

Mass Mose made a sound from his chest that went, 'H-r-rump!' And Zephyr said, generously, smiling at Lennie a little, 'It was my fault.'

The Sisters of Charity, as though acting upon a given signal, got up off the bench together and went inside.

6   SURJUE WAS WEARING a sky-blue sport shirt, a soft brimmed Panama hat and a pair of cream flannel trousers above two-colour shoes when he stepped out into the street.

He walked along jauntily, whistling as he went. A little boy stopped to watch him going down the street, begged him sixpence; Surjue put his hand to his pocket before he could stop to think about it, and though he remembered with an inward wince that he was pretty nearly broke his hand came up with a flourish and he gave the boy sixpence. He had been won with that smile.

And there was something else too, a kind of excitement. He did not know how it came about, or why, but there it was and it went with the sky-blue sport shirt and the two-tone shoes and the whistle on his lips.

He was meeting Buju and Crawfish at a place in a lane off the street to discuss a business proposition, and it wasn't a matter of racing tips tonight. Racing tips made him think of Flitters, and he frowned. It was nothing . . . Flitters hadn't looked in after races that afternoon as he said he would . . . Rema had said something about Flitters . . . you be careful of that guy . . . she was always saying things like that, Rema . . . didn't like Flitters, that was it . . . women were like that, called it intuition.

The lighted shop fronts looked into the semi-darkness of the street and seemed satisfied that there were enough people about to stay open. They looked smug and comfortable as though speculating behind their rectangles of glass and rolled-up steel shutters what effect the latest rise in prices of consumer goods would have on peoples' spending . . . but speculating with an optimism born of past experience, like bandits lurking in ambush, knowing that fat prizes must pass that way; the rolled-up shutters like raised eyebrows sanctimoniously aloof from the sordid existence going past continually on the sidewalks, or in cold-blooded contemplation of possible new and unimagined price ceilings.

And the wind walked sedately down this street, folding back scraps of useless paper left carelessly to lie on unkept sidewalks, or slyly playing with the skirts about little girls' knees, or combing its fingers puckishly in passing through an old man's wispy beard, sometimes going lickity-spit through a crack in an ancient zinc fence or shingle-roof, sometimes scattering a handful of leaves before it like a bent old woman with a feather duster clearing out an attic room.

Surjue went through a zinc fence . . . through a hinged zinc sheet in a zinc fence that looked like a solid stretch of iron sheeting down one side of a lane . . . went through this secret door into the back premises of a Chinese shop, and so into a little side room where liquor was sold after closing hours and without a licence to a limited clientele.

Two men sat drinking at a little table inside the room. The one called Crawfish had a dark red complexion and rusty brown hair, he was tall and thin, his face and neck and hands covered with large reddish-brown freckles that sometimes ran into patches and his uneven teeth showed through lips like a split bladder that gaped a little and was never still. The other, Buju, was shorter, thick-set, black, with little bright eyes and a nervous affliction that made him give off clucking sounds from deep down inside his throat. He had a large, round head, and big hands; on the middle finger of the left one he wore a large gold ring.

'Wha' happ'n?' said Crawfish as Surjue came in.

'Don't happ'n yet,' said Surjue.

He drew up to the table and the Chinaman brought him another glass. Ice clinked and Buju tipped liquor into the glass.

Crawfish, taking a fly out of his drink with his little finger, looked at it, flicked it away, frowning, said, 'Rass, the flies around here don't even know when it's time to go to bed,' made a face and gulped down the rest of his liquor quick.

'Was a piece of cork, man,' Buju laughed.

'Cork, no?' said Crawfish, wiping the back of his hand across his bladder-like lips, 'never seen a piece of cork with little hairs sticking out of its ass.'

'How's a boy,' said Surjue, looking from Crawfish to Buju, grinning, rubbing his hands together as if he had a pair of dice in them, his gaze coming to rest on the picture of a naked woman on the wall, sitting, holding a big pink cushion in front of her shaped like a heart, her eyes and juicy smile privy with sex.

'You got ants in your pants, Surjue.'

'Boy, I'm feelin' so good this evening, I tell you.'

'Let's get down to business.'

'We can talk here?'

'Sure. What's bitin' you?'

'Could do with some Flit around this joint.'

'Never seen a guy so unholy scared of a little cockroach.'

'Cockroaches an' flies, they gimme the creeps.'

'Talkin' about Flit, 'minds me of a joke . . .'

'Let's get down to business, eh?'

'Sure.'

'What's the dope?'

'This here is a sound proposition, Surjue.'

'Safe as a church.'

'What's it, anyway?'

'Black market deal.'

'You wouldn't kid me now, would you?'

'I tell you it's a sound proposition.'

'Yeah man, safe as a church.'

'You wouldn't even have to come in on it as an operator.'

'All we need is somebody put up the dough.'

'What's the merchandise?'

'Beef.'

'We plan to run in the carcases from St. Thomas, leave the Spanish Town end alone.'

'Yeah man, strictly alone.'

'Suppose the cops catch you?'

'It's a fine.'

58

'Stealin' cattle ain't. It's a prison offence.'

'We wouldn't be doin' the stealin'. Be running the market operations, only.'

'I see.'

'All we need is somebody put up the dough.'

'How much?'

'Couple of hundred to start.'

'Half of that even.'

'Couple of good operations we'd be sittin' pretty.'

'We got a plan worked out the cops couldn't touch us.'

'Yeah man, safe as a church.'

'When you got to have it?'

'Soon as we can.'

Where the hell could he raise a hundred pounds? Was he dreaming?

'You figure we could make good money out of it?'

'Double and treble our capital on two-three good runs.'

'It's so easy like turning over on your side.'

Now where the hell did he think he could raise that kind of money? Was he dreaming?

'Well, give me a little time think it over, I'll let you know.'

Out in the street, a hundred yards or so from the gate, he ran into a girl. A swell looker, she was quietly but nicely dressed, she had a bunch of loose pamphlets in her hand and a red hand-bag with a long strap over her shoulder. She gave him one of those slightly intense slightly breathless looks with half a smile, she looked a little bold and a little bashful all together, and every bit nice.

'Good night.'

'Hi-ya, baby . . . Er, good night.'

'I saw you coming out of your gate earlier. You live in that big yard up the street?'

'That's right.'

Not what you might think she was at all. Now what the hell did she want?

'One of these pamphlets would cost you a sixpence, it'll tell you about the most important thing in life, how to save your soul. . . .'

59

Oh, like that.

He smiled evenly. He broke out a fresh packet of cigarettes, took one.

'Oh, I've read up on that already.'

'Have you?'

'You're smilin' like you don't believe me, but I'm tellin' you serious, I got it all fixed up about my soul.'

'Oh.'

'Yes. I been down on my knees an' everything like they said in the pamphlet an' talked with God about it good an' hard. Tell me somep'n, you think he's on the level?'

'What do you mean?'

'Now don't try to kid me, baby, you know whàt I'm talkin' about.'

'I don't. If you mean to say if God is on the level. . . . '

'Yeah, that's what I mean.'

'Well, you didn't get much from your reading if you doubt the wisdom and goodness of God. I mean to say. . . .'

'Well look now, don't gimme that line. I talked to him good an' hard, I tell you, an' he never done nothin' 'bout it. Now what you know?'

'Er, you speak of God as though — as though — ' she sawed the air with her hands, finding speech, but he was off again.

'That's what I mean, baby, you wouldn't think a guy like that would hide the joker up his sleeve or do anything right low down of that sort, would you?'

'Please . . . do you realize what you are saying? . . .'

'Sure. An' what's more I'd like to meet him up face to face an' give him a little piece of my mind one of these days. Look baby, the things you could lay at that guy's door, I wouldn't do like that to a mangy sick rat, I wouldn't.'

'Oh!'

'An' look at me — I'm not God. Now what'd you know?'

'Excuse me . . . someone I want to catch. . . .'

'Sure. I mustn't keep you. All the same I'd like to have a real good chat with you some time. The things I could tell you, you wouldn't believe 'em, an' God's truth, every bit. The way that guy's been short-changin' me an' some of my buddies, you wouldn't believe it. Well, there you are, another time when you're not so busy, eh? Say, what's that book called, *Millions Living Today Will Never Die* . . . well now who would want to go on living for ever with things stewing around like they are today? You tell me. En' if you think it's going to be different under any new-fangled system you're just a sucker for soap-box propaganda, an' that's a fact.'

He had to shout the last bit at her going across the street, and after he had finished he felt so good he wanted to laugh.

Well he'd fixed her, that ought to learn her a lesson, a real nice gal like that going from bar to bar and from place to place selling little pamphlets to people who didn't want to read them, but didn't know how to say so. Mostly men bought 'em, he'd bet. Fellows who talking to her couldn't keep their eyes off her tits, she all sexed-up an' wanting to do things, workin' it off this way. A bloody shame, that's what it was, and for what, to keep some guy with a big belly, and no appetite left for anything, rolling around soft in a swell automobile.

That peculiar excitement in his blood went with him all the way home.

He found the room door wasn't locked, but Rema was in bed, asleep, the lamp on the table turned down low. He could tell she was asleep from the way she was breathing into her pillow, and looking down at her now in the soft lamp-glow, her bare neck and shoulder and the peep of a breast with the top of her nightie pulled down all over on one side, started things coming up inside him, like the kick you get from strong liquor, only different, kind of up and down, and a little like a motor turning over, multiplying revs per minute. He passed the tip of his tongue over his dry lips, without knowing it, with things coming up inside him from way way down, smooth and sleek like a cat coming out of a dark shadow and walking through a beam of light, like music coming up out of a trumpet, rampant, with thin curved horns.

He took off his hat deliberately and hung it on a nail above the table with the lamp, and took it down again, and brushed it lightly with a sleeve, and laid it on a chair. His breathing quickened ever so slightly. He pulled two buttons off his shirt, taking a long time about it, looking at her, and away, and carry-

61

ing the image of her lying there in his eyes, staring at the blank wall opposite the big double bed. His breath came a little faster, like he had been running hard the last bit of the way. He stripped his shirt off and automatically flexed the muscles along his belly, making them roll like a snake.

He eased himself down on the side of the bed, sitting, careful not to awaken her, put up one foot across his knee and pulled off the shoe, the opposite wall with the calendar blacked-out slowly and his mind carried the image of her that he held within his eyes and laid it there.

He could have touched her by reaching out his hand, but he didn't; he sat there and thought for a while, and he lifted the other foot carefully from the floor and pulled off the other shoe.

He stood up.

He did another involuntary belly-roll.

He bent over her and straightened up again, and slipped off his pants. He tossed them so that they fell anyhow across the back of a chair.

And now he stood up in his underpants alone and listened to the horned music singing inside him, and underneath it the beating of drums.

He closed his eyes and passed the tip of his tongue over his lips again.

He leaned over the bed and the fingers of both hands came out stiff and he worked them up and down listening to them crack, and then he put them down to touch her and closed his eyes and felt under the nightdress for the soft of her belly with his taut fingers and still she didn't come awake. And he drew his fingernails lightly across her soft flesh still holding his fingers stiff like talons, and then he let them sink voluptuously into her flesh but with the motions of tickling her, and she opened her eyes and came out of sleep. . . .

And he bared his teeth and laid them to her throat, and gnashed them against her body, and lifted her clear off the bed, and gnashed his teeth against her flesh and threw her down again, and she laughed and struggled and called his name softly:

'Surjue . . . Surjue . . . you will wake up the place. . . .'

62

7 THE SEA IS AN OLD man babbling his dreams
. . . and was there some talk of the stars? . . .
the bright tears of morning drown in a wide
wide sea . . . who is there outside in the dark beyond the door,
knocking, to tell his dreams? . . . there are so many empty rooms
in the shuttered house that is yesterday . . . hamstrung at high
noon, who is it at midnight wakes to madness and rattles his
chains? . . . the sea is a weary old man babbling his dreams.

There were some who accounted the chance sure-footed, and
added their bones to the bleached white bones on the beach . . .
beneath the brinking horizontal horror the calcined shin makes a
dry sound . . . the salt dip rims and blurbles and sucks at hollow
cavities where the arrested genuflections of rocks tell there are
older gods than these . . . and the shin-bone pipes hollow requiems
to the sure-footed chance . . . the sea is a sad old man babbling
his dreams.

Who are they that passed along the weary beachheads and
sang their songs before us? . . . they have hung their harps on
the willows and gone their way . . . this curvature of rock was
limned into being out of reluctant granite . . . these sterile grains
of sand have told their tales before . . . the wind writes its tireless
songs along the stricken hollows . . . and the sea is a weary old
man babbling his dreams.

Two shoes stuck out noses from under the bed like rats explor-
ing an empty room and sniffed separate seams in the floor board-
ing that ran outside through a crack under the door. The light
bulb wearing a kilted skirt of fluted rose-patterned paper swung
on its drop cord from the ceiling with the least threat of wind,
swept light across the floor.

The outer periphery of shadows around the circle of light
swung with it, became an ellipse near the wall where the bureau
stood, and came to rest in its peripheral formation again in the
middle of the floor.

Shag lay on his back on the bed, his head resting in his clasped
hands and watched the slow pendulous swing of the drop light,
tried to forget the brown bilious taste in his mouth, hung one
leg over the side of the bed, and waited patiently for Euphemia
to come in from the bathroom.

She came in with a towel wrapped around her head like a turban, her face dull and expressionless, slumping a little as she sat down in front of the bureau, and smelling of bay rum.

'What's the matter with you, you sick?'

'Nothing much I guess, I took a dose of salts.'

'Salts always makes me feel that way too. Hurry an' come to bed. The light hurts my eyes, I can't sleep.'

'I won't be a minute now, you turn over on your other side.'

'I'm not sleepy really, I want to talk.'

'Talk? At this time of night!'

'How late is it?'

'Anyway you ought to be tired after a day like this.'

'You drop that hair brush a coupla times more you'll have the back off. What's the matter, you nervous or something?'

'I tell you I'm not feeling well tonight. It always makes me feel like this when it happens.'

'You ought to see a doctor, it's not your regular time.'

'What you know about it?'

'I ought to, you forget?'

He could see the shape of her breasts in the big round mirror where the dressing gown came open in front, they were big and round and solid like moons, they filled him with an intense satisfaction, with a feeling of warmth and security. He felt weak and spent after that fit of coughing . . . somehow the comforting assurance of her firm round breasts filled out the empty places inside him, made him warm and secure.

'What you thinking about?' she said, shifting on the stool before the mirror.

'Nothing.'

'I heard you make like a sigh, how you feeling now?'

'A lot better, it's all that dust I take up on my chest down at the tile factory, cement an' such, it's a hell of a place.'

'You be careful, ought to see a doctor yourself.'

'Me, I'm all right. Wish we could move.'

'Eh?'

'From the yard here, I mean. Don't like the place somehow.'

'It's not so easy to get a place to live in these days, where'd you want to go?'

'I dunno. It's the people I don't like, some of them.'

'Yes.'

'What's the matter? You in pain?'

'My belly is hurting me a little. Like who?'

'Eh?'

'Like who in the yard special like, you don't care about?'

'Plenty. Like that Bedosa.'

'Oh him. He's a liar and a sneak.'

'Yes.'

'I could kill him like a cockroach, God's truth. I saw him talking to you.'

'Yes.'

'A man like that is dangerous, I'm scared of him. What did he say?'

'Oh nothing much, a lot of foolishness, I don't pay him no mind.'

'What'd he say, special, to make you think of him now?'

'Didn't say nothing — special. Talked a lot of rot.'

'He's a nasty, evil-minded man.'

'I don't pay him no mind. What's the matter, you look faint.'

'I feel kinda faint, must be the room is hot.'

'It is. Open the window right up, honey.'

'And sleep with it that way?'

'Yes. Why not?'

'I'd be scared of burglars. I don't trust the people in this yard. I hate them, God yes, I hate them . . . like you.'

'You don't have to be scared of them that way, I can take care of you.'

'Oh yes.'

'I don't have a gun, but I keep my old machette under the bed, and it's as sharp as sharp.'

'Shag!'

'What, honey?'

'I don't like to hear you talk like that.'

'How?'

'You mean to say you would — chop somebody?'

'Effen it came to that, yes I would.'

'Effen it came to what . . . what you talkin' about?'

'Effen a burglar was to get into the room, for instance. Or anything like that . . . what's the matter now, you shiverin', you scared?'

'Don't like to hear you talk like that.'

'All right, I was doing it to comfort you.'

'To comfort me . . . ?'

'Yes, you so scared about burglars, an' all.'

'I'm not — not really.'

'Yes, you are, I never seen a woman so scared. You goin' to push up the window for me, honey?'

'I'm not feelin' hot any more.'

'You shakin' now like you got the ague, you sicker'n you think, I bet.'

'It'll pass.'

'You're goin' to see a doctor in the morning.'

'Morning I'll feel better, I know it.'

'That's how the fever comes an' goes. You go an' see a doctor first thing tomorrow, promise me. Effen you was to go an' get sick bad, or somep'n, don't know what I'd do.'

'I'm feelin' better'n better, be okay in a minute.'

'Nothing to be scared about, a good sharp machette is even better'n a gun, I seen a man chop off another man's arm above the elbow with a machette, *wham!* like that, one strike.'

'SHAG!' shuddering, calling his name big, in a voice of pain.

'Sorry, honey . . . Euphemia! what's the matter with you? God, you scared me. Thought you was goin' to faint. You seein' the doctor in the mornin' honey effen I have to carry you.'

The light bulb in its kilted skirt of a shade swung with the wind, dragging its periphery of shadow across the floor. Shag swung his feet to the bare boards, sat up with his hands pressed against the bed either side of him. Euphemia saw his anxious face in the mirror looking at her with a kind of scared uncertainty and a kind of hunger, shut her eyes an instant as though with pain, opened them again and went on with brushing her hair.

'Come to bed now, honey. Time you got to bed.'

'In just a minute.'

'You're more tired than you know, that's it. Worrying about me being tired, was you? Why honey, your eyes are closing down on you. Come to bed now, eh? Come on to bed.'

'If I only knew of a place to go. . . .'

'What?'

'Nothing.'

'You mean — yeah, I guess you could do with a change. Nothing like a change of air.'

'I don't want to leave you.'

'For a couple of weeks yes, honey, it'd do you good.'

'You need a change yourself, more'n me.'

'I don't, I tell you it's just the dust I keep takin' up on my chest that does it, workin' down at that dam hole.'

'So you say.'

'You all wore out, honey. Gotta think of you.'

She stood up now, big and tall and handsome, a fine figure of a woman cast in the classical Greek mould, but ebony all over, like a magnificent carving in ebony. Slowly she shrugged out of the faded dressing gown. Standing like that in her thin night dress the lines of her voluptuous figure were emphasized. He could feel the bitter-stale brown taste in the back of his mouth.

She hung her dressing gown from a hook over against the wall the other side of the bureau and walked over to the bed in her bare feet.

She came and stood before him and looked down at him with a kind of mothering tenderness. She put out a hand and rested it lightly on his head. He took the other and held it in his and looked at it long, as though he didn't know what to do with it . . . where to arrest his searching for her, his reaching for her across space . . . he stood up suddenly and pushed her gently towards the bed.

'Go on now, lie down. You're all wore out.'

She fell across the bed, her body taking its voluptuous folds about it, snuggled down, her legs slightly drawn up, her back toward him. He switched off the light, tiptoeing toward the cord and back as though his bare feet shuddered from contact with the floor. The street light outside cast a faint glow against the frosted window glass.

He got into bed and lay quietly beside her, sat up and tucked the cover about her feet. His hands dragged slowly against the length of her limbs, as though taking assurance to himself that she was there; he sighed, taking warmth and comfort from the bare contact, the certain knowledge of her there.

'Got a good mind send you to the country for a change,' he grumbled.

67

Very quietly she shuffled the folds of the cover from off her feet.

'Got a good mind pack you off to the country . . . clean wore out . . . need a change.'

He yawned expansively, his hand before his mouth, grunted, and turned over on his side.

His knee came up unconsciously and rested against her buttocks. Little by little she stirred as though to ease herself into a more comfortable position, inched away.

The night outside gave up a thousand murmurs . . . unconsciously she listened for his breathing among the other sounds . . . Bedosa had told him something; what? . . . that story about Wallacy and the girl they called Susu he had told around the fire . . . his breathing told her he was not yet asleep . . . wanted to send her off to the country . . . *de ribber ben come down, a-how you come over* . . . he always kept his machette sharp under the bed, would she dare to hide it? . . . you're just plain wore out, that's what, need a change . . . *de ribber ben come down, de ribber ben come down* . . . a cricket set up a shrill racket, it sounded just outside the window but it might equally be down somewhere by the old ackee tree . . . and all on account of that little monkeyshine, Manny; she had lost her temper . . . *de ribber ben come down* . . . his heavy breathing told her he was asleep.

8   MANNY AND TANSY were already asleep on their separate bunks when Bedosa and Charlotta turned in. Bedosa was heavy with sleep because he had eaten more heartily than was good for him, but goaded by a curious perversity Charlotta wanted to talk.

'Effen you don't pull the laces you'll spoil the shape of you' shoes takin' them off that lazy fashion. I saw you and Nanine.'

'What you saying?'

'Saying I saw you and Nanine. With yuh head down on her knee.'

'Cho, you didn't see nothing at all, you only lookin' argument, I'm tired, want to go to sleep.'

'Right out in front of everybody, an' don't care for enything.

You should think better of yourself, don't mind me. I only work my fingers to the bone to make things go right . . . but don't mind me. You married me in a church, you mind? I'm no common gal you picked up off the street. I only want for things to go right, but I'm an old fowl now, chicken is what you want.'

'I want to go to bed. You will wake up the children next.'

'The children, eh? You care a heap about the children — an' me. I'm just an old woman in your way, if I was to die tonight you would be glad. Is young gal you lookin', after all these years, you ought to be ashamed.'

'Where you goin' with that pan?'

'Goin' outside to draw water. What you want?'

'Gimme the ole pan, I'll get the water for you.'

'You! You only want an excuse so you can look in at that gal's door, you stayin' right here, when since you been drawin' water for me?'

'All right, if you want to go out into the night dew an' tek up cold, is your affair. I was only thinkin' of you.'

'When since you start thinkin' of me? We'll be married come October seventeen years, an' I'm nothin' but an old woman now to you. Tek time put down yuh shoes you will wake up the place with yuh noise. Seventeen years . . . an' it's a good thing it's only two children I have for you, the Lawd did know good not to give me any more.'

'Fo' God's sake stop singin' in me ears, Ah want to go to sleep. Go draw you' water an' come back, you don't want go to bed? My God! is fire you goin' mek-up this time of night! Is what matter wid yuh at all?'

'I want some water to hot. Don't mind me, you go on to sleep. Every livin' day I work an' work me fingers to the bone tryin' to mek two ends meet, an' what's the thankee Ah get? The Lawd knows! But no mind, though, the good Lawd knows everything.'

'Effen you goin' start on religion now—'

'Ah say tek time yaw, de Lawd is not asleep.'

She swung the tin can by its wire handle and went out through the door, leaving it ajar. Bedosa kicked it shut with a thrust of his foot.

He took off his outer clothes and lay down on the bed in his merino and drawers. He closed his eyes, but sleep would not come. All kinds of thoughts kept stirring around inside his head. Or was it the cow-heel stew lying on his chest keeping him awake? Every time he belched he tasted that ole cow-heel stew.

He wondered about Shag and Euphemia and Bajun Man. Now that was a set up! And Shag didn't know a thing, poor sucker he didn't even have a clue. Bajun Man was taking his woman away from him right under his nose, and he couldn't see. Wasn't no good telling him nothing, neither, when a guy was that dumb wasn't no good doing nothing at all.

Charlotta came in back through the door. She went over to the wood stove where she had started a fire, set down the pan of water, laid on some more wood to make the fire blaze. She filled the kettle and set it on the stove. Then she went down on her knees before the slowly kindling fire and made her mouth into a bellows and shut her eyes and blew upon the tentative nurseling flames. The wood was green and smoke and cinders blew into her face. She gasped and coughed and drew away, putting her face to one side and taking the weight of her body on her hands. Smothering with self-pity she glared through smoke-reddened lids at the man lying on the bed.

'All you can do is stir up trouble among the people you livin' with in the same yard. What you want to go troublin' what don't concern you for? Ole people say jackass don' hear himself bray, you go on trouble trouble, trouble will trouble you.'

He turned over on his other side deliberately, giving her his back. But weltering in self-pity as she was now she had lost all her fear of him. His very indifference to her suffering goaded her on. She sat down before the fire now, her legs drawn up under her, as though she welcomed the physical discomfiture of the smoke and cinders. She rocked a little back and forth from the waist. She brushed dead cinders from her dress with both hands.

Years of ceaseless toil and suffering had made her become narrow-minded and religiously bigoted, that and the fact that she was terribly deep-down insecure. And Bedosa who was at heart a coward, though he bullied her and drove her unmercifully, would run away every time rather than stand and fight.

'Seventeen years I've stood it, an' only the Lawd knows why. You can turn yuh back give me, an' form sleep, but you goin' lissen to me tonight. Seventeen years, an' you didn't pick me up off de street, you married me in church, remember, but now I'm just an ole fowl in yuh way, you don' have to pay me no mind. Young gal you lookin' — me, I'm just an ole fowl. Chicken pickin' you lookin', no? You mind yuh time. Good fo' nuttin all you can do is mek trouble wid de people livin' in de yard. An' Manny a big bwoy now tekin' fashion from you, you ought to be ashamed though, effen you had any mind at all you would be well an' shame.'

Tears came to her eyes, and they were not all for the smoke, they formed and grew big under her drooping reddened lids and rolled down her sooty face, and a dark mist came up inside her and her bosom grew big with her troubles and the burden of her days and nights. She started to sob, and found that way a little of the tension was released, and there was a slight loosening of the cords inside her breast, and her head fell forward on her bosom and she sobbed some more.

The fire, unattended, grew under the kindling with red and yellow flames, and the kettle on the hob hissed and whistled softly and presently began to sing, and still she sat there unstirring before the fire sobbing to herself, and the big tears made under her reddened lids and rolled down.

Goodie thought it was Puss-Jook but it was Ditty wheezing a little bronchially in her untroubled sleep on a mattress laid out on the floor one corner of the room. Puss-Jook was doing no more than scratching himself systematically and with the greatest economy of effort over by the window staring out into the night when she got back from Cousin Maudie's down the road with the liniment for her knee. Took up cold in it she had from standing long in her rubber-sole canvas shoes on the chill pavement outside the grass-yard early mornings haggling over vegetables she bought from the country people coming in on trucks from the hills.

She had run out of liniment, careless, but really sake of she didn't have time before doctor shop closing to buy it bring home with her. Night fall so soon, you take two turns round the market square with your vegetable barrow, tired, siddung, shet you' eye, open it, Lawd, sun gone down.

An' de ole knee was a sose-a tribulation top of everything wid de ole pain gnawin' her from livin' mornin' till night.

Rheumatism must be, so de doctor-man did say, shore nuff, when she went to de doctor-shop, Auntie Maud advisin' her, an' did tell him 'bout de pain-a-joint.

Scasely can sleep night-time wid de man snorin' widouten a trouble in de world, stretch out side-a her, de bed a-go crips-crips under him every time him turn.

Scasely can sleep wid de pain-a-knee ah-gnaw she, Lawd, jackass say de world don' level, ups-an'-downs, me Jesus, nutt'n but ups-an'-downs.

An' Ditty she a big gal now caan help her, do nutt'n all day long, must deh-traipse de street, lookin' is what? she wouldn't know, but ah-so today pickney stay, me Jesus, gal ah big-up like ooman now scasely can kip de one-room clean.

She sat down on the side of the bed to 'noint her knee and looked dully at Puss-Jook sitting on a stool over by the window scratching himself intimately and yawning into the night.

'Bwoy, why you don't go to sleep, what's matter you tossin' so?' Mack said, raising himself on his elbow and trying to pierce the darkness with his gaze to see if he could what it was made Wilfie so restless in his cot.

'Can't sleep,' Wilfie grumbled back, 'the night is hot.'

'Get up an' go put yuh head under the pipe,' Mack advised, and Wilfie crawled out of the cot and felt along the floor with his feet in the dark for his shoes.

The man grunted and let his head down on the pillow again.

The creaking of the door on its hinge wakened him as he was dropping off to sleep when Wilfie returned from wetting his head under the pipe. He grumbled with his mouth stuck into the crook of his elbow. And Wilfie remembered he had left the comb on the edge of the concrete cistern, and there would be hell to pay in the morning if somebody like Manny was to find it first, for he and Mack shared the same piece of comb. He let himself out again and tried to lift the door a bit as he swung it back so as to ease the weight on the creaking hinges. It made only a little noise, and he breathed easier going outside again.

The night was brittle and cloudless, it had hung out a curtain of stars. A whistling toad went peep, peep, peep down by the guinep tree at the gully's edge, and the whitewashed shacks made converging smudges in the darkness. The street light seen through the leaves of the mango tree was a bright star caught on a pole.

He looked up at the great curtain of night and was oppressed with the stillness, his thoughts were strangely tinged with a sense of guilt, or perhaps not so much guilt as a kind of uneasiness, as though way down he was conscious of having clumsily disturbed some ancient tablets of the law.

He thought of God, and the impenetrable nature of His awful purity and His awful wisdom chilled him to stone. He wondered was it true about God and all those things he had always heard concerning him, wondered did God know in his heart or in his head about things. The awful thought of God lay against his own heart like a chillness, and he was glad with one half of his mind that he only half believed.

He thought of Ditty without exultation, without comfort, without pride in his conquest; it did not weigh with him that it was he who had been ravished by her, because he did not see it in that light at all. All he was aware of was an absence of a sense of manliness as his portion of this act they had shared in secret. There was neither heat nor cold in his heart but a handful of ashes only.

The rectangular window was an unblinking yellow eye looking out with a stolid uncomprehending stare into the indifferent and inviolate night, and Lennie came walking stealthily down the length of the shacks that looked like a smudge of greyness to one side of the slate, the other side of which was held up by the irregular line of the slightly leering picket fence with buck teeth knocked out at unconsidered intervals. The street light seen through the shuffling leaves made a bright asterisk against the darkness. A stammering anvil spoke from across the street where the tinsmith's shop was, he was working late handling some cans for tomorrow's trade.

Lennie came stealthily down the line of the shacks that turned its back upon the gully and so to the concrete-nog structure that stood a little disdainfully to one side looking down its nose at the lowlier barracks, across the inner façade of the house now, always avoiding the open yard space, until he stood outside and facing the yellow noncommittal stare of the window. He rattled on it with his fingernails making a light tattoo against the frosted glass.

Zephyr was in bed reading a book. She got up immediately and threw the window open.

'Why Lennie, you not gone to bed yet?'

'I can't sleep for lonesomeness,' he grinned. 'I saw your light on. Open the window right up, honey, I'm coming in.'

'No big boy, you're not.'

'Why not?'

'Mm-mm.'

'What you doing, reading a book? I'll tell you a bedtime story.'

'Not tonight, I'm clean tired out already.'

'Lissen baby, when are you goin' to quit holdin' out on me? What's the matter with me, I got sores on me neck or somep'n?'

'No. You're a nice boy.'

'Thank you, mamma.'

'Honest, I like you.'

'But what?'

'But nothing, I just like you, that's all.'

'You crazy.'

'Must be.'

'Well, how long we going to stand here arguing?'

He caught her hand, held it, tickled the middle of her palm with his finger. Her fingers shut down hard upon his, she smiled.

'Honest I don't know what's the matter with me, I like you enough.'

'Perhaps if I was to get tough—'

'That wouldn't do any good at all.'

'I got to try everything. Stand back, I'm coming in through the window.'

'No. I won't let you.'

'You can't stop me, honey, unless you goin' to bawl for thief, or somep'n.'

'Wait. Someone is coming.'

'The hell with them, I don't care. Look, I'm tired of your stallin', I'm comin' inside.'

74

He swung himself up on the windowsill and she tried to push him off. He wrestled her halfway across the room until they fell across the bed, and all that time neither of them spoke a word.

9 'YOU THINK AH don't know 'bout you an' Ditty the other night, no?'

Manny leered, his lips drawn back from his big teeth in what was meant to be a smile.

'What you sayin' at all?' said Wilfie.

'Don't try to fool me, man, I was watchin' the two of you all the time.'

They were down the gully a piece knocking down jew-plums off Miss Angie's tree.

'What you an' she was doin' behind the house?'

But Wilfie didn't want to discuss it.

'Eh, what the two of you was doin'? I know bwoy, you can't fool me.'

Wilfie sat down on a stone and stared up at the tree, avoiding Manny's leering face, conscious of a mounting irritation.

'Wouldn't try.'

'What you mean?'

'You dam fool enough already.'

'What you say?'

'You heard me.'

'Say it again.'

'Look Manny, I can't be bothered to quarrel with you.'

'Better not, bwoy.'

'All right.'

'Eh?'

'Anything you say.'

'Know what?'

'Not till you tell me.'

'Goin' lay Ditty meself.'

'You!'

'Yes. What you mean *me*, like that?'

'Mean to say—'

'Effen you can do it why not me?'

Wilfie's face stiffened. His fingers involuntarily clawed at the ground around him, came to rest on a stone. He considered the leering face before him, and his blood was hot, there was also a tingling sensation in his stomach that he did not understand.

'You could try.'

'You think Ah couldn't get it?'

'I'm not sayin' anything.'

'Could have her if Ah was to lift me finger. Could t'row her down any time.'

'All right big mout'.'

'Big mout', nuh? Ah will show you big-mout'.'

'You caint show me nutt'n, bwoy.'

'Ah goin' lay her, watch an' see.'

Wilfie considered this objectively for a moment.

'No, you wouldn't do that. You mean to say—'

'Effen Ah mean to say what?'

'Mean to say you would do that to her — with what you got?'

Manny squatted on his haunches, picked up a handful of pebbles, flipped one at a scurrying ground lizard making away among a sprinkling of leaves.

'You mean the dose?'

'Yes.'

'Why not?'

'You should know.'

'Don't mek me laff.'

'You should laff, wid a thing like that.'

'Bwoy, you don't know nutt'n, they like what I got.'

'You believe that?'

'Prove it to you.'

'Couldn't prove nutt'n to me, bwoy. You gimme a pain. You shore do.'

'Give you a pain, no? Wait till Ah tek Ditty down de gully.'

'You could try. No harm tryin'.'

'Think Ah couldn't lay her, eh? What you consider, you a champion?'

'Nutt'n like that. I ain't braggin'.'

'Shore you is braggin'. But Ah will show you.'

'You caint show me nutt'n. Awe, you gimme a pain.'

'Pain, no? You ain't seen nutt'n yet. Ah tell you they love what I got.'

'Quit braggin'. An' take that thing to a doctor, you know what's good for you.'

'Cho, you nutt'n but a sissy.'

'You gimme a pain.'

'Go chase you'self, bwoy, you ain't know nutt'n.'

'Truth is Ah don't know why Ah bother talk to you at all.'

'What you say?'

'Sometimes you mek me sick in me stomach, Ah want to puke.'

'You want to fight?'

Manny stood up, stretched himself, grinned as though he was pleased about something. Wilfie just looked at him, speaking slowly, deliberately.

'Lissen Manny, don't bring fight to me. 'Member what Euphemia do to you the other day in the yard?'

'Eh? What's that?'

'Ah will mess you up worse 'an that.'

'Say what?'

'You heard me.'

Manny looked at him, his eyes narrowing.

'It look like you want fight, no?'

'Ah tell you don't bring fight to me. Ah got a rock stone under me hand here ready for you. Ah aint foolin'.'

The belligerent look went out of Manny's eyes, he grinned again.

'Cho man, what you talkin' 'bout anyway, who want to fight you?'

'No you start talkin' 'bout fight?'

'Ah wouldn't fight you, Wilfie. Ah wouldn't tek advantage of you.'

'You dam right, you wouldn't, Manny. Ah got somep'n here waitin' fo' you, an Ah aint foolin', you know it.'

'Well Ah don't aim to fight you neither, you is me friend. If it was Pattoo now. . . .'

'Why you have strong fo' Pattoo? What him do you?'

'Dat pulp-eye son of a bitch!'

'What him do you?'

'Cho, forget him.'

'You bring it up.'

'Ah goin' up de yard, you comin'?'

'Goin' back up de yard meself, yes.'

77

Wilfie stood up, getting slowly to his feet, brushed the seat of his pants with his hand, looked up at the jew-plum tree, down at his feet again, appeared to have something on his mind.

'You comin', come on then.'

'Don't wait fo' me.'

'You comin'?'

'Ah say don't wait fo' me.'

Manny shrugged indifferently, his lips forming into that hateful grin.

'No matter. Ah goin' fall Ditty, though.'

'You can try.'

'Think you is a champion, no? Fall her as easy as liftin' me finger.'

'That's your business.'

'An' yours too, think Ah didn't see the two of you the other night?'

'Cho man, you foolish.'

'Foolish, no? Huh! Is what you was doin' behind the house? Think Ah didn't tek notice?'

Bedosa sat on the side of the bed and burped loudly. He made a wry face and bent over a little from the waist bringing his mouth down to his fist. After two or three noisy expulsions of gas he straightened up again, put his wry lips over to one side of his face in a grimace of agony, put his hand inside his shirt and gently massaged the side of his belly.

'God!' he said, and burped, and shook his head and said, 'God!' again.

'You got it bad again, best to lie down an' let me draw you some pepper-elder tea,' said Charlotta.

He yanked off the half-buttoned shirt and threw it to the floor, and was immediately twisted up with another gas pain. When he came out of it at last his face was thinly beaded with cold sweat.

'You got it real bad,' said Charlotta. 'Good thing I have the kettle going,' she said.

He straightened up and looked at her out of a face twisted with agony. 'How you expect me to wear a shirt without buttons on,' he said.

'What you talkin' about shirt?' she said.

78

'Buttons,' he growled, jerking his chin at the shirt on the floor.

'Never mind about that now. You stretch out in bed. I'll bile you some pepper-elder tea.'

'Can't wear . . . shirt . . . withouten buttons on. . . .'

'You keep on about that shirt you give yourself pains in the belly again. Lie still now. Put up your feet, stretch out, an' lie still. Bile you some pepper-elder tea in a minute.'

He lay across the bed, clutched his side, drew up one leg, brought his head down almost to his knee.

She went over to the stove, put some more wood in the fire, blew on it until it crackled and blazed. The kettle sang.

She took some dried herbs out of an old shoe box on a shelf, placed them in a small teapot, poured some of the boiling water over them and set the teapot on the stove to simmer a little beside the kettle.

She went over to the bed and stood for a while looking down at him.

'How you feeling now?' she said.

The new wood in the fire made a thin cricket-sound, and presently rose to a still shriller note, and went out in the dehydrating flames.

'How you feeling?' she said again.

He groaned.

'Rub you up with some of that healin' oil,' she said. 'But you must drink the tea first; tea will lift that gas, you drink it down hot as you can take it.'

She poured out the tea and came back to stand beside him, holding the cup in her hand.

'Come on now, drink it up while it's hot.'

He rolled over, sat up, put his feet down on the floor, took his head between his hands, straightened up with an effort, his face pulled down with pain, took the cup from her hand and carried it to his lips.

'Dam stale patties,' he said, looking at her accusingly, after he had swallowed about half of the liquid. 'Dam stale patties hurt me belly.'

'Those patties I made this morning,' she said. 'You et too many of them, must be.'

'Don't want to see another one of them.'

79

'You shouldn't a-et so many. It's the grease in them.'

He looked at her over the rim of the cup, his eyes full of plaintive accusation, as though he thought she had deliberately tried to poison him.

'Don't want to see another of them as long as I live, you hear?'

He burped long and violently, and at the end of it reached for the pan under the bed.

She went and sat down on a box over by the stove, and watched him with the patient uncomplaining stare of a stone image.

'How you feelin' now?'

'Little better, Ah think Ah get a ease at last.'

'Turn over Ah rub you with some healin' oil. Nutt'n like healin' oil hot to rub with. Ease you plenty.'

'Nutt'n but dem dam stale patties you give me. Ah don' want see another one as long as Ah live.'

'You et too much, is what.'

'Woman, hush you' mout'.'

'All right, tu'n over, bare you' side mek Ah 'noint you.'

'Is account of all de trouble a man have to bear. Ah don't trouble people mek dem hate me, Ah don' trouble nobody, see God.'

'Who hate you?'

'People.'

'People? Is what you talkin' 'bout?'

'Man down the Slaughter House. Slocum they call him.'

'Him hate you?'

'Say is me mek him lose him job.'

'Why? What you do?'

'Do nutt'n at all. See God!'

'Why him hate you then?'

'Don't know at all.'

'Must be you mek trouble fo' him, yes.'

'Never like that.'

'Must be something why him hate you, though.'

'Nutt'n at all. Is just troubles come down on a man. Troubles everywhere you turn.'

'But why people should hate you, you don't do them nutt'n?'

'Tek time rub it, do. Ah feel the pain at me side again.'

'You better go see a doctor.'

'Don't be a dam fool.'

'All right. All right.'

'Gimme ole stale food to it, puff me, all you can do.'

'All right now, don't start fret-up you'self, you will bring on the pain.'

'A-a-ah!'

'Just lie down stretch out easy.'

'Can't even get a button on me shirt. Can't even get you rub me up a little when Ah eena pain.'

'All right, don't start fret, is soon be all right.'

'Troubles on a man from livin' mornin' till night.'

His fear manifesting as dyspepsia surged at him, so that he winced under her hand, instead of taking ease.

'Hush! No mind, it will soon pass.'

Her voice reached him with gentle persuasion in the midst of his spasm, and presently it passed. He expelled gas loudly, and felt better. But even so his fear, compelled upon him by some unseen deep down secret compulsion, surged at him again, beaded his face with cold sweat.

'Man tek oath him goin' kill me.'

'What?'

'Slocum. Say Ah mek him lose him job. Swear him goin' kill me.'

'Who is Slocum?'

'Fellow workin' side me down the Slaughter House. Ah hate the dam place, sickenin' of the smell of blood. Goin' leave the job meself, get 'nother one, that's what.'

'Hush now, frettin' won't help you.'

'Say is me report him to the foreman.'

'You' conscience clear, no need to worry. We trust in God.'

'Ah did see when him hide the cow tail, but see God, Ah never tell no one.'

'Hush then. The man was in temper. Don' mean it. Hush!'

'You don't know him.'

'No mind. In God we trust.'

'Hate de dam place anyway. Goin' get me another job. Sickenin' o' the smell o' blood.'

He groaned with the resurgent pain in his side.

'Hot some more oil.'

'Tomorrow you go see a doctor.'

'No mind that now, you hot some more oil, the rubbin' ease me.'

His deep down fear cloaked in the guise of the pain in his side thrust at him again, and to find relief from it he girded at her.

'Goddamit woman, why you won't hot the oil, rub me?'

'Ah hotten it fast as Ah can.'

'Nutt'n but stale ole patty to give a man it, tired of ittin ole stale food, Gawd judge me.'

'Don't swear now.'

'Ain't swearin', speakin' de truth, tired of ittin ole stale food, Gawd hear me.'

'All right, all right. Comin' over with the oil now, get you'self ready. . . .'

10   STARK SUNLIGHT unsoftened by window frosting invaded the room, lay in white rectangles on the red-ochre stained floor boards and radiated mid-afternoon heat like a brazier through the close atmosphere of the cramped room.

Surjue sat in his BVD's, shuffled the worn pack of playing cards, slapped them down on the table, swore, got up and hitched back the windows wide, struggling with the iron hook that worked itself unwillingly into the rusty screw-eye.

Flitters sitting opposite him surreptitiously lifted one foot and rubbed the toe of that shoe against the other leg of his pants, polishing it under the table out of sight, stared down at the new orange-coloured loafers he was sporting and sucked air audibly through the space between one gold-filled tooth in front and the one next to it. The heat didn't bother him.

Surjue had to get right up into the bed to latch back the other window that let in some desultory air on the back of his neck when he sat down on the edge of the bed facing Flitters. This window had a cracked lower pane of glass in the left hand leaf that was held together with a strip of gummed paper Rema had put there to keep the broken glass from falling out and letting in a draught one day.

(Surjue had said, the hell with it, let the dam place fall to pieces for all I care, we pay our rent regular and that son of a whore of a landlord don't care if the dam place was to tumble down on our heads, why should we? All right, Rema said, I'm not worrying about the landlord but you get a cold draught of night air blowing in on you and you find yourself with a stiff neck or something in the morning, and a lot he'd care.)

He hooked back both leaves of the window now, shuffled into his seat on the edge of the bed facing Flitters again, took up the pack of cards, pursed his lips a little, and dealt the hands.

'Let's shift the table down a bit,' said Surjue, presently. 'I got the sun now right in me neck, an' you look just like a lizard settin' in it there. Yuh blood must be cold man, never see a man sit so still in the sun withouten it botherin' him the way you do.'

'I don't mind it scasely at all.'

'They's lots of things I just can't figure about you.'

Flitters laughed, bearing up with his fingers against his end of the table, and moving his chair at the same time, getting Surjue out of the sun that was near to raising a blister on the back of his neck. His careless laughter irritated Surjue and he stabbed a glance at him as though to question and search him deep down to find the source and cause of his amusement. Nothing gave, and he just grunted, shifting his gaze back to the cards he held in his hand, and shrugging away the little irritation of Flitters and his incongruous laughter. He settled his attention back on the game.

Presently he threw down the cards on the table and reached up his arms behind him, knotted his fingers together, stretched himself and yawned.

'You tired of playing?'

'It don't amuse me any more.'

'Okay. Not so keen, either. Must be the heat.'

'I want to get my hands on a hundred pounds.'

'What?'

'A hundred libras, that's what I want.'

He rubbed his thumb and forefinger together, his fist resting on the table.

'Oh.'

'I got to get it'.

Flitters threw him a swift sloe-eyed look as though to see if he was joking, his lips loosely parted about the gold filling in front, his big hands idly riffing the cards.

'You got something on your mind.'

'Sure I got something on my mind, what you think!'

Flitters put his left hand away in his pocket, and his right hand alone went on riffing the cards.

'I'm not tellin' you neither, so don't ask me nothin', boy.'

'I wasn't askin' anyway, I ain't curious.'

'That's right, you ain't curious at all, I know that way.'

'But a hundred libras, man, that's a lot of money.'

'Who's sayin' it ain't, that's what I got to have just the same.'

Flitters made a thin whistling sound with his tongue against his front teeth and his lips drawn a little over to one side.

'Stop that, can't stand it, makes me blood run cold.'

'Eh?'

'It's the same like scratchin' with a pin against a slate. I beat up a boy for doin' that one time when I was in school.'

'Was I doin' something?'

'Yes, you was. An' don't do it, it makes me blood run cold.'

Flitters' hand came up slowly from his pocket, it carried a large scented silk handkerchief with it to his lips. When he took the handkerchief away from his lips they were drawn into a loose smile.

'I think I got a proposition. Say, you got to have this hundred libras bad?'

Surjue got up and walked across to the dressing table in his bare feet. From there he said:

'What you think? That's what I been tellin' you.'

He came back with Rema's nail scissors in his hand, sat down on the edge of the bed again, hitched one foot up from the floor and started meticulously paring his toe nails.

'Eh? What you think? What's matter you not so bright today.'

He worked over his foot until he came to the great toe nail, and he screwed up his face with the effort of getting that clipped but it wouldn't give, and he tried taking it from the other side but nothing happened for a while, and all the time his face never let go of that screwed-up intentness, until presently the scissors came in two halves in his hand, and he just looked at it in surprise, and presently he started to laugh.

'Well, I be damned!' he said, and laughed some more.

'What you call a thing like this? Well, bugger me,' he said.

And all that time Flitters never said a word.

The cards on the table made a soft riffing sound under his hand and he wasn't looking at Surjue at all, and when he looked up presently he saw Surjue putting down the scissors on the bedspread beside him in two parts, and he opened his mouth to say something, but he said instead, 'Now look what you done!'

Ditty sat on a box in the yard, tilted back against the side of the northern row of shacks using the slanting shadow for shade, shelling green congo peas in a big round pudding pan which she held on her lap, her short skirt drawn well up above her knees. And Manny walked into the yard from down the gully carrying a machette in one hand and in the other a straight green stick which he proceeded to trim, taking the bark off. When he saw Ditty sitting by herself he went immediately across to her.

They fell to chatting and laughing, and Ditty looked at him brazen as you please, taking his chat and giving it back to him twelve to the dozen, and every now and then she put her head back and laughed.

Tansy, a great big axe in her hand, was out in front of the other row of shacks where a short chopping block was that Ras had dragged up from the gully, and she was trying to split some firewood that was too big to go into the stove. The axe was too heavy for her and at length she set it down and leaned against the haft and looked across at Manny at the other side of the yard chopping words with Ditty and she got angry at first with a fierce blazing anger, and then she wanted to cry.

Ras came out of his room carrying the jug to the standpipe for water and he saw her standing there, and he set down the jug on the step and went up to her and said, 'Gimme the axe li'l gal, mek me split the wood fo' yuh,' and he just glanced at Manny once as he swung the axe up, and when it came down *wham!* it split the hunk of wood clean in two pieces, and he spat once on the ground beside him, and took another piece of wood from the pile and set it squarely on the chopping block again.

Tansy took the jug and filled it with water from the standpipe, and she was setting it down on the step in front of Ras' room door just as Charlotta came to her door and said, 'Wha's matter gal, you don't done split that wood yet?'

'Soon done, Ma,' Tansy said, and Ras hunched his shoulders in a kind of shrug and swung the axe up again.

Ditty put her head back against the wall to laugh and Wilfie came into the yard through the street gate. He threw Ditty and Manny a glance and went on inside as though he didn't take notice of anything.

And Ras swung the axe up and brought it down again, and a wood chip split off with the impact and smacked against the pudding pan Ditty was shelling peas into on her lap, and she jumped up and said, 'Lawd Jesus!' And Manny laughed.

Tansy was gathering up an armful of split wood and she saw it happen and wished something wicked deep down in her heart, and it was so wicked she said out aloud, 'Pardon, Jesus!' before she could catch it back, so that Ras looked at her and grinned and nodded with such genuine understanding that it might have been him she was addressing.

She threw him a quick, shy smile, and Ras spat on his hands and took the haft of the axe between them again in a sure grip, and as he swung it up he said, 'Peace an' love, l'il sister, peace an' love!'

'You got a proposition,' said Surjue, 'let's hear it.'

Flitters stacked the cards neatly, squared the edges between the fingers of both hands, and began whistling unconsciously between his teeth again.

'For Christ sake, stop it,' said Surjue irritably. 'One of these days I'm goin' to buy you a whistle to play on.'

'Eh? Didn't even know I was doin' it,' said Flitters.

Surjue started to make a cigarette but Flitters fished a packet of Chesterfield's from his pocket.

'Here, try one of these.'

Surjue took the cigarette, brought his face close to the automatic lighter Flitters held out to him. It broke into flame between his cupped hands and Surjue lit up and drew smoke deep down into his lungs.

86

'It's tricky,' said Flitters.

'Eh?'

'This, er—proposition of mine. There's some risk to it.'

'Oh, that. Main thing is, can we work it?'

'Yeah.'

'Just the two of us.'

'Better that way.'

'If you mean cracking a crib I never done anything like that in my life.'

'I got it figured out all ways.'

Surjue blew smoke up to the roof and leaned back, his head against the windowsill.

'What's the lay out?'

'It's one of them lottery banks in Chinatown.'

'You crazy, man.'

'No, listen to me. They take in plenty of money, these banks. Too late for lodgement in a commercial bank. The place I'm tellin' you about we could get in through the roof, it's a cinch.'

'And you figure the cash would be there.'

'It's bound to be.'

'I don't like it. Never done anything like that before.'

'All it takes is nerve.'

'How much cash you figure they would keep there?'

'Hundreds of pounds, the day's takings.'

'In an iron safe you couldn't open without dynamite. You crazy, for sure.'

'It's one of those old-fashioned safes. You could open it with a hairpin. I seen it, the place I'm talking about.' He leaned forward confidentially, his arms out before him resting on the table. 'Listen, this is the lay out. . . .'

Surjue listened, broke off a half-inch of ash carefully with his fingers, took it in his hand and threw it out the window, his gaze focused on the gold-filled tooth in the face before him.

Zephyr sat down on the side of the bed and her hand went out and touched the other woman on the shoulder. Euphemia was sobbing, but not loudly, and presently the fingers that had bunched up into a fist relaxed and some of the tension went out of her.

'You got to get a good grip on yourself,' said Zephyr. 'No sense to let go like that. Only make things harder, honey. Got to get a good hold on yourself an' let things ride.'

'Let me get up,' said Euphemia, and she sat up, and put her hands up to her face, and took them away again, and said, 'There, I feel better already.'

'That's right.'

'Silly to cry.'

'Well, it helps, you know.'

'No, it don't neither, but God's truth I'm scared.'

'Scared?'

'God, yes, you don't know. . . .'

'Take it easy now. You want to talk it over?'

'Yes, I got to talk.'

'Well, why not. Go right ahead honey, I'm listening.'

'He keeps mutterin' an' groanin' in his sleep.'

'Eh?'

'It—it frightens me. That mutterin' an' groanin' through the night.'

'He is asleep, you mean?'

'Yes. An' sometimes I don't know. Sometimes I think he does it a-purpose.'

'Now you just imagining things.'

'I hate him.'

'As bad as that, eh?'

'Yes, I hate him. God, how I hate him. I lay in the bed beside him an' I make myself into a piece of board, hatin' him to touch me, wantin' to scream. An' he doesn't know.'

'That's bad.'

A mule with a loose shoe went *clip-clopping* down the street dragging a milk cart behind it. Euphemia went across to the bureau and came back and sat on the bed beside Zephyr, a hairbrush with a real tortoise-shell back in her hand.

'And yet he's so gentle and kind and generous to me. He would give me anything I want.'

'I know. He loves you, that's what.'

She looked out through the window when she said it, and for an instant her eyes went hard.

'But it don't stop me from bein' scared of him an'—an' hatin'

88

him that way. When I lie on the bed beside him I'm a piece of board. God, I hate the way he has to do with his hands, and I want to scream, but I'm too scared to do anything.'

'Why don't you break away, clean?'

'I couldn't do that.'

'You mean, you wouldn't know what to use for money.'

She nodded.

'Bajun been out of work a long time, seems to me. I don't see him tryin' too hard to get a job. What does *he* do for money?'

Euphemia didn't answer that one, she sat turning over the hairbrush in her hands.

'I know,' said Zephyr, viciously. 'You take from the man you hate to give him.'

'It's none of your business what I do.'

'Oh yes, it is. You make it my business because you're tellin' me of your own account. I didn't ask you to. It's true, though. You take from one to give the other. My God, how do you do it?'

Euphemia got up, stood up straight before her, by her poise and gesture absolved every inch in her own mind. She didn't even look at the other woman; her gaze was fixed somewhere on the top of the door, taking this assurance to herself, putting aside the other's thoughts about it as something alien.

'You don't understand. You couldn't understand.'

'A thing like that? No. Me, I'm just a whore.'

'I didn't mean it like that.'

'I do.'

'It's no dam business of yours anyway.'

'All right.'

'Yes, I don't mean no harm, but there is things you don't understand.'

'Listen, sister, don't hand me that shit. There's something the matter with women like you.'

'Well, you've turned against me now, so what's the use?'

'If you want I'll go.'

'No. Don't. I—I want to talk with you. Gotta talk to someone.'

'Well talk. I'm listening.'

'Not like that, God, Zephyr, I've got to find someone who'll listen. Look, I'm sorry what I said. You're not any whore. You're a woman, like me.'

'You never said anything, was I said about me bein' a whore. Talk, I'm listening, an' right now you're hurtin' my shoulder.'

'Sorry.'

'Little 'most I'd be black-an'-blue.'

'Oh God, Zephyr, what to do?'

'If I told you you wouldn't do it, what's the use?'

'Yes, I would.'

'Listen, sister, you don't know what I'm aimin' to tell you.'

'Christ. No, not that.'

'Well, you see—'

'I couldn't do that. You—you don't understand—'

'There you go again, you see?'

'I didn't mean anything, honest. I never said anything, did I?'

'You're hurtin' my shoulder again. Get a-hold on yourself.'

'He—he's got a machette under the bed.'

'What?'

'Yes. I could show it to you.'

'Now you're talkin' foolish.'

'I tell you he has.'

'Well, what of it?'

'I'm scared, I'm scared.'

'Sister, you're in a mess, I'm sorry for you.'

'You can talk, you never loved no one—'

'Perhaps, and perhaps not. But leave me out of it, see?'

'You're not any different to anybody else, it's just you never was faced up with a situation like this.'

'All right.'

'Sometimes I feel I could kill myself.'

'Yeah, I know. An' a hell lot of good that'd do.'

'If you could tell me something—'

'Now then honey, get a-hold on yourself.'

'The nights are worst. I lay awake. Can't sleep. Listenin' to him moanin' an' talkin', an' if he's sleepin' himself, I wouldn't know.'

'For Christ sake get a-hold of yourself. Supposin' he was to come in now.'

'An' then he's sick, sick bad, top of it all.'

90

'Yeah, I know. His chest.'

'It's worse'n that. He won't see a doctor. But he's sick, sick bad. Keeps talkin' 'bout it's the dust he takes up on his chest, but it's nothing like that at all, I tell you. An' — an' I'm scared.'

'He won't go to a doctor? But why?'

'Don't know. It's something he's got on his mind.'

'It might be that he's scared to know the truth about himself.'

'No.'

'It might be he's scared himself to face up to the truth about this thing.'

'No, I tell you. No. It's something else. Something he's got on his mind. I don't understand it, an' it's got me scared.'

'You keep on talkin' about it's something he's got on his mind, just to frighten yourself.'

'Why should I want to do that?'

'You're askin' me?'

'I'm not, I'm tellin' you. It's there, an' it scares me. What is he thinking?'

'He's not thinking anything. He's scared like you are, about something else. He doesn't want to know for certain how bad sick he is. Seems people are scared 'bout something or other all their lives.'

'You think so?'

'Yes.'

'You're wrong. He's got something on his mind. One day he's goin' do something bad — '

'You said yourself he was lovin' an' gentle. He doesn't know a thing.'

'He's deep an' cunning.'

'Maybe he's just scared out of his pants about that, too.'

'Why should he be?'

'It's like the sickness he's got on him, it's just something else again that he's scared silly about.'

'I tell you, no. You don't understand — '

'You might be right, at that.'

'Oh God, oh God!'

'Get a-hold of yourself now. No sense to let go like that.'

'I don't want to die.'

'What you talkin' about dyin'?'

'You don't know him, he's deep an' cunning.'

'Or it could be he is simple, an' scared.'

'There you go again. You're only sayin' that to comfort me.'

'I said, might.

'You're not helpin' me much.'

'I wish I could honey, honest I wish I could. Why'n't you make a clean break, come out into the open. It's your mind that's sick, with all that fear.'

'God, I couldn't.'

'All right. All right.'

'Oh God, I couldn't do that. It would mean the end of everything.'

'You're scared for true. God, I didn't know how scared you was. Wish to Christ you hadn't told me all this.'

'You mean that? You say that to me?'

'Yes, I mean it. Don't you want the truth?'

'I want help. I want to know what to do.'

'Yes. Yes, of course.'

'Oh God, I got a pain.'

'Better lie down again. This is a bad, bad business.'

'You can't help me. Nobody can.'

'Don't cry now, no sense to cry.'

'I can't help it. It's — it's the pain.'

'Best to let it go then, put your head down an' cry. There . . . you'll feel better in a minute . . . Let me pull the curtains . . . There . . . you'll feel better now. . . .'

'Ah did see you an' Wilfie the other night,' said Manny, whittling at the stick now with a clasp-knife.

Ditty tilted her head back, and her lips were full and moist, and she laughed.

'Gwan,' she said softly, 'you didn't see nutt'n.'

'Effen you t'ink Ah didn't see nutt'n, yuh wait till Ah tell you' Ma.'

She bared her white teeth in a smile, took her full lower lip between her teeth, and gave him a warm look, knowing what was on his mind.

'You wouldn't tell.'

'Why not?'

'Because.'

'You meet me down the gully after dusk?'

'What for?'

'You know.'

She shook her head, smiling still.

'You tell me.'

He came a step nearer.

'Ah got something to give you, that's why.'

'You can give it to me now.'

'No, Ah couldn't do that, not before all them people, not what it is Ah have for you.'

'What kinda t'ing that could be?'

She held the pudding pan loosely on her lap and her tongue came out a tip and moved slowly back and forth across her lips and went in again.

'Promise me?'

'What?'

'That you will come.'

'Ah can't promise you nutt'n.'

'Why? Count of Wilfie?'

'What you mean?'

'Saw you an' him the other night.'

'Didn't see nutt'n.'

'Ah did, too.'

'Gwan, you didn't.'

She pulled the pudding pan toward her and her skirt came up with it an inch or two, and again the tip of her tongue came out and moistened her lips. She looked up into his face and saw that he was staring at her legs and she made a movement with her hands as though to pull her skirt down and laughed and said, pertly, 'What you want?'

'Want you.'

'You can't want me.'

'How you mean, somebody can't want you?'

'Somebody else want me already, perhaps.'

'Is who? Wilfie?'

'Don't even call his name to me.'

'Ah saw the two of you the other night, though.'

'Gwan, you didn't see nutt'n.'

'Yes, Ah did.'

Wilfie across the yard was helping Tansy to take the firewood inside. Ras leaned against the axe and looked down at them, breathing deeply. His eyes caught Tansy's in a warm friendly look an instant and a slow smile split his bearded face and he said, 'Peace an' love.'

She grinned at him, quickly, confidently, as though they shared a secret, and his big hand went out and just touched her on the shoulder, and her instant bright answering smile warmed something inside him and made him feel good. He laughed and went and sat down on the step in front of his own room door and leaned back against it and scratched his thick beard. And something laughed good and wholesome inside him and came up big with pride and stopped somewhere inside his chest as he watched Tansy gathering up a big armful of split firewood to take inside.

And he said: 'Any time you want wood splitten, sister, you axe me; any time.'

And he looked across at Manny and he gathered the spittle in his mouth and spat big, and said, 'My Gawd!'

And his gaze came back to the girl as she was going through the door hugging the wood to her, and his fingers combed through his matted beard and he said, 'My Gawd!' again.

A little breeze started up out of nowhere and was laid again so that it disturbed only the smoke from their cigarettes, and then a sudden gust whipped in through the window, flipped the three top cards off the deck, two of them falling to the floor, ruffled the calendar which pictured a girl in a puckered nothing of a skirt and brassière against the wall, and snatched a flimsy race programme off a pile of old magazines on a shelf under the calendar and deposited it folded back open and face down on the floor right under Flitters' chair.

'Well, what'd you know about that,' Surjue laughed.

Flitters cracked the fingers of both hands loudly, one after the other, so that it went with a quick staccato sound like the crackling of fire among dry twigs, and he bent over and picked up the cards and set them back on the deck, and he picked up the race programme and put the deck of cards on top of it, and he reached over without getting up, leaning back perilously on two legs of the chair, for a glazed earthenware ash tray on the dressing table that Rema used to keep hairpins and an old razor blade and things in, and set the ash tray on top of the deck of cards to keep them down.

And Surjue, still leaning back with his head against the window-sill, laughed again and said, 'That ought to keep them down, yes.'

'That's what I like to see, a man of action,' he added and grinned.

And Flitters scraped his outstretched foot across the floor drawing it back to him and put it away again under the table; he grinned back at Surjue and said, 'Man of action yes, you talking something now. Like that time when you took the knife away from Manny, an' the kid ripe for murder maybe, out there in the yard, that took a bit of nerve.'

'Cho, that was nothing. Who told you about it, anyway?'

'Ne'mind who told me about it, it's something not one man in ten woulda done, an' that's what I'm talkin' about.'

'Wasn't nothin' man. I learned that trick years ago. Got to be quick, all there is to it.'

'Yeah, I know.'

'It's like you see something going to topple over, you reach out you' han' an' stop it.'

'Took some nerve, too.'

'Well, nobody ever said I was a coward an' got away with it, if it comes to that.'

'That's what I'm tellin' you, it took some nerve. I seen a movie once — '

'Don't bother tell me. I seen plenty movies meself. Seen a man fight a shark.'

'Yeh.'

'It looked good in the movie, sure. So you want to go down to Goat Island some day an' take a header into the water among them hammerheads? No, sir! you wouldn't. Nor the guy in the movie I saw, neither. Not on your ass, he wouldn't. Movies is movies, an' only a bloody fool wouldn't know that.'

'All right, I was only sayin'—'

'I like a man to talk intelligent. Not gimme a line 'bout what he seen done in the movies.'

'I didn't say — '

95

'You did too, said you seen something or other in the movies that took a lot of nerve, like breakin' into a warehouse or a bank, or something, I bet. Well I seen things like that ineself an' they don't give me no ideas whatever, because why, because they don't make bloody sense, that's why. The jails, buddy, are bulging with smart alecks who thought different, they're steppin' on one another's toes.'

Flitters took one hand off his knee and brought it up to his face and coughed a little behind it, and he took out a scented silk handkerchief and passed it across his face but he was as cool as a lizard for all that. And Surjue just looked at him and wondered how the hell a man could keep so cool in all this heat, and he wished to Christ Flitters didn't use that scent, it made him kind of sick.

In the little silence that followed they could hear the Sisters of Charity dropping things and stirring about inside their room at the other end of the next row of shacks, they were all excitement getting set to go to a baptism that night in the hills, where they would be dressed in their white robes and gathered around a pool singing hymns, and the chief elder would wade knee deep into the water and call the initiates to him by name, one by one, and they would come to him to be baptized, and there would be round after round of singing and rejoicing and tromping on the river bank under the round full moon.

Flitters cracked the fingers of both hands again and said, 'Jesus, a man should have to live in a yard like this! Don't know how you stand it, God's truth.'

And Surjue laughed and said, 'It riles you up? I don't let it get on my tits.'

'All the same — '

'Yeah. I could do with a nice quiet place to live in, I guess. Sometimes — aw, forget it.'

'You don't really hate it, Surjue, or you'd get outa here so quick!'

'Yeah, that's right, I don't let it get on my tits.'

'Best thing to do. All the same — '

'If I could get my hands on them hundred libras, now — '

'Yeh. It would change a lot of things for you. Boy, you would-n't know!'

'What you mean?'

'No offence, only I wish you could afford to live different like.'

'What's the matter with the way I live? I like it.'

'Sure. Sure. Didn't mean it that way, Surjue.'

'Don't talk like a dam fool then. Sometimes I get sickenin' of you.'

'Didn't mean anything to rile you.'

'Awe, forget it. An' for Christ sake put that handkerchief away in your pocket. A man used scent like you do, they think he's a pansy, didn't you know?'

'Don't care what folks think, I like it. They'd only be jealous of me.'

'Jealous of you? For what?'

'Oh nothing. Forget it.'

'I ast you for what folks would want to be jealous of you, man! What you talkin' about, anyway?'

'Awe, forget it, can't you?'

'Forget it my ass, sometimes you get me sickenin' of you.'

'Awe, didn't mean to get you riled-up, Surjue.'

'Shit no, you didn't. Jealous of you!'

'All right man, don't get all riled-up that way. What about a little game?'

'The cards don't amuse me any more.'

'Me neither, was just somep'n to do.'

Surjue sat up suddenly, threw the cigarette stub out the window, flexed his biceps, thumped on his chest, let his arms lapse to his sides, stared down at the floor.

'If I could get my hands on a piece of money, though.'

'That's what I say.'

'There's lots of things I'm fed-up with.'

He looked at Flitters hard, and the other's gaze came to rest on the table top in a hurt, embarrassed way.

Surjue laughed suddenly and slapped him on the shoulder.

'Not meanin' you.'

'I wasn't thinkin' nothin',' Flitters grinned.

'You gimme a pain sometimes, but I like you.'

'I'm kinda worried about you, that's all. A guy like you ought to get on, 'stead of bein' stuck down in one place.'

'Boy, I ain't stuck down in nutt'n. Not Surjue.'

'Yeh. I know. All the same.'

'There's crowds of women chasin' me right now.'

'Yeh.'

'They get a hankerin' for me.'

'I know. A chap like you.'

'I don't mess myself up with them, though. Don't want no strings. Let them do the worryin', see?'

'Yeh, I know.'

'Could pick a dozen women, just walk down the street. They'd give me money to sleep with 'em, if I wanted. I'm sickenin' of them, that's the truth.'

He looked down at the great muscles of his thighs and flexed them, and let them go slack, and flexed them again. He looked across at Flitters and light flowed into his eyes.

'Say that over again. Gimme the lay-out.'

Flitters' eyes came suddenly alive.

'What you mean?'

'What you was talkin' about. Gimme the lay-out again.'

He snapped his fingers together eagerly, and Flitters' hands came up from his knees, and he thrust them out across the table before him and leaned a little toward Surjue.

'Well look, it's thisaway — ' he said, and he began to talk quickly, and Surjue sat down on the edge of the bed again and took the cigarette Flitters held out to him, and lit up and smoked with his elbows up on the table, his eyes narrowing a little to keep the smoke out of them, and Flitters knew he had all Surjue's attention now, and he talked softly and quickly, and watched Surjue's face.

Bedosa was out in the yard under the mango tree when Shag came in through the street gate. He took a few steps toward Shag and asked him something, and Shag stopped and pulled out his gold watch which he had brought back with him from Colon, and said something to Bedosa and put it away. And he was going on again toward the house and Bedosa just fell into step beside him, and he was talking to him in a close and earnest undertone, and Shag listened to him and looked away, and made to go on toward the house again, and Bedosa put out his hand and took him by the sleeve, and all the time he kept talking and talking, with Shag making like he was trying to shake him off and go on his way inside.

And Bajun Man who had gone across to the bar up the street a piece to buy two cigarettes, and had stopped, looked at the change from the two shilling piece he had tendered, holding it in the palm of his hand and decided, hell, he might as well have a white rum, came in through the street gate, now wiping his mouth with the back of his hand, spat, put one of the cigarettes between his lips and paused to strike a match, and Bedosa stopped talking suddenly and looked up into the ackee tree and pointed out something to Shag, and Shag looked up into the tree and nodded his head and brushed his sleeve absent-mindedly and went on inside, leaving Bedosa standing there in the yard with a stiff kind of smile on his face as Bajun went past him going toward his room in the northern row of shacks, and he was humming a tune.

The curtains over the window by the bed twisted suddenly as though by an impulse of their own, and went limp again, and suddenly whipped in with energy, and the gust of wind came after and blew a tall vase with some yellow marigolds stuck in it over on its side on the table, and Zephyr jumped up and caught the vase before it rolled off the table and looked down ruefully at the water that was making into a little pool on the floor.

Euphemia sat on the side of the bed staring down at her hands folded on her lap, and she didn't even look up, or move. And presently Zephyr came back and stood before her and she was holding the red tin of Cusson's talc in her hand, and she said, 'Now then, take a-hold of yourself and don't think about it too much, this thing is bound to work out some way.'

'You can say that, it isn't happening to you.'

'You best to lie down an' rest a while, anyway.'

'Don't want to rest, I lie down I get a headache.'

'Well get up an' make the room tidy then, that'll be something to do.'

Euphemia got up heavily and stood for a while looking straight out before her like a person not quite awakened, coming out of a long sleep.

'Go on now, get a cloth and wipe up that water off the floor.

99

I'd stop an' help you put the room straight, only I think it'll do you good havin' something to put your hands to, help you gather your thoughts.'

'It's no use. I can't go on. Something bound to happen soon.'

Her lips began to tremble again and her hands made into fists at her sides, and just then they heard Shag's step coming down the passage, and Zephyr pushed her so that she kind of fell on her knees before the pool of water on the floor, and she grabbed a towel and threw it at her just as Shag was coming in through the door.

Shag looked from Zephyr to Euphemia on the floor, and said, 'Wha' happen?'

'Nothing much, the vase blew over, it.didn't break.'

Shag sat down on the side of the bed and started pulling off his shoes. And he looked up at Zephyr, standing there holding the red powder tin in front of her, and he gave a little wry kind of smile and said, 'You're standing right in front of my slippers, just kick them across.'

He worked his foot into one slipper and started pulling off the other shoe, and suddenly Zephyr realized that Shag was looking very sick indeed. When he had looked up into her eyes and smiled that time there was something in his look that made her deep down sorry for him, she didn't know why.

'I'm all done in,' he said. 'Why the hell can't people leave a guy alone?'

'Eh?' said Zephyr.

'Oh, I don't mean you,' said Shag easily, the way she instantly knew he meant it. 'People who keep hanging around.'

Euphemia got up off the floor and went across to the other window and leaned out and wrung water out of the towel.

'Well I best get on now,' said Zephyr, going toward the door.

And Shag said, 'Why?' quickly. 'Thought you an' Euphemia was talkin', hope I'm not in the way.'

'Course you're not, what an idea. I was on my way out an' everything when you came in.'

The look she saw in his eyes told her as plain as anything he didn't want to be left alone with Euphemia now, he wanted to talk.

'Well, I could stop for a minute, I guess, there's nothing I got special to do.'

Euphemia came back to the water on the floor, tucked up her skirt a bit, went down on one knee and started swabbing at it again.

'I got a book of sweepstake tickets from across the way,' said Shag, 'I want you to pick one for me, gimme some of your luck.'

'Luck!'

'Yes. You never buy them, you ought to be lucky.'

'On the showing of my luck you'd be chucking your money away,' Zephyr laughed. 'Gimme the book, I'll pick one if you want.'

Euphemia got up from the floor and carried the wet towel across to the window again. From there she said:

'You want to talk with Zephyr private, I could go outside.'

Shag looked at her quickly.

'What you say?'

'Say you want to talk with Zephyr private, I could leave you, you heard me the first time.'

'You crazy, no?'

'I must be crazy yes, wipin' up slops off the floor for you.'

'Euphemia —'

'You keep out of this, Zephyr, you hear, you don't know anything.'

'Well, I be damned!'

'Yes, an' be damned to all of you, you all against me in this place, I know. You want him, you can have him, I don't care.'

Zephyr stood up suddenly straight and taut like a sapling hardwood tree.

'You say that to me, I knock your teeth down your throat, so help me God! You hear?' She took two steps toward Euphemia. 'For two cents I'd do it now, you bitch.'

Euphemia dropped the wet towel and her fingers gripped the window ledge and her lips started to tremble uncontrollably.

She said: 'H-hit me if you like, I wouldn't care.'

Shag sat up in the bed, 'What the hell is happening?' he said. He struggled up to his feet and went and stood between them.

Zephyr turned away.

'I'm getting the hell out of here.'

'Euphemia, there was no call to insult her.'

'Stand away from me, I hate you, you hear?'

'Good God!'

'Why don't you go after her, what is holdin' you?'

'You bitch! You bitch!' Zephyr said through clenched teeth, over against the door.

'Wait Zephyr! I got to get to the bottom of this. Don't go.'

'Christ, if I was to stop one minute longer in this place I'd do something I'd be sorry for.'

'Hit me, kick me, why don't you beat me up like you want to do?'

'Euphemia!'

'God, I hate the sight of you! There, I said it, why don't you knock my teeth in like *she* wants to do?'

'God a'mighty! What the hell's happened here? Euphemia, honey, will you stop talkin' like that, I'm askin' you.'

'Well I be damned!' Zephyr started to laugh, choked it off. 'Look, I'm gettin' out of here.'

'No, Zephyr, please. I want you to stay.'

'Some other time, Shag, not now. This is no place for me.'

'You could go on with her an' leave me, I wouldn't care. Why don't you leave me alone, can't you see I'm sickenin' of you?'

'All right, honey. You don't know what you're sayin', an' I'm not even listenin' to you.'

'I'll make you listen to me, my God, I will. I hate you, you hear me, I hate the sight of you. All you do is get in my way, all an' all you ever do —'

The door slammed loudly, punctuating her outburst. She stopped speaking suddenly, with her mouth still open.

'All right, she's gone now. You didn't have no call to insult her that way.'

Suddenly all the quivering anger went out of her, she staggered across to the bed, slumped down on it, and started to cry. She made no sound, but the tears gathered in her eyes and formed into big drops and rolled down her face. She took the hem of her skirt between her hands and twisted it this way and that, and always her gaze avoided his.

Shag put his hands in his pockets and paced up and down the narrow room. Then he went to the door, stood there uncertainly with his hand on the knob an instant, and went out, closing it quietly behind him.

11 IT CAME DUSK quickly and light flushed the sky with a nice palette of colours where some thin transparent clouds spread in the west took the reflections of late sunlight and mixed them and made broad splotched and stippled horizontal lines of wash against a paper sky.

The wind that was restless before came to a sudden hush and the trees in the yard and by the gully's edge stood still and gathered shades of darkness under their leaves. A few twigs pushed out making tentative arrested gestures against the sky.

Some shredded wisps of clouds let down a fringe that started nowhere and ended in nothing, and the *chip-chip* of a late twit dropped into the silence that made nothing of the noises that went by continually in the crazy street.

A little breeze freshened once, twice, riffed the drooping leaves, walked in a whirling dance among the dropped scraps of paper and other unswept litter in the yard, left the whirling scraps abruptly to lie under the stolid gaunt ackee tree like a dancer suddenly letting her skirt fall, turned and went scuttling across the slanting tin roofs, and settled as suddenly again.

A lost naked-necked chicken came up from the gully, put its head to one side, *peeped* anxiously and jerked it back and forth as it made a panicky circuit of the yard. It came to a dead stop in front of the uneven fence, *peeped* once loudly, and flew in a sudden excess of panic clear over the palings and into the street under the wheels of a passing automobile. Somebody kicked it into the gutter and there it was found by a small boy who picked it up, tucked it under his arm, and ran straight home with it.

Wilfie could hear Manny whistling loudly going down toward the gully and he couldn't finish eating his supper, for all of a sudden the food tasted like dry ashes in his mouth, and he got up from the table and went toward the door and Mack said to him, 'Where you goin' to, bwoy?'

'Outside,' said Wilfie, holding on to the door knob.

'Sit down an' eat you' supper.'

'Don't want any more.'

'Don't gimme none o' you' lip, you feelin' sick, or somep'n?'

'Yes. I got a pain.'

'You got a pain, so you goin' outside. What you want outside? You must be tek me fo' poppy-show.'

But Wilfie didn't stop to argue, suddenly he felt he hated to be in this closed-in space, he wanted outdoors. He went through the door without bothering to wait for Mack to finish.

'Well, I be damned!' said Mack, and he started to get up as though to go after the boy, and it was as though his will to action deserted him halfway through the motion and he sat down again, and still chewing on the same mouthful cast a glance at the door. He shrugged and said, 'Hm!' and went on eating his supper of bread and fried sprats from the shop across the way.

And when he was finished what was on his plate, he reached out a hand and took Wilfie's plate and transferred the whole sprats with his fork to his own; the heads and tails that Wilfie had broken off and set to one side he left alone, but the whole sprats he had helped himself to he ate them heads and tails and all.

Wilfie did not clearly know what it was that gave him the impulse to come out into the yard, but as he did so he saw a figure whip behind the shacks and he knew it was Ditty, and that she was going down the gully to meet Manny, for now it was dark.

He thought of Manny and the dose, and Ditty, all together like that, and pictured them embracing somewhere down the gully and suddenly a rush of water came to his mouth as though he was going to vomit. He didn't want to be sick and lose his supper for nothing so he swallowed and swallowed, but each time his mouth filled with water again, and every time it was harder to swallow, and at last he had to run to the lavatory, and he got there just in time to hold his face over the bowl, and he was sick as he had never been since last August when he had stood in the sun too long watching a parade on Emancipation Day.

Rema sat before the dressing table in flesh-pink panties and matching brassière alone, fixing her hair the way she always did for going to bed, and Surjue lay on his side in his BVD's in the bed and tried to read a book.

Rema with her mouth full of hairpins tried to tell him that the lamp was smoking and she couldn't do anything about it because right then her hands were full, but she only succeeded in making unintelligible noises which didn't get any rise out of Surjue at first, but presently he put his finger down against the book to mark the place where he had stopped reading and looked up and said, 'What's the matter honey, you swallowed something?' And then he saw what it was she wanted, that the lamp was smoking and he jumped out of bed and took the shade off with his bare hands. It burnt him so that he nearly dropped it, and when he set it down he said, 'You know honey, that dam shade was kinda hot.'

'You should have taken something in your hand to hold it.'

'Yeah, I know now. Comes from livin' in a dump like this without even electric wiring. Flitters is right.'

'Flitters? Was he here?'

'Yes. What's the matter you jumpin' on me like that?'

'Honey, I didn't mean to jump on you. What'd he want?'

'Who? Flitters? Oh, he just dropped around for a chat.'

'Don't get mad at me, but every time I see that man or hear his name even it gimme the creeps. There's something about him that makes every drop of blood leave my body, it seems, when he's around. If you was to ask me I couldn't tell you why.'

'I know you don't like him, but he's my friend. He never done me nothin'?'

'Don't like him? God, it's not that. It's not I don't *like* him, it's my heart is standin' in my mouth an' I freeze up stiff.'

'You imagine things.'

'I guess so, just can't help it. I've tried.'

She caught his wrist in a grip of so much energy that it made him stand still a minute and just stare down at her.

She said: 'God, Surjue, if — if anything was to happen to you!' like that, and looked away.

'Don't take on like that now,' he said, laying his hand on her bare shoulder and caressing it between his finger and thumb.

He said: 'Honey, you don't want to worry about anything. I can take care of myself.'

'Yes, I guess so.'

'What you mean, you guess so?'

'I mean, you can all right, only — '

'There you go again. If you scared about Flitters so much, why don't you forget him.'

'What he want here, anyway?'

'I told you, he just dropped by for a chat. Lissen, you don't aim to be messin' in my affairs, do you?'

'Oh Surjue, it's not that, no.'

'All right then, forget about Flitters an' be yourself.'

They could hear Charlotta and Bedosa going at it over in their room in the same row of shacks; not what they said, but the sound of their voices.

'We don't want to get to be like *that* couple over there,' said Surjue, his hand gently massaging her bare shoulder.

'Oh, God, no!'

'That's right, honey. Don't let's get to bickering at each other, then.'

'I couldn't live with that. Honest, it'd drive me crazy.'

'Me too.'

'I mean really crazy. Clean out of my mind.'

'Hush, don't even say it.'

'Oh God, Surjue!'

'All right, hon, everything's going to be all right.'

'I pray for it honey, honest I do.'

'Well, if it makes you happy, why not?'

'It kinda comforts me, I can't explain it. I been a few times to the meetin' house down by the Race Course; you come with me some time, eh?'

'Wouldn't do no good.'

'You never can tell.'

'To make you happy, I could even do that; but it wouldn't do no good at all.'

'With the two of us together, anything could happen. I feel something inside me — '

'Look, honey, you get yourself saved, I don't care, so long you remain just the same as you are to me, but don't you bring God inside this door to make life miserable for me — else out I go, you get me?'

'I wouldn't ever do that, you know it. You have no call to say like that to me.'

'I'm just tellin' you.'

'I'm not crazy for nothing in the world beside you. Lissen, honey, you not vexed with me about goin' to the meetin' house without tellin' you?'

'You can do anything you like. We never stood about in corners watchin' each other come an' go.'

'Oh, God, no. I would never want to do that.'

'That's right. Nor me.'

She felt suddenly nearer to him now than if they were in bed. It was such a strange and wonderful feeling that she would not look up at him, fearful of breaking the spell. She just sat in front of the mirror holding the hairbrush in her hand, scarcely conscious even of her own breathing.

And as though the strange beautiful thing she was feeling was communicated to him, he just put his face down to her hair and said, 'Oh God, Rema — honey,' softly, and it was the most wonderful thing she had ever heard in all her life.

Goodie groaned as she pulled off the rubber-soled canvas shoes to ease the pain in her knee. She pulled her skirt up and a cotton stocking down, unstoppered the liniment bottle, poured some out on to her hand and began to rub the rheumatic knee. She sat on the side of the bed, rubbing her knee and groaning, and she looked dully across at Puss-Jook who yawned and scratched himself sitting on a stool over by the window.

'Where Ditty?' she said, presently.

And Puss-Jook looking out at the moonshine silvering the leaves of the male guinep tree over against the gully just shrugged his shoulders and put his hand over his mouth to stifle a yawn.

'What's matter, you sleepy? Didn't finish out you' nap, an' you been at it all day!'

He looked at her without resentment, grinned, looked away out through the window again, and the fingers of one hand clawed at the bristly red hairs on his chest, and the other clawed at his front.

Goodie tried to stretch out her foot before her and she groaned and set it down on the floor beside the other.

'Don't even sweep out the room.'

'Done that already this mornin',' Puss-Jook said. 'She was in here with the broom.'

'Hm! Effen that's the way she sweep out a room only Jesus know what use she have. Big gal a-look tu'n ooman now caan do nutt'n de livin' day.'

'Cho, you naggin' at de pickney too much now. Give she a chance, no?'

'Is whe' she gone? Gal must be a-look somet'ing, is what it, I don't know.'

'God a'mighty, you gone 'pon dat again?'

'Must gone 'pon it, yes. Me wukin' at de grassyard from livin' mornin' till night, nutt'n but tek-up pain a-me knee, lef' gal-pickney home she caan even hold a broom in her han', an' you lay down do nutt'n but scratch-you'self-so-sleep, sleep-so-scratch-you'self all day.'

'Is what you have with me? You better leave me out o' yuh argument, you hear? Is Ditty you havè-up, so beg you put me down. Is yore pickney, she is nutt'n to me.'

'She is nutt'n to you, no? You always talk dat way.'

'She couldn't be my pickney, or she woulda catch higher colour, look 'pon my skin.'

'Effen she is not your pickney, she is fo'-who pickney den, I'da like fe know.'

'Ooman hush yuh mout', don't mek we go over dat argument agen, Ah tired to hear it. You start it up, Ah will go-weh lef-you.'

'Go-weh lef-me, Ah wouldn't care. You go-weh lef-me you come back quick-quick time like you done before. Is who goin' mind you, big man do nutt'n but scratch-himself-so-sleep all day? Ah wonder is-whe' dat gal-pickney gone dis time o' night, at all?'

Puss-Jook laughed coarsely.

'Must be gone look it, she no big-nuff now?'

Goodie looked at him with pain-dulled eyes.

'You would say that, Ah wouldn't wonder!'

'Say it yes, after Ah don' waan she.'

'Man hush yuh mout', you could want you' own daughter? Is what you sayin', anyway?'

'She not me daughter, an' Ah don't want her all the same.'

'Is you' own daughter, though. You kip t'rowin' it in me teeth —'

'Look at my colour, an' look at she.'

'Hush yuh mout', you don't know what you sayin'. Effen she not your daughter, is fo'-who daughter she?'

'You askin' me!'

He laughed again.

'Me Jesus, is the thankie I get wukin' out me life fo' a good-fo'-nutt'n man like you! No mine, though, God know everything. It hot, but hush!'

She groaned loudly, and went on rubbing her knee.

White-robed figures, mostly women, stood around a pool in the hills and sang hymns and clapped their hands, and some shook tambourines, and they tromped, jumping and grunting rhythmically, and waited for the rising of the moon.

Presently a hush fell over the assembly, and they waited with breath held in while Brother Eccles with his great white beard waded out knee-deep into the water, his robes girt up about his waist, coming to stand still about the middle of the pool.

And some of the people knelt on the bank, and some stood up, all frozen in arrested gestures, like a mural. And Brother Eccles held up his hands, and kept them so until the full round moon topped the most easterly mountain, and all the people shouted with one voice.

And they sprang up, those that were kneeling, and shook their tambourines, and others clapped their hands together, and the rhythmic jumping and grunting commenced again, and they sang a song that said about how the floods clapped their hands, alleluya, and the hills were joyful together . . . a song which they had pieced together out of some lines from one of the Psalms.

And while the singing and tromping was going on on the river bank, the initiates for baptism came down one by one from a high rock over against the other side of the pool, as their names were called, and waded out to Brother Eccles standing waiting in the middle of the water, and surrendered themselves into his hands for baptism into the only true faith, and it had come out of Ethiopia and was given to the Black Messiah, and him only, Brother Eccles said.

'Who dat!' said Ras, sharply, putting his hand behind his back.

'Is all right, man, is me.'

'Shag! What you doin' outside this time o' night? What's matter, can't sleep?'

Ras was sitting on a stone under the male guinep tree overlooking the gully. The moon had come up high in the sky.

'Worse'n that, man,' said Shag, thickly, 'ain't ever goin' sleep no more.'

'Eh? What's matter, you look like a ghost.'

'I feel like one. But it's no use, is still me.'

'Here, sit down side me, rest you' feet.'

He moved over to make place for Shag beside him on the stone, and Shag sat down.

'You want to talk, is all right,' said Ras, understandingly, 'nutt'n like talkin' to get yuh mind at ease.'

'Talkin' can't help me, man. I got troubles to walk me into me grave.'

'Hm! Sounds bad. But take it easy, brother, peace an' love,' said Ras.

And Shag said after him, 'Peace an' love,' and he smiled into the semi-darkness and shook his head. And then he said, 'Peace an' love,' again, taking the words in his mouth, turning them over, assaying them, as though wondering what they could mean.

His hand went automatically to his pocket and came up with the makings and he commenced to roll himself a cigarette. But he fumbled it so that the tobacco spilled out of the paper on to the ground between his feet, and he looked down at it and began to laugh softly, amusedly, as though it were the funniest thing in the world.

'What's matter with me is right, I can't even make meself a cigarette again, an' I could roll one of them things in me sleep.'

'Here, let me help you.'

Ras took the makings out of his hand and started to roll a cigarette neatly and deliberately. He paused with the paper up against his tongue in the act of licking it down.

He said, looking at Shag's face intently: 'Now, man, you don't want a cigarette.' And he put his hand to his pocket and took out a spliff and said, 'Try one of these.'

'What's it?'

'A spliff.'

'Oh.'

'Go on, take it; do you good.'

'Well — '

'What's it, you scared? Don't be a fool.'

'Well — '

'Look, there ain't even much of the stuff in it, mostly tobacco, I roll them meself. You got troubles nothin' in the world God made for them like this.'

'All right, brother, give it to me.'

He took the spliff and lit up, dragged long at it, drawing the smoke deep down into his lungs. And he let it out again, slowly, and he didn't feel any different.

Ras was telling him how he made them, just like a cigarette, you mixed some of the weed with tobacco and made it up into cigarettes, and there was nothing in this world God made that could help a man let go of his troubles no matter what like it.

He started to say, 'What you talkin' about man, there's nothing to it,' and suddenly it seemed to him that Ras was a great way off and talking down to him from a high place, and he wanted to laugh.

He laughed too, happily. And Ras said, like God talking to him out of a cloud that was like the stone they were sitting on, 'That's better. You feelin' good already.'

Charlotta moved up and down the room with a kind of restless energy which set Bedosa's nerves on edge. Tansy was lying on her pallet in the next room trying to sleep but the moonlight coming in through the window and forming into a pool on the floor embraced the part of the room where her pallet was, and what with the moonlight making her restless and the sounds from the next room she couldn't sleep.

'You got to speak to Manny good an' hard,' Charlotta kept saying as she moved restlessly about the room picking things up and putting them down, swapping places with them as though it was a kind of game. 'You are the man, an' it's a man he needs to take him in hand, God knows it's more'n I can manage.'

'You worryin' about Manny, I got heavy things on me mind.'

'I got Manny heavy on me mind too, I tell you, just as heavy as anything you got on yours.'

'I don't care what the hell he wants to do, prison was made for his kind, an' prison'll take care of him, an' it's all the same to me.'

'My God, I should live to hear you talk that way! I wouldn't wish it for the worst enemy I ever had.'

'I don't care a dam what happens to Manny, I tell you, an' it's no use naggin' at me, I got heavy troubles of my own.'

'Well, we all have troubles, an' Jesus knows I try me best to make things go the way they should, till it seems no use tryin' any more.'

'Stop naggin' in me ears, will you? Only God knows how I keep from goin' outa me mind. Don't do people nutt-'n an' they hate me, don't trouble nobody at all, see God, an' they out for me blood, an' only Jesus know why.'

'Hush now, don't start on that again, you start frettin' you'self, you sure as anything bring on that pain.'

'Don't get no sympathy from nobody, nutt'n at all, nobody ever 'preciate all I try to do. All I ever get from blessed mornin' till night is naggin' naggin' in me ears. Try to live lovin' with people, all they do is hate me, 'buse me, tell lies on me, out for me blood.'

The droning voices went on and on in the next room, and Tansy tossed restlessly on her pallet, and wondered what was going to happen to Manny, and to them all, sighed, turned over with her face to the wall, and wondered weren't they ever going to get to bed at all tonight and would she ever get the chance to go back to school.

Shag came down the passage slowly, feeling his way to his own room door. It seemed he had come a long, long way in the darkness ... but now he was standing with the knob of the door in his hand.

Images danced inside his head and he was happy. He went in quietly through the door.

Moonlight lay across the floor and stopped at the side of the bed and it seemed too bright to bother to switch on the light. He watched Euphemia's form gathered in sleep, lying outstretched across the bed.

Poor Euphemia, she had troubles ... good thing for her to sleep ... let her sleep. ...

Without thinking about it he snapped on the light switch.

A nerve in her face twitched although she was breathing

heavily . . . the lovely images formed in his mind, as though at
his own bidding, taking their form and excellence from him . . .
let her sleep . . . they went out across the darkness that was like
an abyss . . . and they came again when he commanded them,
like a hawk or a dove . . . let her sleep . . . '*I hate you! I hate you!*'
. . . the voice sounded as though it was muffled under layers and
layers of soft cotton wool . . . and the words that were as a shibboleth to him leaped sheer and terrible out of his consciousness . . .
'*peace an' love*'. . . .

He came and stood beside the bed looking down at her as
from a great height . . . like God looking out of a great white
cloud that was like a stone for its stoniness . . . let her sleep . . .
way back something had happened and it had drawn a dark
cloud over the shining face of God that was his face looking
benevolently out of his cloud over all the world and Euphemia
stretched out in the unconsciousness of sleep across the bed. . . .

Words flowed and took forms and made into images in his
mind . . . and in his hands he held the tokens of them and he sent
them forth and they did his bidding and returned like doves
to his hand . . . the words themselves were a shibboleth, and were
without meaning other than that which he endowed them with,
so that they became the most beautiful, whole, perfect, sheer,
excellent words in the world, like the secret names of God . . .
and they were also of a strange ruthlessness and power . . . and
he said them over and over and sent them forth to flower into
the most excellent images of his mind . . . and he called them to
him again . . . the same words over and over . . . '*peace an' love*' . . .

Someone laughed, and Euphemia opened her eyes wide and
sat up, and she stared hard at him standing there, and her fingers
clutched the cover and drew it up to her throat.

'Why — why you laugh like that?' she said, at last, in a choking
kind of voice.

And Shag sat down on the side of the bed, still smiling that
inscrutable smile, started pulling off his shoes, and said, 'Me, I
didn't laugh.'

He climbed over her and went to lie down at his side of the
bed. Euphemia looked timidly into his face, wondering what it
was that could make him smile like that; had he been drinking?

He lay on his back with his eyes wide open, and presently the lids drew down of themselves over that fixed stare and he was asleep.

The heaviness of his breathing reassured her and presently she closed her eyes out of sheer nervous fatigue and was soon herself fast asleep.

And his spirit wandered dreamlessly out over vast spaces that were without end, and were in truth a reality out of which there was no waking, only he had not come upon it in truth, but another way.

His over-burdened mind had found release as by the lifting of a latch and walking through a hidden door. He had just stepped over the threshold into otherness and found peace.

12   IT WAS WILFIE who told Pattoo that Manny had his knife.

'I seen him with it,' said Wilfie, 'an' he's braggin' what an' all he'll do to you if you try to git it from him.'

'Huh!' said Pattoo, and went in search of Manny.

He found him as he was coming up from the gully, and Pattoo said, shaking his head angrily and spluttering, with saliva flecking his lips as he talked, 'Gimme me knife. Yuh have it. Gimme hit, I say.'

And Manny just grinned and hitched up his pants and spat in his hands, rubbing them together, and said, 'Come an' git it, you pulp-eye son of a bitch! Ah got yuh knife, yah, so what?'

Pattoo blubbering with rage humped his shoulders, clenched his fists, walked around Manny in narrowing circles, gibbering at him. He said, 'Gimme hit, you hear? Yuh got me knife, gimme hit, I say!'

Manny grinned harder, watching him warily, waited with a mounting kind of exhilaration, enjoying in anticipation beating up the other boy to a pulp with his fists. He was bigger than Pattoo by a couple of inches and knew that he was stronger and could beat him any time. And this was it, if only Pattoo would fight.

Wilfie stood by, his hands in his pockets, looking on, and he wasn't enjoying it. He felt as though he was responsible for it in some way and he wished he had not become involved. And yet for all that there was a certain excitement, and he hoped deep down that Pattoo would get in one good blow and perhaps bring blood from Manny's grinning mouth.

Pattoo, blubbering like that, circled two three times round Manny, and then he suddenly veered off at a tangent, and Manny saw him stop, his eyes searching for something on the ground, bend over, but before he could take the stone in his hand and hurl it Manny read his intention and closed in on him with great strides.

He kicked Pattoo in the side while he was still bending over and the smaller boy fell to the ground, rolled over, tried to get up, was suddenly drawn up with pain, and Manny fell on top of him. He hit him with both fists sitting on top of him like that, and blood trickled out of the corner of Pattoo's mouth, but he was dead game.

His hand, clutching the stone, smashed into Manny's side, and a look of instant surprise bulged Manny's eyes, and the next instant his face twisted with sharp pain, for Pattoo had broken one of his ribs with that blow, although he didn't know it then, knowing only that sharp instant stabbing pain that made him keel over and fall away from Pattoo.

They both got to their feet slowly, coming up about the same time, and now Pattoo didn't circle any more, he came straight at Manny, his hands out before him like an ape. He did not hit Manny with his fists but clawed at him and his hand came away with skin off Manny's face under his fingernails, and Manny hit him in the face again and he went down, sobbing.

Manny kicked him once, and he twisted up, but more to protect himself than with the pain because it didn't catch him squarely, Manny was too eager to make use of his advantage, and he kicked at him again and this time Pattoo caught his foot under his arm and brought him down. As he fell Pattoo twisted and got Manny's foot under him and he put his mouth down snarling like an animal and bit hard.

Manny screamed with pain and kicked out hard with the other foot, and Pattoo let go, and there was an ugly bloody gash in his head that started above the hairline and ended well down on the forehead where Manny's boot heel had broken the skin.

He came up quick, some dry twigs snapping brittle under his bare feet the only sound he made, lips puffed and drawn back from his teeth making him snarl; came straight at Manny again with the lumbering motions of an angry ape, and Manny was there to meet him.

Manny was bigger than he but he fought with a snarling gibbering ruthlessness, a narrowness of intention that made the other afraid; he would have been glad for a pretext to break off the engagement now, but, compelled to go on to the end, was unable to back down now and save face.

He had had no idea that Pattoo was so strong and tough, that once aroused to that pitch of battle, his mis-shapen awkwardness covered a berserk rage, that underneath his lumbering clumsiness was an unquenchable fire and energy which he focused to the narrow point of his immediate purpose that was unassuagable in its urgent rage.

Pattoo came straight at him now and something gave at the pit of his stomach as he fell automatically into a crouching stance of defensiveness, hit out with both fists, blindly, feeling the impact against his opponent's puffy flesh, but without exhilaration now, without zest for it, acting upon the urgent impulse of fear.

He hit out blindly and saw Pattoo go down again, jumped on him, hoping to crush all resistance out of him under his feet, saw something that increased the urgency of his furious assault, Pattoo's clawlike hand reaching across the hard trodden ground for the knife.

It had slipped from Manny's pocket when he had fallen, unseen, and now Pattoo's quick eyes had apprehended it, a God-sent chance.

Manny felt his stomach turn over inside him and for a moment he was sick, his body went slack; conscious of an instant stab of pain in his side where the two ends of the broken rib gritted together, he held his breath for the spasm to pass, felt the same sharp thrust of pain in his side again when he resumed breathing, and stood now with all his will to fight cancelled out in a cold sweat of fear.

The blade flicked open in Pattoo's hand, and Manny, his eyes going suddenly wide, backed away; Pattoo, rising to his feet somehow, stood before him swaying a little from side to side, his eyes going cold and dead like a snake's with his purpose, came in, crouching from the waist.

Manny screamed like a girl when Pattoo struck at him with the knife, threw his arm across his chest, twisted his body, felt the razor sharp blade go knifing through his shrinking flesh, but with less sharp pain than he imagined, saw Pattoo's eyes suddenly look as though they were going to pop from his head as blood spewed up from a severed artery, and turn with a great sob and go crashing blundering away across the gully.

He felt faint and sat down, and must have lost consciousness; came to again after seconds, to find Wilfie crouching beside him, trying to get him to his feet.

'It's only the arm,' said Wilfie, 'you got your arm in the way, you lucky. But it's bleeding like hell. How you feelin' now, think you can walk?'

13   THE SWAG LAY in a flour sack on the flat concrete roof between them, and the roof had a low ridging that went all the way round it on four sides, and green painted pipes went down to the street to take the rain water away.

They worked quickly without talk, gathering up the tools Flitters had brought in the bag to make the hole in the roof with, dragged the rope ladder up, rolled it into a neat packet and put it into the sack with the other stuff, and hefting it with one hand Surjue found it was quite a weight.

It was about three o'clock in the morning and dark, and the street was quite quiet, but even so they were careful not to show a light from their electric torch.

Wind blew from across the sea and rattled a loose zinc sheet on a building across the street, and Surjue stiffened a little first, and then shivered, suddenly feeling cold.

He looked up at the night and drew a deep breath and saw above him a dark cloud trailing a scattered handful of stars behind it, and Flitters touched him on the elbow and said, 'Let's beat it, hey?'

'We'll just unsling the rope ladder, hitch it on one of those concrete pillars that side and let it drop into the lane. Got to look first to make sure nobody is around, it ought to be okay, but you never can tell.'

They moved like two shadows in the darkness on the roof, and suddenly a single shot ripped across the stillness and chipped a piece out of the concrete pillar out in front overlooking the street.

Surjue dropped down instantly, and found Flitters beside him, and he was shoving something into his hand, which he grabbed without thinking. It was a gun.

He started thinking fast then. The shot from the street . . . it was the cop on this beat . . . no doubt about that . . . and the way they had it figured out he should be somewhere at the corner of King Street . . . damn that cop! if he was walking his beat properly he wouldn't be here until they left the roof and got clean away . . . damn all cops! he hated their guts . . . what the hell to do now? . . . must get away. One thing he wasn't going to lay down on his belly and wait for that damn cop to come up here and get him . . . one thing sure.

He was thinking fast . . . only one thing to do . . . and he started to do it. . . .

'Lissen,' he said to Flitters, whose teeth were chattering so loud he could hear them, 'I'll hold him out front. You get down the ladder into the lane, take the stuff with you. You get that clear?'

'Yes.'

'When you get into the lane whistle, loud so I can hear. I'll drop you the gun. It's dark as hell up there. Get behind cover an' shoot to hold him off — not to hit him if you can help it. It would go bad against us if we was caught. We gotta be nippy to get outa this with our noses clean.'

Even before he'd finished speaking he let rip with a shot, and he heard it ricochet off the pavement and smack against one of the steel shutters across the street. It brought an answering shot almost instantly from the man in the street. It came so close that a concrete chip clipped his cheek and it started to bleed.

But it showed him exactly where the cop was shooting from, behind a telegraph post, one of those thick hardwood ones that bolted solid to a stout base; it gave him all the cover he needed.

He was thinking fast. He was not afraid. When he got action like this he didn't have time to be scared. The cop, he figured, didn't bother to blow his whistle because he knew he was the only cop along this double-beat. Labour troubles on the sugar estates down country had drawn cops away from the city force, Government was using them to lend aid and comfort to the sugar barons who had decided to fight the union, and as far as he was concerned it was all to the good.

Out of the corner of his eye he saw Flitters like a shadow go over the ridge of the roof to the lane side, and thought, good, he'll be okay in the darkness of the narrow lane, all the time keeping one eye on the base of the telegraph pole across the street where the cop was taking cover.

Another shot hit the concrete projection beside him, not so close this time. He didn't bother to waste an answering shot, waiting to see if the cop should try to get from behind cover and cross the street. He was prepared to stop him from doing that until he'd heard Flitters' whistle from the lane below, or until he'd used up all his shots.

A whistle from Flitters and he would crawl flat on his belly across the roof to the lane side and drop him the gun, take his chance of getting safely over the ridge and on to the rope ladder. Once in the lane it would be an even chance of their making the break.

What the hell had happened to Flitters? . . . why didn't he whistle him? . . . he must have got down into the lane by now. What the hell did he think this was, a picnic?

A dark shadow edged cautiously a little from behind the telegraph pole across the street. He smiled grimly and let drive, and almost chuckled to see the shadow leap back behind cover again.

The dark cloud had dragged away from its scattered waggon-trail of stars and the wind blew gusty and cool and shook the loose zinc sheet on a building across the street, and Surjue crouched behind the concrete projection and waited for something to happen.

It was a long time before he could make himself believe that Flitters had abandoned him here on the roof, and that he must try and make his own get-away as best he could. His mind shied at the chill reality again and again, and he resolutely shut it away.

But at last he had to admit it to himself and try to figure a way out of his dilemma. He got down on his belly on the cold concrete roof and inched his way across to the lane side. He counted on the chance that the cop would be watching the spot where he had been under cover, put a hand up and over and made sure of the rope ladder. Then he held his breath and came up crouching on his hands and knees.

He scarcely fumbled it going over, but he must have given something away, or else that cop was extra smart for he was nicked in the fleshy part of the shoulder by a .38 bullet and a lucky thing for him it wasn't deep. He ripped down the ladder so fast that he could scarcely hold the rope between his hands much less feel it with his feet. He fell sprawling and a little stunned into the blackness of the lane, and moved quietly, tentatively at first to see if there were any broken bones, and then he got up into a crouching position. As he did so a beam of light from an electric torch picked him out from among the anonymous dark objects in the lane, and a voice said as cool as anything, speaking from the corner, 'Put 'em up, buddy, an' don't try any funny business!' And as he straightened up with his hands raised above shoulder level, the voice said drily, 'I'd sooner put a bullet through a hole-in-the-roof burglar who packs a gun, than jug him alive.'

The cop was smaller than Surjue, but he was lean and hard; one look into his eyes and all ideas about trying to pull anything faded away.

'All right,' said Surjue, trying to make his voice sound easy.

'Where's your buddy? You didn't go up on that roof to play a game of hop-scotch with yourself, did you?' the cop said, smiling wryly, sizing up Surjue.

'Know any more good jokes, buddy?' Surjue said out the side of his face, and suddenly he saw himself acting like a tough crook out of some third-rate gangster picture, and he laughed and said, 'That was lousy!'

And the cop said, 'Hey?'

'What happens now?' said Surjue.

It amazed him that he could feel so cool in a situation like this; the fact was he was reacting to it in a moment-to-moment way that didn't give him any time to think. That would come later.

'Turn around and bring your hands down slowly, and buddy, I'd drill a hole into you just as soon as not, remember. That's all right. Now put your hands behind your back, I'm gonna put these pretty little bracelets on to you.'

14   THE WOMAN ON the bed shivered, stretched out stiff like a piece of pitchpine board, a wet handkerchief laid across her forehead lent her face a shut look, and only the hands nervously clutching the sheet at her sides gave any sign of feeling.

Zephyr sat on a chair drawn up beside the bed, a bay rum bottle in her hand, and now she leaned across and gently took the handkerchief from her forehead, wet it generously with bay rum and gently laid it on again.

'Close you' eyes tight honey, how you feelin'?'

'About the same.'

'Try not to worry too much, you can't mend anything by worryin'. Shut you' eyes now, an' go to sleep.'

'I can't sleep. I tried that already. Talk to me.'

'Gosh Rema honey, I wish I knew what to say.'

'Anything. Just talk. It stops me from thinking. You want me tell you somep'n, I knew it was goin' to happen.'

'You knew?'

'Yes, I felt it coming for weeks. I had dreams, I was scared, I begged an' begged him. He wouldn't lissen to me.'

'Don't tighten up so much honey, relax a little, try to let go.'

'I even prayed. But it didn't do no good. That Flitters. I tried to warn him about that man, he wouldn't lissen to me.'

Outside the sun shone brightly, down the gully, far in the distance, the birds were on a spree. The *chip-chip* of twits could be heard just outside the window; two nightingales were having an argument in a divi-divi tree.

'Why didn't they hold Flitters too, I wonder?'

'I wouldn't know.'

'Guess he must have run away.'

'I tried to get bail for him, was no good. They said for me to come back tomorrow.'

'But they can't hold him like that, it's against the law.'

'Maybe they can't, I wouldn't know, but they done it.'

'You get a lawyer go down an' bail him, honey, they can't hold him like that, it's against the law.'

'Against the law or not, they wouldn't even let me see him.'

'They can't do a thing like that an' get away with it. You try to get feelin' well again, and go see a lawyer. How are you fixed for money, if there is any way I can help you let me know.'

'Thanks Zephyr, gee, you're the best friend I have in the world, it seems.'

'Don't talk about it, honey, we got to help one another; in things like sickness an' trouble it's just natural for people to help one another, it seems to me.'

'Yeah, I know that's the way you feel about it, Zephyr, an' you're the best friend I have in the world withouten a doubt.'

'You try to get well anyway quickly an' we'll both go see a lawyer, holdin' a man like that without bail is against the law.'

'He had a gun an' was shootin' at a cop, they say; seems to make a hell of a difference, an' it might be in the law like that, I wouldn't know.'

Talking like that made the tension let go of her little by little, and hope built up within her again.

'Yes, you'n me will go into town tomorrow, get a lawyer handle this for me.'

'That's right, honey, now you're talkin'! Make them cops sit up an' take notice, you bet your bottom-nickle on it, sister, that's what we're gonna up an' do.'

Zephyr reached over and removed the handkerchief again.

'No need for that now, I'm feelin' better.'

'You mean that; already? Well now, wadya know!'

Rema sat up slowly in bed, raising herself on her arms, put her head down on her bosom, cupped one hand over her forehead, shook her head a little, and took her hand away.

'Little bit of a headache left, but nothing to keep me in bed.'

'You better rest still a while yet, honey, get you' strength again.'

'Do me a favour, push up the window? . . . Right up . . . Ah, that's better . . . room gets so hot an' stuffy in the afternoon.'

Zephyr saw Wilfie wandering forlorn and lost down the gully, and at the same time she could hear Charlotta and Bedosa talking across in their room.

'What you lookin' out the window, thinkin' about?' said Rema. 'Pass me the hand mirror from the table, please.'

Zephyr turned away from the window slowly, took up the mirror, wiped powder off the back of it against her dress, handed it to Rema.

'I was thinking,' she said, slowly, 'life has got a stick to beat us with — every last, lonesome, sufferin' mother's son.'

'Is why you vex-up?'

'Not vex-up, nutt'n.'

'Yes, you is.'

'Not. You crazy wid de heat.'

'Crazy, nutt'n, you well an' vex-up.'

'Vex-up over what's it?'

'I wouldn't know.'

Ditty shifted the basket from one arm to the other and came a step nearer to Wilfie. She had come down the gully to pick jimblins for stewing and on her way back up to the yard had come upon Wilfie, and he looked lost.

A sudden gust of wind went shouting through the tree-tops. A lizard came out and sunned himself upon a stone.

She came nearer to him and said, 'You don't need to be vexed-up 'bout nutt'n. Not about Manny, or anyone at all.'

He moved back from her a step, involuntarily, without thinking about it, and stood with one foot on a stone.

She was smart and saw that unconsciously he was still holding something against her in his heart, and she did not press him, but her tongue came out a tip and wetted her lips, looking at him closely, and her high breasts under the tight sweater moved visibly with her breathing, up and down.

'You goin' up the yard?' she said, and dropped her voice a register and said again, 'Walk with me up to the yard.'

He tried to balance on one foot, the uneven stone teetering

under him, and he had to throw his arms wide to keep from falling, she put a hand out as though to help steady him, and he stepped down off the stone, moving away from contact with her. She bit her lip, and let it go, and smiled.

'Effen you not vex-up is what matter with you, then?'

'Nutt'n matter with me, what you mean?'

'Somep'n must matter with you, is all right, though.'

Something goaded him.

'Why you don't go look fo' Manny, him must be want company. Poor Manny up at the room all alone.'

'Ah could look fo' him, yes, after is nutt'n. Could look fo' anybody sick in de yard.'

'Yes. You could an' do that.'

She stuck out a hip and set the basket astride it to ease her arm, looked at him intently, as though she would read his mind.

He pulled a seeding grass stalk, put the soft pithy end to his lips and nibbled it between his front teeth, looking away.

She said, changing the subject, 'Ah got some starapples up the house. Goodie brought home from the grass-yard, you want some?'

'No.'

'Eh? You don't want some?'

'Ah said no.'

'You not vex-up 'bout nutt'n, Ah see dat now.'

She smiled, caught his eye as his glance was going deliberately past her, and pressed home that warm seductive smile, using all the play of expression she had come upon by intuition, and had improved upon by studied use. She breathed deeply, her lips slightly parted, her sharp pointed breasts lifting and falling consciously under the tight sweater. He pulled another grass stalk to him, slowly, and looked away.

'You goin' up to the yard?' he said, coolly.

'Yes.' The smile widened a little. 'But I ain't in no special hurry, takin' me own time.'

'You could give them to Manny.'

'Eh?'

'The starapples.'

'Oh.'

'He'd be proud to have them, I bet, comin' from you.'

124

'Sure he would be, I know it. Manny wouldn't be keepin' up malice, like you.'

'I ain't keepin' up malice with no one. How you feelin' now, okay?'

'What you mean, Ah wasn't sick!'

'Sure, sure. Maybe Ah was dreamin', never mind.'

'Is what you talkin' about, anyway?'

'Oh nothin', nothin'.'

He dug his bare toes into the yielding top-soil, watched her as she turned to go away.

She was part way up the gully side before he realized that she really meant it, leaving him with a feeling of incompleteness, going on up to the yard. He bent down quickly, acting upon a sudden compulsion, took up a little round stone and threw it at her so that it hit her on the backside.

She put her hand quickly to the place and turned, her lips half open, not knowing whether she ought to be angry, or laugh.

'Why you did that?'

'Gwan, you well an' sick, only you don't know it!'

'Bwoy, is what you sayin' at all?'

'Gwan, you sick! Better tell you' Mammy befo' ambulance come to tek you to Bumper Hall.'

She set down the basket at her feet suddenly, put her arms akimbo at her sides.

'Wilfie! You know what you sayin' any at all?'

'Effen Ah know what Ah sayin'? Why, suttinly! No mind, you wait little, you will soon find out.'

He squatted on his heels, grubbing voluptuously at the yielding top-soil with his toes, he grinned from ear to ear with a fierce satisfaction, chewing vengefully on the tender grass stalk.

Without another word she picked up her basket, and walked proudly disdainful up the gully side toward the yard.

Wilfie rocked back on his heels in an excess of abandon, until he went right over on his back, kicking his heels in the air.

His voice, taunting, strident, followed her up the foot track.

'Manny gi' Ditty him dose oh! *Eh-heh! heh! hey!*'

He kicked his heels and laughed raucously like that, and all the time something inside him weighed like a stone.

125

15 SHAG RETURNED home unexpectedly early that afternoon and went straight to his room. There he found Bajun Man stripped down to his BVD's lying stretched out in his bed, and Euphemia in her dressing gown alone was sitting on the stool in front of the dressing table applying perfume to her body, and the front of the dressing gown was open and Bajun could see her reflection clearly in the big round mirror from where he was lying across the bed, 'catching his second wind' as he said, and Euphemia laughed.

And it was just as she was laughing into Bajun's face grinning at her in the mirror that the door knob turned in Shag's hand, and he came quietly into the room.

He stood in the middle of the room with his hands in his pockets and his lips were white, and he didn't look at either of them but at the crack in the floor boards under his feet, and he said to Bajun, still without looking at him, 'Get you' things quick an' get out before I change me mind.'

Bajun didn't wait to be told that twice, he just picked up his things that were lying on a chair at the foot of the bed and passed out into the passage that way; and Euphemia sat before the mirror and never moved. Even her big hands clutching the dressing gown in front of her were still and cold without feeling, as though they had been turned into salt.

When the door closed behind Bajun, Shag raised his eyes a little and they were staring straight out in front of him at a fly-spot on the opposite wall. He went across to the bed, presently, and sat down, like a man who was suddenly very tired, and didn't know until just then how tired he was, and he took his head between his hands and started to laugh.

Then he checked himself suddenly, and said to Euphemia in a voice of surprising quietness, almost gentleness, 'Get up,' and she got up immediately as though all her will waited in a void of negation and chaos, and waited only on the command of that gentle voice.

'It come into my mind to kill the both of you,' said Shag, quietly, 'but I'm not sure about anything in my mind now, and I got to be dead sure.' And he said, 'I want to be alone a spell, so take your things an' go into the bathroom, because I want to be alone.'

She gathered up her things, and turned to go from the room.

And when she came to get her shoes which were beside the bed she had to come close to him and bend down, and the front of her dressing gown fell open and he just looked at her and looked away quickly and she saw that a muscle was twitching in the side of his face, and she shuddered, thinking about the thing under the bed.

When she got to the door he stood up suddenly and said, 'Wait,' and she stood stock still as though all of her own will had been cancelled out inside her and she was powerless to move or think until that soft voice gave her leave.

He came and stood before her, and he said, 'Look at me,' and she lifted her face slowly and looked at him, full, and he saw that nothing lived within her eyes.

He said, 'Good,' and she didn't understand him, and he said again, 'I don't even hate you, aren't you glad to hear?'

But she said nothing at all, and he said again, suddenly, 'Get the hell out of here.'

When he was alone in the room he went across to the dressing table and he stood for a while looking at the things on it as though he was searching for something that he would never find. And his hand went out, blind, and fumbled among the things on the dressing table, and presently it closed about the handle of the tortoise-shell-back hairbrush, and he took it up and looked at it and turned it over, but it didn't tell him anything he wanted to know, and he put it back again.

All along from way back further than he could remember he had told himself he mustn't do this, he must never never do this, and then something had got into him that day and he said, 'The hell with Bedosa, if I wanted to I could go home I guess.' And he had searched around in his mind for a reason, and the real reason drew its lips back from its fangs and grimaced at him and said, 'You would do it yes, sucker, if you wasn't scared. Weak in the pants, that's what you are, weak in the pants for a woman, and scared.' But he thought of another reason, that there was the book that he made up the workmen's time from, that he had taken home with him the day before, and God knew it wasn't true that he had forgotten it this time on purpose.

The rubber knee-boots impeded his running and he cursed them, slog-slogging along the asphalt road, but there was scarcely time to think of anything now, but the immediate urgency of putting distance between himself and the crazy man behind him with the meat chopper, wanting his blood.

He was out through the big gates out in front of the Slaughter House and down the street, yells of people, sound of people, running, yelling, filling his ears . . . he threw one look over his shoulder and sure enough it was Slocum, his eyes reddened and crazy, staring out of his crazy face . . . said it was he caused him to lose his job . . . and he had come back to the Slaughter House yard today, pay day, to take his revenge.

A mule dray from the City Cart Stables jogged along lethargically ahead of him going down the street; the driver straightened up and twisted around hearing the shouts and yells of the people, men and women, as though they too had joined in the chase, but not really, intent only that they should not miss anything, not thinking about it that way, but wanting to be in on the kill, crazy for the sight of blood. The drayman too, as he was going past him panting and fugitive, gathered up his reins, took his cowhide whip in his hand, laid it across the startled back of the somnolent mule, bringing him suddenly to a resentful canter, the drayman too not wishing to be left out of the race.

His feet lifted heavily, encased as they were in the unwieldy rubber knee-boots, but he thought little of that now, fear spurring him on, God knows where, getting away anyhow from the crazy man who had snatched up the heavy meat chopper, shouted a wild oath to heaven as he came staggering drunkenly out of the Slaughter House yard . . . people shouting in his ears, screaming, urgent voices, men and women . . . 'quick, run man, him coming after you with a meat chopper . . . Slocum . . . crazy as hell . . . Christ a'mighty . . . murder . . .' following after him as he came out of the gate, goaded by panic, slog-slogging in the heavy clumsy rubber knee-boots, going down the straight asphalt way.

Sounds all around him rang and echoed and screeched in his ears, but he scarcely heard them, panic taking complete possession of him, scattering his senses in confusion . . . a steam whistle over by the cornmeal factory shrieked, sending in workmen on a new shift, calling others off to queue up outside the pay office window . . . clatter of mule hooves, iron-tyred dray wheels, stirring up the settled dust along the hot asphalt stretch . . . a shunting engine across the railway yard suddenly slamming on air-brakes . . . the hiss of exhausting steam, and the gathering of energy to send the same shunting engine with its coupled waggons loaded with bananas shuttling toward the docks where the S.S. *Jamaica Producer* was tied up for taking on cargo at No. 1 Pier . . . honk of a car horn coming round the corner . . . it barely missed him as he rounded the bend; trying to pull over more to the sidewalk, he slipped in the gutter and he went sprawling on his face . . . the man in the green two-seater jalopy shut his teeth hard and swung the steering wheel, trusting to luck, hit the four-inch concrete ridge of the sidewalk with his left front wheel bending an axle, straightened up, said, 'Christ Jesus!' and wondered why his steering had suddenly become stiff, the jalopy inclining now to one side of the street, decided he'd best pull up anyway, on account of the yelling crowd . . . 'Now what the hell goes on here, some more labour troubles?', and wondered was the police tear gas squad somewhere up the street.

He moved about the room examining objects and putting them back. He was pulling up his roots one by one, and it was the only thing to do.

He fetched a suitcase from under the bed, and a steamer trunk from under a hanging press to one corner of the room. He dusted them carefully and put such things as he would need more immediately into the suitcase; the others went into the trunk.

There was only one decent thing to do, he had to pack up and quit.

He got down on his hands and knees and brought out the machette from under the bed. He put it away in the trunk.

He could chop the woman up, yes, but somehow he didn't care that much. He toyed with the idea for a moment, sitting down on the side of the bed, and wondered was it that he was wanting in manhood that he did not care enough to kill her? He saw her standing nude before him, magnificent and nude, and he thought, what a lovely bitch to chop up, but he didn't care that much. To do a thing like that a man had to be dead certain in his mind. And he wasn't.

He felt an emptiness at the pit of his stomach, as though his bowels had dropped out of him and he was inching toward death, and he sat very still on the side of the bed and took his head between his hands. He coughed a little and wiped his lips with his handkerchief, and there was blood on the handkerchief, and he folded it carefully and put it away in his pocket.

He locked the steamer trunk with a little key he kept on a ring attached to his watch chain, and he pushed and hauled the heavy trunk until he got it over in a corner, out of the way. And he took up the suitcase off the floor and stood it on a chair.

He looked around the familiar room . . . this was a part of his life that he was turning his back upon, leaving it today for ever . . . a lovely bitch to chop up . . . a man had to be dead certain in his mind first . . . truth was he didn't care enough. He couldn't have loved her as much as he thought he did, he was going away.

He took up the suitcase, feeling that emptiness at the pit of his stomach. He went out through the door.

A cry went up from the pack running after him when he fell. There was tension and hysteria in that concerted cry. And other things too, but he scarcely thought about it at all. Three women fell out of the race and clutched their sides and laughed; one of them fell on the sidewalk laughing like that, her belly puffing up huge with laughter, and subsiding again, letting it go.

He scrambled up to his feet, their cries in his ears, spurring him on, he must run, run until he dropped, going God knows where. He scrambled to his feet, his fingers clawing at the asphalt, stumbled on, sounds filling his ears . . . shriek of a locomotive whistle . . . coming up, rising to a pitch, and going away . . . he turned the corner into the street that was at right angles to the one he had come down from the Slaughter House gates . . . he was running blind before, reacting only to the compulsion of his fear . . . but now he saw his objective and it lent his effort purpose . . . a long train of freight cars was coming down from the railway yard along the lines that ran across the street, going toward No. 1 Pier.

The gates were lowered across the street stopping traffic, all he had to do was to get across the lines before that string of freight cars. They would cut off pursuit for the time it would take that long train to cross the street. Trains always slowed down going into the dockyard, sometimes stopped, straddling the street. All he had to do was to get across.

The man operating the gate yelled at him. He paid no heed. He had balanced it in his mind to a nicety, figured he'd just have time to get across. He went under the gate. Voices shouting in his ears . . . the scream of the locomotive whistle rising to crescendo . . . he paid no heed. The end car was hurtling toward him, but he had time, he could make it.

He was going across the lines, had one foot over . . . the heavy, awkward rubber knee-boot on the other tripped against the metal rail . . . he was flung sprawling across the lines.

Slocum, his eyes reddened and crazy, came to a dead stop before the gate . . . saw his quarry sprawling across the lines, bunch himself up in an effort to scramble over on his hands and knees . . . saw the signalman standing on the roof of the end car raise his flag and signal frantically . . . heard the racket of air-brakes slamming on . . . the cars bucked and jolted, came to a shuddering stop . . . but too late . . . he shut his eyes and reeled against the gate . . . he was trembling like a leaf . . . sudden pandemonium of voices . . . he scarcely heard them . . . 'God!' he said, 'God!' and put his head down against the bar and started to vomit.

'God! Oh, God!' . . . he had never been so violently sick in all his life.

16 THE NIGHT SPEAKS with a thousand whispers, but a single voice . . . the wind comes, and questions, and passes on . . . the acclamation of the stars does not disturb the stillness . . . so it is with the night . . . brother, are you there, waiting your turn in the darkness beyond the door? . . . you will be announced with the others . . . our ghosts will keep company at the board . . . will applaud and be silent and wait with the waiting companions . . . each will await his turn and be quietly astounded . . . the night calls with its thousand whispers that is a single voice.

Anonymous in his cloak of darkness each waits with the night . . . the thunderous acclamation of the stars does not disturb the stillness . . . what waits with such aplomb as the brother outside the door? . . . all the guests are gathered beneath the same anonymous shadow . . . each answers to his name, and all with one voice . . . do not be deceived by the multiplicity of sounds that ring and jingle like laughter . . . do not be dismayed by the myriad murmurs that possess the night . . . we halt on the same tread and are quietly astounded . . . death speaks with a thousand whispers, but a single voice.

The day wore on listlessly to afternoon, and it was hot and close and brought the desire for sleep out in the open under the shadows of trees. A strong wind had blown earlier and swept all the scraps of clouds from the sky, leaving it naked and washed-out and debauched.

A dead cat someone had slung down the gully brought out a multitude of vultures, and as they circled and banked and came slanting down to earth their wing-spans cast shadows that crawled silently across the dusty yard surface like restless ghosts.

A strange hush had come over the yard and its inmates, and Zephyr coming upon Euphemia, whispered, 'What happen? I seen Shag go through the gate with a suitcase.'

And Euphemia said with the first show of feeling, 'Thank God, he's gone!'

Zephyr looked at her as she stood in the passage outside the bathroom door fastening a belt around her waist and she thought, 'What a hell of a mixed-up business life is, anyway,' and she said out aloud in response to Euphemia, 'Yes, I guess you must be right,' and that was all.

They took Surjue from his cell and brought him to the guard room, and everything was quiet there; that is to say there was only the Sergeant and three other policemen there, and Surjue.

The Sergeant sat at a desk and two of the policemen sat on a bench which had been dragged away from the wall and set in the middle of the room. The other one stood behind Surjue and between him and the door. The Sergeant looked at Surjue, and one of his hands played with the brass buttons on the front of his tunic and the other rested on the desk in front of him, and he said, gently, 'You better behave yourself in here, let me give you a piece of advice.'

'Yes,' said Surjue.

'Sir,' said the Sergeant.

'Eh?'

'Say "yes sir", when you're speaking to me.'

Surjue made no answer. He saw that the fingers of the hand on the table had tightened about a round black ruler and the other had unbuttoned two buttons of the tunic, but the voice was so gentle it almost purred.

'You got that?'

'I heard you,' said Surjue.

'He's a dunce, Sarge,' said one of the policemen on the bench, 'he don't catch on quick,' and he stood up and took a hitch at his belt and unbuckled it and took it off. He put it across the back of a chair, and began taking off his tunic. The other policeman got up and stretched his arms and arched his back, stretching up, as though he was stiff from sitting in one place too long, and he too unbuckled his belt and took off his tunic and laid them carefully over the back of another chair. They stood in their shirt sleeves facing him.

'I don't believe he's going to give us any trouble,' said the Sergeant. 'I think he's going to be real good with us, you boys are too hasty.'

'Give him a drop of ju-ju waps, Sarge.'

'Yeah, limber him up a bit.'

'No boys, let ju-ju waps stay inside the wall.'

They chuckled over this as though it was a joke. Surjue looked from one to the other, faintly puzzled; what was this, what were they talking about, were they practising up some kind of vaudeville act?

'Tell me something,' said the Sergeant, smiling affably, leaning across the desk, pressing his fingers together, 'who was with you on this job?'

Surjue didn't answer.

'Well?'

The Sergeant's lips were smiling, but his eyes were not amused at all. One thing Surjue noticed about him, and he wanted to laugh — he put out the tip of his tongue and wet his lips just like he always saw Ditty do, and to Surjue it was very funny. And then he looked from the Sergeant's grinning lips to his eyes, and suddenly he didn't want to laugh.

133

'Well? Aren't you going to tell us? Who was with you on this job?'

'Nobody.'

'Tsk! Tsk!' the Sergeant clicked his teeth together, still wearing that smile. And then he said, quietly, 'You're lying. Who got away with the stuff? Who was the other guy on the roof with you?'

'Must have been me shadow.'

The Sergeant made a wry face. 'You mustn't make jokes like that, if you want us to laugh. Who was on the roof with you?'

'Nobody.'

'Who was on the roof with you? Try and remember.'

'There was nobody, I tell you.'

'There was somebody on the roof with you, who was it?'

'Musta been Santa Claus.'

The Sergeant made a wry face again.

'I told you you mustn't make jokes like that here. We hear bad jokes like that every day. Who was on the roof with you?'

No answer.

'Well?'

'I told you already there was nobody.'

'You're not so smart as I thought you were. The boys were right. Who was on the roof with you?'

No answer.

'Tsk! Tsk! A dunce.'

'I told you, Sarge.'

'Maybe he's just scared, that's why he won't talk. There's nothing to be scared about, nobody's going to hurt you.'

'Don't kid yourself, I'm not scared.'

'Who was on the roof with you?'

No answer.

'He's not scared, but he won't answer.'

'Maybe he's just stubborn.'

'He's a dunce, that's what. Judd was right. Come on then, who was on the roof with you?'

'Ask me again.'

But he didn't. He shook his head sadly, rubbed his hands together, blew on them and rubbed them together again as though he was cold. He said, quietly, 'Maybe he has forgotten. Bring out Big Ju-Ju from inside the wall.'

One of the cops went across to a locker against the wall, opened it, took out a big rubber truncheon.

'Big Ju-Ju will limber him up, make him make water, an' not a broken bone to show for it.'

So this was it. The third degree.

The cop with the rubber truncheon came and stood beside him. He was grinning too, and the tip of his tongue came out and made that same gesture, licking his lips, and because of its mental association it was the most horrible thing he had ever seen.

'All right buddy, I'll ask you again. Who was it on the roof with you?'

He would jeer them and taunt them and curse them to keep from screaming; one thing he wouldn't tell. When the time came for him to settle with Flitters he would settle for everything.

'All right . . . I'll ask you again. Who was on the roof with you?'

'Cho, they do it better in the movies.'

The cop with the rubber truncheon hit high up on the arm, and a sharp pain burst inside it and it went dead.

He screamed, 'They do it better in the movies! Yah! You lousy bums!'

The cop hit him with the rubber truncheon again, and again, and the others held him. All the while he cursed and swore and jibed and screamed at them . . . and he took his tongue between his teeth and bit it until he tasted blood . . . and the next blow he let it go and screamed with pain.

They gathered up what was left of Bedosa the best they could and conveyed it in a handcart to the Public Hospital, and there they laid it out on a slab in the morgue.

'Got to communicate with his family . . .' 'Identification . . .' 'How you say he got his? What was he doin' on the lines? . . .' 'You can't identify that! . . .' 'Crazy guy chasin' him with a meat chopper . . . ' 'Got to get someone identify the deceased. . . .'

The porter and a couple of attendants and the handcart man plus some members of the heterogeneous crowd that had followed the handcart, and a policeman, stood around and talked it over.

'Never seen a man messed-up like that in all me life . . .' 'Fellow was chasin' him with a meat chopper . . .' 'Pukin' his daylights out in the gutter by the gate . . .' 'Seen a man and a

woman chopped clean in two down No. 1 Pier one night . . .'
'Never seen nothin' like that, though, never seen a man messed-up
like that before, I bet . . .' 'Train took the outside lines beside
the shed 'stead of goin' straight down the middle . . .' 'Just
settin' there in the midst of all that rum-vomit . . .' 'Hell of a way
for a man to die, Christ a'mighty! . . .' 'Was dark . . . night . . .
two of them was goin' it hard cotched up against the lines . . .'

Up at the yard Charlotta was singing because of the fullness of
her heart. She had what once had been a sweet contralto voice,
now it had become a little tired and frayed at the edges, but in
moments of deep emotion or quiet exaltation it could still carry
a tune.

> Lo, when the day of rest was past
> The Lord, the Christ, was seen again;
> Unknown at first, he grew to sight:
> 'Mary', he said — she knew him then:
> *Alleluya!* . . .

In her heart there was a great heaviness. The Lawd knew it
was a heavy burden a poor body had to carry . . . what with
Manny gettin' himself into all kinds of bad mischief, and nobody
knew what it might be next he would be in . . . 'people like Manny
mek fo' prison, an' prison'll get him one of these days' . . . hush,
do, ask God pardon, you don't know what you sayin' at all . . .
Bedosa was hard an' bitter against Manny . . . still his words sent
a chill through her heart . . . Please God, don't mek anything
happen . . . de burden is 'most too much for a poor body to carry,
me Jesus, is you alone know. . . .

> And dimly in the evening light
> He joined two friends who walked alone —

Jesus, touch their hearts and melt their hardness with your
love . . . touch the hearts of Bedosa and Manny, both, so that they
may know the sweet gentle love of Jesus, an' let him in. . . .

> A stranger, till he stayed to sup:
> He brake the bread, and he was known!
> *Alleluya!* . . .

She went about the room singing softly to herself and dusting

136

and setting things straight. The cow heel that Bedosa had brought home last evening had been singed and scraped and was on the fire already, gently simmering to a stew. She would have it ready to set before him against his return.

'Who was with you on the roof?'

They had him now straddled across the bench that had been dragged from against the wall. He was strapped securely to it, because he had fought so hard it was impossible for them to hold him down. Each time they hit him with the rubber truncheon he screamed. At first he had screamed taunts and jibes and obscenities at them, but now he just screamed when they hit him.

They didn't care about his screaming because the doors and windows were closed and little sound could reach outside. And anyway it didn't matter, nobody paid attention in this place to prisoners screaming. He wondered how long this would go on before he lost consciousness. One thing he made up his mind about, he wasn't going to tell.

'Who was it up on the roof with you?'

The question was repeated again and again in that same flat, not unpleasant voice, almost without inflection, until he could hear it, the same question over and over, even when the voice was silent and he was screaming and writhing and twisting under the blows.

'Who was it up on the roof with you?'

One of the policemen had armed himself with a cow cod — the dried and cured sex organ of a bull which was a tough length of gristle that could cut a man's flesh like piano-wire — and he was practising shots with it where Surjue could see him, making it whistle as it cut through the air.

'Lemme a chance at him; Little Ju-Ju will mek him let go his water; limber him up better'n anything, I bet, Little Ju-Ju.'

They stood aside and the man with the bull-thong stepped up and swung at him . . . once, twice, three times . . . he could feel it cutting into the flesh of his back, ripping the shirt off him . . . and the Sergeant suddenly shouted, 'Stop!' and he went up to the cop with the bull-thong and took it away from him angrily and threw it into a corner, and it was the first Surjue had seen him angry all that time.

'Don't be a dam fool, Judd, that cow-cod leaves marks behind, didn't you know?'

'Hell, Sarge, it don't matter.'

'Well it does, an' we're not having any more of it, you hear?'

And the words of the cop kept sounding in his ears, 'Hell, Sarge, it don't matter!' And it brought him nearer to real panic than he had ever been. What the hell did he mean, it didn't matter? They could do anything to a man in here and nobody cared? If it didn't mean that, what the hell else could it mean?

'Untie him,' said the Sergeant. And when they had untied him he said, 'Take him back to his cell and put him on B ration.' And Surjue knew that meant bread and water. They were going to lower his physical resistance and work on him again. That meant he wasn't going to get bail!

He was taken to the cell by the same cop who had wanted to have a go at him with the bull-thong. When he unlocked the cell door he jerked his head sideways for Surjue to go in, and as he was going through the door he put his foot out and tripped him. He fell, and the cop came in and kicked him in the side, and the sharp stabbing pain in his side made him so mad he got up, and the cop kicked him again and again while he was trying to scramble to his feet, and once when a favourable opportunity offered he stamped him with the sole of his boot, and the nails on the heel raked his side and tore some skin away, but Surjue managed to get to his feet and a blind rage came over him and he closed with the cop and mauled him up bad until they had to come inside the cell, hearing his yells, and drag him away.

The Sergeant said, 'Serves you right, Judd,' and Judd looked down shame-faced at his boots, but the other cops just looked grim and one of them was smiling a little, and Surjue knew exactly what he meant by that smile.

He had seen a man beaten right out in the yard that morning with the buckle-ends of belts and bull-thongs and batons until he was a mess. He didn't know a man could stand so much beating, it made him sick to see it. This man was a habitual criminal with twenty-one previous convictions, and they called him Cubano; and Surjue figured he must have spent most of his life in jail.

The cops who gave Cubano that unmerciful beating that morning were smiling like that cop was smiling now outside his cell. Surjue had had little education but he had a quick alert mind.

He had said to himself, if you give people that kind of power over other people, what'd you expect? It came like second nature to them to knock the prisoners around. A prisoner, a criminal, was a man who had lost his right to be considered a man, he was just an animal; but they treated animals better, and it was only because the law protected animals. A man could get into trouble for being cruel to an animal. But there was no law protecting criminals, as such, and nobody had ever heard of a man being jailed or hanged, or even fined, for something he had done to a criminal under his charge. Yet criminals had died of the beatings and the B rations and the dysentery and the further beatings they got, and the doctor made out a certificate of death by pneumonia, or death by something — he didn't talk with Buju and Crawfish for nothing.

Of course the doctor wasn't wrong when he put down pneumonia, or whatever it was, on the death certificate. He wasn't required to set down that the pneumonia or the gangrene was brought about by the man's ribs being broken, say, and his lying for three days in a dumb-cell without seeing a doctor, and a piece of one of his ribs sticking into his lungs.

He had never been to prison before, but he had not talked with Buju and Crawfish for nothing. And now they had him, and he knew what to expect.

He didn't know the Sergeant was off duty that afternoon. All he knew was that they came for him later and led him across the yard to a cell in another building where it was dark and further away from the guard room. And they beat him as he had seen them beat Cubano that same morning; and he knew when something inside him let go and there was nothing to make him contain the faeces in his belly, so that it came away from him with a rush, as though something had burst inside him, and the contents of his bladder with it.

And they beat him to the ground, and they beat him to make him get up; and they beat him until he crawled like an animal dragging himself on his hands and knees, among them, blind, clear outside the cell and into the dark passage; and they beat him until he crawled back into the cell again, clawing and groping for

139

the entrance with his hands, because he didn't know where he was or what he was doing, he was so stupid with pain.

There were six of them, and when they were tired of beating him they went away locking the cell door behind them. And one of them said, 'That'll learn you to beat up a cop, me man,' as he was going out. And they came back again and unlocked the cell door and told him to get up. And they had to kick him hard to make him get up, because at first he felt as though he couldn't, and then he got up and they marched him down the dark passage between them and out on to a little patch of green grass to one side of the yard. And they took two other prisoners out of their cells and gave them buckets, and they made him strip off the clothes he had fouled himself in, and the two other prisoners stood off and threw buckets of water on him, and then they made him dry himself and put on some clothes they had brought for him. And they marched him back and locked him in his cell again.

That night he developed high fever, and he wasn't even able to eat his bread and water. And the next morning he was removed to the Public Hospital under police guard.

The sounds slackened, rose to crescendo, spaced out, subsided, rose up strident, hung in the air a space, and went on down the street . . . a boy whistling shrilly a song about love was one of them . . . a snorting, hustling, arrogant, outsize omnibus with hissing air-brakes was another . . . the ceaseless, strident, casual chatter . . . the laughter that was like fire-crackers going off by the packet . . . two women greeting each other, shouting intimacies across the busy street . . . automobiles . . . the usual contingent of trucks and bicycles and handcarts and barrows . . . a country woman from the hills driving her donkey with loaded panniers before her down the street.

A petrol-truck with cylindrical sausage-body rumbled over the asphalt ruts, the chipped patches where the road was pock-marked, defaced, dragging a chain.

That was in the street.

Inside the yard a gloom had settled over everyone and everything, it was as though a dark cloud had gathered immediately overhead, casting a shadow over this place. Two little speckled birds came hop-stepping, picking up ants, in the middle of the yard; they stopped to look at a hungry lean rail of an alley cat, said *chip-chewee* and flew away toward the gully.

Tansy had been taken with hysteria when she learned what had happened. Rema made her lie down on the bed beside her, her own trouble forgotten for the moment, and wet her head with some of the bay rum and talked to her gently, soothingly, until the frantic sobbing diminished to a hiccup. Rema, a nerve in the side of her face twitching, sat up and took her head between her hands, and listened to the sounds going past in the street.

> Lo, when the day of rest was past
> The Lord, the Christ, was seen again;
> Unknown at first, he grew to sight:
> 'Mary' he said — she knew him then;
> > *Alleluya! . . .*

That was Charlotta over the ironing board inside her room singing to keep from breaking down and weeping. It was she who gave Zephyr most concern when the terrible news had reached them.

'Is there anything I can do?' she asked from the door.

And Charlotta just looked at her, and drew her arm across her forehead, and shook her head, and said, 'No', and went on to singing the next verse of the hymn.

Manny, grumbling to himself, got up, although he shouldn't, made a face of pain, hesitating a little, and went on outside into the yard.

Charlotta continued her ironing.

Presently she set down the iron on the ring as though to let it cool a little, and stopped singing in the middle of a verse.

She sat down on a stool, bent down and pulled up a stocking that had fallen halfway down her bony shin.

Zephyr came a few steps, hesitantly, inside the room.

Charlotta said, in a flat, steady voice, 'He always kept up his Burial Scheme Society dues, so that won't give me any bother; one thing he was always a careful man.'

She shut her mouth as though she had caught herself talking out of turn. She took the end of her apron between her hands. Slowly at first, she started to gather it up and wring it . . . and wring it, and wring it . . . and the sharp angular outlines of her face softened a little, the outlines becoming slightly blurred, and her lips twitched, and she started to cry.

Zephyr sat down beside her and put her arm about her shoulders. Charlotta let her body relax for an instant, but presently she sat up straight again; she gently pushed the other woman away, and stood up. She said, as though chiding herself:

'Cho, what's matter now, you goin' to cry?'

And she took up the iron again and held it close to her cheek, testing the heat, and started to iron the damp sheet on the board.

> And dimly in the evening light
> He joined two friends who walked alone —
> A stranger, till he stayed to sup;
> He brake the bread, and he was known!
> *Alleluya!*

She sang.

And Zephyr got up and walked quietly with head bent, as it were, reverently, through the door.

What comfort could she hope to offer this woman?

She felt of a sudden little and daunted, overawed by a courage she could not hope to reach.

BOOK TWO

1 ZEPHYR SAT DOWN, linked her two little fingers together, tried to pull them apart without unhooking them, her face stiffening with the effort; watched Lennie go through the door.

There was a knock.

'Who's that? Come in. Oh, Euphemia. Come right on in, I'm all alone.'

'I couldn't sleep. The place is full of sounds.'

'Sleep?'

'I went to lay down. Tired. Tried to go to sleep—'

'Yes. There's trouble enough in this yard. What's happened to God? Don't he care any?'

'God? Hush! You mustn't say it. Ain't you scared to talk that way?'

'No. Not again. I seen too much in my time.'

'Already . . .'

'What you mean, already?'

'I—I don't know . . . know somep'n, Zephyr, wish to Christ I could get away.'

'You?'

'Yes. It — it feels — I feel just like I was in prison.'

'I don't get you. What makes you feel that way?'

'I should have gone when you told me.'

'When I told you what?'

'To go away — leave everything — start all over again —'

'I did that? Told you to go? Oh yes. That was a long time ago. What's happened?'

'All right, I'll tell you. We had a row. He's gone for good this time.'

'Bajun Man?'

'Yes.'

'Well, ain't that just too funny!'

'All right, go on — if you want to laugh.'

'I'm not laughing. Honest Euphemia. It's just — just I can't figure nothing, that's all.'

143

'He packed up an' left. He — he ain't coming back. I know it.'

'The dirty swine!'

'No.'

'What you mean, no? He left you flat, didn't he?'

'Don't say it like that. You —'

'Yeah, I know, I don't understand. You gimme a pain in the guts. Honest you do.'

'I don't know —'

'You sold or pawned everything you had. Didn't you? You needn't lie to me. An' now he can't get nothin' more outa you, he's packed up an' quit.'

'Please don't say it like that.'

'You poor, snifflin' little fool. I could be sorry for you.'

'Don't, Zephyr —'

'All right, all right.'

'I wish I was dead.'

'Sure. But what's the use wish'n, you alive, ain't you? An' you just got to take it.'

'I could kill myself.'

'Don't — don't make me say it.'

'What?'

'Let it go.'

'I don't know what to do.'

'You said I never loved a man, I couldn't.'

'I said that?'

'Yeah, a long time ago. I couldn't figure you then, now I know what you mean.'

'Don't turn against me, Zephyr, please. You're the only friend I've got.'

'Turn against you? No. Only I'm sorry for you, I can't help it, an' God! I don't want to be.'

'I could kill myself, I got no use in the world.'

'You ought to go down on your knees to Shag an' beg him to take you back.'

'Good God, no.'

'You couldn't do that, eh?'

'No, I couldn't.'

'Who's going to look after you?'

'I could get a job.'

'You could? Well, I'm glad you thought of that.'

'Only I don't know what I could do.'

'You could hire yourself out to cook for somebody. Go an' hire yourself out an' cook for a family, somewhere.'

'You think so?'

'Yes, why not? It's the only thing you can do.'

'An' then — an' then, maybe —'

'Eh?'

'Oh, nothing.'

'Christ, I could be sorry for you!'

'Don't look at me that way, Zephyr. You — you're the only friend I've got.'

'Look, you had supper yet?'

'Supper? I'm not hungry.'

'Well, I am. Here's some money. Could you go out to the shop an' buy some bread an' sardines or something — and a pear?'

'How much?'

'Enough for three of us. Lennie's here.'

Lennie's voice from the door.

'Yeah, Lennie's here. An' I nearly tripped over a stool coming down the passage.'

'I'm sorry, I must have left it there.'

'My God, what a place to leave a stool! Sister, would you mind pullin' your feet in outa the way?'

'Why don't you look where you're goin'?'

'Excuse me, but you must be crazy. A heluva place to leave a stool!'

'All right, I'm going, you don't have to insult me.'

'Say, what's this?'

'All right, Lennie. She's a little upset, that's all. Go on, Euphemia, get those things an' hurry back. I'm hungry.'

'All right. You — you sure I won't be in the way?'

'Go on now, honey. There's a good girl.'

The door swung on its hinges again, clicked shut. The silence breaking on a brittle note.

'Say, what's the matter with her?'

'She has troubles, Lennie. God, life has a stick to beat every one of us with.'

'You said it, honey. You said it, for sure.'

'I read in the papers the other day where a woman died at a hundred an' four. She had ninety-seven grandchildren an' great grandchildren. What'd she have to be proud of, I'd like to know.'

Manny was at the gate as Euphemia was going through. He had his arms up on the top rail, his chin resting on his hands.

'You going to the shop?' he said.

Euphemia just looked at him in passing, and looked away again, as though he wasn't there.

He said: 'What you want there? I'll go get it for you.'

'It's all right. I wouldn't trouble you.'

'No trouble. I'm going there anyhow.'

'You were going to the shop on your own account?'

'Yes. I mean it. Want me carry the basket for you?'

'No. I can manage. I wouldn't trouble you.'

'Awe, don't be like that. Don't — don't be bearin' up malice.'

'Who's bearin' up malice? Me?'

'All right. I didn't mean to say anything to vex you.'

'Do me a favour, Manny. I don't feel to talk.'

'Blow. That's what you mean?'

No answer; her head held straight before her all the time.

'Oh, all right. I guess I'm poison to you.'

'I didn't say that.'

'I guess you have a right to say it, too. I'm not blamin' you.'

People passing down the narrow sidewalk elbowed them into the street.

'You could walk ahead. I would carry the basket.'

'It's nothing at all. I wouldn't trouble you.'

'I guess you don't feel like talkin' to me; I'm not blamin' you.'

'Oh God, don't bother say you're sorry for anything, I couldn't stand another blessed thing tonight.'

'I'm sorry all the same. I wanted to say it.'

'You're sorry? I don't give a damn, it's nothing to me.'

'All right. All right. I just wanted you should know.'

Silence between them. People thrust them apart, going down the street.

'Anybody could use a friend. That's what I want to be.'

'Oh Christ, don't bother nag me tonight, I beg you. You would do me a favour truly? I want to be alone.'

'All right, I guess I can get what I want in the shop across the street there. You going further, walk good then; walk good, hear?'

Manny ran into Wilfie as he was coming in through the gate. Manny had a lighted cigarette between his lips; he was puffing at it with a bravado.

'You coming from the shop?' said Wilfie.

'Followed Euphemia part way up the street.'

'Oh.'

'Oh, nothing. She don't even want to talk to me.'

'No mind that, man, she'll come around, don't worry.'

'I could be the dirt under her feet.'

'She should be sore at you too, remember?'

'Yeah, I remember all right. Want a smoke?'

'Sure, gimme a draw. Look, I can bring it through me nose.'

'It's not as if I want anything from her, either. Anybody could use a friend.'

'Yeah, I get you. Never mind, she'll soon forget it.'

'No. I guess she won't — ever.'

'What's the matter? You feel — that way about her?'

'What you mean?'

'I guess you must be in love with Euphemia for true.'

'My God, you said it. I'd give her anything she asked me — just anything, you hear?'

'Yeah, I figured that. Gee Manny, you're crazy for hell!'

'Sure I'm crazy. Think I don't know it? So I'm crazy, an' what the hell gives?'

'You askin' me!'

'Know somep'n? I'd lie down in the dirt an' let her walk over me. I wouldn't give a damn. People laffin' at me? Let 'em laff, I should care.'

'Boy, you sure talkin' somep'n. How's·the job, you like it?'

'Eh? The job? Oh, yeah.'

'Shoemaker trade is a good trade these days. Better'n renovatin'. More customers, I mean.'

'You helpin' your Pa dry-clean, an' all?'

'Yeah man, I'm doin' it all meself now. How you gettin' on with Mass Mose?'

'Oh, he's all right. He's a regular guy. I can talk to him 'bout anything.'

147

'That's good. I'm glad to hear.'

'Just like he was my own Pa, only more.'

'Yeah, I get you.'

'Yes sir, I'd lay down in the dirt -- in the dirt, man — an' let her walk over me.'

'Awe hell, Manny, forget it.'

'Forget it? Forget it, you say?'

'Er — you got that thing better yet?'

'Eh? Oh sure, sure. Told Mass Mose 'bout it. He made me go to the doctor shop, get something. It fixed me up, all right.'

'I know. You told me when you were going to buy it. Remember?'

'Yes. That's right. Said I was to be careful. Mass Mose. Careful! Christ, you bet I am.'

'You don't — you know?'

'Sure, a guy gets feelin's. Every now an' then. But you got to be careful, that's all.'

'Seen Ditty? She went down the street just now.'

'Ditty! You not thinkin' about her that way, are you? Her Old Man's layin' her, didn't you know?'

'For Christ sake, man! Don't say a thing like that.'

'It's God's truth.'

'How do you know?'

'She came braggin' to me about it, an' all. Said he was makin' passes at her, anyway.'

'Makin' passes at her! Her Old Man?'

'She says he isn't her Pa. He says the same.'

'What the hell you talkin' about man, I don't get you.'

'Tellin' you what she told me, that's all.'

'You know somep'n, Manny, there's somep'n about that Ditty I'll never understand.'

'Don't even try, man, she isn't worth it. Just a little white-livered tramp.'

They stopped talking and Wilfie turned his face away and tried to whistle a tune. Manny took the cigarette that had burned down to a stub from between his lips and flicked it away.

'You'd think anybody could use a friend these days, now wouldn't you? It's not as though I wanted anything from her. Gee, I'd just want for her to ask me to do something for her, that's all.'

'Man, you sure crazy to be in love with Euphemia. She's plenty older'n you.'

'All right. So what? I didn't say it wasn't crazy, did I? All I want is a chance for me to show her, that's all.'

'Man, you crazy for hell, withouten a doubt. Awe, I wouldn't make a woman ball me up like that, I'd see her dead in a ditch.'

'You can talk like that, nothing like this ever happened to you.'

'What happened, tell me?'

He waited for Manny to answer, still looking away.

'Dunno. Must be something like how lightnin' strikes. You get a feelin' inside you an' first you don't understand it, an' then something happens, like — like an egg hatchin' out — an' you know.'

'What?'

'What I been tryin' to tell you. You remember my Old Man?'

'Yes. Sure.'

'I used to hate his guts. I don't any more.'

'He's dead. You couldn't hate him still. What you talkin' 'bout?'

'I hated him worst after he was dead — for a time. Then I got to figurin' things out, an' a lot of things come plain to me. First, why did I hate him? I don't rightly know. He never did me nothin'. I think he was scared to try. I was 'most as big as he was. He was always scared. He never did things like other men. That gave me a clue. I guess I wanted to be proud of my Old Man, like any guy would want to be. I couldn't. It got so I wanted to act opposite to him all the time. He was scared to do things. I went out an' did them. It got so I wanted to act like a man before my time. You follow?'

'I'm hearin' you.'

'Well, that's about the size of it, I guess.'

'When did you start figurin' all this for yourself?'

'Don't rightly know. Perhaps it was his dyin' like that did it. An' this other thing. Like lightnin', you get me? Just like lightnin'.'

'You mean about Euphemia?'

'Yes.'

'Manny, you know somep'n, you got your hands full.'

'I know it man, I know it.'

'She wouldn't even look your way.'

'I know that too, but it don't make no difference. It's not a thing you can control, ever — your feelin's about a woman, I guess.'

'You know, you got the same force-ripeness in you still? Only different now. A bit worse, I should say.'

'Yeah? Well, if it be so it just happened, an' that's all.'

'I don't get it. I don't get it at all. The last bloody thing I'd figure for you.'

'I didn't figure it either, it just happened, I tell you.'

'Don't look, there she is now, just comin' in through the gate.'

'She wouldn't even look my way.'

'She got troubles plenty, I guess.'

'Anybody got troubles like that you'd think could use a friend.'

'You know somep'n boy, she'd piss you up. That baby she's tough. She'd make you piss.'

'She piss me up . . . anything . . . just so long she let me be her friend, I wouldn't care.'

2   THE DARK SHADOWS beyond our ken crowd in upon us and stand and wait unseen . . . they wait in silence and drink us up in darkness . . . they wipe their hands across their lips and pass the cup . . . they are the dark company that keep eternal vigil over life unto death . . . we are endlessly lost amongst a host of shadows that stand and wait.

The grisly profile bulks in the likeness of stone . . . it runs four sides of the closed compound . . . when evening comes it lengthens its shadow . . . it lies across our utmost dreams . . . the sun rolls down the sky without stay, without sound . . . the shadows close in, creeping noiselessly across the gravel of the compound . . . they are always in waiting somewhere against the wall.

A man might go mad in the stillness, in the darkness . . . a man, come to the end of his dream, alone . . . a man might go mad with terror when the great aloneness and the utterness of night about him weigh like stone.

The clink of a tool in the night — and then silence . . . they cut a tunnel in the darkness working with a pan handle only . . . underneath the great stone building they burrowed like moles in darkness . . . the hole came up in the gravel yard outside the kitchen . . . there were men with guns waiting for them in the shadow of the wall.

A row of single iron beds running down two sides of the long ward, dark grey blankets rough and uniform drawn up over recumbent figures stretched out in sleep or tossing restlessly between episodes of uneasy slumber and intervals of itching torment where chinch bugs sucked loathsome full bladders of blood from unwilling hosts, counted sixty-six; thirty-three iron cots on either side.

Little sounds fell into the deep well of silence that was not aware of them until they were gone.

A goods train sounded its whistle down the railroad track going away from the town, the quickening stroke of the pistons pounding like a racing pulse shuddered through the night . . . bells chimed in the church yard beyond the wall and went out, were merged in the multitude of small carrying sounds . . . an electric motor whined in the distance, and a buzz saw sang, bit deep, worried its way angrily through a chunk of wood, and came up again with a singing twang like that of a plucked chord.

Surjue turned over on his side but couldn't sleep.

The man on the cot beside him was Cubano. They had both gone down with dysentery the same day, working on the prison farm, and had been sent to hospital. This was the prison hospital and already it was overcrowded. Mattresses were spread on the floor between beds, and down the aisle. Nearly a hundred prisoners had to be squeezed into the hospital ward. The air carried a sickly breathed-over odour.

He could see that Cubano too was not asleep; and presently the man turned over on his side facing him, and spoke in a low undertone.

'It's dam hot an' stuffy in here, I can't sleep either,' said Cubano.

He had a swarthy, sullen face, and his eyes were hard and black, and gave nothing away.

'I know what you want,' he said, 'a cigarette.'

Surjue's eyes signalled, 'The Warder', and Cubano said: 'He's all right. He won't trouble us. He's one of the good ones.'

Surjue said: 'Ain't nothin' like a good warder, they don't come that way.'

'This one won't trouble us,' said Cubano, chuckling. 'He'll stay up the other end of the ward where he is an' mind his own business. Want a smoke?'

'Sure.'

Cubano's hand went under his pillow. He took out a crumpled packet of cigarettes, passed one to Surjue, put one to his own lips. He pulled the blanket up around his head like a hood and struck a match. The sudden spurt of flame didn't make much difference, because there was always some light inside the prison ward.

They lay on their sides and smoked, hiding the glow from their cigarettes under cover of their blankets, felt better for the comfort of nicotine, human companionship, talk. Their conversation was carried on in the same undertones as before; the warder leaning against the barred window at the other end of the long ward, never stirred.

'It's your first time inside?'

'Yes.'

Cubano was silent for a moment, digesting this.

'All the same you shoulda known better'n to trust a rat like Flitters, I heard all about it. What you goin' to do?'

'Do?'

'Yes. He ought to be rubbed out, a guy like that.'

'Don't worry,' said Surjue.

Cubano looked at him, but his head was withdrawn under the blanket as he took a long drag at his cigarette.

'Ah, you got friends outside.'

'You bet I got friends. What's more they know the whole story. I sent word to them. They'll know what to do, an' they'll do it. If they don't do nothing I'll get Flitters myself when I'm out of this. I'll get the bastard if it's the last thing I do.'

'Yeah . . . I know a chap once squealed on a buddy. He got away to Panama.'

'Flitters won't get away, don't worry.'

'I'm real worried about it all the same.'

'What's it to you?'

'I'd hate for a rat like that to go on living.'

'You can quit worryin' right now.'

They smoked in silence for a time. Cubano coughed. Down the other end of the ward a prisoner waked, groaned, turned over on his other side, groaned again, louder.

Surjue said suddenly, 'I hate this blasted place.'

'Me too,' said Cubano, and then he said: 'Fletcher is going out next week. How'd you like to be made hospital orderly?'

'Who, me?'

'With a bit of luck you could get it.'

'How you mean?'

'Well, they usually take a long term man for an orderly. You got five years.'

'That don't mean anything, man.'

'Yes, it do. You been of good conduct. It's your first time inside. You're the fittenist man for hospital orderly when Fletcher goes out.'

'Don't make me laugh.'

'Okay. Just wait an' see.'

Surjue heaved himself upright, threw off the blanket, put his feet down on the ground.

'Where you goin'?' said Cubano.

'To the can.'

'Here. Take a cigarette with you.'

'Thanks, buddy.'

'It's nothing. I like talkin' to you. Say, don't you have anybody outside you'd like to get a letter or a message to?'

'Yeah, sure. I'd like to write a letter. Private.'

'Write it. I can get it out for you. Don't ask me anything. Just give me the letter, that's all.'

Surjue looked at him closely. 'You mean that?'

'What you mean, do I mean that? Sure I do '

Surjue smiled.

'Okay, I'll take you up on that,' he said.

Why did he talk to Cubano, tell him all his mind? He didn't know. Coming out from between the beds he stubbed his toe, swore sibilantly, sat down suddenly on the end of the cot, took his foot in his hands.

'Shit, I never get used to that dam bed foot always tryin' to trip me up,' he said, and Cubano laughed.

'Takes time to get used to things in here. I'm gettin' out.'

Surjue knew he had heard him right the first time . . . the words themselves, the tone of quiet assurance that went with them. But he said, 'Eh?' before he could catch back the ejaculation.

'Don't kid yourself, I'm not stayin' here,' said Cubano.

'You goin' to break jail?'

'Hold your tongue, man. You want to tell everybody?'

'Sorry . . . It's all right. Nobody heard me . . . You must be crazy,' he whispered.

'Crazy, no?'

His face twitched into a kind of smile, twitched with hardness, and relaxed again.

'It'll be the third time I done it. Twice from the other place . . . we was out on the brickyard. Once from here. I went over the wall.' He added as an afterthought. 'I want to see my woman, that's what.'

Just that, and Surjue felt something come up from inside him and take him by the throat.

Someone moved at the other end of the ward. It was the guard, changing his position. He took a few paces down the aisle, stepping carefully to avoid the men sleeping on mattresses on the floor. He swung his stick in the air as though to restore his circulation, and went back to his post by the window, dragging up a stool.

Boots crunched on the gravel outside, and further down the compound a voice challenged in the night, was answered by another . . . the sound of boots crunching across the gravel in the yard again . . . silence. . . .

'They can't do nothin' to me, boy, they done everything already. This is your first time inside . . . you don't rightly belong here at all.'

'They caught me, though. . . .'

'Shit, you got carried down by a rat, that's all. The skunk! Somebody ought to get him for it.'

'Don't you worry 'bout nothing at all.'

'Okay. You write that letter soon as you're ready. I'll get it out for you.'

Rema was sick, bad . . . she needed him . . . he had four years and two months to go, if he earned all his remission of time . . . good God! . . . four years and two months! . . . he wanted to laugh.

Boots crunching on the gravel outside the hospital . . . a clock in the town chimed the half-hour . . . the waves of sound vibrated and went out . . . a dog suddenly woke and barked hysterically in the distance out by the other end of the town . . . silence, broken by a scampering movement of rats on the roof . . . Cubano was speaking.

'. . . you better watch out for that bastard anyway, he'll move heaven to get you.'

That could mean only one person . . . Aaron Nickoll. The louse! He'd never done that warder anything, why did the man hate him, try to make mischief for him, bawl at him on the least occasion? He couldn't tell. Maybe it was just that he was mean. Just a skunk, that's what. He was just plain mean and ugly everybody said, but he seemed to take a special sneaking spiteful interest in him, Surjue.

'You be careful of that guy,' said Cubano.

'Don't worry, I've got his number.'

'Remember, a prisoner's word don't mean a thing against the word of a warder.'

'I'll watch my step.'

'If a warder wants to frame one of us, beat him up, get him a billet in the dumb cell, he can always get away with it.'

'I know. I'm careful.'

'Careful don't help you sometimes. Not if a warder hates your guts bad enough. Keep out of his way is the best thing.'

'Yeah. I'll keep out of his way all right.'

'He hates your guts for nothing. He's mean like that.'

'Maybe I'll meet him up outside when I leave this place. I can wait.'

'If he could fix it you wouldn't leave here alive. You don't know him.'

'Well I mean, he couldn't do anything like that.'

'Quit kiddin' yourself, there is nothing he couldn't do. This is your first time inside. You got a lot to learn.'

'My God, yes. But I'm learning fast. How you feelin' in the guts?'

'A little weak, that's all.'

'The sulfa tablets make me feel sick.'

'They turn my stomach too, make me want to vomit. But the dysentery is worse.'

'What's this dysentery about anyway? Everybody's gettin' it.'

'I guess it's the food.'

'Yeah, all that rancid ole sunflower oil an' the hog-nose, I guess.'

'Good for feedin' pigs, about all.'

'Good enough for you an' me too, so they think.'

'Ever seen inside the kitchen?'

'Me? No.'

'Well just as well, wouldn't make you feel any better,' Cubano laughed.

'I hear the cockroaches chase you if you don't stand up an' fight 'em off. Is true?'

'Sure do, man! They'd climb right up your chest an' bite you if you wasn't careful. The copper they boil the soup in is bricked-in above the furnace. They swab it out to clean it.'

'You don't mean that!'

'They clean it like you clean a floor. I mean it.'

'Christ!' He gagged. 'Don't bother tell me any more.'

'The visiting committee, they take 'em to the kitchen on visiting days. They make 'em sip little cups of soup. They say, Mmm! that tastes pretty good; fine healthy food . . . sure, an' if they had to drink it every day like we do they'd come down with dysentery too, you bet!'

'Yeah, I know.'

The crunching feet passed down the gravel walk again. A couple of screech-owls made a circling flight above the compound; they were hunting for rats. A man screamed and came suddenly out of his sleep, gibbering and moaning, in one of the cells on the ground floor in the building to the west of the hospital. The sound survived for a few moments and then was put out by a warder rattling his baton against the steel bars of the man's cell.

A voice said: 'Shut up, there, or I'll take you out an' give you something to groan about.'

The sound subsided to a kind of sobbing, and went out.

Cubano said, softly: 'I hear they caught the two men who made their break yesterday from the prison farm. They're bringing them back tonight, or tomorrow.'

'You mean that! They got 'em quick.'

'Yes. They shouldn't have done it that way. Broad daylight

156

. . . you got to go through the town. You can't do it in these prison clothes. Me, I'm goin' over the wall.'

'Over the wall?'

'Yes. Guys have done it before.'

'But how?'

'You got to figure it out, that's all.'

'An' get shot.'

'That too. You got to take a chance.'

'I'd like to see somebody do it, that's all.'

'It's been done already, I tell you. I guess it can be done again. It's the only chance you have of makin' a break from this place, really . . . some dark night . . . then you can get through the town.'

'With all them guards around! Man you must be crazy. They'd shoot you down without 'quintin'.'

'Sure. It ain't no picnic. You got to take your chance.'

'Well buddy, I wouldn't ever try it.'

'You never can tell. Wait till you've been in here a little longer. A man can't tell beforehand what he might do.'

'No bloody fear! A man would have to be crazy to try a thing like that.'

'Maybe they was crazy, but they did, those others. They got away.'

'What? All of them?'

'Christ, no.' A pause. 'You plan, and wait your chance, that's all. If luck is with you, you can do it. A man has got to play his luck sometimes.'

'Yeah. I guess so.'

Silence . . . as though the night stood still with breath held in.

'Ever heard of Sam Leg, Rigin, Manhurst?'

'Yeah, of course. Who hasn't.'

'They played their luck as long as it held. But they weren't smart.'

'Perhaps their luck was played out.'

'Bloody fools, all of them. Just bloody fools.'

His face went dark and secret. Surjue knew he wasn't going to say any more. He wasn't sorry. He didn't want to listen to any confidences; didn't want to have anything to do with it at all. Why the hell did he want to tell him about his plans, anyway? Why did he want to involve him in this thing any at all?

157

In the distance the saw whined and cleaved its way through the wood . . . the sudden veering of the wind brought the sound nearer. It screamed, biting into the wood, and the scream came down to a growl . . . and then it came out at the other end . . . singing free.

A bevy of rats scampered across the ceiling.

Surjue lay on his back and stared up at the blankness above him.

Somewhere out there in the town a little dog set back on his haunches, and put his muzzle up, and bayed the moon.

3   EUPHEMIA WAS engrossed in reading when a shadow fell across the paper. She looked up to see Manny standing beside her. Her eyes went back to the paper folded on her knee.

He stood like that, breathing down his chest, his eyes searching the ground at his feet, stood there cancelled out, not knowing what to do, whether to go or stay.

'You readin' the papers?'

His awkwardness prompted him to say the idiotic words, thinking in some remote half-conscious region within him, 'My God, what to say now? She wouldn't even look at me!'

She didn't look up, kept her head down giving him no sign at all. It was always like this at first . . . sometimes if he kept on, sweating in his uncertainty, she would give some sign . . . sometimes nothing ever gave in the smooth wall of passive resistance she set up between them, surrounding herself with it, like a wall around a high unassailable tower that daunted him, cancelled out his manhood and left him trembling and unassuaged.

Suddenly he blurted out: 'You want me to go?'

'It's the open yard,' she said, 'it don't belong to me.'

'If you want me to go you can say so, I don't want to push myself on to you.'

'You can please yourself about it, it is nothing to me.'

She was going to talk to him then, thank God she was going to talk.

'You readin' about the murder case, I bet.'

'Why you should think so?'

'Nothing special. Ain't it, though? Where the woman saw the man with what she called "the shining blade"? Him runnin' with it in his hand after he had done the deed?'

'I didn't see that.'

'It's there though. She saw him going through the crowd, and as he passed under the lamp light she saw something shining in his hand. He was tryin' to cover it up, but she saw it plain when he was passin' under the street light.'

'Yes?'

'So she said. That was the evidence she give. They couldn't get her off it. The shining blade.'

He moved awkwardly, until he stood now directly in front of her where he could see her face. She still acted remote, withdrawn, as though he was not there. Sometimes he felt as though she took a deliberate delight in making him suffer, as though the sight of his suffering gave her a sense of power, and negated her own insufficiency and insecurity, and he didn't care.

He searched his mind for something to say that would get a rise out of her.

'You not afraid a green lizard might drop on you out of the tree? There is green lizards up there, plenty of them.'

She shuddered involuntarily and looked up, but that was all.

'No need to be scared of them really,' he said, 'they don't bite,' thinking of her comfort, not wanting to scare her away.

'I'm not scared of them, I hate them, that's all.'

'You scared of them a little, yes, that's why you hate them.'

She said, 'You know a lot, don't you?' Then she said, again, 'Anyway, I wouldn't like for one of them to drop on me.'

'They wouldn't do that a-purpose. They scared of you more, I bet.'

She looked at him then, as though his words veiled a double meaning.

'Why you say that? Why should they be scared of me?'

Her eyes searched his face, and for an instant her look seemed bold and inviting, but he didn't believe even what his eyes told him, he put it out of his mind.

She was looking at him still with that half-bold, half-sullen look, and she said, 'Eh? Aren't you goin' to answer me?'

'What was it? I don't remember?'

'Why should they be scared of me?'

'I don't know. They always run away.'

He sank down on his haunches before her now, was conscious of the fact that Wilfie was still working on the chicken coop they had been making as though he wasn't aware of what was happening under the tree . . . sank down on his haunches slowly, tentatively, as though he didn't want to do anything overt that might scare her away.

His fingers fumbled along the ground in front of him and he gathered three little pebbles in his hand. He tossed one carelessly in the air and caught it, then he tossed it in the air again, and caught it in his mouth this time; and spat it out into his hand again. He leaned forward doing this and he realized that he could see right up her dress, see all the way up, the cool, smooth, voluptuous curve of her legs under the skirt that she had inadvertently drawn up above her knees, mindful of her own comfort only, but scarcely conscious of it now.

He had had just that one quick glance, and he burned with desire to look again, but he dared not. If he did anything like that it would only send her away. The desire needled him until he could scarcely withstand it, but he resolutely looked away.

Wilfie was straightening his stiff neck — stiff from a boil he had got on it — with a wry effort, his face drawn into a grimace of pain. Their eyes met, and exchanged a kind of intelligence, and Manny looked away.

His ears were burning hotly, there was a kind of twitching in his belly that was like hunger, and he realized that she was looking at him, but for some inexplicable reason he could not meet the challenge of her eyes.

'A lizard run on you it means you goin' to have a baby,' she said.

It was the first time she had made a voluntary observation to him like that. Other times she had only barely retorted to something he had said. He felt the subtle significance of this, and it made him bold.

'That's when they run up your legs, so old time people say.'

He couldn't resist the sweet torment any longer, and he stole another glance. The curves of her thighs were like the folds of hills with the cool valleys between . . . they made a strange, almost savage assault upon his senses . . . the back of his throat became suddenly dry and hot, and it was like sharp needles going through his groin. His tongue too was dry and heavy. There were chill little spots behind his burning ears.

She laughed, and he looked at her face quickly to see if she really meant it, and he grinned back at her, and tossed up a pebble in the air again, and caught it in his mouth.

'I can do that every time,' he boasted.

'Cho, that's nothing,' she said, 'give it to me.'

He spat the pebble into his hand, rubbed it between his palms, passed it to her.

She tossed it in the air, leaned far back on the box, missed, it fell behind her with a faint clink against the gravel.

'I missed it,' she said, as though she could scarcely believe it had happened.

Manny laughed.

'Here, you would like to try it again?'

She said, petulantly, 'No.'

'Look,' he said, 'look, I'll show you how.'

He tossed another pebble in the air and caught it expertly, spat it out into his hand, rubbed it between his palms, held it out to her.

She shook her head. The old sullen look had come back to her face, but there was a kind of smouldering look deep in her eyes. He felt better, and better, he felt a curious rising exhilaration, there was a chorus of strange noises ringing inside his ears. The image of deep cool valleys nestling among the folds of gentle hills . . . an oasis of sweet cool valleys after a wide waste of thirsty sand . . . sand . . . he could feel the grits at the back of his throat . . . hot and dry . . . like a man consumed with the ultimate thirst . . . coming blindly toward the pleasant oasis with the sweet cool valleys nestling among cinnamon hills. . . .

He saw that she had on a pair of white pumps with the straps unbuckled, and seeing him look at them she gave a little laugh, pulled up her dress a few inches further and bent down to buckle them. He could see right down the top of her dress now . . . now then the image of the full bosom inside the thin dress and nothing on besides. When she sat up again she forgot to pull down her dress. She had moved somehow closer, and her face seemed to glow at him with a warm smile.

He shut his eyes as though to put out a vision from them,

and he bent forward and set his lips to the flesh just above the nearer knee. And it was as though a kind of fierce hunger swept him, so that he put out his tongue and caressed the soft flesh above her knee with it. And suddenly she laughed awkwardly and thrust at him with her foot, pulled her dress down primly, stood up . . . realized now, from his silent writhing on the ground, that her foot had caught him unintentionally in the groin . . . but something flamed within her and went out cold, and she felt no pity . . . stood up, looking down at him, his hands shut upon his hurt, laughed awkwardly again, pressing the folded newspaper to her bosom, turned and walked quickly toward the house.

Wilfie was concentrating hard on hammering a bent nail into the wooden frame of the chicken coop. Manny came and knelt down beside him, without words took the hammer from his hand. He was breathing hard, and his face wore his hurt and his shame, and Wilfie was acutely conscious of the embarrassing silence that was laid upon them, and the dull throbbing in the back of his neck, which was another thing again.

Goodie came in through the gate. She passed them, limping wearily, a basket on her arm, her face puckered with worry and with weariness.

Manny took a bent rusty nail and straightened it with the hammer against a stone. He hit his finger with the hammer and the pain welled up inside him but he pretended he did not feel it at all.

Wilfie crouched on his haunches, looked at him and looked down at a piece of box board he held in his hand as though speculating about it. He didn't say anything.

Goodie went by, clip-clop, dragging a pair of old shoes loosely attached to her feet. She went slowly up the steps and into her room.

'Hold this piece of wire down for me, the dam thing wants to fly back in my eye,' Manny grumbled.

Wilfie held the wire in place, and Manny drove home the straightened nail, using more force than was necessary. He clinched the nail head over the wire to make it hold. His hands seemed extra big and awkward, and they were trembling a little.

He took his upper lip between his teeth and bit it until he could taste the salty taste of blood in his mouth. He beat on the ground with the hammer, and Wilfie just looked at him, still without saying a word. He opened his mouth as though he was going to speak, and shut it again.

Hot tears blinded Manny's eyes and he shut them tight and hit the ground with the hammer and bit his lip hard.

'Don't do that, Manny,' Wilfie said, presently.

And Manny said, 'God dam and blast!'

And then they heard the noise inside Goodie's room. It sounded like someone was trying to break up things inside. Then they heard like Ditty's voice, begging and screaming, and through it all the sound of heavy blows. Then Puss-Jook's voice, raised in anger . . . and a heavy blow . . . then Ditty's voice again, imploring. . . .

'Lawd God! Do! Do!' Ditty begged. Then she screamed, and there was the sound of more blows.

They didn't hear Goodie's voice once, and there was something terrible and meaningful in that fact. The blows went on, and there was the sound of bodies struggling inside the room, and another sound, bigger than the rest, and it was like the table with plates and dishes on it upsetting and crashing to the floor.

Ditty screamed again, and it went up high, and tailed off to a low moan. Then there was the sound of a dish shattering against the wall, and suddenly the door opened, and Puss-Jook staggered out. His hands were up to his face, and his face was bleeding, and there was bright blood all down his merino front, and he was dressed only in his merino and drawers.

He nearly fell down the steps coming down into the yard. And the blood was pumping all over his hands. It came from a great gash in his forehead.

Then the blows again . . . and the sound of Ditty moaning.

And all that time they didn't hear Goodie's voice at all.

Then they saw Ditty sliding on her bottom toward the door, and she only had on about half of her clothes. And what she had on was dragged up about her clear up to her waist, and Goodie was standing over her beating her unmercifully with something that looked like a broken bed lathe. Ditty dragged herself to the doorstep and tumbled out into the yard. She lay there on her belly, moaning.

163

Goodie was coming down the steps after her, dragging the bed lathe behind her, but Mass Mose came out of his room same time, and he went up to her quickly, and said something to her. And he took the bed lathe from her hands. And she just sat down on the step and covered her head with her apron, and started to bawl.

Manny said: 'I saw it comin' a long way off. Goodie was bound to catch them at it one day.'

Wilfie said: 'What you talkin' about, man? You mean — you mean —' but he couldn't bring himself to say it.

Manny laughed.

'Sure I mean that. Claims he isn't her Pa. A jerk like him would say anything. A man who do nothin' but lay down an' sleep, an' nourish himself up like a stud all day! What you expect?'

Manny laughed again.

'Stop it!' Wilfie almost shouted.

And Manny said, 'Eh?'

He saw Wilfie standing over him with a strip of old packing case in his hand that had an edge to it like a knife, and he was trembling.

Manny just looked at him and said, slowly, 'Say, what the hell is happenin' to you?'

Wilfie threw the piece of packing case from him and turned and went quickly from the yard, going in the direction of the gully.

Manny stood up and looked after him with a puzzled expression on his face. His fingers loosened about the hammer and it fell with a dull thud to the ground.

He said, softly: 'Well, what'd you know!'

4 WALKING BETWEEN the wall and the wall we come to a question with the baffled wind . . . the moon in crescent looks over the blasted branch of a duppy tree . . . twenty centuries of Christ has not assuaged the world of violence . . . we listen to the jangling laughter of our chains about us and are consoled.

The multi-calculator, the machine wonder of our age, can duplicate our thinking . . . can find the robot answer to the streamlined robot question inside the second . . . we have made great advances in this glorious mechanical age . . . we have walked the ultimate ways of annihilation to the last . . . the nuclear theory has cracked the last difficult equation . . . now we can sit on a stone and juggle a handful of glass balls.

Within the ruin of walls we question the wind and it makes answer unto us . . . the rats have eaten our inheritance in the wide world . . . the young moon in crescent comes to the gate under the duppy tree . . . all our dreams are gone before us into the stillness of evening . . . she looks over the ruin of our wall and confounds us with her silence.

We are quietly disembarrassed of our dreams in the midst of ruin . . . this moment arrests us in the last stone-gesture . . . it will come to disingenuous anachronism with the next . . . the wind walking between the wall and the wall will make the same eternal question . . . the moon from the duppy tree waits to press our stone-lips in darkness . . . all life waits to drink us up to the last shuddering breath.

Rain made a steady patter on the roof. And with it wind — gusty, thrusting wind that strained at the corrugated zinc sheets and made a thin whistling noise as it whipped across the damp unyielding metal sheets of the slanting roof, searching out every knot-hole and crack in the sodden board walls that smelled strangely of mildew and the dampness of leaves that have lain a long time close to the earth.

The woman lay stiff and straight in the bed and made no movement whatever. She just lay there listening to the rain and the wind. Her thin wasted blue-veined hands clutched the edge of the sheet that was drawn up under her chin. Her eyes stared out into the darkness about her, wide with fear.

Outside the window with the broken pane of glass held together with gummed paper the lightning criss-crossed like the blades of a scissors, and stabbed down into the ground. She shut her teeth hard and waited for the crash of thunder that seemed, when it came, to concuss through her body. Her hands that clutched the sheet to her throat jerked, and tightened, and went still.

After a bit the rain lulled and she pulled the sheet off her, sat up, passed her hands down her bare arms, got out of the bed, crossed the cold damp floor in her bare feet, went over to the little table against the wall where the oil lamp stood, felt cautiously for the matches, found them, struck one, guarding its flame carefully between her hands and lit the lamp.

She turned from the table, put both hands up to her head, running her fingers up into her hair, shook her head as though trying to think what she was to do next.

She went down on her knees beside the bed, felt under it with sweeping gestures of both hands, and drew out an old shoe box. She sat down on the side of the bed and took the old shoe box on her lap, started laying out its contents on the bed beside her.

There was an old discoloured handkerchief that had been used for cleaning shoes. One corner of it was crumpled up and stiff with dried-up shoe polish. It had a stuffy, resinous smell.

There was a little bundle of old bus tickets, held together with a doubled elastic band, that she had collected when the bus company was running a kind of free lottery where a certain ticket number, picked at random, would bring anybody who presented it at the bus company's office, a cash prize. Surjue had made her save all their bus tickets saying, hell it don't cost nothing an' anybody can win, and then it was announced in the papers that the Attorney General's office had said that it was illegal and amounted to a public lottery, and that it was contrary to the law. But the little bundle of bus tickets with the elastic band slipped twice around them was still there where she had dumped them and forgotten them in the old shoe box under the bed.

There was a slim handout memo pad that carried advertising for a company which sold 'sparkling aerated waters', on which she had made some notes.

And there were two separate parts of a pair of nail scissors that Surjue had put away carefully to repair some day.

These and other things she laid out on the bed beside her. And then she got up and went across to the bureau and took a pair of scissors from the drawer and came back to the bed and sat down again and began cutting these things up deliberately and methodically, as though they represented a part of her life that she was finished with for ever, and was never going to return and look upon any more.

A lick of lightning far off daubed the bunched-up clouds in

the sky a dirty yellow outside the window an instant and went out. Spent rain water dripped from the tin roof and hit the sodden earth with a dull wet repetitive sound.

The smell of damp rotting leaves and sweet wet earth mingled, invaded the room when the wind came in with a little draught through a knot hole beside the door. The other smells gave way to one of orange peel fermenting in the garbage box outside in the yard. That sickly sweet smell prevailed above all the rest and clung damply about the little room.

She put away the shoe box under the bed again, thrusting it far under, and to one corner, and went and sat on the stool in front of the moisture-blurred mirror, and started combing her hair.

She saw a picture of herself suddenly as a little child going to the spring to draw water, and standing there by the edge of the pool she could see the still reflection of the clouds in the water, and at the base of the clouds the dark shadows of the trees. And as she stood watching them the cloud masses broke up into fantastic shapes and sped across the sky, and went out before the scudding wind that told of storm.

And she was saying over inside her the words of the poem they had learned by heart in school that week:

> Little lamb, who made thee?
> Dost thou know who made thee? . . .

And as she said the words over to herself softly her heart grew big inside her and she was filled with a curious kind of exaltation that made her want to sing and laugh and cry together . . . she lifted her skirt and waded out into the water, trying to stand with the bright image of the clouds about her feet. But always they moved away from her, eluded her. She stood with her skirt caught up about her, laughing and crying at her own childish folly in the middle of the pool.

As she sat before the mirror combing her hair she had the same kind of mixed-up feeling inside her now.

'They are hurting him . . . hurting him . . . they do not understand about him . . . us . . . how loving and gentle he can be . . . how to bring the best, that is warm and good, out of him . . . how could they?'

She started to laugh, softly, inwardly, without mirth, and it came up to her throat and broke there, and it made a queer kind of choking sound, and before she knew what she was doing the hot tears began to fall.

One fell on the back of her hand that held the brush, and she looked at it with surprise, and another and another fell, even as she was wiping the first one away. And she began to feel more and more mixed-up inside her, and all kinds of images and notions started up in her mind, and they seemed to have no connection with her or each other.

And her lips were saying softly, of themselves:

'Nobody in all the world . . . just nobody at all . . .'

And she couldn't think what it was all about.

A light drizzle made a blur of the window when the lightning struck straight down into the ground, and after the splitting, rocking burst of thunder that followed immediately upon it there was no sound in all the world . . . saving that of the wet roof dripping, dripping on the sodden ground.

She went on brushing her hair.

Big, solitary drops of rain hit the roof with a metallic sound, and then blew away with the big wind that followed. And again the night let down silence all around her. A ship's siren sounded from far, far away across the harbour, and there was the *swish* of an automobile's tyres going at high speed through the puddles of rain water that had settled in the street. And then the silence again.

Her hands lay limply on her lap, the hairbrush still held in one of them. Her stare was big and vacant on the murky shadows on the floor. A mouse came out from under the bed and moved with quick starts and sudden stops among the shadows. She stared at it, unmoving, and was not afraid.

It went under the bed and came out again, and stopped and looked at her with bright eyes, and darted noiselessly toward a dark corner of the room.

She got up presently, walking like one in a trance with that same wide sightless stare, and went across to the table where the lamp was. She blew out the light.

She turned away from the table, her hand knocked against the match box, swept it to the floor.

She went down carefully on her hands and knees and felt for the match box in the dark. She made little sweeping gestures with her hands in front of her, all around her, but she could not find it. And then she straightened up, still on her knees, and put her hands up to her face, and a shudder shook her body.

For a long time she knelt there like that. And then she started creeping on her hands and knees, silently, stealthily, as though she must take the greatest care not to make the least sound. She reached out in the darkness and clutched the edge of the bed. She raised herself slowly, cautiously from the floor. She sat down on the bed and tried not to hear the creaking of the springs.

'Nobody in all the world . . . just nobody at all . . .' Her mind kept saying the words over, but they held no meaning for her . . . 'Just nobody in all the world . . .' but it meant nothing at all.

She could hear the far-away gurgle of water from up the spring, and it sounded like the muffled clapping of hands . . . and the hills put aside their veils and came out from behind the clouds, and they joined hands together and started to dance. They went dancing like that right down to the edge of the sea . . . and all the sea rose up in waves and they clapped their hands. . . .

Most of the water on the roof had run off now. There was only the occasional sound of a drop falling outside. The violent blades of lightning no longer disturbed the darkness. The storm had passed as suddenly as it had come.

She sat on the side of the bed in her thin nightdress and shivered with cold. She thought of getting back under cover of the sheet, but she felt suddenly very weak, like one who is spent with fever.

And she remembered the match box on the floor.

With a sigh she went down on her hands and knees again, started making the same blind sweeping futile passes with her hands out in front of her and beside her as before, until one hand knocked against the stool in the dark. Her hair came down into her face and confused her. She felt all mixed-up and tremulous inside. She knelt up straight and put her hands up to her face and tried to remember, to gather her thoughts out of chaos.

She started to weep, and she said, weakly:

'Light the lamp . . . *please* light the lamp.'

And then she remembered about the matches again, but she was too far gone with weariness to bother about looking for them.

The night let down silence around her, and she lost all sense of the passage of time. Her feet felt very cold but she couldn't think what to do about them. And presently the numbness came up from her feet and passed into her body, and she was too numb to move or to think about anything at all.

She heard a sound as of someone whimpering, and the sound disturbed her, as one is disturbed deep down in a dream without understanding it. The cold and the darkness seemed to make one, and draw in upon her, and gather her up to itself.

She wished the whimpering would stop . . . that someone would light the lamp and set her free. She wanted to creep back into bed where she could be snug and warm.

The loneliness and the night overlaid her, and she was defence-less, like one in a deep sleep menaced by the terror of a dream.

'Nobody in all the world . . . just nobody at all . . .' but the words didn't mean anything, they were just part of the confusion inside her, part of the jumble of mixed-up images and sounds.

The darkness and the cold and the stillness lay upon her like a great crushing weight.

Time passed.

From across the other end of the town a cock woke in the false dawn and crowed.

5   'STOP THERE! Where are you going?'
        The growling challenge rooted Surjue to the spot, made him turn automatically. He saw the warder Aaron Nickoll coming toward him, swinging his stick. He knew that this particular warder had conceived a dislike for him, had sworn to get him. And he figured this was it. He felt his skin stiffening all over. He knew a warder could get away with anything, any assault upon a prisoner. Always the warder's bare word would be taken against anything the prisoner might say. It was a situation you just had to accept because there was nothing you could do about it.

But watching Nickoll swinging his stick, striding toward him, a nasty smile of vicious triumph on his face, a hot rage went through him, and almost immediately after he went as cold as ice, waiting . . . so this was it . . . he felt curiously relaxed, waiting.

The warder's thick-soled boots made a crunching sound against the gravel that was ominous in itself . . . curious how that sound could assume so much importance at this moment . . . he had heard it so often before . . . it had never meant anything special to him. But now there was a special significance to it. That purposeful crunching gait, the stick swinging easily in his hand.

He had been on his way to the block of cells facing the hospital, east, where a prisoner was sick. There was no room in the hospital for him. He was taking him some sulfa tablets the doctor had prescribed. As hospital orderly he had special privileges. None of the other warders troubled him.

He should have asked one of them to accompany him to the prisoner's cell, but there had been none around when he came out from the dispensary. The dispenser had sent him to the sick man's cell with the tablets. Technically he was breaking a prison regulation, but it was merely a technicality, the splitting of a disciplinary hair. Nickoll, he knew, would make the most out of it.

He stood before him now with that vicious triumphant look on his face.

'Why didn't you stop the first time I called to you?'

'I did stop.'

'Say, Sir, when you speak to me. Why didn't you stop?'

Surjue was quietly resolved about one thing, if he hit him with that baton, he wasn't going to get away with it. With that settled in his mind, he felt wonderfully relaxed, almost at ease. In moments of action like this he never had time to be afraid, because he wasn't able to think too much, or too far ahead, he was too absorbed in the active immediate. He was relaxed now, but it was a very physical kind of relaxation, all of his body was very alert. It was the kind of relaxation that an athlete has before he gathers all his powers for a supreme effort.

'I asked you a question.'

'I answered you.'

'Say, Sir, when you speak to me.'

Surjue was watching his eyes, knowing that the moment would come when his eyes would give Nickoll away, the exact moment when he would strike.

'Did you hear me?'

'I heard you.'

'Sir.'

It was coming now. Surjue almost smiled.

'Say, Sir, when you speak to me, damn you!'

Nickoll's hand went up with the baton, and Surjue just stepped in with his left. His fingers were spread and he just pushed his hand into the warder's face. Simultaneously he brought the other hand down sharply on the wrist above where the fingers were clenched tightly about the baton. The baton fell with a clatter among the loose gravel. Surjue bent forward quickly, and stood up now holding the ebony heart baton in his own hand. He was actually smiling as he faced the furious Nickoll. But it was a tight smile of terrible resolve. Nickoll, however, didn't see it that way. He was too angry. He had lost the initiative completely, and it made him angry.

Surjue knew all the tricks of rough and tumble fighting that he had picked up in back alleys among the gangs of tough urchins that had peopled his boyhood. He knew he could take the bully Nickoll, he wasn't worried a bit.

Nickoll coming at him now, the look in his eyes turned to low vicious cunning, felt he had the prisoner just where he wanted him; assaulting a warder; he had a just and righteous cause to avenge; now he could really dish it out.

He put his head down, hitched up his belt, moved in on Surjue. Surjue dropped the baton, took him by the shoulders, shifted one foot forward, seemed to give his body a slight twist, Nickoll was tripped neatly, he fell to the ground, the shock of impact with the gravel jarring his whole body.

When he tried to get up he realized that his ankle had been badly twisted, he didn't know how badly until it took his weight, turning over and pressing up on his hands and feet; when he was only halfway up, conscious of his hurt, the ignominy of his position, the cool smiling face of the prisoner above him, his right hand clawed at the gun concealed in his side pocket. And then Surjue really got going. He had Nickoll by the wrist before he could pull the gun. There was a brief tussle and a savage thrust and twist, and Nickoll screamed with pain, and dropped the gun. He thought the man had broken his arm.

Almost with the same movement Surjue neatly tripped him again. And now when Nickoll looked up from the ground Surjue was standing over him, the gun in his hand, and murder in his eyes. Nickoll lay there, resting on his elbows, just looking up into the face of the other, his own face seamed with fear. He didn't try to move.

Three warders passing saw what was happening. Two others, marching a platoon of prisoners on to the parade ground saw too, but they dared not leave the prisoners to do anything. They ordered the platoon to halt. The three warders coming hesitantly toward Surjue had only batons in their hands. Only at night were the special guards allowed to carry firearms.

Surjue knew this, knew that Nickoll had committed a serious breach of the prison regulations by having a gun on him without being on special duty, knew that this was the one circumstance in all this that was to his advantage, decided to play it to the limit. He wheeled and faced the advancing warders.

'Stick 'em up!' he said.

He was actually trembling with excitement.

Their hands shot up above their heads. They were taking no chances with a prisoner armed with a gun on the open parade ground.

'You too,' he said, waggling the gun at the two warders with the prisoners. 'Come over here. An' don't fool with me, I'll plug you just as soon as spittin'.'

They shuffled over and stood beside the three warders with their hands in the air.

'Get up, you!' this to the thoroughly frightened Nickoll sprawling at his feet. 'Go stand over there with them. And get your hands right up in the air.'

Nickoll limped across the gravel and joined the other five.

Surjue said to the prisoners who had been halted on the parade ground: 'Boys, you keep out of this. This here is my show.' And by that single act saved himself, although he didn't know it then.

An Overseer in the Assistant Superintendent's office saw what was happening, jumped out of the chair on which he was sitting, tilted back against the wall, his boots up on the table, blew his whistle, and pulled a gun out of a drawer in the desk. He kept on blowing the whistle, and that brought other warders running, blowing their whistles as they ran. It brought the Superintendent from his office, too, because the blowing of whistles like that could only mean one thing, a prison riot, or an attempted prison break.

Three of the Overseers, or senior warders, what would correspond to commissioned officers in the army, had got themselves guns. Except for his swagger stick the Superintendent was unarmed. By the time he had located the trouble Surjue had backed the six warders up against the wall of the building that housed the Superintendent's office and that of his clerical staff, upstairs. He placed them so that they would be between him and the direct line of fire, their backs turned to the men with the guns.

He said in a clear, controlled voice: 'If anybody starts shootin', I'll get these first. Now don't anybody move.'

One of the Overseers, a young man who had come into the prison department straight from college and had been given rapid promotion over men longer in the service, said: 'I could try a dash for the stairs. I could get on to the balcony and get him from there.'

'Don't be a fool!' the Superintendent snapped.

He had to think of the men who stood to lose their lives.

One of the older Overseers said: 'That man is dangerous. I know when a man is in that mood. He'd shoot at the drop of a hat.'

The Superintendent said, 'All right, Surjue,' he knew many of the prisoners by name, 'what's all the shooting about?'

He spoke very quietly, in an even, conversational tone.

'I don't aim to do any shootin', Super, not unless somebody tries to rush me. Anybody who tries that is goin' to get it, I promise you.'

'All right, man, nobody is going to rush you. We can settle this, what's the complaint? You're not trying to make a daylight break, are you?'

'No, Super, nothing like that.'

Surjue secretly admired the man for his cool nerve in the face of a situation like this. He had to hand it to the Super, he was the coolest of all of them there.

Already the initiative had passed into his hands. He had spent most of his adult years among men like these. He was a hard man, a rigid disciplinarian, some said a cruel man, but he knew the men he had to deal with. A prisoner, he knew, doesn't arm himself with a gun and go berserk and try to shoot his way out single-handed in the middle of the day for nothing. He didn't get that crazy over a matter of routine discipline, or because he didn't like what he had been given for breakfast.

He said again: 'We can talk this over in my office, if you like.'

'Hold it, Super,' said Surjue, warningly, 'don't you move. If I go to your office how do I know you won't clap me in irons an' let them take me down to the dumb cell, an' look the other way while they are beatin' the shit out of me?'

'Fair enough. You'll have to take my word, though.'

Surjue considered this a while.

'Excuse me, Super. No offence, but I just don't think I'll take the chance.'

'What are you going to do, then? Figure to shoot your way out? You can't get away with this, you know.'

'I don't know about that, Super, I could try.'

'Listen man, I give you my word, in the presence of all these officers and prisoners, that I will give you a fair hearing, and a square deal. Not according to the book, either, as man to man.'

'Listen Super,' Surjue said, turning it over in his mind a moment. 'It's all on account of a little argument between Warder Nickoll here, an' me. You goin' to take that warder's word against mine every time. I could square it by blowing a hole through him first.'

'When we talk, Surjue, there'll be nobody there but just you and me.'

'Word of honour, Super?'

'I give you my word.'

'I got to think it over.'

'You think you've got the handle, but you're wrong.'

'I know what I've got, Super. An' I'm not throwin' it away. I'm playin' this hand meself, see? Don't try to rush me.'

'Where did you get the gun?'

'Took it off the warder who tried to pull it on me. Warder Nickoll here.'

'Is that correct, Nickoll?'

'Yes, sir.'

'Mmmm. I see. The offer still holds, Surjue. You'll get a chance to tell me all about it, what made Warder Nickoll try to pull a gun on you, everything.'

'Okay, Super. Send your men away. Tell them to go back into the office over there. I'll send these here to join them. Then meet me on the parade ground.'

'He'll shoot you, sir! Don't do it. It's a trap!' said the young Overseer.

'Shut up!' the Superintendent snapped, without looking at him. 'When I want your advice I'll ask it.' He said to the prisoner with the gun pointed at his belly: 'Okay, Surjue. That suits me. I'm sending them in. You will release the two officers in charge of that batch of prisoners, and they will march them straight to their cells. Then you will let the others go over to the office, where they will remain until we have concluded our talk. Fair enough?'

'That's okay by me, Super. I'm takin' a hell of a gamble on this. But I'm seein' you.'

A few minutes later they met on the parade ground. The Superintendent's body covered Surjue's from the direction of the office, and Surjue was holding the gun and it was pointing at the Superintendent's tunic just below where the Sam Browne belt buckled in front.

'Give me the gun,' the Superintendent said.

'That's no part of the bargain,' said Surjue.

'I can't talk to you while you are covering me with a gun in sight of the whole prison. It's bad for discipline. What do you say?'

Surjue looked at him steadily, searchingly, for about a second, and handed him the gun.

'That's better,' said the Superintendent, taking it, drawing a deep breath without knowing that he was. 'That's being down-right sensible, now. I think you better come with me up to my office, we can talk better there.'

'Okay, Super, I'll follow you.'

They crossed the parade ground, went up the stairs, and into the Superintendent's office.

The Superintendent sat down on the swivel chair behind his desk, unlocked a drawer with a key on a key case he always carried with him, put the gun away, pushed the drawer shut, and locked it again.

'Sit down, Surjue.' He waved Surjue to a chair.

Surjue hesitated a moment, sat down.

The Superintendent spoke rapidly, in a terse, military tone.

'Now I don't mind telling you that this is highly irregular, but I've given you my word. This is the way I see to deal with this particular situation, which in itself is highly irregular all the way through. So just forget anything that I might say to you inside this office, as I will on my part in respect to you. I am stretching a point of discipline a long way to fit this case.'

6   HE HAD A FEELING of bigness and strength that awed him . . . some day it would burst out and he would not be able to control it . . . there was a tiger lurking inside him, he could feel its mighty purring going through his body, and he was afraid. There was a great force like a mighty coiled steel spring inside him, and some day it would slip the safety catch and shiver him and sunder him in a thousand pieces. It was a terrible feeling of power and bigness . . . so terrible that it dwarfed him, and made him afraid.

The way it made him feel now he was light-headed, and his feet dragged along the pavement as though he wanted to hold back. He saw people look at him in passing, and he smiled deep down inside him, knowing that if they knew the truth about him, in the terms of bigness and strength and terror, all wrapped up within him waiting to announce itself, they would blanch with fear. He smiled because of this terrible secret he carried inside him that none of these people knew. If they knew they wouldn't just look at him casually, and away, in passing, or not at all, they would gape, and shake, and turn and trample each other in panic, as they would coming upon a tiger stalking through the dark lanes and alleys at night.

Terrible thing to know all this, and to be the only person who knew it. Terrible to be a tiger and dangerous and cunning, and to be strung with the steel sinews of a tiger, and nobody know. It was an awful thing for a man to hold such knowledge of himself, in secret, and he only of all the people in the world. He smiled that terrible smile because people could pass him like that as though he was nobody, just a down-at-heels brown man walking the streets at night . . . because they could look at him casually, or not, in passing, and not gape and be taken with panic and run screaming in the opposite direction.

And he dared not tell anyone this terrible secret . . . only hint darkly at it, sometimes, and watch them closely to see if they could take his meaning. He could not tell anyone because someone might see underneath his skin, inside him, and it would be out with that knowledge. It would be out like a flash, roaring and lashing about in its terrible rage and strength and bigness — and he was afraid.

He walked right into a policeman and he didn't see him. The impact shook him, and he lurched away. But the cop caught him by the arm and pulled him up.

'Here, what you think you doing? Can't see where you going? You must be drunk, no?'

'No, no,' he shook his head violently, impatiently. 'Not drunk. Oh no.'

'Here, lemme get a good look at you.'

'Yes.'

'Hm! Your eyes look funny. Must have been smoking the weed.'

'Oh no. Not that at all. It is on account of the bigness —'
There, he nearly gave it away.

'The bigness? Say —'

'You are not afraid?'

The cop laughed.

'Afraid of you? Don't make me laugh. I have a good mind to take you in. Would too, only I'm in a hurry. Got any of the stuff on you?'

'Oh, no, no. Everything is under control; under control, you see.'

'Hm! hopped up to the eyebrows, that's what. If it wasn't that I was busy, I'd sure run you in, buddy. You take mighty good care, that's all I advise you. On your way!'

'Don't mention it. Thanks.'

The cop laughed.

'All right. You look a decent enough chap. Take my advice, don't mess yourself up with that stuff. Go on now, an' sleep it off.'

'It's not what you think. It's just on account of the bigness — you know — the size!'

'If I wasn't in such a hurry I would take you in, you could be dangerous runnin' around loose. You look a sight! What a jagg you must have been on to get that way. You be careful now. I'm giving you a chance this time.'

'That's all right, officer. You wouldn't guess unless I told you. That's all. Good night.'

He went on down the street. The policeman's gaze followed him. He made as though to stop him, looked at his wristwatch, shook his head, clicked his teeth, turned, went on his way.

Shag was pleased with the clear poetic imagery that formed in his mind. A woman, he thought, was like a tree. They were full of sweetness and fruitfulness. And if the tree got out of hand, and did what it ought not to do, like a grapefruit tree bearing sour oranges, you cut it down at the root and made an end of it, and that was a lovely, tantalizing thought.

There was nothing of it that didn't make sense in his mind that was as clear as a bell, and the officer was in a hurry, he was going to see his girl; it all made sense like a beautiful poem, like fruit hanging heavily and voluptuously from a tree, making the words of a poem, and the cop was really a nice man, a very very nice man, he was in a great hurry to take his woman in his arms . . . and that was the nicest thing about him, he would understand all this about women, each lovely with her promise of sweetness, and bitterness, when it went wrong and ugly, like a double-dealing tree.

Go and sleep it off . . . he was such a nice man . . . if he went to sleep now he would have to lie down, and the great angry purring musical beast would rise up and creep out from under his skin, and walk all over him, and lick his face . . . he would come awake and the bigness would be loosed within him, and the terrible strength that could uproot a tree.

That was it . . . and the nice officer was on his way to see his woman . . . to lie in her arms, and go to sleep on her breast . . . and he would wake again, and the tiger would be laid . . . and the great snake like a coiled steel spring that raised its head and stared out of eyes like great glass marbles would be coiled about the root of that tree.

The cop was a nice man, he would have a long, long life and learn a lot about women . . . he was a woman-man, he would always have the upper hand of his women, he would break their arms above the elbow . . . break their teeth . . . but one thing that nice cop would never learn, the most important thing of all . . . a woman was a tree . . . and vulnerable . . . vulnerable like a tree.

Vulnerable was a nice word, a nice, nice word . . . it was round — no, not round, but oval . . . an egg-shaped word . . . a bridge-word, and a woman-word . . . a word like the egg hidden away inside a woman . . . and a word like a tree. It was a word that was strong like the buttresses that held up one end of a bridge he had seen, and a sweet-brittle word, like the sound of wind going through a woman-tongue tree.

Some people didn't understand about words. They did not know the meaning that went with the sound. The meaning of the sound of a word like *vulnerable* was like a great anaconda snake coiled around the base of a woman-tree. Oh, *vulnerable* was a lovely word, a lovely, lovely word; a sweet, full, round word nippled like a woman's breast; and it went into the poem about woman in his mind, and the purring in his blood, and the beast.

A man always thought, I don't care if she stings me to death, meaning a woman, and he would knock until she opened the gates of heaven and hell and let him in. And they were all the same, though one was a serpent and the other a beast, they were all the same in this, they were each vulnerable in the end . . . vulnerable like a double-dealing tree.

He passed shop fronts that had their shutters down for the night, and people brushed shoulders with him on the sidewalk. And a piece of brown shop-paper, grease-marked and creased and wrinkled, that had been wrapped around a sugar-bun, went walking down the pavement in front of him a matter of yards . . . until he stamped on it hard to hold it down, and a coil of orange peel left to lie on top of a tumbled heap of garbage snug against a pitch-blackened buckled and sagging corrugated zinc sheet fence, leered up at him like a round, disembodied, sardonic face.

The wind whipped at his back lifting his shirt and flapping it against his clammy skin, and he started to cough. He had to stop walking and lean against a telegraph post, and he felt weak and dizzy. It was as though his chest was gripped hard in a vice, and it was trying to squeeze the breath out of his lungs.

He spat blood, and steadied himself, holding himself upright with a great effort, because of the blackness and the dizziness that overcame him when he leaned forward. And the blood trickled thinly from the sides of his mouth, down his chin, and dropped on his shirt front. And he didn't care.

He held himself propped up like that against the cold telegraph pole until the fit of coughing passed. Then he took a soiled, crumpled, and damp handkerchief from his trousers pocket and wiped his mouth. His hand took a long time coming up from his pocket with the handkerchief to his lips, and back to his pocket again.

He knew he was a very sick man, and in a way it worried him that it should be so, though in another way he couldn't care less. He was not frightened about it for himself, its consequences to himself, but he was scared stiff that people should know. He knew that his sickness was one of the notifiable diseases, that meant there was a law which said it should be reported to the health authorities, and they would put him away in a sanitorium. He didn't want to be put away in any sanitorium, he wanted to live the rest of his days a free man, free to come and go, free to think and dream and act, and to eke out his life and wander up and down the streets of the city at night as he pleased, and as the spirit moved him.

He had on a pair of wide, baggy blue-jeans, and something hard inside it pressed against his right thigh. He was reminded of it now because he tried to bend that knee to hitch his foot against the base of the telegraph pole. He was reminded of it, and the grimace that was his accustomed smile these days came back to his bloodless thin yellow face.

He decided it was time for him to move on down the street. He did not wish to attract attention, and he certainly would if he was to stay propped up against this telegraph pole too long, looking like a drunk. He eased himself off the pole and stood with only his hand barely resting against it, rocking slightly on his feet. With an effort he straightened himself up and walked slowly, but still a little rockily, down the street.

He looked up at the electric lights above him on their tall black poles, strung on wires hanging in space. They seemed incongruously detached from the rest of the street, they were impersonal, and made him feel he could detach himself like that too, even when he walked with the crowd. It was a good, safe, comfortable feeling, it made him feel sure of himself again.

He went slowly up the steps, coming abreast of the yard, and went in through the gate.

Euphemia was sitting alone under the mango tree, out in the yard. She did not look up when he came in. Ras was in the yard too, and as he saw him he said, 'Shag!', and came toward him.

'Long time no see,' said Ras. 'How you keepin'?'

He saw that Shag and Euphemia were staring hard into each other's eyes. She had risen suddenly. Her hand was at her throat. But her face had a strange, dead look about it, and it wasn't altogether fear. There was something of weariness and resignation in it too. Shag started to laugh; quietly, not letting himself go.

Ras stopped suddenly a few feet away and looked at him. And then he looked at Euphemia standing with her hand to her throat, under the deep shadow of the tree, and one foot came out and made a feeble gesture in the dust, as though he had spat there, and was wiping it out.

Shag leaned against the gate. His face wore a wide, bland smile.

He said: 'Hi, Euphemia.' But he didn't move.

He said: 'What's matter? You not goin' to say, "hello"?'

'What you want here?' said Euphemia, and her voice sounded strangely tremulous, and husky, and low.

'Just come to look for you. You not glad to see me?'

Shag noticed that the house and the shacks were in darkness. People had either turned in, or they had gone out. Everything was strangely silent inside the yard.

'I kept away for a long time. I didn't bother you,' he said, conversationally.

Ras cleared his throat.

'How you feelin', Shag?' he said, 'you feelin' all right?'

'Tired,' said Shag, 'I been walking some. Been walkin' a long long way tonight.'

'Want to sit down a bit? Catch you' wind, like?'

But he wasn't paying any attention to Ras. He heaved himself up off the gate post and took a few steady steps toward Euphemia.

She did not move. She might have been carved statuesque and exquisite out of a hunk of wood, the trunk of a great tree, she was so still.

His cheeks looked queerly hollowed-out and yellow in the reflection of the street light. He moved another step nearer.

Only her hand tightened a little at her throat. And then he stood very still in front of her, his mouth twisted into that wide, bland smile. It seemed to cancel out the hard stare in his eyes.

The fingers of her other hand were clenched upon a pucker they had made at the side of her skirt.

Shag said, looking at her with that wide, bland smile: 'A woman is like a tree.'

He turned to Ras.

'Eh, Ras?' he said. 'You know that way?'

He stood staring at her for a long time, until the tears started rolling down his cheeks.

'You don't have to be scared of me,' he said, quietly, matter-of-factly, except for a slight tremor in his voice. 'I wouldn't hurt you for anything in the world.'

He made an effort to swallow. And then he said: 'I only came to tell you — you are vulnerable — that's all.'

'Vulnerable,' he said again, after a little silence, and brought his sleeve up to wipe the tears from his face.

He was conscious again of the machette in its leather sheath resting hard against his right thigh under the soiled blue-jeans.

'Now then, you better go inside.'

Still she didn't move.

'Go on, get inside now,' he urged. 'Get into bed and lock the door.' He spoke gently, urging her with the very gentleness of his voice.

'There are things inside me that are too big to speak,' he said. 'Go on in, go on now like I say.'

She moved slowly to do his bidding, like one in a dream.

Shag turned when she was halfway to the house. He saw Ras looking at him, embarrassed, and he said.

'Walk with me to the gate.'

Together they went down to the gate, down the steps, and out into the street.

Shag put his hand up and touched Ras on the shoulder, as though he wished to tell him something in great confidence.

'I wouldn't hurt her,' he said. 'God knows I wouldn't hurt a hair of her head.' He paused, drew a deep breath. 'But sometimes the bigness inside me. . . .'

He gestured with his hands.

'It's—it's too, big . . . you know that way?'

He turned and went slowly, and with a kind of wistful dignity down the street.

7   THIS IS THE STORY of man's life upon earth that formed him . . . it shudders throughout from cover to cover with terror and pity . . . the demons of light and of darkness inform all his days and nights . . . it has been attested that he is of threefold dimensions . . . all his being is encompassed about from birth with dying . . . his separate death matters nothing . . . it matters all, that he has turned his back upon life.

Things were settling down for the night inside the hospital ward. The warder on duty, Surjue, Cubano and Chippie were playing a quiet game of dominoes. Most of the other men were asleep, or lying quietly on their bunks. All except one — an old man. He groaned, and although the warder ordered him several times to be quiet, every now and then he would groan again, and whimper inarticulately. He had made frequent trips to the bathroom at the south end of the hospital, at least three times in the last half-hour, to make water.

'What's the matter with him?' said the warder, testily.

'He's scared, that's what,' said Surjue.

'That's what he's in hospital for, scared?'

'The doctor is keeping him under observation, that's why he's here.'

'Oh, I see. Your play, Cubano.'

'Think I'll just block this end with a *tres*. Pass you, Warder?'

'You give me hell, man, you make me knock.'

'Me too,' said Surjue.

'You see how you give you' partner a pass?' said Chippie. 'No mind, I'll make him open his trey-end by lickin' him with a big-six up here.'

'Man, yuh t'ump me way!'

'T'ump you way, no? You don't see nutt'n yet,' said the warder. 'Sixes about!'

'Pass me again,' said Surjue. 'Is me, yuh pardner you gi' pass, you know? Well, is up to you.'

'Is all right, pardner. Effen him got six-five him win de game. Otherwise, *hm!* — him goin' count with me.'

The old man hobbled past them going toward the bathroom again. The warder looked up at him, and said:

'What's matter, Pappy? You goin' piss again?'

'Yes, sah,' the old man said, drawing himself up in the middle. 'The bladder can't hold water at all.'

'He's scared, Warder, that's what's the trouble.'

'Yeah. Twelve strokes of the cat! That's what he's pissin' himself about.'

'You mean that? An old man like him!'

'Yes, sah. The judge give me twelve lashes with me sentence. An ole man like me.'

'Was you raped the little gal, no?'

'No, sah! Me, Ah wouldn't do a t'ing like that. Look at me, sah. An ole man like me?'

'What's it you in for?'

'Practisin' obeah was the charge.'

'Pappy, you ought to know better than to do that. They goin' flog yuh ass withouten a doubt.'

The old man clutched his middle and groaned as though he was seized with cramp.

'I got pains in me body. All over. They shouldn't flog an ole man like me.'

'Don't you know is wrong to practise obeah?'

'Yes, sah. Is true. But an ole man, sixty-two . . . daughter left me . . . nobody to mind me. What to do?'

'Ah sorry fo' yuh, Pappy. Them goin' cut yuh bottom. Bad t'ing, obeah. Sorry fo' yuh fo' true.'

'Ah begged the doctor to give me a chance. You t'ink him will help me?'

His eyes searched their faces for some sign — some least prop on which to pin his hope. But their faces were blank, and gave nothing; of pity, or anything, there was not the least shred. Only blankness, and an unwillingness to meet his searching gaze.

He said, shuffling off: 'Excuse me . . . can't hold me water . . . oh, Jesus Christ . . . eh, what to do?'

Somebody was snoring loudly down the ward. A big, rasping sound, like a buzz saw. It filled the place. The four men sat tight. They seemed to have forgotten the game.

'The doctor thinks his heart is good,' Surjue said, presently. 'The test for sugar was negative, too.'

'Shit, you mean he's goin' let them cat that poor ole bugger?'

'He only makes tests, man. Puts his report down on a printed form. What the hell can he do?'

'He could tell them nothin' doin'. Hell man, in his department there's nothing Doc can't do.'

'Cho, there's nothing the matter with the old bugger, he's only scared,' said Cubano. 'Guess if I had twelve strokes of the cat coming to me I'd be pissin' meself too.'

Chippie laughed and said: 'He won't even feel it. He's only skin an' bones.'

'Suppos'n it was you?' said the warder.

'I'm a young boy. Look on the flesh on me!'

'You ever seen them cat a man?' said the warder.

And nobody said anything at all. They curiously avoided each other's gaze, as though they were secretly ashamed about something.

The snoring down the ward seemed to gather volume in the silence. It went see-sawing across the stillness with a hard rasping sound.

Suddenly Chippie giggled as though he couldn't contain himself. He tried to stop, with the questioning gaze of the others' eyes upon him, but he couldn't help it; he just wanted to laugh.

'A man cut my bottom once with a cowhide whip,' he said.

'Shut up, Chippie!' said Surjue.

'We goin' finish the game?' said Cubano.

'It don't amuse me no more,' said Surjue.

The warder stood up, and hitched up his trousers.

'Goin' take a turn down the ward,' he said. 'Nickoll is on night duty. Inspection time coming up. He's out for my shirt.'

'You had a gun on him an' didn't kill the bastard!' said Cubano.

'Oh kiss my ass man, you go bump him off yourself,' said Surjue.

'All right, all right, I was only kiddin'.'

'He caught me one bright moonshine night with his daughter,' said Chippie. 'We was hidin' under the tarpaulin on top of the dray. I heard his steps coming down from the house, but she wouldn't kip still, the tarpaulin was shakin' an' rearin', like a couple of cats was shet down underneath it.'

'He ketch you with his young daughter, he shoulda cut out yuh stones,' said Cubano, shortly.

'He dam near did that, man!' Chippie almost shouted. 'He wasn't careful where he threw the lash.'

'All right, Chippie. Pipe down, or you'll have to go back to your bed,' said Surjue. He gathered up the dominoes and put them away in the box.

'All right. All right. I'll be quiet,' said Chippie, contritely. Then he said: 'I was holdin' my pants up, an' runnin' like hell for the gate. The first lash the whip caught me I started runnin' in circles, then I was lyin' on me belly drawin' meself along the ground.'

'I bet you wet you'self too,' said Cubano.

'Wet meself! Man, Ah was makin' water like a hydrant . . . Funniest dam thing, Ah couldn't find the gate.'

'Wrap it up now, Chippie,' said Surjue, tersely.

Suddenly he felt very irritable, he didn't know why.

Chippie said, 'What's bitin' you?' looking at him, wonderingly.

The old man stumbled past them, going toward his bunk.

He sat down on the side of it, groaned, shook his head, as though he was trying to find the answer to a problem that was too profound for him.

Surjue looked at Chippie like he was going to say something, changed his mind. He shrugged, turned away, walked slowly over to the old man's bunk.

'Better turn in now, Pappy,' he said.

The old man shook his head again, as though he didn't understand. His hands came up from his knees and they made a wavering, uncertain gesture in front of his face.

'Sixty-two years March gone,' he whimpered. 'Fifty-eight she was when I buried my wife. Las' year daughter up an' lef' me.'

'All right. All right,' said Surjue.

The irritation crept into his voice again, but the old man went on, unheeding.

'Nobody to mind me,' he said. 'What an ole man to do?'

'What, you askin' me? The hell I know!'

'I got hernia,' the old man said, 'you tell the doctor for me, no?'

'Tell him you'self,' said Surjue, shortly. 'You get to bed, now. You ought to be asleep long ago.'

'All right,' said the old man. 'Tek time wid me, do.'

The warder came halfway down the aisle. Then he stopped, hesitated, and went back up to the other end of the ward again.

'What the hell is bitin' him?' Chippie said to Cubano.

'Dunno,' said Cubano. 'What you worried about?'

'I'm not worried about anything, man. Don't like him talkin' to me like that, that's all.'

'You tell him good, boy,' said Cubano. 'Mek him talk to you polite. Tell him up an' down.'

'Shit to you!' said Chippie.

'Shit to you again,' said Cubano, without heat.

'Awe, I'm gettin' outa here in three weeks time, the hell I should worry!' said Chippie. 'A lot of crazy bums, the bleedin' lot o' you.'

'Three weeks, eh?' said Cubano. 'When you see you' wife tell her howdy fo' me.'

'Ain't got no wife, buddy,' said Chippie. 'Try again, Mister Ass-hole, you not doin' so good.'

'Not married, eh? Cho man, mean to say you don't have a woman?'

'What the hell is that to you?'

Cubano chuckled. 'Go to sleep,' he said, 'you ain't got nutt'n to worry about.'

A loaded truck went up the narrow lane out in front of the prison in reverse. They could hear the motor whining and fretting in that gear, backing up the lane.

'Goin' get me back me ole job drivin' an ice-truck,' said Chippie, laughing. He sat down on the end of his bunk and made a noise like a truck, gunning the motor, shifting gears.

'Ice-truck no?' said Cubano. 'Better get down off it now, an' go to sleep.'

'Well anyway, I was sideman on one of them for a time,' said Chippie, 'an' Ah was learnin' to drive one of them Fordson vans. I give a fellow ten bob to teach me.'

'Yeah. An' effen yuh didn' grab the woman's han'bag, mebbe you would be drivin' one of them now.'

Surjue stood waiting for the old man to crawl into bed. He felt his impatience with him mounting. He felt he could go across and hit him in the face with the flat of his hand to make him shut up.

'Come on, Pappy, get busy. I can't wait around here all night.'

The old man drew himself into the bed, pulled up the blanket around him, he kneeled up with his bottom sticking in the air, like he was going to say his prayers, and slowly subsided, grunting and groaning, on to his belly, like a sick cow.

'I got gran'children . . . son an' daughter, the second one, in the States . . .' he said, muttering half to himself. 'Me, an ole gran'fader . . . eh, Lawd Jesus! . . . what an ole man to do.'

Surjue went back to his own bunk.

Cubano was lying quite still under his blanket. Chippie came in from the bathroom.

'Pissed all over the floor,' said Chippie. 'The ole bugger; wouldn't wish myself in his shoes for anything.'

'Save it,' said Surjue, shortly.

Chippie opened his mouth as if to say something, changed his mind. Surjue waited until Chippie had pulled up the blanket around his head, then he too rolled into his bunk.

He lay there for a long time without sleep.

He turned over on his other side, but it was no better.

They treat prisoners worse'n animals, he thought. You wouldn't strap an old mule to a wooden frame and take the flesh off its back with a cat-o'-nine-tails twisted with rawhide and piano wire . . . hell, you wouldn't do that to an old mule.

The moon came up big. It made him restless. A nightingale sang from the top of the church over beyond the wall.

All of us are guilty . . . equally guilty . . . that was the Padre.

The Padre was a funny bloke. He liked him.

The sound of snoring drew louder and louder. It came from many quarters. It filled the ward.

Underneath it another, gritty sound . . . sound of someone groaning.

The nightingale trilled and trilled from the top of the church.

The snoring of men — rising up from the voluptuous depths of total sleep . . . the deep-down guttural sound, the thin high whistling, mingled. . . .

Lawd Jesus . . . what an old man to do.

All of us . . . equally guilty. . . .

Why were there people like him and Cubano and that stupid, blubbering, bladder-weary old man in the world!

8   FLITTERS THREADED his way through the crowd and walked on slowly down the street.

Some things he tried not to think about, but they kept coming up inside him. Especially when he was alone. What the hell did he have to worry about, anyway? Was he losing his nerve? He kept thinking about those dreams.

They had him backed up against a wall like the high prison wall he was passing on his right now . . . the wall of the General Penitentiary . . . they had backed him up against this wall, and he was fighting for his life. He had gone through agonies in that dream. He woke out of it washed in cold sweat, the sheets rolled up under him, and damp from contact with his skin.

A cold wind whipped against his face, going past the grim prison wall, and he shuddered. Christ! what it must be like shut in behind those high walls!

He tried to shake off these thoughts; took comfort from other things. The visa from the Cuban authorities in Havana may come through any day . . . the Consul had made him cable them . . . he had written out the words himself, the Consul in Duke Street had . . . on a half-sheet of notepaper . . . and he had handed it in at the Cable Office yesterday. You ought to get back a reply in ten days, said the Consul. He would feel better when he got aboard that plane.

The little woman who ran the restaurant where he ate . . . Lucille . . . she didn't know anything . . . she didn't have to know . . . nobody knew what his plans were, and that was the way it should be. The little woman was a stroke of luck . . . he was lucky, that's what . . . he could eat free . . . just the kind of cooking he liked too . . . her real name was Lucille, they called her Estina . . . what a name!

He went on down the street, taking comfort from these thoughts, putting the others behind him. He would go on down to the end

190

of Paradise Street. He would sit on a boat by the beach, perhaps sit on the little wooden pier, smoke a cigarette, look out to sea. Across the water lay Cuba . . . another nine days he should hear about the visa. Cuba . . . Santiago . . . Havana . . . one of those foreign places he would put down his roots again . . . shuck the old life behind him, start a new life, be free.

Something seemed to pull his gaze over to his right again. The prison wall came almost right flush up against the street here. Only a few iron railings around it divided it from the sidewalk. You felt as though you could put your hand out and touch it . . . the dark, forbidding wall.

He wondered if Surjue was in there, or if he was at the other one in Spanish Town. Spanish Town, perhaps . . . or else somebody had told him so . . . he couldn't precisely remember . . . funny, that . . . well, what the hell difference did it make!

Sunlight went slanting up the brick-grey of the old prison wall, searched out a dark seam that ran irregularly, zig-zag across the uneven surface like a duck-ant trail, picked out here and there occasional metallic glitters in the old masonry that flashed back light like a scattering of broken glass, traced out the slight indentations that came to its stony surface like wrinkles to an ancient face.

Below the sunlit triangular space shadows drew up from the brick-paved street, they huddled against the damp and gloomy wall.

Overhead John Crows circled and banked and glided beneath the thunderheads in the slate-grey sky.

A little head-on wind came thrusting down the street.

A schoolgirl in a middy blouse coming up the street and over-taking him, had her skirt blown up above her plump smooth knees. She tried to fight it down with one hand, clutching her satchel to her with the other.

Flitters walked on with easy swinging strides. He was whistling a tune.

He reached the corner of Elletson Road, felt hungry, stopped and bought a couple of lobster patties from a woman with a lunch cart. They were hot and spicey with curry, tumeric, leek; the pastry was light, buttery brown, crisp, flaking away between his fingers. His mouth watered freely, waiting for them to cool a bit, so he could bite deep into them, not just nibble at the crust. There was nothing like good food when a man was feeling low.

He walked on, down to the bottom of Paradise Street, and sat on an upturned fishing canoe. Finishing the patties, he rested his elbows on his knees, and stared out to sea.

The little waves wrinkled with laughter, sunlight, a lick of foam; they were thrust up lightly, and as lightly laid again.

A sea-gull circled and dipped. It skimmed the water; came up with a flying fish in its beak.

Behind him the nets were strung out upon poles, drying in the breeze.

A man came up silently behind him, coughed. He sprang up as though he had heard an explosion; his heart went wild, he could feel it thumping inside his shirt.

'What the hell —!'

'Sorry.'

The man cleared his throat, and said, 'Sorry,' again. He grinned. He had two teeth missing in front. He said: 'You got a cigarette?' rubbing his hands together.

Flitters remembered about the cigarettes. He too wanted a smoke. He broke open the packet, took out one, passed it to the man. He noticed he had one trouser leg rolled up to above the knee. The lower part of his leg showed a long, jagged, white scar. The new skin over it looked like thin shiny paper, slightly wrinkled. He did not like to look at it. It gave him a queer feeling inside his stomach. He looked away.

'You got a light?' said the man.

He grinned affably. The gap in front gave his face a gaping, incomplete look. It made him look slightly foolish.

He held the lighted match out to the man, trying to treasure the flame like a precious thing in the hollow of his big hand. The wind put the match out, just snatching the lick of flame off the split stick, like a mischievous child having a game. He handed the man the match box instead.

'Windy,' he said.

'Yah,' the man said, 'a bit.'

He said, 'It's goin' to blow.'

And Flitters said, 'Oh,' as though that explained everything nicely.

The man sucked once or twice at his cigarette, grinned, nodded, limped away.

'Probably got that from a barracuda,' Flitters said aloud, but not loud for the man to hear him. 'One of them barracudas must have got at his leg.'

'Wonder how it happened?' he said, blowing cigarette smoke out before him, against the wind.

He sat down on the bottom of the canoe again, and stared out across the sea. The gull was circling low above the water again.

A shower of gleaming fish started up out of the water in a short hopping flight, as though they were being chased by a bigger fish.

Flying fish.

They gleamed like quicksilver in the sun.

They spouted up out of the water, suddenly, took a short flight through the air, and dropping back into the sea, hit the water like a spattering of rain.

The waves made the same even rhythm and pattern across the restless face of the sea.

A tidy looking nursemaid wheeled a perambulator before her down to the end of the street. When she stopped the near wheel of the pram rested in a puddle of water. A little pink blossom of a baby nestled in the pram.

The baby put its tight little fist up to its face and sneezed.

The nursemaid looked at Flitters, caught his eye, looked quickly away.

She made baby-talk with the pink-and-white bundle in the pram. The baby put its legs and arms in the air and made baby-talk back at her.

It sneezed again, and its nose was wet.

It looked like a starfish tossed up on its back on the sand.

The nurse lifted the end of the baby's dress and wiped its nose. She looked at Flitters, their eyes held a second, she looked away.

Flitters sat quietly, smoking, his elbows resting on his knees. He looked down at the ground between his feet, knew that the nursemaid's eyes were upon him, but didn't bother to look up.

He wished she would go away.

The baby sneezed again, and started to cry.

He thought: 'She oughtn't to bring it out here. It's got a cold. This kind of breeze isn't good for a baby with a running cold,' and as though projecting the thought out to her, 'Why the hell don't you take the kid home?'

The nurse said, 'Coo-coo, den whaste mattah nowee?' to the baby.

It only bawled the louder.

She stooped, picked up a shell, held it close to the baby's face. The baby put its head back, braced its feet encased in shapeless knitting against the side of the pram, and screamed.

The nursemaid began to look flustered, un-poised, uncomfortable; her loss of *savoir faire* expressed itself in a growing petulance with the child.

Flitters smiled, and shook his head. She saw him. She yanked the pram toward her, wheeled it around, and started up the street.

'That's right,' he said, projecting his thoughts out to her, 'that's right, go home with the baby. Can't bring my mind round to things like that today.'

He stared out before him, across the tops of some coconut palms further down the beach.

A pale star hung like a spent candle in the sky.

Water gathered in his mouth again . . . he swallowed, but his mouth filled as fast as he swallowed. He put his head down between his knees and spat on the sand. He felt sick at his stomach . . . a sweeping wave of sickness, suddenly . . . he started to vomit.

He vomited watery stuff, and after some green slime.

The green stuff tasted bitter. He wondered if his gall bladder had burst inside him. He felt scared.

He took a large scented handkerchief from his pocket and wiped his lips. He held his head up, groaned, put it down again quickly, and spewed some more slimy green stuff. Jesus Christ! He was glad the prim nursemaid had gone away. Wouldn't of cared for her to see him like this. Seemed somehow unmanly. He felt about the same.

Christ! for weeks now he had felt it coming on, this sickness. All that cold sweat at nights, those dreams. He wondered had someone set a ghost on him. His thoughts turned to Surjue.

Hell, he didn't believe that nonsense about ghosts. *Duppy know who to frighten* . . . an old Jamaican proverb . . . hell, he didn't believe that foolishness about ghosts. Nobody could set a ghost on him, one thing certain . . . you had to believe in obeah for it to work for or against you . . . old time people had a saying, Duppy know who to frighten. Shit to you, Surjue! Ain't scared of no friggin' ghosts.

Ain't scared of ghosts, you hear me!

He put his head down again, and the front of his belly seemed to come up slap against his backbone. He retched and retched, but nothing came. Only a thin trickle of clear water.

Damn fool to be thinking about ghosts at all . . . nothing but those old patties. Old warmed-over patties the woman had sold him . . . get the hell out of here, why don't you go home? . . . good thing the nursemaid had left the beach . . . wouldn't care for her to see me looking this way . . . damn that woman with the lunch-cart, should lock people up for peddling stale food. Dangerous stuff, old warmed-over patties . . . ptomaine poisoning . . . clammy, just like he got at night when he had those dreams . . . all right now, hold everything a minute . . . soon be feeling better . . . *duppy know who to frighten!* . . . shit to you, Surjue!

An hour later he was dragging himself up the stairs to the room where he lodged. The landlady came out into the hall just as he reached the landing halfway up.

'Two men were here looking for you.'

'Eh? What's that?'

'Two men . . . didn't leave their names . . . looking for you. . . .'

Christ! Oh Christ Jesus!

'Say, what's the matter? You feelin' sick?'

'Yeah. What they looked like? Can you describe them?'

'Oh, they looked ordinary enough. I didn't take special notice.'

'Yeh. Yeh. I get you.'

'One was a sambo man, the other was black.'

'The black one was hefty, chunky, big gold ring on his finger? Big ring . . . big as that . . . gold?'

'Don't remember, didn't take notice.'

'Oh, all right. All right. I'm goin' up to bed.'

'What's the matter? You look sick as a turkey pee-pee.'

'Nothing much. Must be something I et.'

He held on to the railing tight, and pulled himself along, his feet dragging up the stairs. His stomach soured on him, he made grey hairs going up those few steps.

Inside his room he threw the window open, pulled back the counterpane, kicked off his loafers and stretched out on the bed.

Cold sweat pricked all over his skin. He got up and took off his shirt. He drank half-a-tumbler of water into which he had stirred a teaspoonful of soda bicarbonate. He went to lie down again.

All the time thoughts kept surging up inside him. They grew big with his fear.

Two men to see him . . . might have been anybody . . . didn't mean anything, two men to look for you . . . the breeze blowing in through the window was chill against his back. He got up to close the window. The breeze whipped in petulantly and swept some old letters and things in a heap off the table and spread them out untidily on the floor. He stooped to pick them up. Among them was an old race programme. He took it up from among the heterogeneous lot and looked at it now.

He grinned, memories flooding back upon him . . . that day he had won some good money on Battle Song . . . Surjue had given him Rock Water . . . didn't even place, Rock Water . . . nearly had a row that time . . . dam' pig-headed, cantankerous cuss, Surjue . . . he could afford to smile now, thinking of Surjue's pretentious knowingness, the airs he gave himself, thinking himself no end of a guy.

He put the things back on the table and went to lie down again. He belched once, big, and it made him feel better. He lay on his side and gathered the pillow under his head, nicely thumped-up, held in place with the crook of his arm.

Something uncomfortable under his side made him get up. He pulled his merino up, loosened his pants, took off the money-belt he wore next his skin. He pinched up the skin where the money-belt had marked it, he saw that it looked pimpled all over between his fingers. It was on fire with itch like a rash. Must do something about this damned money-belt, he thought, as he went across the room to hang it up in the clothes closet. Then he thought better of it, reached for the tin of talcum powder, dusted himself freely around the waist, put on the money-belt again. He wouldn't be able to rest with it anywhere but next his skin, he must bear it. It gave him a kind of stitch in his side, but he must bear it. A week more . . . nine days . . . he would have his Cuban visa . . . everything was going to be all right.

He thumped-up the pillow, gathered it up under his head again, held in comfortably with the crook of his arm.

The wind rattled the window lightly like someone trying to get in without disturbing him.

'Awe, shit to you, Surjue!' he murmured against the pillow.

The sickness at his stomach had passed. He drew up one leg to ease the stitch in his side.

He fell asleep.

9   '. . . WHAT HAPPENS TO people when their lives are constricted and dwarfed and girdled with poverty . . . things like that and that and that come out of it . . . moral deformity, degradation, disease . . . there I go again, talking the way I shouldn't . . . heaven help us all, for all are guilty before heaven . . . God forgive us all, for all of us stand, with these, in need of forgiveness . . . I must hurry, I have to burn some wasps . . . ah well, God's mercy on us . . . see, I have bought you some books.'

The Chaplain's face shone with perspiration, and the rim of his collar was wet and frayed. He sat down at the foot of Surjue's bed and watched him do his exercises.

'That's right, my lad, keep fit, eh? Keep fit. Don't stop. Please continue. Don't let me disturb you.'

'I guess I was just about through, anyway, Padre,' said Surjue, pulling on the top-piece of that uniform that seemed specially designed to degrade the human body, with its sheer ugliness and unfittingness. He tucked the tail of this unsightly monstrosity into the waist of the three-quarter-drop trousers.

'Thanks for the books, Padre,' trying to be at ease.

'I hope you like them. There are a couple by Agatha Christie, and there are also some by Erle Stanley Gardener. I believe those are among the, er — best known exponents of the literature of mystery and suspense. I see you are wearing shoes. Congratulations.'

Surjue looked down at his feet, almost self-consciously.

'Yes, sir,' he said, 'doctor's orders.'

'Yes. Yes. Very good of the doctor, I am sure. A man, even if he wore shoes regularly outside, must wait until the doctor in his infinite wisdom and compassion prescribes them for him when he gets in here. Dear me! Perhaps I should have studied medicine instead of theology. Perhaps then I should have been able to do more good in the world.'

He looked closely at Surjue.

'Do you think it strange?'

Surjue didn't answer.

'I mean, my talking like this. I am serious.'

'You want an answer?'

'Oh yes, yes.'

'I think you're okay.'

'Well, bless me. Er — that was very kind.'

'Not at all, Padre. You were askin' me.'

'Dear me, dear me. I've still got those wasps to burn.'

'Wasps?'

'Yes. Horrible creatures. No respect for property. They nest on the roof of the church. Somehow I don't feel they ought to be there. I am told the way to go about it is to burn them. Horrible!'

He went and stood by the window, looking at the ceaselessly circling John Crows.

He said: 'John Crows.'

'We have them with us all day, every day,' said Surjue.

'It's on account of how the place smells,' he added.

'Yes, it stinks, doesn't it. I have often wondered why it is that a prison always stinks.'

'Well, this one does anyway. Three hundred men live in here, Padre. Many of the cells carry three prisoners to them. They were built to hold one. A lot of men together like that are bound to raise one hell of a smell, excuse me, Padre.'

'Yes. Yes, of course. In a sense a prison like this is a very interesting institution, it provides a curious sidelight to the human character. It was conceived as a place of detention and punishment. Not as a hospital for morally sick people, a place of rehabilitation. It is like taking your consumptive old grandmother, and burying her, to cure the disease.'

Surjue laughed. He wasn't amused.

'John Crows,' said the Chaplain, looking out thoughtfully through the window. 'I believe they got their name from a minister of the Anglican Church. The Reverend John Crow. In the old days, way back, the garrison at Port Royal nicknamed the red-headed black vultures John Crows. Apparently the reverend gentleman wasn't very popular with the men.'

'I guess not,' said Surjue, without enthusiasm.

He passed his hand across his chin, looked down at his feet.

The Chaplain turned away from the window and went back to it again. He looked out across the roof of the next block of cells.

'What is worrying you, son?' he said from there.

His voice had a far-away, melancholy timbre to it.

Surjue didn't say anything. He took up one of the books and thumbed the pages carelessly.

'Perhaps you would rather not talk about it with anyone. I understand that. I do, indeed.'

The wind coming through the window rumpled his untidy long hair. He put a hand up, unconsciously, and tried to make it stay down on his head. He gathered up a hank of it in front and twisted it, and twisted it, between his thumb and forefinger.

He said: 'I have got to climb up a tall ladder to get to the roof. Perhaps it's a bit too windy to burn the wasps today. Eh?'

'What do you think?' he said, when Surjue made no answer.

'I've had bad news, Padre,' he said now, slowly, keeping his voice low, speaking as though he had considered it carefully, and had made up his mind to share this confidence with the other. 'Very bad news.'

'Yes. I could see that. You want to talk?'

'It's about my — my wife. She's sick. Bad.'

'I am sorry to hear. Is there anything I can do?'

'No. They're going to take her to the madhouse. She's clean out of her mind.'

A long silence.

'Are you sure?'

'Yes. I've got to see her — before.'

'How?'

Their eyes met. The Chaplain looked away.

'That's no good, you know. There must be some other way.'

'Don't try to kid me, Padre. You know their ain't.'

'Isn't there any such thing as a parole?'

'I don't know. An' even if there was you'd have to have pull in the right place.'

'I know. Still it's worth trying. I've got to think about this. Don't — don't do anything in a hurry, eh?'

Another silence. Presently:

'Thanks, Padre,' said Surjue. 'Thanks for takin' an interest in me.'

'Don't say it like that, Surjue.'

'It's no good, Padre. It won't work. I'd like to believe it would. It'd be something to take my mind off — off the other. . . .'

'Yes. I know. But it's been done before, I believe. Chaps have been granted parole before this, I should imagine. You have plenty to recommend you. Your first slip . . . you haven't got a criminal record behind you. Your record in this place has been exceptional. In spite of that unfortunate affair with the warder. You came out of that all right. Full marks. Full marks. I will talk with the Superintendent. Perhaps it is not such a good day for burning wasps, after all.'

10 SURELY LAUGHTER must lighten, now, somewhere in the world to put the shadows asunder . . . waits, like a young girl, untaken, waits for her first kiss . . . waits like the unspoken beginnings of desire . . . waits like the sap waits to burst with bud from a tree.

The clouds walk in their bright new apparel against the sky . . . they are close and secret . . . the shadows walk shoulder to shoulder between the lichened walls . . . they are closer than the clouds, and still more secret . . . they have drunken their fill of our lives in darkness . . . they are heavy with sleep, like men filled with wine . . . where in all the world will they come again to lie, untroubled . . . unshaken by any doubts at all, and take their rest in peace?

The gleaming spears point toward all mornings . . . and things turn back to their beginnings again . . . the stone-lips have spoken their last meaningless equivocation . . . the grinning skull on the wall improves the aim of the small boy with a handful of stones . . . the speech that flowered in epigrams gives over to the sound of wind speaking through an empty eye-socket.

Somewhere in the world something to redeem them . . . resolve their doubts, blot out their deeds . . . resides something . . . like love trembles on a young girl's lips, unspoken . . . waits laughter to lighten, now, and right them . . . redeem them, resolve them . . . redress them . . . somewhere in the world.

Manny and Wilfie were standing at the gate, looking out across the street, chatting. They had been standing there for a long time, with nothing special to do, and they were still there when Lennie and Zephyr came out from the house together and went out through the gate and down the street.

'Bet they are going to see that show at the Tropical,' said Wilfie.

'Know somep'n,' said Manny. 'That woman is a friend to everybody.'

'What you mean?' said Wilfie, quickly.

'Nothing like that, man. I mean it genuine, not *mean*. She is a real good woman.'

'You bet she is.'

'Better'n plenty who would look down at her.'

'She's on the square, that's what. Others are doin' the same as she, only they are on the crooked.'

'You said it, man.'

'Lennie is crazy for her.'

'Lennie is all right, too.'

'But she is holdin' him off.'

'I wonder why?'

'Women are curious. You can never understand a woman.'

'Yeah. You never know why they do things they do.'

The moon came up big beyond the roofs of the shacks across the street. It was as clear as a looking glass. You could see the mountains like dark shadows across the face of the moon.

'Boy, ain't that a moon!'

'Yeah, that's somep'n, all right.'

'Don't 'member seein' it so big and clear for a long, long time.'

'I'd like to be walkin' out meself with a woman, with a moon like that ridin' the sky.'

'Man, oh man!'

'I wonder can she see it through her window?'

'Who? Euphemia?'

'Yeh. Know somep'n? I'm goin' to knock on her window, an' tell her look at the moon.'

'You crazy for hell!'

'Just tell her, that's all.'

'You sure an' crazy.'

'Goin' do it just the same.'

He moved off with the words, speaking them as he went. Wilfie looked after him, shook his head. Somehow he felt sorry for Manny, as you would for a whipped cur. And it made him angry. He did not want to feel sorry that way for his friend.

He saw him go up to the window and knock.

Nothing.

From inside the room you could hear the faint rumble of a sewing machine. Euphemia had hired the sewing machine from Cassie.

The sewing machine kept on grinding away inside the room.

Manny knocked against the window again. Harder.

Everything went suddenly dead still inside the room.

Manny knocked again. Still louder.

Presently out of the silence a voice that didn't sound like Euphemia's at all said, 'Who's there?'

'It's me, Manny.'

The voice said again, 'Go away.' But it still wasn't Euphemia's voice. It sounded choked and thin.

'Euphemia,' said Manny. 'Are you all right? It's me, Manny.'

Silence again.

Suddenly the window flew up.

Euphemia put her head out and said: 'What the hell do you want?'

Manny opened his mouth to say something, but Euphemia screamed at him: 'What the hell you want to come frightening me like that for, hey?'

She put her hand to her breast, and laughed suddenly.

'God!' she said, 'you gimme a scare!'

She laughed again, as though she had suddenly discovered a wonderful release in laughter. As though all she ever needed to do, when things were too much for her, was to laugh.

'What's the matter, Manny?' she said, not unkindly. 'Eh? You want something?'

'I only came to tell you, look at the moon.'

'Eh? The moon? My, ain't it bright an' pretty!'

And Manny said, looking at her: 'Ain't it? Yes!'

She leaned further out of the window, and giggled.

'That's all you wanted, Manny? To tell me, look at the moon?'

She looked at him, and Manny was suddenly covered with confusion.

He laughed, and said: 'Like that, yes.'

She half-sat on the windowsill now. She reached a hand out toward him, as though to steady herself.

She said: 'Come here. Let me lean on you' shoulder.'

She said: 'You think you can bear me weight?' and laughed again.

Manny took a quick step toward the window. Her fingers against his flesh burnt him like a live coal.

The way he was standing, the weight of his body was not evenly distributed, was awkward, but he didn't dare to move.

'Never seen a moon like that for the longest day,' he said.

She giggled: 'You say it so funny. For the longest day. Ever see moon in the day?'

'I said that? It must be I am crazy. Euphemia. . . .'

'Eh?'

'Oh, nothing.'

'Must be something. Tell me what you were going to say.'

'Was nothing. Something about moonshine. I forget.'

'Forget nothing! For that I'm goin' inside back.'

'No, stay!'

She took her hand away. He made a clumsy grab for it. She pulled away quickly, laughing. She drew down the window slowly. She leaned against it, laughing, inside the room.

He could see her full silhouette clearly outlined against the frosted glass.

He stood outside the window, nonplussed, shaken. Stupid, suspended, he stood, not knowing what to do.

He was trembling like a man taken with an attack of ague. He felt flustered, and shamed, and cheated.

A foolish, idiot smile came to his lips. He lifted his hand

and held it before his face, and looked at it. He scratched the palm, grinned sheepishly, shook his head, and moved away.

The sewing machine started up inside the room again. Euphemia was singing. It was a song about moonlight and roses. She was very gay.

Manny scuffed his feet in the gravel, walking slowly toward the gate where Wilfie stood. He was looking down at his feet all the way.

'Man, how you do it?' said Wilfie, softly.

'Eh?'

'Me, I would hate her guts. I couldn't take it.'

'Don't care what she does, I like it,' said Manny, his face set obstinately. 'Just so long as she'll talk to me.'

Wilfie looked at him. The moonlight shone on his face and made it look greenish. Manny felt his gaze on him, but he didn't meet his eyes.

He was drawing figures on the gravel with his foot and erasing them.

'The hell with moonshine!' said Wilfie, suddenly, 'I'm goin' inside.'

'You can go if you like, I can't keep you,' said Manny.

And Wilfie said, presently: 'Awe hell, just as well to stay.'

'It's too early to go to bed, anyway,' said Wilfie.

Manny looked at him now.

'Tell you what, let's go talk to Mass Mose,' he said.

And Wilfie said, 'Yes. His light's still on. He can't be asleep.'

'Maybe just readin',' said Manny.

He cleared his throat and said: 'Don't bother say anything to anybody, you hear?'

'Man, what you take me for?'

'That's all right, Wilfie. I guess I'm just all kinda screwed-up like.'

A door at the end of the shacks at back against the gully opened. Rema came out of her room.

She stood on the step. The two boys stared at her, their mouths gaping.

She looked up at the moon.

She laughed, and came down off the steps, and stood in the yard.

They gazed at her in dumb astonishment. She was stark born naked.

Her two breasts curved up in front of her like the two horns of a crescent moon. Her skin shone in the moonlight, tawny.

Wilfie thought he had never seen anything half so wildly beautiful, and melancholy, in all his life.

He felt nothing else, for the moment. Only this sadness, this sense of desecrated loveliness. It weighed inside him like a stone.

She came a few steps down the yard, and stood still. She put her face up to the moon, and laughed again.

Her breasts were like the horns of a young moon, curved exquisitely upward . . . the moonlight turned her all tawny, tawny. . . .

'Jesus Christ a'mighty!' someone said hoarsely at his side.

'Jesus God, she's crazy. We got to do something. Quick!'

Rema turned and walked back toward the shacks, slowly, past them, going toward the gully.

She looked lithe and wild . . . like a wild, wild thing, coming suddenly into the open, free.

'Christ a'mighty, man, wake up! What we goin' to do?'

It was Manny, tugging at his sleeve.

Wilfie looked at him and shook his head, his mouth still halfway open.

'I know what,' said Manny. 'I'm goin' to call Mass Mose.'

'You watch her, Wilfie,' he said. 'Don't lose sight of her. She's headin' for the gully. Keep you' eyes skinned. Goin' fetch Mass Mose.'

Wilfie moved over the ground in his bare feet quickly, silently, as though if he made the least sound he would startle that vision, make it take flight and vanish. He went after her quickly, rising like a dancer on his toes.

Round behind the shacks she went, walking slowly. And then she started to run, going toward the male guinep tree.

What was she going to do now? Wilfie's heart was beating wildly.

His lips shaped the words: 'Oh God! Oh God!' without sound. They seemed to go from him like a prayer, with the wild beating of his heart.

'What to do now? Suppose she takes to the gully!'

And he said, 'Jesus have mercy!' feeling pity for her coming up inside his throat.

She reached the tree, and crouched down, hugging her knees. She seemed not to notice how cold was the air. She crouched down as though she wished to hide herself against the ground, to take something of it to herself, or give herself up to it utterly.

The wind came and rustled the shadows lying thick as velvet underneath the tree.

It seemed a long, long time he stood there, waiting. He was panting hard from holding his breath so long.

Mass Mose and Manny came quietly from around the angle of the shacks. Mass Mose was making a little noise with his tongue against his teeth, '*Tsk! Tsk!*' like that. He was carrying something white over his arm — a sheet.

'Wait here. Mustn't startle her,' he whispered to Manny.

Manny went and stood beside Wilfie.

Mass Mose went on, on tip-toe, carrying the sheet.

When he got near to her she sprang up quickly. Her eyes were wild, wild, her nostrils wide, like a thing at bay.

'What you come after me for, to beat me so kill me?'

'No, honey. I jus' fancied you mus' be feelin' cold.'

Mass Mose' voice quavered a little at first, before it steadied . . . but it was gentle, gentle . . . talking to her like you would coax a child.

'See, I brought something for you to cover with.'

He put the sheet around her.

She was docile under his touch. She even smiled.

'I just came out for a walk,' she said. 'Don't be angry.'

'Hush, honey. Nobody's angry. You come with me inside.'

She went quietly with him, his arm across her shoulder, holding the sheet around her . . . they walked past Manny and Wilfie side by side.

She said once: 'I don't want to go inside yet.'

And Mass Mose said something they didn't hear.

When they reached the step she sat down, and he sat down beside her. She put her head down on his shoulder and started to cry.

'Don't let them get me. Don't let them take me away. You won't, will you?'

206

'Hush, honey. There's nobody goin' to hurt you when I'm around.

She said: 'You seen the man come out after me with the long knife?'

'Hush, honey, don't even talk about it now,' he said.

'You were out there with them dancing, too?'

'Eh? Yes, yes. It's goin' to be all right.'

'No, you wasn't. You're only foolin'. You think I'm crazy, must be, but never mind.'

'The horns,' she said, 'they were pointing up like this.'

She raised her arms straight up above her head.

'And they were dancing all down the long valley . . . the hills . . . but you weren't there.'

She suddenly turned, and threw her arms about him, knocking the spectacles off his face.

'Oh God!' she cried, 'you won't let them get me. They would trample me to death, you know? The hills.'

'The hills, yes honey, they won't ever get to hurt you.' He set his spectacles straight on his face again, with some difficulty, still holding on to her with one arm.

'So they were joyful so they were dancing. They come prancin' down from up yonder with a thunder-roll.'

She laughed, and put her hands up to her face, pushing the wild hair out of her eyes.

She said, looking at him earnestly: 'They were tramplin' everything down into the ground before them.'

And he said, patting her shoulders: 'It's all right now, though. They've gone away. Gone back where they come from . . . won't ever get to hurt you, honey. It's all right, you hear . . . trust the old man.'

'And he out in front of them, dancin' naked, with the long, long knife.'

She put one hand to the crook of her elbow, showing him the length of the knife.

'Yes, yes,' he said, 'rest now . . . no need to worry . . . you lissen me, honey . . . lissen the old man . . .' crooning to her, as to a child.

She laughed and said: 'That's nice. You like me?'

She said, shaking her head at him: 'You sweet, sweet Mass Mose. I want you to myself, can't done.'

207

He said: 'Let's go on inside the room. You can't stay out here all night like this, talkin'.'

'No. Don't want to go inside.'

'You come with me, then. Make you warm an' comfy. Come with me, yes? The old man won't hurt you.'

His voice grew suddenly husky, and tears came to his old eyes.

'You wouldn't hurt me, no. You would help me — help me in the dark.'

'Yes, honey, sure the old man would do anything for you. You come with me.'

She stood up suddenly.

'All right. You follow me inside.'

She turned and went in through her own room door. And Mass Mose went in with her, holding the sheet around her, and talking to her gently all the time.

11 SURJUE FELT his stomach turn against him. He set his food tin down quietly and looked out through the window. He hoped to Christ he wouldn't have to vomit. He hoped if he did it would come up without that tearing sound.

He would go and wash his mouth in the bathroom. Perhaps if he was to take a little walk. . . .

'What's eatin' him, I wonder?' whispered Chippie.

'It's always the same thing,' said Cubano, wolfing his food hungrily. 'Bad news.'

Walls, walls, and all that passed between them . . . a man un-manned, un-countenanced, given over to the naked stare of self-pity . . . society, and the cankering, unyielding sore . . . en-closed within these walls a man was shut from light, like a seed struggling toward the sunlight from between damp stones . . . shut away like this a man lost his manhood and became a cypher, and lost his spirit and became insensible stone . . . shut in like this, with the rats scampering in the ceiling, and the stale smell of human waste and offal, and the vultures circling eternally in the

sky, a man became at last lost to himself utterly and to the world
. . . shut away a man like this and all you had was his skin —
stretched tightly against his body that knew the pang and torture
and bitterness and degradation of whip and bludgeon and ankle-
chain, and his shame, and the shame of others with him, all . . .
all of the man that you shut in here was one with the bricks that
went into the hideous walls, never to come out again, like the
bricks that held together the hideous cells in darkness, and the
mould that grew and ripened on the damp and reeking walls.

All of the men enclosed within these deadening walls, within
this sightless, unfeeling darkness stayed here with the generations
of lost men that were brought here damned to insensible negation
out of sight of the world . . . the lost generations came here, were
taken up, caught up, lost without memory of the living world . . .
lost without end in darkness, the spiritless, succeeding generations
upon generations, the murderers and rapers of young girls, the
spoilers of others, the arsonists, the cut-throats, their manhood
slowly squeezed from them, to be drunk up at last by the screaming murderous walls.

The vultures circling eternally outside made shadows on the
trampled parade ground . . . the vultures seeking offal, drawn
there by the close stench, by the reek of dead men stood up, stink-
ing to the sky. They were free, the vultures, coming to rest on the
parade ground, they eyed the stood-up dead contemptuously,
they hopped and cawed and fought over hideous refuse, and were
free . . . they flapped their wings and circled low and lifted and
topped the wall . . . free as air, the contemptuous vultures, the
bald, hornbeaked, beady-eyed, the respectable, clerical-looking
reverend John Crows.

He took water in his mouth, cupping his hands under the
bathtub tap, swished it around, and spat it out again. But he
couldn't spit out the taste of hopelessness and moral degradation
that had come to stay.

Special Location — they called it with the contempt of familiar-
ity, the Bull Pen — Special Location was a big animal cage, fitted
with solid steel bars buried deep in concrete . . . below the hospital
ward, running almost its full length . . . a piece at the end walled
off to house the dispensary, all . . . a jealous prisoner had stabbed

another to death with the blade of a scissors there . . . he was in a murderer's cell now, waiting for the hangman to open the door six o'clock one chill morning, waken him out of dreamless sleep . . . 'Wake up, buddy; I've come for you.'

He had a quarrel with his friend about another man . . . only the worse characters were herded together inside the Bull Pen . . . he accused him, in anger . . . his anger swam red before him, drowning out his friend's denial . . . 'What you an' him was doin' then, down at the Brickyard? Eh, answer me. What you was doin' together down there?'

The friend denied it again and again. He was past anger. Something more than anger stared from his eyes.

'If you mean it, get them put you back in the Bull Pen. You hear?'

The other shook his head without speaking.

Blind with jealous rage he plunged one blade of the scissors into his friend's chest. It went right in up to the hilt, which was the other blade, held like that in his hand. The blood spurted out and spattered him all over. He had wrapped a towel round the wrist of the hand that had held the scissors behind him.

Looking down at the blood on his chest, he laughed.

The sickness in his stomach surged at him again.
He swallowed some more water, and tried to forget it.
A little after that he began to feel better.
He went over to the window and stared dully outside.

He saw the teeming thousands of lost men who had been processed between these walls . . . their faces gaped and grinned at him, their gnarled and twisted bodies, their sick bodies, their bodies hunched above crutches, were without human form, as their faces were . . . they grimaced, and wore their faces like masks, and were cowed and broken, without pride or humility . . . only negation, that was all . . . their eyes stared up at him out of those lost, negative faces, and they gave no witness of life . . . they were glass balls, staring and globular, and without hope in all the world.

Their feet made a soft scuffling sound in the gravel, without shoes, as they walked. He could not bear it, and tried to put aside the vision that he might hold on a little longer to his hope and his reason. After all, five years was not all of a man's life. What could they do to him in five years inside here, that he could not undo when he took his life again?

And it seemed to him a voice whispered in his ear, '*They make animals without hope of the men who pass through here.*' And he shuddered and stared across the rooftops of the cells beyond, and was afraid. For the first time since he had been inside he felt this fear.

Deep, deep down inside him he knew it, and it went with a halting sound like the soft scuffling of bare feet in the gravel in the yard.

His gaze went over the top of the wall, where another world altogether lay, outside . . . he would be old coming out of here . . . he would be old and halt and vicious like the dead old men you met in the streets who had somehow shed their youth without growing up in wisdom and years . . . *Lawd Jesus, what an old man to do!* . . . the man, sixty-two, who couldn't hold his water . . . they had taken him out and beaten him the other day.

Suddenly his eyes went wide. He stood rigid with his mouth open, trying to shout. His throat was dry. No sound would come. And then something loosened inside him, and his throat became slack and capable of issuing sound.

He shouted, screamed: 'Fire! Fire!'

First a cloud of thick smoke, and then a great flame shot up from the roof of the ancient church over beyond the wall.

It made a big, terrifying backdrop, against which you couldn't see the sky.

'Fire! The church on fire!' he screamed.

The sound of heavy, booted feet running over the gravel . . . whistle blasts!

He smashed a pane of glass with his bare fist in his excitement, put his arm through the hole he had made, screamed at them, waving his bloody hand.

'The church! Not here! Fire on the church!'

And then they looked up above the high wall from the ground, and saw.

But they didn't know what to do about it. Inside here they, too, felt shut off from the outside world. They went rushing round in circles like frightened rabbits. Like chickens in a hen coop, with a mongoose inside.

He was screaming at them again: 'Do something! For Christ sake do something! Oh you bloody fools! Phone the fire brigade ... don't you know where the phone is ... what the bloody hell do you know!'

And then someone got the idea, because of what he was swearing at them, or he got it on his own, he went sprinting back across the gravel toward the office.

And another smashed the glass of the fire-box in the yard.

Lucky thing all the prisoners were locked inside their cells, at the noon hour. In the confusion there was no chance of a jail break.

Surjue thought, what the hell would they do if a fire was to break out in here, or an earthquake got going? And he held his bleeding hand by the wrist, and laughed.

12   IT WAS LATE when Flitters left the back room of Mosey Joe's. The outer bar was closed long ago.

He let himself through the side gate into the lane. He put his hands in his pockets and whistled a little as he sauntered down the street.

As he went east past the prison wall a chill wind met him full on. He glanced up at the gloomy old wall, going past it, shuddered, looked away. He had learnt that this was not the place where Surjue was working out his sentence. They had taken him to Spanish Town. Something about the gloomy wall towering some thirty feet or more against the sky, gave him the creeps.

A dark shadow, and then another, detached itself from the other shadows up a lane the other side of the street.

He didn't see them. The wind blew against his face that was beaded with sweat and clammy. He took out his handkerchief and wiped the sweat away.

He had been scared back there ... a moment more and he would have talked to Mosey Joe ... would have told him all he wanted to know ... Mosey was a smooth one, he had been working on him, giving him the third degree . . he wanted a share of the swag . . . Mosey was a deep one . . . shit to you, Mosey Joe! . . . he wasn't going to let on about anything to anyone . . . he could take care of himself . . . he wasn't scared.

He decided he would walk home by way of Paradise Street; instead of going up Elleston and along Victoria Avenue. It was a little out of his way, but he liked Paradise Street. It was wide from sidewalk to sidewalk. It went right down to the sea. Sometimes he would stand at the bottom of it and just stare out across the water. The gentle lap-lap of the little waves was like a hand smoothing out your ruffled nerves. He loved the sea, he should have been a sailor. There were a lot of foreign places he would like to know before he died. He would know those places yet. Only give him a little time.

The streets were deserted this late at night. He thought he heard a footstep behind him scuffing in the gravel at the side of the road. He looked round quickly. There was nobody there. Must have been his imagination . . . something to do with the state of his nerves. Hell, he must take a good grip on himself. His nerves were all shot. Fact. He'd have to do something about it. Wouldn't do him any good now to lose his nerve. Mosey Joe had made a crack back there about him using people and playing his hunches. Well, he had a hunch tonight everything was going to be candy.

When he had looked behind him just now he had thought he had seen a dark shadow moving against the wall. Most of the houses in this street had high walls. He didn't like that. He would go down the next lane, on to McWhinney Street, or whatever they called it, and over the bridge. That would take him right out to Paradise Street.

Must have been his fancy playing him tricks, that shadow . . . there were a lot of big old trees in front of some of these old houses. They cast shadows against the sidewalks. This part of the city must have been built a long, long time ago. It hadn't changed very much in all these years. A lot of these old houses high up from the street, with their solid brick walls, must have survived the 1907 earthquake. He wasn't even born then. A long way from it. One hell of an earthquake that was! He had heard people tell about it. Men and women and children pinned down

213

by fallen masonry, burned alive. Some were pinned down, quite conscious, but helpless, waiting for the fire to get them. A hell of a way to die!

One man he knew had had his arm pinned down like that. The fire was going to get him. Only his arm pinned like that up to above the elbow. The rest of him free, but held like that, as in the grip of a vice. He hacked and tore at his arm until he got away, leaving half of it in the wall. He lived to tell the tale. Died only a few years back . . . knew him well . . . had talked with him many times . . . old man Duperley . . . was a photographer. One of the two best known photographers in the city, those days.

He was going across the bridge that spanned a gully course, going toward Paradise Street, when he saw the two men following him. They were walking quickly, closing in on him now. He knew instinctively, the moment he saw them, that they were following him. He didn't even have a gun on him, nothing at all.

The two men were closing in on him now, and he was unarmed. He threw one panicky glance behind him and started to run.

He was trying to gain the gully over beyond Paradise Street, by the lunatic asylum. It was one of those cemented gully courses. It went alongside the asylum grounds. If he could only make the gully perhaps he could shake them off. He knew that dark gully course like the inside of his hand.

Running like that he broke out all over with cold sweat. It was the jaundice he was having, he told himself. He was a sick man, fact, if only people knew it. The breath was making a thin whistling sound going into his lungs.

He was across Paradise Street and over the fence now. He went over the barbed wire fence in one stride. Must look out for crab-holes. Get your foot caught in a crab-hole . . . twisted ankle . . . would be all over with him in a minute, then.

Beyond the cemented gully course down by the beach the fishing nets were still hanging in the breeze. They cast a deep blue shadow this side, the moon over beyond that.

A man sitting in darkness by the nets jumped up, shouted, challenging, 'Who you?' He was smoking a spliff. He could smell the weed.

His pursuers were running as quickly as he. He hadn't gained on them any.

His feet hit the bottom of the cemented gully course. There were a few inches of water at the lower end, by the sea. The water had a stale smell of fish. He started running up the gully course, keeping close to the wall. He listened, but he couldn't hear the sound of his pursuers behind him. He thought with a sudden increase of terror, he couldn't hear them because they were running in their bare feet. The sound of his own shoes would give him away. They could run blind, and never lose his trail.

Jesus Christ, what a fool he was, what a bloody fool! Better if he had kept to the street. In the street he could have leaped somebody's fence, gone over a wall, hidden in one of the yards, come out again in a back street somewhere, shake them off that way. What the hell had made him think of the gully? Christ, what a bloody fool!

His breath came now with a sound like sobbing.

He couldn't hear his pursuers, but he knew they were there, somewhere behind him, closing the distance between them with every stride. Already he was almost out of breath. He was a sick man, fact, if only people knew!

Surjue came awake out of a bad dream.

He turned over on his back, and swallowed his saliva, and made a face in the dark. He didn't like the taste in his mouth.

'Oh God!' he groaned, involuntarily, thinking about the dream. Funny thing, he couldn't remember it. It had something to do with ferocious, bristling, razor-back wild-hogs. His hands and face were clammy with sweat. 'Oh God, what a dream!' He lay on his back and stared at the blank ceiling. He was scared to go back to sleep.

He wondered what a dream like that could mean, and if dreams really had any meaning. Meaning or no meaning, that was one hell of an uncomfortable dream. A man's body and mind suffered agonies, having a dream like that.

The more wide awake he became, the more the outlines of the dream blurred, faded. He couldn't make it hold together at all. All he was left with now was a horrible reluctance to go through the agony of a dream like that again . . . that, and the taste in his mouth.

Damn that toilet! It had started up again. That was what had got him awake . . . must have been that knocking set up by the faulty valve in the bathroom, like somebody taking a sledge hammer and knocking the water pipes.

He turned over on his side and saw that Cubano wasn't in his bed.

That awful taste in his mouth. He would go and wash it, brush his teeth, gargle with some water.

When he got to the bathroom door Cubano was just coming out.

'What the hell is the matter with you?' growled Cubano.

'I had a bloody awful dream . . . just got awake . . . must have been the toilet woke me . . .' Somehow he resented the new brusqueness of Cubano. The other just brushed past him now and went on down the ward, back to his bed.

'Hell,' he thought, 'everybody's got troubles in a place like this.'

Mustn't mind it, he thought, maybe some days he acted worse than that himself.

He brushed his teeth, took some water in his mouth, gargled, spat it out. Another luxury the doctor had allowed him, his toothbrush. He thought grimly, if he didn't look out they would pamper him till he got soft in this place.

He thought: 'The hell with Cubano!'

He went back to his bunk, and lay down.

Flitters had stopped running now . . . stopped, and pressed himself flat against the cold, sheer wall. He listened intently. He couldn't hear a sound. Nothing but a little whistling noise of the wind going down the gully . . . going down to the sea . . . the tiny, far-away *wash-wash* of the little waves. Not a whisper of footsteps . . . not the least whisper of any other sound. Something had happened, they had broken off the chase.

Cold terror shook him. Oh, you bloody fool! They were creeping up on him on their bare feet in the dark. Of course he wouldn't hear any sound. Any moment now he would see their dark shapes coming round the corner.

He leaned his back against the wall, pulled off his shoes. He tied the laces together and slung them round his neck.

The wall was too high here for his purpose.

It was a good plan . . . he had the advantage of them there . . . he was a good bit taller than they . . . Now. . . .

He could see their dark shadows creeping round the jutting angle of the wall. They were advancing cautiously, slowly, closing in for the kill. They were more than twenty yards away when they came from behind the jutting angle of the wall.

Something whispered inside him: 'You can't get away from those killers. Not a ghost's chance in daylight of getting away. They'll never give up until they have made crow-bait of you. What's the use trying to run away, stand here and face them.'

He bent over from the middle and started to run. He gained another few yards lead that way. They didn't think he was going to run any more. Thought he was done for, winded. Or thought he was armed, at bay.

He could hear the sound of their feet now, padding after him. He ran, crouched over, keeping close to the wall.

The height of the wall fell away considerably here. He knew it, and this was the spot he wanted. He would show them a trick or two yet. He still had plenty on the ball.

He ran diagonally across to the opposite wall. Stopped, gathered himself, ran, crossing again . . . took a running jump, his arms straight up, his fingers clutching for the edge. God! made it! Just made it!

He pulled himself up, over . . . sprinted across a short stretch of grass . . . over the barbed wire fence again . . . and out into the street.

Across the street, running like a hare for his objective . . . a low wooden fence of palings . . . over . . . into somebody's yard.

Maybe they hadn't even got out of the gully yet. He daren't stop to take a backward glance.

Oh God! if a dog was to start barking now it would give him away. But he was acting on a gambler's hunch now, he would play his hunch to the end.

He ran halfway round the house and went over the back fence into another yard. He was going over back fences from yard to yard, picking them out by instinct . . . playing his hunch for all it was worth.

He was heading in the general direction west all the time, and getting further and further away from the sea. He ran across an open lot pocked with crab-holes. He ran until he was exhausted.

He sat down suddenly on a sidewalk, thinking, 'What a frightened bloody fool you are!' He figured he had shaken off his pursuers long ago. They would never know where to look for him.

'Wonder if they have got out of the gully yet?' he thought.

He wanted to laugh.

'I know why you weren't enjoying yourself,' said Lennie, 'too many soldiers.'

He was saying good night to Zephyr at her door.

'What you mean by that crack, too many soldiers?' She spoke quickly, defensively.

But he didn't notice anything. He went blundering on.

'All wantin' to make a pass at you, yes. Boy, I didn't want to start a fight with the army, but I was gettin' good an' ready to punch somebody's nose.'

'I didn't notice anything special. I only saw you weren't happy.'

'I hate that Silver Slipper crowd. Don't like soldiers. Seems to me women always go for men in uniforms.'

'All right. Good night, Lennie.'

'What have I said now, honey? What you vexed-up about?'

'What you aim to do, stand here all night an' argue?'

'No baby, I'm comin' inside.'

'No, you're not. Good night, Lennie.'

'Look honey, what you want to get vexed-up with me for? Awe, have a heart.'

'I'm not vexed.'

'I said, I don't like soldiers. Well hell, I don't like 'em. I don't *have* to bloody like 'em, now do I?'

She stood with one foot hitched up behind her, her head resting against the jam of the door. She didn't say anything. Just looked tired.

'Awe Zephyr, honey, don't act like that.'

He tried to take her hand. She pulled away.

'You think you can say any old thing to me, I just got to take it.'

'What have I said to you, honey? It's the dam army I'm beefin' about.'

She said, defiantly: 'Well, what's wrong with the army?' And then, very deliberately, so as to hurt him: 'I like soldiers just as well as other men.'

'Don't talk to me like that;' he said, hotly.

She saw he was angry now, and laughed.

'Well, just get that straight, an' don't let's have an argument every time a man looks at me when we go out.'

He said, very slowly, 'All right, I get you.'

She said, bitterly, 'I wonder, do you?' And turned, and went in through the door.

He sat down on the sidewalk and got back his breath. He felt of a sudden safe, secure. He had fooled them. Did they think he was easy game? They'd find out different. He'd slip them, get away, they'd be beating the air. He felt of a sudden a great upsurge of confidence, it filled out his sagging ego.

He felt a ridiculous desire to thumb his nose at nothing. He did so now, and laughed. They thought he was easy game, did they? Well let them guess again, he'd show them something.

He took his shoes from around his neck and started putting them on. He realized his feet were bloody and swollen. His shoes were too small for them. God! he didn't realize how hard he had been running . . . only now he was beginning to realize the impossible hazards he had taken in his stride.

He stood up to test his feet. Okay, they could still carry him. He slung the shoes around his neck again, and started to walk.

He stopped suddenly, panic making him prick all over.

God! what a bloody fool!

After his wonderful escape he was going to give himself up . . . just like that . . . fall right into their hands. He was going to walk straight home, and they would be just inside the gate, in the shadow of the house, waiting for him. God! what a bloody fool! Fear made him prick all over with itching, like a rash.

Couldn't go home. What the hell was he thinking of.

Only one thing to do. He'd have to knock up Lucille. She lived in a little two-room apartment above the restaurant. She would ask a lot of questions, but he would fob her off with something.

Thinking, planning, he started to walk. He went up a street, across, and up another. He climbed a fence and was inside a cemetery.

Got to put his shoes on. His feet were sore, tender. Got to squeeze them on, couldn't get anywhere like this all night. He sat down on a grave stone, took the shoes from around his neck, and squeezed them on to his feet somehow. He stood up, tried to walk in them. Found he could make it. He would force himself to walk in them until his feet settled down, grew accustomed to the shoes.

He picked his way across the cemetery, careful not to trip over any of the graves. He was glad for one thing, the sky was heavy with dark clouds. The clouds were part of his luck, they put out the moon.

He went over the other boundary fence of the dark cemetery, and out into the street again. This street, like the rest, was almost deserted. Two dogs trotted single-file up the sidewalk. A drunk went staggering past, dead to the world.

He was a young man, slender; he seemed a decent sort of fellow. Or was, sober. Some kind of a clerk in an office, he would guess.

The sight of the drunk, blundering home, blind, in the early hours of the morning, made him feel superior, somehow; it was like a shot in the arm. Made him feel a special kind of person, different from others. Born with a special kind of luck, taken care of by a special kind of providence. One of the elect of mankind, not just one of the herd. All this gave a big boost to his confidence. He felt so good he wanted to laugh.

He had to do something he didn't want to, standing on the sidewalk outside Lucille's front door. He had to make a noise enough to wake the whole street. Lucille slept so soundly.

Standing over against the opposite sidewalk he could see her window was open, pushed up from the bottom. He whistled . . . louder . . . louder . . . but nothing doing. My God! she slept like a log.

He took up a handful of gravel and threw it against the window.

Some went right though and must have fallen on top of her in the bed. Still nothing happened. Jesus Christ! how could anyone sleep so hard!

She was there all right, he knew it. She always slept with the window open like that, from the bottom. He had tried to argue with her about it, told her it was dangerous. She only laughed. She was one of those fresh air fiends. She had been listening to some crank-talk about tuberculosis. If she wasn't in the window would be securely closed and bolted down.

Eventually he had to take a stone and go and beat on the door to make her hear him.

After a bit she got awake. She put her head out through the window, sneezed three times, yawned with her hand before her mouth, and said, 'Goodness! It's you!'

She said: 'I'll be right down, just let me draw on something.'

'For Christ sake!' he said.

But she had pulled her head inside.

She said, as he sat on the side of the bed and took time pulling off his shoes, wincing, 'What happen? Why you come so late? Goodness! you know it's morning! What *have* you been up to now, you look like you've been in a fight.'

He let her talk herself out of breath, asking a lot of dam fool questions. He went on pulling off his shoes.

He got up and went across to the wash basin and washed his hands and face. He came back to the bed, took off his trousers, hung it up on the accustomed hook behind the door.

Still she kept on talking, asking question after question.

'Look baby, I'm tired, tell you all about it in the mornin'.' He got into bed and pulled up the cover around him. 'Aren't you gettin' back to bed, baby? Don't you want to sleep?'

He thought he heard knocking!

He woke, sat up in bed, listened for the sound.

He must have been dreaming.

He put out his hand in the darkness, and found Lucille was not in the bed beside him.

He was suddenly tense, listening, wide awake.

Voices downstairs . . . she was speaking to someone at the front door. He got out of bed quickly, his bare feet making no sound at all on the naked floor. He went across the room on tip-toe, found his clothes in the darkness and pulled them on.

He could not hear what they were saying . . . only the rumble of their voices below. He knew that summons at the front door three o'clock in the morning could mean only one thing. They had traced him here.

Oh God, oh Jesus, what a bloody fool he was!

They knew where he lived . . . the places he went . . . everything about him. They knew he had gone to the Cuban Consul for a visa. Oh God! of course . . . they had been shadowing him, checking up on him for weeks. They had sat in judgment on him, according to their own code of justice, and had found him worthy of death.

He tore the sheets off the bed, knotted their ends together. He tied one end of his improvised rope to the bedstead . . . lucky thing the bed was close up against the window, and the window was open. He would let himself out into the street without making the least sound.

He let down the end of the sheet through the window. He squeezed on his shoes quickly, wincing with pain. He threw one leg over the windowsill, gripped the sheet between his hands, brought up the other, eased himself through, and over, cautiously, testing his rope. It held.

He was swinging in space, his clothes making a soft, scratching sound against the rough pebble-dash on the outside wall.

Suddenly a dog, sleeping on the sidewalk, woke, started barking, backing away across the street, barking . . . and then it seemed all the dogs in the street got awake at once and started to bark. He heard, underneath it, a sound like scuffling at the front door.

He went sliding down the length of the sheets so quickly, it took some skin off his hands.

He landed on his feet on the sidewalk.

Without looking behind him, he was sprinting, as fast as his legs could take him, down the street.

Outside the Salvation Army lodgings in Upper King Street he paused to draw breath. He had been running hard, it seemed for an incredibly long time. Once he thought his strength, his wind, would fail him. They were gaining upon him. Panic gave him new strength, a third breath.

They had gained on him so much, on account of his injured feet, that he could hear the breath rattling in their lungs, giving him chase . . . actually hear them breathing . . . and it had lent him strength, to know that they were weakening. The pace he had set was too hot for them. He thanked God for the length of his legs.

He knew something else too, that they didn't have a gun.

That latter knowledge didn't bring him much relief, however, because he realized, picturing it vividly in his mind, that they were going to settle his hash with ugly weapons — like blackjacks and knives. Much better to be shot with a clean hole through you, to go down riddled with bullets than — oh God! to die that way!

These men were wolves. They were wild beasts. They knew no pity. They knew no law but the law of the jungle. He had betrayed one of them. He had been weighed, and found worthy of death.

He had raced up dark lanes, twisted across narrow alleys, throwing them off his track. Now he had shaken off pursuit completely; had left them, floundering, behind, confused, not knowing which turn to take. He was safe.

He had only to put up at the Salvation Army Hostel for the night. In the morning he would get away to the country. He would send a forwarding address to his friend Repole. Ask him to collect the visa when it came . . . only a matter of days now . . . he would get to the airport and hop the first plane for Havana.

They were full up at the Salvation Army Hostel . . . no room for the night . . . sorry buddy, not a spare bunk left . . . look like you could do with a cup of coffee, though . . . too bad the kitchen's closed . . . come a long way? . . . excuse me, didn't mean to ask no *un*-necessary questions . . . forget it . . . sorry, can't even offer you a cotch.

Well, that was that.

It was plenty.

He put his hands in his pockets and went slouching wearily, brokenly, down the street.

He would have to take his chance sleeping on a bench in the Park, or something . . . might even be lucky enough to get pulled in by a cop. He never realized that the prospect of arrest could be so inviting. It was the very best thing could happen to him now.

Better thing, if he could risk it, go to Hanover Street . . . sleep with a whore . . . he wouldn't mind sleeping with one of the younger flossies . . . was a girl named Betty — part East Indian — in one of those flop-joints down that street . . . had seen her once . . . gone there looking for a sailor who wanted to do a deal with a watch . . . didn't mind the idea of putting up with Betty for the night, but Christ, he couldn't do that. If he should go that way now, sure as anything he'd walk right smack into them. He had shaken them off back there some place. No, Jesus! he couldn't take that risk.

Going past the Ward Theatre now . . . on the sheltered pavement out front people slept . . . rows of dirty human bundles, looking like cast-up flotsam on a lonely beach . . . oh Lord, oh Lord, what luck! . . . all he had to do was to pick himself out a spot between them. They would never think to look for him here.

He stepped stealthily among the rows of sleepers spread out like bundles of old clothes on the pavement. He lay down between a stout woman who breathed asthmatically, and a thin man with a stunted, peppery kind of beard. The hair on his chin sprouted thinly, curled up into little balls like blackpepper grains.

The night was warm. He was bone-weary. He pillowed his head on his hands, stretched out on the hard concrete, and went straight to sleep.

Lennie walked on down the street feeling unaccountably angry with everything. He was taking his own time going home.

He had begged her to leave that yard and come and live with him. He had the very place in mind, a quiet little bungalow, two rooms, standing in the same grounds with a bigger house, but separate from it. It was a modern little bungalow, with a veranda two sides, as pretty as a coloured picture postcard. Had its own little pocket-handkerchief-size garden plot out front, and all.

Funniest damn thing about women, they all went crazy for a uniform!

Way back he had thought of joining the police force. He wouldn't mind being a cop. Cops got a pension when they retired from the force. Didn't know much about the pay, though . . . always seemed to be some grousing about the pay.

There were other things, too, that made him decide against being a cop. There was the question of the promotion. Seemed there were things wrong with the police force. They were ca ling for an enquiry, a commission of enquiry, to go into the whole set-up. You bet things were bloody there, or they wouldn't be doing that. What was it he read in the papers? Four suicides among high-ranking officers. Men quitting the ranks to join up as farm workers. The Elected Member of the House who had called for the investigation complained detectives had been set to watch his office, his telephone wires tapped! Hm! Things in the police force didn't look so good to him, in fact.

Wonder what they went and bumped themselves off for? Would the Commission report on that?

Then there was that business about that acting corporal . . . what was his name now? . . . he forgot. Got himself shot up three times in circumstances he should have been given the V.C. for each time . . . or anyway the highest police award. Was reading about it in the papers only the other day.

This chap, whatever his name was, first occasion he was on beat duty along Slipe Road . . . back in '37, that was . . . near Wolmer's gully . . . getting on for dawn . . . saw a suspicious character carrying an attache case . . . called to him . . . guy jumped into the gully . . . gave chase . . . guy suddenly turned and fired point blank at the cop . . . missed . . . swung an uppercut to his jaw, the cop . . . knocked him out clean . . . like something out of a third-rate movie . . . only this happened to be true. What you know!

Next time, about two years later . . . was with a buddy on patrol duty . . . two men came along carrying a box . . . stopped them for questioning . . . one of them jerked out a .38 revolver, plugged this cop through the chin and throat . . . another guy would have had himself taken in an ambulance to the hospital . . . this chap grappled with the gunman, disarmed him, marched him to the lock-up. After that this cop was in the hospital two weeks. Spent three months at home convalescing from that scrap!

Third time . . . this was just September gone. Early morning . . . he was riding a bicycle alone . . . saw two men, looking suspicious, carrying sacks . . . hid himself in the shadow of a building . . . challenged the men as they came abreast . . . chaps started to bolt . . . cop grabs one . . . they start fighting . . . other man comes back to help his pal . . . so he is fighting with the two of them now . . . the fight ends when the cop stopped a slug from a gun with his guts . . . the men get away.

Somehow he managed to get to the station and make his report, before collapsing . . . was rushed, dying, to the hospital . . . during the next two days he put up the biggest fight of all . . . this time for his life, with death . . . two operations failed to remove the bullet from his belly . . . he's still carrying it around inside him as a sort of souvenir.

The man who shot him was arrested the same morning by another cop. He was still carrying the gun on him.

The jury, months later, in sentencing this thug, made a special point of complimenting this cop for his exemplary bravery in the performance of his duty. Rose . . . that's what his name was . . . goes around with a stick now . . . Acting Corporal Rose.

Eighteen years in the service.

Highest he could get up to was Acting Corporal.

Acting Corporal!

Shit!

The woman's strident screaming jerked him violently out of sleep.

Everybody had got awake; there was a hum of excited conversation going on around him.

The stout woman sat upright, hands clutched to her bosom, and kept on screaming. . . . Her money gone!

Somebody had robbed her while she was asleep.

She carried it in a threadbag tied with a string around her neck, the bag nestling between the ample folds of her bosom.

He realized that they were all looking at him suspiciously.

'Who you?' someone said.

He sat up. Rubbed his eyes. Stared around him.

226

'Who you?'

'I —'

They drew closer around him, menacingly.

The hell with these people! How could he explain to them?

They were a hideous bunch, taken all together. A child the other side of the woman had its two eyes stuck down with matter. He was trying to force them open with his fingers, whimpering, choking, his nose running with a three-days cold. One man had no nose at all, only two holes in the middle of his face, the legacy of a dose of syphilis. Another had running sores all the way up one leg, to his knee, and that foot was about three times the size of the other. He hadn't looked at them too closely at first, now he was really seeing the kind of company he was keeping for the first time. It made him physically sick. He felt as though he had found himself among a colony of lepers.

He scrambled urgently to his feet.

'What! Yuh waan run-way?'

They clutched at him. He had to kick at the thin old man to make him let go of his leg. Someone grabbed his arm. He closed with him, pitched with him, clear off the sidewalk into the street. He brought up his knee suddenly, jabbed the man in his groin.

He was up on his feet again. But they had surrounded him. He hit out right and left. The noise was enough to wake the dead. He fought them off with a sick desperation, not making a sound. Right and left his fists smashed at them. Blood was running down from a gash in his forehead into his eyes.

He saw somebody was coming at him with a knife. He broke through the ring of men and screaming women like a bull out of a pen, and went sprinting down the street.

They were too close upon him . . . closing in upon him . . . he had run too much already . . . his muscles ached, his feet were sore . . . he cast a fearful glance behind him . . . saw the pursuer who was gaining upon him was alone. He slowed down and allowed him to catch up. Then he turned and felled him with a blow just under the ear.

He went on down the street, and up the next lane.

He kept heading west through the silent streets that were given over to darkness. He dared not turn back the way he had come.

227

He was walking through back streets and alleys of gloomy, interminable slums.

Stark old tumbledown two- and three-storey houses rose up out of the palpable shuddering greyness, seemed to totter together in a nightmarish huddle above the narrow, evilly-leering, gutted streets.

The smell of wet tar-roads scarred and sun-blistered and night-sweating rose up to his nostrils, mingled with the odours of rancid vegetable oil stale with cooking, dry-rot in old timbers overlaid with the liverish green of damp mildew.

The wind blew across the carelessly swept-up heaps of untended roadside garbage where dogs, scuffling, snarling, fighting, had been before.

There were nice people who thought, ain't old slums awfully quaint-looking and romantic, and in their own way beautiful? . . . people who had nice manners sitting in restaurants eating, and smelt of expensive toilet water, and spent the afternoon, by appointment, at the hairdresser, or sitting smoking cigarettes and reading the latest Book-of-the-Month selection steaming their pores in hot scented baths.

Saliva thickened in his throat, stuck his tongue hard up against the corrugated roof of his mouth; he hawked and spat, trying to get rid of it, trying to get a clean sweet taste back in his mouth. The thick phlegm roped-up, knotted itself around his elongated palate, slipped back, resisting his every effort to dislodge it; he fought it, gagging at it, scraping at it with a great tearing strangling sound.

The thick wads of hardening mucus gave way, parted reluctantly, were coughed up at last with great expense of energy; he leaned against the high wall of a built-up, bricked-in yard, where rows upon rows of stark lean-to tenements hived, high above the leprous street, and smelled to heaven, and swelled the bank balance of a big-gutted heavy-jowled dyspeptic whose only son had committed suicide to save his family-honour . . . couldn't let it down, his old man wore the Order of the British Empire, was a Justice of the Peace, had successfully disputed all medical theories relative to the hardening of the arteries, and was a pillar of the Episcopalian Church.

He was heading out to their part of the city, he thought grimly.

228

They wouldn't dream of looking for him out here. He was playing his luck for all it was worth. His only chance. Double or quits. He walked on, scarcely thinking of where he was going, or what he was going to do when he got there.

His feet were dragging with weariness. They were swollen so bad he didn't know how he would take off his shoes . . . die with his boots on, perhaps, he thought grimly . . . ground his teeth with sudden passion . . . thought again, his rage getting the better of his terror, 'Shit to you, Surjue!'

There was a patch of light down the end of this street. He went toward it like a man lost in a desert coming upon a green oasis amid that sterile waste of sand. His feet actually lifted from the pavement now, as he tottered along.

The sign outside said: UNITED NATIONS COLD SUPPER SHOP — Opens All Nite. A cup of hot coffee, he thought, gratefully, wouldn't hurt him any at all.

He pushed the wire door and went in.

He sat down at a table, looked around the place.

It was almost empty.

Buju and Crawfish sat drinking steaming coffee from a couple of chipped blue mugs across the room.

The devils had each a pitchfork, they had tails, and chattered and grimaced like monkeys. She regarded them coldly, and dispassionately, as they scrambled up and down the wall. She was not scared of them. At times, watching their antics, she wanted to laugh.

They had broad blue patches over their little behinds, as though somebody had pinned a blue diaper on each of them. They were really funny. They reminded her of a coloured picture she had seen long ago, in her childhood, in a book.

The words, 'Come to Jesus!' stuck out from among the untidy jumble of thoughts within her mind.

The little blue devils chased each other, grimacing horribly, up and down the naked wall.

She lay in bed with the yellow sheet drawn up tight, and clutched about her throat. Her fingers felt hot and stiff. They were like pieces of dry stick. She worked them at the hinges of the joints to see what would happen. They made a dry brittle sound to her ears, or else she imagined it. Laughter choked at the back of her throat.

She tried to laugh, but instead found herself weeping, with her hands pressed hard against her eyes. She whimpered, and drew herself up by her hands, holding on to the iron rail of the bedhead. Her knees came up of themselves, and were rammed hard against her chest.

Her teeth started to chatter, as with cold, but she shut them tight. Her body shook and shook, until she could hear the bed shaking with her. She couldn't keep still.

The little blue devils came down off the wall.

They were lost in darkness among the shadows on the floor.

The lamp on the table, turned down, smoked, going out, giving up to the darkness, for the want of oil.

Her teeth chattered against her will. She gained control of them and shut them against her trembling lower lip. They bit down hard, and there was the salt taste of blood in her mouth.

The little devils dragged themselves up from the floor, one by one, holding on to the sheet, drawing it taut about her. They sat down in a gibbering semi-circle around her as she huddled in the bed.

The lamp on the table across the room smoked up, gave a little puff, the tiny yellow flame went up in a thin arc. It left the wick altogether and drew into a thin curved pencilmark of blue flame that hung on nothing.

The lamp made *puff*, again, and went out.

She crouched huddled up in the darkness . . . a voice croaked, 'Come to Jesus!' . . . the blue devils closed around her silently . . . she could see their eyes . . . she was sobbing, sobbing, with the wild laughter shaking in her belly . . . they squatted on their blue-patched bottoms, waiting for her to drop asleep.

She knew what they had come for, to haul her screaming and scratching at them with her nails, and naked and trembling, before Massa Jesus . . . she was shaking with terror from her head to her toes . . . the darkness thickened about her . . . 'Come to Jesus! Come to Jesus!' . . . the little blue devils were hushing it in a low, whispered chant . . . her hands clutching the iron above her head grew tighter and tighter . . . her thin arms were straining beyond their strength . . . she shut her teeth, and drew away from them, as far as she could . . . *'Come to Jesus!'* . . . she shut her teeth, and gathered her strength to fight them off.

The chase had led them here, the same as him.

So this was it . . . the end . . . after all he had been through . . . he had had it now.

He shivered with hot and cold spasms. Impotent fury and horror shuddered through the vents and inlets of his being . . . they went with the thundering tumult of his blood.

They came across the room without a word, and sat down at the table, either side of him. They didn't say anything at all. They had brought their coffee mugs with them. They just sat, drinking their coffee in silence.

He looked across behind the counter where the proprietor had been. He had gone into the kitchen, out back, behind a screen door.

He tried to get up, casually. The two men walked with him, on either side of him, close, toward the street door. He wanted to stop, turn back now. They wouldn't let him. They held him each by an arm, just above the elbow. They walked him out between them, through the swinging wire-screened door.

Out on the narrow sidewalk he said, trying to hold his voice down, steady: 'Wait a minute; where — where are you taking me?'

Of all the dam fool things he had to say that now.

'You were goin' for a walk, weren't you? We're just comin' along.'

'Don't — don't —' he sobbed, his sobs choking him.

'Cho, come on man, you goin' start cryin' now?'

'Look, I got money — I'll split it with you.'

'Well, just look at him. He's goin' start to cry!'

Oh God, what a bloody fool he was! If only he'd had the sense to buy him a straight-razor . . . carry it around in his back pocket . . . he looked around him wildly for a weapon to use against them . . . to fight back at them with . . . anything.

'Look, let's go back inside the restaurant — talk this over —'

'We can talk walkin'. What you got on your mind?'

A little wind blew down the street. It went through him like a knife. He was trembling. They tightened their grip upon his arms.

'Don't kill me,' he begged, 'don't — don't kill me.'

'I'll do anything you say ... I'll give you money ... I'll go to prison for you ... I swear to God! ...'

'Just look at him, will ya! Snivellin' like a baby!'

'Shit! He's yellow all through his stinkin' guts.'

'It gimme the creeps havin' to do with a guy like this.'

'Yeh. I want to cry meself. I must be soft.'

He tried to bear himself like a man, but his terror wouldn't let him. It bore him down, down, went over him like a flood.

He was talking quickly, breathlessly, through a dry mouth, that had suddenly gone dry on him.

'Don't — don't kill me — listen, no — we can talk. Don't — don't do it — I got a proposition — wait an' hear me out — just gimme a chance — gimme time to talk — '

His tongue came out to moisten his lips, but it felt curiously corrugated now, and dry. It felt rough, and thirsty, like a piece of old paper ... he talked on in a thin piping voice, with sand in his mouth.

'Listen boys ... I'll make it good for you ... let's talk it over ... I got money ... money in the bank ... I swear it to God! ... I wouldn't try to fool you ... Christ, no ... wouldn't try to fool with you boys. ...'

'Tell you what buddy, you save it till tomorrow. We're busy, we got plenty to do tonight.'

'Yeh, we can set down an' talk it over in the mornin'. Over a cuppa coffee an' coupla poached eggs on toast. That suit you? Nice hot cuppa coffee, like that one you didn't get inside.'

They were playing with him like a cat with a mouse. He knew it. Some memory of manhood deep down within him rose up in revolt.

He tried to walk calmly forward between them, to his death, in dignified silence.

He couldn't take his feet up off the pavement. They were half-carrying him, half-dragging him between them.

His tongue was dry and swollen and heavy. It got itself stuck hard against the roof of his mouth.

His eyes rolled back in his head. They made a quick half-circuit of the heavens. A few bright stars stuck out from among the heavy clouds.

'Oh God have mercy ...' he started to pray, in earnest.

Only a garbled, unintelligible mutter crackled from his tight throat.

'Lissen Buju, bwoy, him prayin' . . . lissen him good.'

Buju spat in the gutter. 'Mebbe God wi' hear him. Bwoy, big-'fraid mek a man do two things, dem say — shit himself an' pray to God.'

Crawfish let out a big laugh that rang raw across the stillness of early morning.

'Bwoy, dat's good. Is whe' you hear dat one?'

Suddenly a blind rage against his fate and its manifest and terrible injustice swelled up within him. It burst upon him full and berserk. He gathered his strength and started to struggle with them.

He fought them blindly.

It was as though a madness was upon him. It lent him super-human strength.

He shook them off. He was free. He hit out at a face. Felt the dull, puffy contact against his fist. Saw Crawfish go spinning over the edge of the sidewalk, slip, go down in the gutter. The stocky Buju came in charging with his head low, like an angry bull. He hit him with both hands . . . heard him grunt an obscenity . . . saw him stagger sideways . . . he stepped in quick and hit him hard in the back of the neck. He thought he had broken it.

Out the corner of his eye he saw Crawfish getting up from the gutter. A long knife blade gleamed naked in his fist.

He turned and went sprinting down the street . . . up the first turning on his left . . . a dark and narrow lane.

The breath came whistling into his lungs. A wild, heady exultation raced like music through his blood.

He was running again with that swinging stride, a free man. He would outstrip them again. Shake them off again. Give them the slip. The thick, sodding bastards! Thought they were a match for a man like himself!

He ran, keeping close to the dark wall on his right. The blood went singing madly through his veins. He could hear them behind him, blundering along, growling, cursing, coming blindly up the middle of the lane.

In his full stride his foot struck against something. He tripped, fell heavily over an old pitch-blackened garbage box.

Before he could come upright, they were upon him. He backed up against the wall.

He had nothing to fight back at them with but his fists. His breath came from him with a hoarse, rasping sob. But he was fighting with the bitter end of that berserk rage. He hit out blindly with both fists, his breath jerking from him with those big rasping sobs.

Something crashed against his right shoulder. His arm hung dead and useless at his side.

He saw Buju raise the blackjack to hit him again. He dodged it. Crawfish stabbed him in the side of the face with his knife.

The point of the blade went in just below the eye. It laid his cheek open to the bone, came to a jarring stop against the teeth in his lower jaw.

The knife struck him again . . . in the neck, and sheer through the jugular . . . the point came out through the other side of his throat.

He started to scream . . . it came up high and thin . . . broke off . . . ended on a curious kind of rattling note.

He slumped to one side, and pitched like that across the open garbage box, reeking with its three-days sour garbage smell.

The lower part of his body kicked and bucked, spasmodically. He was still conscious. With the third strike Crawfish sent the six-inch blade through his back up to the hilt.

Buju came around in front and split the skull open with his blackjack. It gaped, and the grey matter, streaked with blood, spilled out.

They left him lying there and walked, unhurried, down the dark lane.

The moon broke from a heavy cloud, threw a gleam over the shoulder of a tin-patched building on their right. It lighted upon the huddle above the reeking garbage box an instant only, and went out, drawing under its dark shroud again.

The two men walked shoulder to shoulder down the empty lane. They went without once casting a glance behind them, unhurried, without ever speaking a word.

BOOK THREE

1   'OVER FOUR HUNDRED people vomiting their lives away ... men and women and children, all over the country ... more than fifty deaths already ... the doctors can't save them ... malnutrition has been found to be the cause of this annual vomiting sickness. It is the vengeance nature exacts from them for being poor. ...'

The Chaplain was speaking, looking out through the window, his hands in his trousers pockets, and he might have been speaking his thoughts aloud.

Surjue said: 'You think it's a sin to be poor, Padre?'

He said: 'Yes, poverty is a sin. It is contrary to nature. All things were provided abundantly for man's use.' He turned away from staring out through the window bars, looked closely at Surjue, as though he was trying to weigh him in his mind.

'You saved the church,' he said, 'by your quick action, the other day. I love that old church so much. I want to say again, thank you.'

'It's nothing, Padre. Anybody would have done what I did.'

'Yes. Yes. Perhaps. If they had the quickness of wit to do the right thing in an emergency. How is your hand?'

Surjue automatically held up his injured hand and looked at it.

'Coming along fine,' he said, and put it away, self-consciously, behind him.

'Good,' said the Padre, 'good.'

He cleared his throat, shifted his weight from one foot to the other, passed one hand lightly across his unruly hair.

'I have seen the Governor.'

'Yes?'

'Had a long talk with him about your case. He listened carefully to all I had to say. He was very sympathetic.'

Surjue waited. His good hand gripped the edge of the bed. The Chaplain's words came slowly, jerkily.

'He is in a pretty difficult position,' he said. 'You see, there is absolutely no parole system in this country. It is not provided in the penal code. You must understand that.'

He hesitated, and Surjue said, 'Go on — please.'

He was surprised at the coolness of his own voice.

'The only thing the Governor of this colony could do in your case is grant you a free pardon. He is not prepared to do it on the facts submitted to him.'

Surjue said nothing.

'I put your case to him as strongly, and as well as I was able. Told him except for this you had a clean sheet ... fine prison record, everything. I took with me a letter from the Superintendent of this prison. I had more than one interview with His Excellency. The first time he seemed to be favourably impressed. I confess I had hopes after that first interview of being the bearer of very different news this day. He said he would need a few days to consult with his advisers. He made another appointment. The next interview I had with him I knew we had lost. It was almost as though I was talking to a different man. To be perfectly frank, I did not find him the kindly disposed, sympathetic prince willing to act with graciousness and liberality in the exercise of his absolute powers of clemency. I found him now intractable, brusque, almost evasive. I am sorry, Surjue, I tried my best. I failed.'

Surjue stood up. For the life of him he could not meet the Chaplain's gaze.

'It's all right, Padre,' he said. 'Thank you.'

He said, breaking the little silence that followed, 'I know you did all you could, Padre. Please don't worry about it.'

The Chaplain said: 'I am going to try again. Don't think I'm going to quit so easily. I am going to see the Director of Prisons and get a recommendation for a pardon from him. He can't refuse it. You may have to tell the name of the man who was your accomplice. What really happened is that you just took the rap, while the other fellow, who was doubtless the ringleader, got away with the swag.'

'Don't bother about it, Padre,' said Surjue, turning away.

'You mean — you still won't tell this fellow's name?'

'That's right, Padre.'

'Well, I'm not going to weary you with questions. You must

have your good and sufficient reason. I have not the smallest doubt but that it must be worthy. I respect you for your silence. It has cost you so much.'

'Oh, it's nothing like that, Padre.' Surjue laughed. It wasn't a pleasant laugh. 'I could tell his name now. It wouldn't hurt him at all.'

'You mean — he is no longer in the country.'

'Somep'n like that, I guess. He just isn't around. That's all I'm sayin' about it.'

'All right,' said the Padre, quietly. 'I am going to see the Director about that recommendation just the same.'

'I wouldn't bother too much about it, Padre.' Surjue spoke lightly, almost flippantly.

The Chaplain looked into his eyes quickly, and looked away.

'Your wife is very ill, Surjue,' he said. 'I called to see her three times while I was in town.' He paused, then said more slowly. 'The second time I had a doctor along with me, an old school mate of mine. She will have the very best attention that the circumstances will allow. She absolutely refuses to be removed.'

'She's crazy, ain't she, Padre? Come on now, tell me the truth.'

'Yes. You have a right to know that, certainly. It is feared she might go completely out of her mind.'

'In that case . . .'

'She would have to be removed to an institution.'

'They'd put her in a straight-jacket an' take her to the madhouse. Well, I can't do anything to help her. I beg you leave me now, Padre. Sorry, sir. I — I want to sit down an' figure this out.'

'I can't help thinking,' said the Chaplain, as he sat facing the Superintendent across the desk in the other's office, 'that they are punishing an innocent, helpless woman, much more than they are this guilty man.'

'Of course. We know it. Cases like this often happen. But what can we do about it?'

'Nothing under the present system. No.'

The Superintendent looked across the desk at him, tolerantly, even kindly. He doodled with a pencil on the green blotter-pad before him. He felt a little sorry for the painfully distressed, futile but kindly man who slumped like a frameless scarecrow in the opposite chair.

'Well, it's the best system that human ingenuity has been able to devise,' he said, not without pride.

'Human ingenuity! Just another sophistry. What in God's name does that mean? I'm not swearing. I mean it literally. Can you tell me?'

'Well, I mean this. Outside of those fancy prisons where they spoil and pamper hardened criminals, what other system do you know of that is more humane than ours, in dealing effectively with crime?'

'I am sorry, I cannot answer you. I have not made a study of penology. But I tell you this, we make criminals out of men and women and children in the kind of society we are satisfied to put up with. We are just as much criminal, in a sense, as they.'

'Excuse me, Padre. That is not fair. You use words extravagantly. Forgive me if I must say it, but you talk just like one of those Communists.'

The Padre gathered himself and stood up. He was taut, and shaking with anger deep down.

'Fools!' he said, his voice quivering slightly. 'We are all fools. We are smug and satisfied, and let the Communists beat us to it every time.'

The Superintendent fidgeted uncomfortably in his chair.

'No, get this straight, I am not a Communist,' said the Padre, 'but I can tell you a thing or two. Why do you think Communism grows and thrives among underprivileged people? You sit back in your swivel chair and shake your fist at it, can you answer that?'

He sat down as suddenly as he had got up, and passed the back of his hand across his brow.

He said in a gentle voice: 'Forgive me. I am a little upset today. I should not have lost my temper. Here,' he felt in his pocket, took out a little crumpled pamphlet, it was titled THE UNIVERSAL DECLARATION OF HUMAN RIGHTS. He held it up and thumped its leaves, his hands still shaking slightly. 'Ever seen one of these? It is issued by the General Assembly of the United Nations. Date, March 1949. Already it has come to mean nothing to us but more words in a book. But here it says, on page 6, Article

22, "Everyone, as a member of society, has the right to social security and is entitled to realization . . . of the economic, social and cultural rights indispensable for his dignity and the free development of his personality." That is what it says. And that is the crux of the whole question here, the basic approach to penology in a civilized state. The population of our prisons is made up almost wholly of people who had no other alternative but to commit these crimes for which they are being punished, and what is more shocking still, they will be forced to commit them again and again, each time they are outside. For they have no other means of putting food into their hungry bellies, let alone all consideration of dignity and the free development of their personality. In this country of less than 50 per cent literacy about one-third of the population is unemployed.'

'But my good Chaplain, what are we to do?'

The Chaplain looked at him, and said quietly:

'Sit back comfortably, and fold our hands, of course. Never give the little suckers an even break. Do as we are doing now, entrench ourselves securely behind the defences of reaction, and leave it to somebody else to save the world.'

'You talk like a soapbox politician. I have no time for that. I am just a man doing a difficult job.'

'Och mon! Who is talking about you? Forgive me. I said we — *we* are all guilty, everyone of us. Myself no less than the other man.'

The Superintendent stood up slowly, tidied some papers on the desk before him, to signify that the interview was over. He said, without looking at the Chaplain: 'Since we've been so frank with each other, I'll say this, I think you're mad.'

Surjue lit a cigarette, in defiance of all prison regulations, lay back, with his head resting against the iron of the bedhead, pulled one knee up, let the other foot drag on the floor, and smoked, his face set, staring up at the whitewashed ceiling.

Somewhere down the long ward a prisoner coughed.

What the hell use to hope for a miracle to happen . . . God damn it, he just got to see Rema . . . just got to get out of here.

The veins along his temples stood out on his still face like weals. His face was flushed and hot, it pricked all over with little beads of sweat.

239

From down the long corridor, the same coughing . . . the wind blew under the projecting iron of the roof making an eerie sound.

Outside the prison wall a man driving a coconut cart creaking on its ungreased axle down the lane, cracked his whip loudly above the gall-backed straining mule staggering under the load. The sound of the whip came up to him like a pistol shot . . . again the coughing . . . the wind made *woo-ee woo-ee* going over the slanting iron roof.

The cigarette had burned down almost to his fingers. He crushed out the smouldering end against the back of his naked hand. The smell of scorching flesh seared his nostrils. The set of his countenance, the fixed glass stare in his eyes, gave nothing away.

The Superintendent scraped back from his desk, the paper-knife that he had used to open the last batch of incoming mail still in his hand. He pushed a button under his desk and presently a clerk from the prison office stood before him. He was dressed in civilian clothes. He didn't salute.

'You rang, sir?'

'Yes, Hogan. I have here, ah — a communication. It says leave to appeal to the Judicial Committe of the Privy Council in England has been declined by the Chief Justice, in the ah — Buckshire case. That means the execution will be proceeded with according to programme. Attend to the necessary formalities personally, will you, Hogan?'

'Yes, sir.'

Hogan took the letter from the Superintendent's hand, glanced at it through his bifocal spectacles, looked again at the Superintendent.

'Is that all, sir?'

'Yes, Hogan. Routine matter. No special instructions.'

'Yes, sir.'

He cleared his throat.

'Er — if you will pardon me, sir. About that matter of my departmental leave. . . .'

The Chaplain let himself in through the side door; he suspected there were people in the study waiting to see him. Old Mrs.

Browntree about the Girl Guides' rally . . . Mr. Watling about cricket pads for the Church Lads' eleven . . . a deputation from the Steering Committee about the projected bridge drive . . . Mrs. Whitfeather about her little boy . . . he didn't wish to see any of them today.

Just inside the hall down the end of the passage, he ran into the cook. He said, 'I am going upstairs for a minute. Don't bother about the coffee. Doctor said I shouldn't drink so much coffee, not good for the nerves, anyway.'

She stopped dusting the furniture to look at him, with a sort of proprietory nod of her greying head.

He turned and went slowly, heavily, up the creaking stairs.

The maid, Suzan, came in from the study.

'Oh, Parson. . . .'

She started to skitter up the stairs after him.

Cook called her back sternly, with one finger raised.

'Suzan.' She crooked the finger at her.

The girl came down back quietly, soberly, her hands folded about the apron before her.

She said: 'Yes'm, Mrs. West?'

Cook said, laying a hand kindly on her shoulder:

'Can't you see, chile, there's something troublin' the good man? He wants to go apart an' pray.'

He climbed the steep flight of narrow stairs leading up to the attic, breathing like a man who had just run a hard race.

The attic door was never locked. He turned the knob, and the door swung back quietly under his hand.

He went in, drew the blinds, threw open a window from the bottom. He stared across the tops of some trees to the scarred roof of the old church in the distance . . . behind it, towering, the sheer prison wall.

On a little ledge behind him there stood a heavy crucifix, and before the crucifix an ancient prayer stool. There was some old tapestry hanging against the wall. The crucifix, the stool, the tapestry, most of the things inside this attic, reached back into the past, to the grim old days of slavery. The place haunted him with all its austere beauty and its ugliness. He came here often, alone, to pray.

He stood at the window a long time, looking out across at the ancient, historic church. The wind blew his untidy hair about his head. He put his hand up, automatically, to smooth it down.

Some thin, starved-looking, ragged children came running up the street, laughing, shouting, swearing, skylarking. They had their slates and books with them, coming from school.

His lips moved as though he would say a prayer for them; bless them. He shook his head, hesitating, as though the sense of his own helplessness, unworthiness, rose up like that terrible wall between him and heaven.

He turned from the window and went and stood, dumb, weighed down as with a sense of guilt, before the crucifix.

He said aloud: 'Hów many Messiahs must be crucified to save the world?' and wondered if he had spoken heresy.

The cries of the children in the street were going away in the distance . . . the church bell in its ancient tower started telling the noon angelus.

The wind came in and shook the old tapestry against the wall.

2

THE TRIFLING SPRIGS of chance confound our footsteps . . . the events that make tomorrow quit themselves today outside our ken . . . brother, do you pause long in this square of the chess board to consider? . . . do you wait to log the thousand perils smirking in the dark?

Morning kneels barefooted and without covering for her head . . . kneels upon the mountain to discover the molehill . . . kneels before the toadstool to discover the lily . . . stands erect like a bright drawn blade.

We pursue our personal history without the niceties of punctuation . . . and set up a few stone images in the likeness of our own image along the way . . . discover our dreams between arresting parallels . . . these are the longitudes that contain the ends of hope and desire . . . they go with us the longest way to the end of our dream.

Midnight.

The clock struck the hour from the church across the way, beyond the wall.

The hospital slept.

All except the warder on duty, a man dying alone in the night, and Surjue, lying on his bunk, sleepless, waiting for the man to die.

He hated death as he hated sickness, only worse. He wasn't a good hospital orderly. A good hospital orderly wouldn't let things keep him awake all hours of the night, just lying there hating them, he would get his night's rest.

God! how he hated this place!

He remembered the first day he came here.

And in the midst of all that he could remember Rema. The taste of her mouth. Her breath. Lying on a soft mouldy bank of dry leaves under the gloom of dark trees at the bottom of the pasture. The first time he had taken her. Late afternoon. Under the silent trees. . . .

He had shivered all that first night in the dark, chill cell, without any blanket to cover him. The mosquitoes bit like hell. It was a choice between the cold and the mosquitoes, and having something to put his head down on. Lying flat on the bare mattress with nothing to raise his head a little, he found he couldn't sleep. Funny dam things like that happen. You wouldn't believe it if somebody was to tell you. If somebody was to say to you, lying there I couldn't sleep because there was no pillow under my head, you would just laugh.

You would say, boy you crazy for sure, you want to sleep nothing on earth can keep you awake, don't tell me.

But it was a choice between folding his one blanket and using it as a pillow, or sheltering under it from the mosquitoes and the cold.

He had folded the blanket and put it under his head, and so snatched a few moments of uneasy sleep out of his long vigil of misery.

That was his first night.

The next morning the cells were unlocked all down the line. You could hear the steady rattle of bolts stammering all down the length of the wards as the warders let the prisoners out of their cells with the coming of dawn, and mustered them outside in the yard for bucket-parade.

The men standing in long lines, each man with his night bucket.

Jesus God! the stink it raised!

The line moved slowly along as they went past the big buckets one at a time and each man tipped the contents of his bucket into it until it was full and then they took it away and shoved another one in its place, and the line moved along slowly until they got to the last man. That was he.

Men carried the big buckets on long stout poles between them, hefted on their shoulders, to the dump-pits, way down beyond the wards.

After bucket-parade, breakfast.

The breakfast was brought in buckets, too. Coffee, and bread. These buckets looked the same as the others.

That morning he didn't eat any breakfast.

Later in the day he was sorry for that.

After breakfast the prisoners who had come in the evening before were stripped naked and mustered out in front of the dispensary.

They were marched one at a time into the dispensary while the doctor examined them, and a report was made out on a separate printed form for each man.

After examination they were made to put on their prison clothes again. They were detailed, some to the prison farm, some to the various workshops, some to the kitchen. A few went into hospital.

He was one of them. The doctor had written down on his sheet that he was suffering from shock. Also his ear was bad. It was leaking a lot of stuff.

He didn't see the sheet that day. It was not until many months after. He was hospital orderly when he saw his own sheet. He came across it, with his name and number on it, among an old batch.

But that's how he came to know he was suffering from shock. He wouldn't have known it if he hadn't seen it written down on his sheet. He only knew that standing out in the blazing sun, stark naked, he suddenly had to fight to keep standing up. Things became dark before him. He was trembling all over. He wanted to break out of the line and run. He was filled with a dark, unreasoning panic.

The sun felt as though it was burning a hole in the back of his neck.

They were all bunched up together, naked, like a lot of animals in a pen. In the midst of his panic he felt his shame and his degradation, it went with the bitter taste at the back of his throat.

And in the midst of this he could think of Rema. Rema and himself, together, making love for the first time, under the silent trees.

He remembered the taste of her mouth, her passionate response to his kisses, all the bright sweetness of her, the way she closed her eyes with her head back against the crook of his arm, his mouth pressed to hers, and how she opened her eyes slowly again, and he could see the light golden flecks in the dark pupils, and how the corners of her mouth came up a little as she made her lips ready for his kiss.

And later as they sat side by side on that thick bank of leaves smelling of deep forest mould, far away he could hear like someone *halloo-ing* to them, and when he called her attention to it she laughed and said it was only the sound of the wind going through a hole in an old breadnut tree down by the hollow.

And he listened hard again, scarcely believing her, and it sounded now like someone blowing on a cow horn, far, far away.

Presently she got up and said it was time for them to be going back up the hill to the house. She held out both hands to him, and he made her pretend that she was pulling him up to his feet, but really he was pulling her down to him again.

She lay on the bank, breathing heavily against him, and he remembered most of all the way her mouth came up to meet his and how she kissed him back urgently, giving him heat for heat and flame for flame and passion for passion, as though it was not sufficient for her to lie underneath him and suffer his kiss.

He had always bragged a little about the women he could have had. And all in all it was nothing. An empty boast to utter among men. For all the time there was never any other woman in the world for him, beside her, and it would be like that, without question in his mind, until death.

A low gurgling sound came from down the ward, where the man lay dying.

Surjue got up and went on his bare feet down the aisle to the bunk where the dying man lay.

One look at him and he could tell he was near the end now.

A hell of a thing for a man to die alone in the night.

He suddenly felt he must do something for him.

What?

This man was a stranger to him. There was nothing he could do.

He put out his hand to straighten the blanket about him. He saw that the man's eyes were on his face. They had a fixed, ghastly, glassy look about them. They seemed to be begging him to do something. He couldn't understand what.

What do you say to a man in a situation like this?

He couldn't think of anything to say.

He just stood beside the dying man, meeting his stare.

He felt uneasy, wanting it to be over.

Why the hell should this man's dying mean anything to him?

He wished to Christ he could get it over and be done with.

A hell of a thing to die in the night like this, for all practical purposes, alone.

Her breath was like the good sweet smell of the deep forest mould.

Why should he have such a deep hatred of death?

The man was a stranger to him. Why should he personally resent the fact of his dying?

Rats scampered across the ceiling, making an eerie sound.

One came out of a hole in the wall on the floor by a bunk across the aisle.

Its eyes were like glass beads, its nose inquisitive. It ran out of the hole, and in again, as though it had been going some place special, in a hurry, but had suddenly changed its mind.

The dying man made a rattling sound deep in his throat.

Surjue, looking at him, saw that the stare seemed glassier, stonier than before. As he looked the man's mouth fell open. He knew he was dead, and he was glad of it.

The rats went squealing and skittering across the ceiling.

The warder nodded on a stool at the end of the ward.

The dead man lay with his mouth open. His lips snarled back from his teeth, making him hideous.

He tried to close it with his hand, but it fell open again.

He saw that the man's teeth in front were pocketed with pyorrhea, his upper gums were swollen and scarred and indurated with running, purulent sores.

He turned away, feeling slightly sickened.

With his hand withdrawn the dead man's mouth gaped **again.**

246

Why the hell should he care about this man dying? A stranger. There were things worse than death. A thousand times worse.

They were going to take her and put her in a straight-jacket, and lock her away in a padded cell in a madhouse, out of sight.

He pulled the blanket up about the dead man's face.

Should he wake the warder?

Yes. Certainly.

He went down to where the warder nodded on the stool. Shook him.

The man nearly fell off the stool. He came to attention, settling his helmet on his head.

He even started to say, 'All correct, sir!'

And grumbled, irritably, 'What the hell!' instead.

'There's a man dead, over there.' He pointed to the bunk where the dead man lay.

'Good for him. What you want to wake me for. I was havin' a nice little doze.'

'Yeh. An' the next thing you know it would be inspection. Nickoll's on duty tonight.'

'You damn right, man. Got to be careful.'

He said: 'Man dead, you say? What kill him?'

'What the hell do I know.'

They were goin' put her in a straight-jacket. A straight-jacket. A man on the bed beside the dead man snored loudly.

It seemed somehow indecent for a man to be snoring so loud.

The warder yawned and stretched himself.

'*Yow!*'

He said, 'In this place if it's not one damned thing, it's another. The hell with this prison life!'

He said: 'No life for a dog, let alone a man, lemme tell you.'

And Surjue pinned his lips back a little, and murmured:

'You don't say!'

3   IT WAS LATE afternoon.
The sun went steeply down beyond the western wall. It made long, slanting shadows across the hospital beds of the iron bars that grilled the windows.

Surjue lay on his back, his head in his hands, his hands up

against the iron bedhead. Cubano sat on his bunk, doing a belly-roll with his hands pressed against his lower abdomen, his feet on the floor.

'You blow out through your mouth when you tighten. You suck in you' stomach, an' it roll right up before you,' he was telling Surjue.

'Nice,' Surjue commented drily, 'if you like it.'

Cubano laughed.

Presently he said, 'I can't figure you at all.'

'Awe shit!' said Surjue.

'Like that. Sure, I get you.'

'I'm gettin' the hell outa here.'

'Say what?'

'You heard me.'

'How? You serious?'

'What you think, I'm jus' talkin' to sweeten me breath?'

'You got any ideas?'

'Ideas? I got ideas a-plenty.'

'I know. Mean about gettin' out.'

'That. Well, I been figurin' somep'n.'

'I guess you mean it, too,' said Cubano.

He looked at him closely. 'I'm takin' a chance on you.'

'Takin' a chance on me? What you mean?' said Surjue.

'Lissen me man, you can't get outa this place unless — unless you have a plan.'

'I'll get one. Don't worry. Been figurin' hard the las' coupla weeks.'

Cubano laughed. 'You can stop right now.'

'Eh?'

'Stop figurin'.'

'What for? Who's goin' stop me, I'd like to know.'

'I got it all figured out already,' said Cubano, quietly. 'I been figurin' it a longer time than you.'

'You mean —'

'Hush! Tonight, after dark — when they're gone to sleep, we'll talk.'

'What's matter? We can talk now. Nobody can overhear us.'

'You got to swear a pact with me first. So help you God.'

'You can cut out that,' said Surjue, calmly. 'It wouldn't mean nothin' to me.'

'Eh? What's that?'

'Just don't believe in God.'

Puss-Jook came in through the gate.

He walked with a swagger. He was carrying a new suitcase. Not the old straw one with the belt around it because the latch was useless, that he had walked out with. This was a new, grained leather travelling case. He wore a Panama hat on his head, and he was carrying a supple sort of cane.

When he had left the yard after the fight he had had with Goodie she had said, contemptuously, 'Cho, him wi' be comin' back soon enough.'

Now he walked in through the gate looking like a brand new nickel.

Ras, sitting under the lime tree, watched him going past.

Goodie was inside her room, humming a hymn, when Puss-Jook pushed in through the door. Ditty had gone down the gully to look for brambles to make up the fire with. Goodie alone was inside the room.

The moment she saw him she stopped humming. She looked at him with the expression of a fish that has been drawn out of the water. She had forgotten to close her mouth.

He went straight across the room, put down his new suit case. Took off his hat, looked at it, gave the black silk band a quick rub with his sleeve, hung it up on a nail against the wall.

He turned then and faced her.

'Where Ditty?' he said.

'Down the gully, lookin' brambles.'

'I'll tend to she later,' said Puss-Jook, and he laughed.

He came two steps toward Goodie. She backed away toward the door.

He caught her by the wrist, pulled her to him. He struck her with the supplejack across the broad of her back. The blow made her drop to her knees, as though he had felled her with an axe. She didn't make any sound at all.

He beat her with the supplejack until she was a thinly whimpering bundle of old clothes writhing on the floor. He stepped

249

over her to get to the door. With his hand on the knob he turned and said, quietly.

'That'll larn you who is the man in this house.'

He opened the door and went out into the yard, still carrying the supplejack with him. At that moment Ditty was coming up from the gully, dragging a dry tree branch behind her.

Ras stood under the lime tree, his hands in his pockets, looking on.

When Ditty saw Puss-Jook standing before her, she gave a little gasp and dropped the dry limb. One hand clutched the front of her blouse.

He took two steps toward her. She turned and fled in terror. She ran straight up to Ras, standing under the tree.

'Save me, do. Him goin' kill me. Do, Ah beg you. Don' mek him get me, do!'

She threw herself on him, twined her arms about him, trying to get behind him at the same time. She twined her legs about him now, like she was climbing a tree.

He said, 'Tek it easy, gal,' trying to reach her, to disentangle her from about him, gently but firmly. She resisted him, sobbing her terror, clinging to him with all the strength in her body.

'All right, hush! Tek it easy, now.'

Puss-Jook looked on, a smile of amusement curling his lips.

He came slowly across the yard, making the cane whistle through the air.

Ras stood waiting for him, his arm about the trembling girl's shoulder. He could smell her fear rising up from her armpits to his nostrils. He held himself easily, waiting for Puss-Jook to come up to them.

Puss-Jook stood a few feet away. He brought the point of the cane to rest on the ground. He looked on with that same amused, contemptuous smile.

'You can have her if you want, Ras.'

Ras said: 'Howdy brother. Peace an' love.'

'Say you can have her if she tek you' fancy. High time fo' she to get a man.'

'Yuh words are wantin' in wisdom an' elegance,' said Ras quietly, as though he was speaking a sermon. 'They flow from de mout' of a fool. They not deservin' an answer. But brother, don' try to draw me anger. Go-long yuh ways befo' yuh tongue trip you. Peace an' love.'

Puss-Jook opened his mouth as though he was going to retort, but changed his mind.

He turned and went toward the room where Goodie was.

'What you goin' do, daughter?' said Ras to Ditty.

She clung to him, plainly in terror.

'Is a little beatin' you 'fraid fo' so? Cho, mek up yuh mind an' get it over wid.'

She looked up at him, her eyes big and misty. She smiled a little, getting her courage back again. Her tongue came out, a tip, and moistened her lips.

She said, presently: 'Ah not 'fraid him. Him caan kill me. But when Ah did see him yonder, me heart did stan' in me mout'.'

'Is all right now,' he said, coaxing her. 'Go inside an' mek you' peace wid you' Pa. 'Member him is you' Pa.'

She shook her head, still resting her body warmly against him.

'Him not me Pa. Him is nutt'n to me at all.'

'Hush! You don't know what you talkin'.'

He felt suddenly uncomfortable. He wanted to break away from her.

'Yes. Yes,' she said, quickly. 'Ah tell you him is not me Pa. Somep'n 'bout him, don't know what it is. . . .'

Tansy came down the steps into the yard.

'You got any smokin'?' said Cubano.

'Cigarette? Yes. A couple only,' said Surjue.

He reached inside his pillow and brought out a cigarette.

'Is all right, I won't rob you,' said Cubano.

'Rob me nutt'n, I got another. Go on, take it,' said Surjue.

'Won't smoke it now, anyway, till later.'

'Jesus Christ, if only we could make it,' said Surjue.

'Sure we can. If we have some luck. Man, in a business like this luck is everything.'

'I know. Anyway, we can try it.'

'That's the stuff. You got to risk somep'n. One t'ing, we mustn't mek it more than jus' the two of us.'

'Man, you t'ink I'm a fool no? This here is a two-man team.'

A silence. Presently:

'Christ Jesus! I don't care if they kill me. I got to get out if it's even for a night.'

'Once you get out, man, you'd be foolish to mek them catch you.'

'What I got to do, I got to do, no matter what should come.'

The toilet bowl started up its racket.

'Hear the toilet?'

'Yes. What about it? Don't bother me nutt'n, only at night.'

'Night time I just love it.'

'You mean it's got somep'n to do with the plan?'

'Hush! Tek time. Ah'm goin' tell you all about it. After dark meet you in the bathroom. We mustn't be there together for too long.'

Surjue bent his head near to the window to see what Cubano was showing him. He gasped his amazement. He saw that Cubano had cut almost halfway through one of the steel bars.

'How the hell did you manage it, man?'

'Hacksaw an' file,' said Cubano. 'I got them in me mattress now.'

'How you got them in here?'

'Hush! You ask too many questions. Maybe I laid them like a hen. Fact is they come over the wall.'

'Over the wall?'

He nodded. 'I got friends outside. They come over the wall when nobody was lookin'. Later, I found them. The hardest thing was to hide them safe, but I did that too.'

'How?'

Cubano grinned.

'Piles in me ass.'

'Eh?'

'I had them up me ass, man. Was them gimme the piles.'

'Jesus Christ! You mean it?'

'Had to break the hacksaw blade in two. A pity.'

'Man! Ah jus' can't figure it.'

'Wrapped them in a piece of oilskin, greased, an' got them up, all right. After a bit, I got used to carryin' them around — you know, inside me. Hell, in this business man, you got to take a chance.'

'You plugged the mark in the bar with somep'n ... Say, what's that stuff you got in you' han'?'

'Soap, coloured with lampblack. Was a good idea of yours that, washin' the hospital. It looks jus' like the bar itself, unless you examine it close.'

'Who would think of doin' that.'

'I rubbed the bars first with a little of the lampblack. Mixed it up with some vaseline.'

'Man, you shore do think of everything.'

'Tell you what, we need some more vaseline an' some methylated spirit. You got them both down in the dispensary. You get some of that stuff up here, little at a time, eh? Bring it up inside you' shirt. When you get it here I'll hide it.'

'What you want methylated spirit for?'

'You'll soon find out.'

An owl screeched in the night, flying low over the roof. Cubano crossed himself. Surjue looked at him and smiled.

'What you laughin' at?' said Cubano, gruffly. 'Maybe you don't believe in God. But don't you go braggin' about it, man — not when you're planning something dangerous like this.'

4   THE LIVIN' CLOUDS o' witness come to de sky ... de moon, brudda, is a shim-sham eena prickly-yaller tree ... den you tu'n yuh eye look behin' you, nutt'n ... an' nutt'n de befo' you jus' de same ... de livin' clouds o' witness come to de sky bim-by, brudda ... an' bim-by come peeny-wally stars a-plenty ... no mine de jubba-jubba moon a-mek him shim-sham eena cottonwood tree ... rockstone bruk bear-foot a-pass, *hm!* but hush! ... look up so see de livin' clouds o' witness standin' in de sky.

Charlotta made up the fire, put the kettle on the coal pot, and went on tidying the room.

The sick child on the cot started to whimper, and its mother sitting on the stool beside it wiped its face with a damp kerchief that smelt of bay rum.

'You put a little soda in the mint tea, Daisy?' Charlotta said.

And Daisy, her cousin and the mother of the sick boy and two girl children besides, said it wasn't mint tea she had given the baby that morning but cirace boiled down with a little John Charles bush and coloured with condensed milk.

'The soda is good for the vomiting,' said Charlotta.

'Ah goin' mek some mint tea now with a little pepper elder in it, so put in the soda, half-teaspoon, no mo', an' if that don't stop the vomitin' then we have to call the doctor,' she said.

Daisy did not say anything. She only knew she had no money to call the doctor with, and rather than wrap her baby in a blanket and sit with it sick, for hours, in the waiting-room at the Public Hospital, and likely have to come away with it untended at the end of the day, she would go on trying all the remedies she could think of, or that kind neighbours might suggest. Go on like that till the end.

She had had two other children come down with the mysterious vomiting sickness in past years. One had died, but it was the will of God that the other should live, and now Effie was a big girl, going on six, and always such a help to her in the care of the other two, her little sister, Bernice, four, and the baby just eighteen months, that she didn't know what she would do without her, at all.

The kettle sang on the coal pot. Charlotta made ready to draw the tea.

The sick child cried again, and started to vomit. The mother held him over the pan, and her face showed nothing of what was going on inside her, while she waited for the spasm to pass from that taut small body she held in her arms.

Charlotta, looking over the mother's shoulder, saw that the child was going into convulsions. She felt suddenly weak at her knees.

Outside in the yard Effie and Bernice sat in the sun and wriggled their bare toes in the dust. They drew their short shifts way up their bellies and fell to an interested speculation concerning their navels.

It was the noon hour, and after the midday meal the whole prison was resting. The prisoners were locked securely in their cells, their bellies full.

In the hospital ward Surjue, Cubano, a man named Jerredan and Cuffy, were playing a quiet game of dominoes.

It was hot. The guard, who was up at the other end of the ward, took off his helmet and mopped his forehead. He held it between his knees for a while, and was grateful for the cool breeze that blew against the side of his head that was to the window. It was against all prison regulations for him to be on duty without his helmet on, so that technically he was breaking a rule, but to tell the truth, as long as they didn't catch him at it, he couldn't care less.

A man up his end of the ward turned over on his side and groaned.

They could hear him down the other end of the ward where the domino game was in progress.

'Pass you, Surjue?' said Cuffy.

'Pass nutt'n,' said Surjue, laying down a piece.

'Ah see you' mind not on de game, man. Ah thought Ah did pass you.'

'Wha's de matter wid him, him groanin' so loud?' said Cubano, when the sick man let out another long, low moan.

'That's the man dem beat-up tother day,' said Jerredan.

And Surjue said loudly, 'Play.'

'Pass me,' said Jerredan.

'Pass you, no? You don' pass nutt'n yet! Hm! Ah goin' mek you run like a dose of salts next time, bwoy. Watch out.'

The game proceeded, and talk went on all around the table. Only Surjue seemed preoccupied, his mind elsewhere.

Jerredan started telling them a story about a girl-friend he had who, unknown to him, was the girl-friend of another man. She had left him, but he wanted her back.

'One day him meet her up out Coronation Market Way,' said Jerredan, and he gave that curious self-conscious laugh which sometimes accompanies the telling of a painful, brutal, ugly experience.

'What happen?' said Cuffy.

'Him bit off her nose.'

'Say what, man?'

'Bit off the nose off her face. Clean.'

'You was present?'

255

'No, Ah wasn't present, but somebody see it, tell me all 'bout it afterwards.'

'My God! Man wicked, sah!'

'Him ketch her by de ears an' put him mout' to her face. First people thought them was kissin'. Some l'il gal an' bwoy start to laugh. Then the woman start bawlin' you could stan' outa Grass Market hear her. When him bite off de nose clean down to de face, him pitch her 'way, spit out de nose, so run.'

'Mi Gawd!'

'Man wicked, sah!'

'What happen to de gal?'

'Go hospital. She get better. De man him doin' time still fo' it, though. Judge gi' him big sentence. Well after dat Ah leave her out. She send tell me the other day she have baby, an' de baby is fo' me, me mus' mind it.'

'What you do?'

'Is de man pickney, yaw. Me, sah! Me naw mind 'nodder man pickney. After me no fool!'

'What a t'ing deh a-world, doh eh?'

'True wud, bra' — true wud.'

Suddenly there was a piercing blast from a whistle. Repeated again and again. The warder at the other end of the hospital had his bare head up against the window bars, blowing blast upon blast on his whistle.

Other whistles answered from outside. The sound of boots crunching in quick time across the gravel. Men shouting. Pandemonium abroad.

'What happen?'

The warder shouted: 'Men going over the wall!'

So that was it. A prison break. Men trying to make a dash for freedom in broad daylight, under the very eyes of the guards.

'The bloody fools!' thought Surjue.

He rushed to the nearest window, where he could command a good look-out.

The baby had stopped trying to vomit. Too weak. It lay like a dark wilted flower in the middle of the bed. It scarcely breathed at all.

The mother bent over it, wiping its face with the damp kerchief.

She said nothing, did not become hysterical, only sat down on the side of the bed, leaned over him, looked down into his face, from time to time dabbed at it with the kerchief.

Charlotta went up and stood behind her. She rested her hands on her shoulders. Her throat was tight, as if a hand clutched it.

The child opened his mouth a little and gasped for breath.

The mother tried to gather him in her arms, tried to lift him and hold him against her bosom, to breathe into its mouth. The head fell back across her arm. She propped it up with one hand. She stared down into the still face.

Charlotta reached down to take the baby from her arms. She knew it was dead.

Death had come so suddenly to it. The little mite! So lookin' like a flower it was.

When she laid it out on the bed it looked exactly as though the child had fallen asleep. The face like a dark flower was beautiful, composed, relaxed. Not drawn and crumpled with pain.

The mother gave no sign that she knew what had happened. She said nothing at all.

Charlotta sat down beside her, put an arm around her shoulder, drew her gently aside.

She looked up into Charlotta's face and saw that she was weeping.

'Why you takin' me away?' she said.

There were three of them.

The warders charged down on them, closed in on them from every side, with batons drawn. The men turned from the wall and ran under a savage rain of blows.

They penned them on the parade ground.

They moved in on them with their batons going. The men were like animals, surrounded, frightened, unable to break out of that circle.

They were beaten to the ground.

They fell on their knees, the blood pouring from them, beaten, dazed.

They beat them until they fell on their faces and writhed on the ground.

One man scrambled to his feet and tried to run, anywhere, just to get away from the blows.

'Get that man!' the Superintendent shouted.

His voice sounded like the crack of a whiplash.

They knocked the man down again. He fell with a thud they could hear upstairs in the hospital. Blood went spinning from a gash in his face.

They beat them until they crawled on their bellies like wounded animals, dragging themselves along by their hands, like insects that have been crushed underheel but are not quite dead.

A low groan went up from one of the men. He lay flat on his belly on the gravel, his face down in the gravel. Not even a tremor went through his body, he lay that still.

One man was still crawling strongly, using his hands mostly. His buttocks sometimes lifted in the air as he tried to get up on his knees. But the effort failed him. Then he couldn't drag himself along any further, and only his buttocks worked up and down now.

The third man lay with his right knee drawn up close to his belly. It straightened out slowly, and he lay perfectly still.

'Attention!' the Superintendent shouted. 'Make them get up, and bring them here to me.'

They yanked the men to their feet.

They had to prop one of them up between them. He couldn't hold upright otherwise. If they had let him go he would have dropped to the ground.

'Who let you out?' said the Superintendent, standing in front of the three men with his swagger cane.

None of them answered.

'Speak up, who let you out?'

None said a word.

'Somebody must have let you out of your cells. Who was it?'

No answer.

He picked on one man as the ringleader. He was the strongest, toughest, most intelligent of the three. He came a step nearer and stood directly before him.

'Who let you out of your cell? Answer me.'

He struck him in the face with the swagger stick. The man

groaned, and his head fell forward on his chest. He didn't even try to avoid the blows.

He beat him across the head and face until the swagger cane splintered and broke off short in his fist.

A prisoner from one of the cells cried, 'Shame!'

Two or three other prisoners took up the cry. They were all new to the place.

The Superintendent turned quickly.

'Get that man. And that man, and that. Go take them out. Bring them here.'

They fell on them with their batons as before.

The same thing all over again.

The Superintendent swung round on his heels. His eyes searched the faces pressed against the bars, and swept the cells three sides of the parade ground, the windows of the hospital.

'Any other sympathizers?' he shouted, while the warders were still working on the three prisoners. 'Eh? Eh? Anybody else want to sympathize?'

Surjue felt Cubano's breath against the side of his face. He drew away from the window. He felt sick.

'Just a smalltime bully,' he said.

'Take it easy, man.'

'Stand him up against any of those men in an empty alley. Think how different he would talk!'

'Hush man!' said Cubano quickly. 'In a place like this you don't even think it, much less say it out aloud.'

5 THE MORNING WAS cold and bleak. The man, stripped, stretched out tight, was strapped to the wooden frame so that he could hardly twitch. A bored Overseer and a couple of warders stood by, beside them the man with the whip.

The doctor stood alone, a little apart. He looked irritable, ill-tempered. He didn't wish to be present at these floggings, but the regulations required it. Damn this whole show, he hated it!

'Ready, Butcher?' said the Overseer.

The man with the whip smiled slowly, his eyes looked like he was just coming awake.

'In a minute Mr. Millicant; just gettin' Betsy limbered up.

He swung the whip with its nine separate thongs around his head, and brought it down with a whack, against a grass covered bank. The place where it fell looked as if a lawn mower had gone over it. He grinned, swung it around his head again.

The doctor said: 'Come on, man. Get on with it. I can't stand around here all day.'

He spoke irritably, moved a few paces this way and that, came to rest in the same spot, his hands in his pockets.

The Overseer said in his bored voice, 'Ready? One.'

The man on the frame stiffened a little — not much; he found that if he stiffened hard the cords that lashed him to the frame would cut into his flesh.

On the word 'one' the Butcher swung the cat above his head, took a step forward, and brought it down across the naked back that twitched on the frame.

There was a short silence. And then the man screamed. He had been holding his breath, bracing himself against the shock, but all the breath he held in him came wrenching from his body with that scream.

Great livid weals stood up against his flesh, made into ridges that were broken at the ends, and wet. The Butcher had drawn blood with the first lash.

The Overseer looked at the doctor. The doctor nodded his head. The Overseer sang: 'Ready? Two.'

The Butcher had stepped back to his former position. He took the thongs in his other hand and drew them through his fingers as though he was caressing them. Actually he was loosening them up. He let them hang down before him, giving the whip a little shake.

His eyes were dull and expressionless. He looked like a man who had just come out of sleep, was not yet fully awake.

On the word 'two', he swung the cat up and took that short quick step again.

The man on the frame jerked his head up. As before the scream stuck inside him a little at first, and then it seemed to come wrenching from him, as though he was reluctant to let it go.

When the Butcher came back to his original position the man on the frame groaned and made other involuntary slobbering noises. He made water freely. The blood glistened in gobs on his back.

The Overseer looked at the doctor.

The doctor said, 'Wait.'

He went up to the man on the frame and took his wrist between his fingers to feel his pulse.

The Overseer put his hand before his mouth. He shivered a little. The morning was cold.

The Butcher drew the thongs between his fingers to loosen them. His tongue came out and moistened his lips. He paid no attention to the doctor, the Overseer, the warders standing by, or the man on the frame. He gave all his sleepy attention to the cat in his hand.

The doctor stepped back from the man on the frame. He went and stood in the same place as before, and put his hands away in his pockets again. Without looking at the Overseer he said, 'Okay.'

After the sixth lash the man on the frame stopped screaming. He made those curious, involuntary, animal-sounds only. His back looked like a slab of raw meat in a butcher's stall at the market.

On the seventh stroke the doctor made the same cursory examination. He turned away and said, shortly, 'Enough.'

'But he's only had seven. He's to get twelve.'

'Don't tell me what he is to get. I know my job,' the doctor said, brusquely. He put his hands in his pockets, and deliberately walked away.

The warders looked at the Overseer. The Overseer shrugged.

There was nothing to do about it. They could not proceed with the sentence of the court unless the doctor was present. Those were the regulations.

He said: 'All right. Pull him down. Put him back in his cell.'

The Butcher stood looking down at the ground before him, all the while gently stroking the cat.

6   THE MOON RISES red from out the still water of the bay . . . the hanging nets throw a dark shadow on the beach . . . the serried rows of nets have come to rest under the trees . . . and only the water is unquiet with the pull of the tide.

The dark palms lean over the water's edge beyond the wall . . .
night creeps on shadow by shadow and the world is still . . . a man
sits under the blue gloom beneath the nets . . . he watches the slow
moon rise, and the tide coming in.

The shark-tooth scar on his leg sets up an infernal itching . . .
he sees the light cresting the waves, spangling the sea with moonshine . . . he thinks upon the lobster-pots beyond the gleaming
bar . . . he lifts a spit-wet finger to try the wind . . . and is content,
scratching himself, untroubled by any dreams.

It was Sunday afternoon, and the whole yard slept.

The sun was well past the meridian, rolling like a ball of fire
down the sky, when Zephyr got up, feeling hot and sweaty.

She washed her face and tried to read, but her heart was not
in it. The afternoon was oppressive. She felt lonely and miserable. It would be so nice if Lennie should drop in.

Lennie. . . .

Her gaze fell on the gramophone on the little table across
the room. Lennie's portable gramophone. He had lent it to her.
They had often played it, danced to it. But not since. . . .

She remembered that at the bottom of the pile there were some
sacred records.

She went over, brought the pile of records back to the bed with
her, sat down, took them on her lap, read the titles, turned them
over, checking through them.

She found one with 'There Were Ninety and Nine', on one side.
On the other side the same choir sang, 'Rock of Ages'. She remembered it. It was a sweet Southern choir, she had listened to them
singing on the gramophone many a Sunday afternoon with
Lennie.

She put on 'There Were Ninety and Nine' first. She lay back in
the bed, clasped her hands behind her head, shut her eyes, the
better to hear it.

Manny and Wilfie were just sauntering past the shacks on their
way to the gully when Euphemia came into the yard. She had an
ice pitcher in her hands, a chunk of ice at the bottom of it. She
was going to the pipe to fill the glass pitcher with water. The
afternoon was hot and it made her thirsty.

262

She saw that Manny looked back at her, hearing her come out into the yard, and looked away quickly again.

She laughed.

Poor Manny! The little monkey. Perhaps she tormented him too much. But serve him right, he shouldn't come bothering her like that.

She went toward the stand pipe, drew water in the pitcher, swung the pitcher around in her hand two-three times, listening to the cool tinkle of the ice, looked up, and saw Shag coming toward her from the gate.

She just stood there watching him, unable to move, frozen to the spot.

The choir sang on, as from a great way off . . . 'There were ninety and nine . . .'

He came slowly toward her, a kind of smile twisting one side of his face.

'Howdy,' said Shag, standing before her. So close he stood he could have put out his hand and touched her. She stood motionless before him, held in a kind of spell.

'What you want?'

The words sounded alien to her ears, as though it was not her own voice she was listening to.

'Just to look at you.'

His eyes stared from his head oddly. Gave her a strange feeling of unreality. This was the residue of a dream of horror she had dreamed before. She would waken . . .

The ice tinkled in the pitcher.

'Standin' like a tree.'

'W-what?'

'Ah got something fo' you. You want it?'

If only he would look away for a moment.

'You want it, yes an' no.'

What foolishness was he talking? Why did she stand so still, listening to him?

'I want you, yes an' no. An' you want me too.'

She knew then that it was fear that held her rooted to the spot.

He shifted his weight from one foot to the other. She noticed for the first time how thin and wasted he was.

His hand went inside his shirt and stayed there. She didn't

even notice it. All she saw was his eyes, staring from his head with wide, unmoving pupils, that were altogether visible all the time, like those of a lunatic.

'Don't bother go 'way,' he said. 'I come from far, far. I want talk with you.'

A faint breath of wind blew cool against her face. It brought a curious, fugitive scent from him to her. It was his scent, and not. Something she had never experienced before, but knew now, instantly, intuitively. It was the smell of death.

And he was drawing something from inside his waist. She watched him, almost impersonally, still rooted to the spot.

The gramophone needle scratched drearily, hoarsely against the inner groove of the record.

Zephyr got up with a sigh.

The music had a wonderfully soothing effect upon her. She didn't want it to stop. She turned over the record and started playing the other side, 'Rock of Ages'.

She sat down cross-legged on the floor before the gramophone and listened to it. It made her heart grow big inside her with all sorts of strange mixed-up emotions.

As she sat there listening to it, she heard underneath it, sounds like voices in the yard. But she didn't give it any mind.

The record had a tiny crack across it, but that didn't matter either, much.

'Don't bother try run away,' said Shag, conversationally, 'I want to look at you.'

He was looking at her all the while. Never once did his gaze leave her face. The whites of his eyes were bloodshot on a background of dirty yellow. The pupils were dark circles without any irises whatever. The front of his shirt had dark brown stains on it as though he had killed a chicken and it had spattered him with blood.

'I don't want anything,' he said, as though in answer to a question. 'I have only come. You not glad to see me, eh?'

He put one foot up against the edge of the cistern.

Her hand shook slightly. She could hear the tiny musical tinkle of the ice in the pitcher.

The unseen choir sang, 'Rock of Ages cleft for me, let me hide myself in thee . . .'

The trees in the yard stood breathless with witness.

The whistle of a peanut-vendor's cart went shouting its brash note down the street.

He said the one word, 'Vulnerable', and laughed.

She put her tongue out slowly, drew her lower lip in a little, held it between her teeth. Her bosom rose and fell rhythmically, and nothing else about her moved at all.

'Standin' with bearin' like a tree, eh? Don't it? Yes an' no.'

He shifted his foot a little against the rough concrete surface, as though to give himself better purchase.

Little perspiration pricked and pimpled on her face.

She knew that she must do something. Now. But what?

She let go of the pitcher and it broke into splinters on the flag-stones at her feet.

She turned with a sob, her hand to her throat, and ran toward the house.

Her hand was reaching for the door knob when she felt something strike against her shoulder, close up to her neck. It bit deep into her flesh.

She screamed and fell on the step.

Shag was standing over her with the machette raised aloft. It was stained with blood.

She put up her hands as though to ward off the blow.

Three fingers were shorn off clean. They fell into her lap.

She screamed again, long and high-pitched. And that was the last time. The very next blow severed her windpipe, and the point of the machette travelled diagonally in a straight line across her right breast.

But she was still alive, and her eyes stared up at him in horror as he slashed and slashed at her with the machette.

One blow lopped off the left arm clean, above the elbow, and laid her abdomen open. Her entrails spilled out upon her lap.

People stood at doors, windows were thrown open. They looked on in horror, unable to do a thing, while he hacked and hacked at her woman's flesh in a frenzy of murder.

The scratchy gramophone played on, 'Rock of Ages' . . . women screamed . . . a man's voice behind him said, '*Shag!*' . . . a forearm closed about his throat from behind . . . he was savagely pulled back, half-strangled.

Suddenly all the strength went from his body, and with it the frenzy, and the will to resist.

And then he was sitting down on the flagstones by the cistern among the glass splinters, the bloody machette between his knees, and he was gasping for breath with short hacking sobs.

Women all around him went on weeping, wringing their hands, talking, making strange noises.

He felt this weakness overcome him. He put his head down between his knees and brought up great gouts of blood.

He was dying, he knew it, this was his death warrant signed on the flagstones between his feet, in blood. And he couldn't care less.

7 THE MOON WAS UP. It was a splendid moonlit night.

The two men stood before the steel-barred window stripped, looking out. They were in peril of discovery every moment of the time. Any moment the guard on duty inside the hospital might take it into his head to come down to the bathroom.

They were prepared for such an emergency. They would have to silence him to save themselves. They wouldn't scruple about it. It would be risky, it might raise an alarm. They were desperate, but they didn't relish the thought. It would suit their purpose better if he were to remain where he was, at the other end of the hospital ward.

Having removed the single steel bar they discovered it was possible to squeeze through. But they had to take their clothes off and grease their bodies thoroughly, all over, one helping to grease the other.

Everything was in readiness. They had knotted sheets together to form a rope. The sheets were also knotted in the middle so as to provide hand and toe holds for climbing when they were going over the wall. They had rigged up a primitive grappling hook out of bucket handles. This was tied to one end of the rope.

The other end was attached to one of the steel bars across the window with a slip-knot. A length of string was tied to the other end of the slip-knot, so that they could release the rope when they had completed the first operation, getting through the window and to the ground below.

It looked pretty much as though they would need to have all the luck on their side to make it. But they were desperate men, resolute and determined, they were strong, active, tough, prepared for all eventualities.

They stood by the window now, alert, waiting for the moment to come when they would make their gamble against odds.

The way they had it figured out, it looked fairly simple. It depended largely upon timing. The time would be midnight when they were changing guard.

There was a military precision and ritual about this business of changing guard inside the prison at midnight. They had watched it night after night, and had built their whole plan around it.

Precisely at midnight the new detachment of guards that was to take over was marched smartly down the compound and brought to a halt near to the wall. Almost immediately after the guards on duty came down to the wall and were mustered near to where the relieving detachment was made to fall out and take up positions.

It was in those few moments when all the guards within the prison compound were mustered by the wall that they had to get through the window, to the ground. And that would be the first move in the game. The next was to create a diversion sufficiently spectacular to throw everyone into confusion.

They were going to set fire to the opposite building against the western wall. The plan was to fire the end cell which was empty. That was what the methylated spirit and the bundle of rags were for.

There were some forseeable hazards. These had to be taken care of. The first one was the hospital guard. He would be the only guard who would not be among the muster by the northern wall. It would take a little time for the man who would relieve him to get the keys, climb the steps, unlock the double set of doors, surrender the keys to the outgoing guard, and be double-locked in himself.

It was possible that the incoming guard might insist on a check before taking over. If it was discovered then that two prisoners were missing, the alarm would be given at once.

To counter that they would have to be quick. If they could start the fire soon enough it was quite likely in the excitement and confusion which the outbreak of a fire in a place like this would create, that the fact that two prisoners were missing from the hospital would be overlooked for the first few moments, at least.

The second big forseeable hazard was the guard who would take over the patrolling of the western block of cells. Cubano had given himself the job of starting the fire. But this guard might turn up on the scene too soon.

Well, in that event they must be prepared to surprise him and silence him before he could give the alarm. That would be Surjue's job.

Barring accidents the rest should be comparatively easy. A fire breaking out mysteriously in a block of cells at night would be sufficiently strange and exciting to cause all the guards to rush to the spot. It was just one of those things that would humanly happen in the circumstances.

They would be naturally curious, wondering what could have started the fire. A prisoner smoking, perhaps. A man gone out of his mind in the silence of the night, and the loneliness and isolation. Spontaneous combustion. They would abandon their posts for a few moments, feeling that the prisoners were all securely locked in their cells. They would naturally want to help to put out the fire. If there was any so disinterested as to remain at his post, then he would represent one of those unforseeable hazards they would have to take in their stride.

Surjue could hear Cubano breathing inside him as the church clock struck the hour of midnight.

The relieving guards were coming down from the main gate where they were always mustered. The two men could hear the crunching of the gravel under their thick-soled boots.

A voice challenged. The counter-challenge was given.

The detachment swung out in front of the Assistant Superintendent's office, and across the parade ground.

'Here they come,' whispered Cubano.

And Surjue whispered back: 'Yes. Here they come.'

268

'Help me get up,' said Cubano.

He tried to hoist himself up against the grill. Surjue held him back, pulled him down beside him.

'Wait,' he whispered, 'they'll see you.'

'You dam right, man,' said Cubano, 'never thought of that.'

Surjue wondered if he was all right . . . his nerve . . . his teeth were chattering with excitement.

'As they go past the corner of our building,' said Cubano. 'The same moment they get past.'

'Okay,' said Surjue.

He realized it was the excitement before the race. Like a horse jumping off before the flying of the tape. He felt better. Cubano was all right. He was betting on Cubano. He had to.

They were holding a nine-night in the yard. The three Sisters of Charity had dragged a bench from their room. Dressed in their white robes and head dress they sat on the bench and presided over the proceedings.

They led the singing of doleful hymns to the accompaniment of their cymbals and tambourines, and exhorted and prayed. The people in the yard gathered in a semi-circle facing them. They looked appropriately mournful and their voices were lush with wailing.

'Come down Lawd Jesus an' cleanse the world of wickedness,' Sister Mattie prayed, and the others groaned and said, 'Amen!' They rocked themselves backward and forward and from side to side. Their eyes swam with a kind of religious ecstacy. They rolled their eyes to heaven and beat upon their breasts.

'Lawd Jesus come down out of your high mountain, an' lead us up out of this wilderness of sin,' she intoned.

'Come, Lawd Jesus, come,' they intoned after her.

Then someone raised a hymn.

> Hark the sound of holy voices
> Chanting as the crystal sea
> Alleluya, alleluya,
> Alleluya, Lord, to thee!

The three rose and rattled their tambourines, and half-turned and rattled them, back to the same position, rattled them again.

Multitude, which none can number,
Like the stars in glory stands
Clothed in white apparel, holding
Palms of victory in their hands.

And always the three kept time with their tambourines, making a half-turn this way and that.

And Sister Mattie cried in a high-pitched voice that was almost a scream:

'The stubborn and rebellious generation shall be scattered like chaff. And the Lawd will not let his face shine on the righteous until they have put them away from their midst.'

They all together groaned and said, 'Alleluya,' and 'Amen.'

And then they sang some more.

Zephyr bent down and whispered in Mass Mose' ear, 'Havin' a good time?'

He looked up at her and smiled, and nodded.

'I like the singin',' he said.

'Sure. Me too.'

She sat down on the box beside him, holding on to his arm.

'Bow down thine ear, O Lawd, hear me, for I am poor an' needy,' Sister Evangie shouted in a loud, hoarse voice.

And they groaned together, and said: 'Amen!' again.

'You believe in all this nine-night business?' said Zephyr.

'Child, it depends on what is in de heart,' said Mass Mose, reverently.

And Zephyr said: 'Yes. I suppose so.'

'It's all in de heart,' he said, looking at her. 'Not in de head.'

'Yes.'

'Some people mek a loud noise about it, an' it don' mean nutt'n 'tall. Some have it in here,' he tapped his chest, 'an' it is everyt'ing.'

'I guess you are right. You would know.'

There was a table spread with refreshments. It was presided over by Charlotta and Goodie, but the time for serving them had not come yet.

'By the time they get through they'll be awful hungry,' thought Zephyr. But she didn't say it out aloud.

They had started singing another hymn.

Cubano went first. He squeezed himself through the bars, his head first, then his arms. He drew the rest of his body through like a snake. He didn't hesitate or falter once. He went through the bars and down the rope with the precision and neatness of an act that had been carefully rehearsed.

Surjue was squeezing himself through the bars before Cubano's feet had touched the ground. He came down beside Cubano, and the other jerked at the cord attached to the slip-knot. He pulled the rope down.

They could hear the boots of the guards crunching against the gravel up by the northern wall.

They passed silently under the shadow of the little porch effect out in front of the dispensary, peered carefully around the wall.

All was in order. The place was deserted. At the extreme northern end of the building they crouched down again, close against the wall. Cubano was down on his haunches, working on the bundle of rags on the ground between his knees. The acrid smell of methylated spirit rose to Surjue's nostrils. He nearly sneezed.

They didn't have to speak. Each knew what was expected of him, and of the other.

Surjue was relaxed, waiting, in case the guard should come around the angle of the building before Cubano could cross over to the opposite block of cells, reach the end cell, where a condemned murderer had recently spent his last days, nip around the protecting angle of the wall. He was alert, tingling with excitement, yet perfectly cool, relaxed, without fear.

Cubano got up from his crouching position, holding the bundle under his arm.

'You got the matches okay?'

'Yes.'

'Good.'

Cubano moved away from the wall. He ran quickly, crouching from the waist, across the gravel without making any sound, on his bare feet.

Surjue could hear the guard rattling the lock of the Bull Pen door now. He knew only a few yards separated them. Any moment the man would be coming around the corner of the building, crossing over to try the other locks on the other side.

He took a deep breath and waited, crouching against the wall.

Four blazing bamboo torches were planted firmly in the ground around the bench where the Sisters of Charity presided. Now the three together sang a song to the accompaniment of their clashing tambourines and the others squatted around and clapped their hands keeping time, and swaying their bodies from side to side, and grunting. All of them now.

Zephyr too.

The words of the song went like this:

> The floods clapped their hands,
> Alleluya!
> And the hills were joyful together . . .

Refreshments had been served, and plenty of rum had been consumed. Some of the inmates of the yard, as well as visitors, were still gathered around the refreshment board. There was one there who was particularly boisterous with argument. He stood beside Bajun Man. The two were drinking heavily, and Bajun nodded his head every now and then, as though agreeing with him heartily, and every now and then he laughed.

He was having a good time.

Ras stood a little apart, brooding under the lime tree. Manny came down from the shacks at the back with Wilfie. Between them they were carrying an old packing case. They set it down near to where Ras was, a little apart from the semi-circle of worshippers which was presided over by the Sisters.

Ras, watching Nanine closely, saw that she was gyrating and swaying and clapping with the others, but it lacked zest. She looked slightly drunk. He hoped that everything was all right. He didn't bother pay much attention to Cassie. He knew that she revelled in this sort of emotionalism. But she was strong, she could take it. She never seemed to get too excited about it, and fall into fits. But he knew that with Nanine it was different. He figured that perhaps one kind of spirit counteracted the other. Or so it seemed to be in the case of some. He had adroitly plied Nanine with much rum, around the board, as a measure of precaution.

Tansy hovered around the board, helping Charlotta and Goodie as best she could. They were taking care of the guests now, and the guests were beginning to get noisy.

'John Crows,' said Manny to Wilfie. 'Jus' like a lot of ole John Crows.'

'You dam right,' said Wilfie. 'Bwoy, took a good two swigs o' dat ole rum. Feel it inside me belly now. You didn't try some you'self?'

'Yes. It don' do me nutt'n. Don' feel no different.'

'Bwoy, it don' hit you right yet, jus' wait.'

'You know somep'n,' said Manny, presently. 'Goin' get drunk tonight. Good an' drunk.'

'Man, now you talkin' somep'n. Les you an' me get drunk together. Raise all kinds o' hell.'

'Bes' thing to do.'

'Yeh. Tha's right. Let's.'

'Wish Ah had a drum,' said Manny.

'Wha' you wan' a drum fo'?'

'Mek noise, man, mek noise.'

'You don' need no drum to mek noise, man. You watch me.'

'De kinda noise I wan' mek would stop dem, mek dem lissen to me.'

'Don' wan' stop nobody, man. Jus' mek noise go-long, raise hell, ease you'self, no mine dem.'

'Wish Ah had a big, big drum, all de same.'

'Bwoy, Ah goin' get me some o' dat punch Tansy dippin' out befo' it all finish,' said Wilfie. 'Comin' wid me?'

They got up off the packing case, went up to the table, stood either side of Tansy, close up to her, nudging her to get her attention.

She gave them each a cup of rum punch.

'Have some you'self,' said Wilfie. 'Go on now, lively-up you'self.'

Tansy shook her head, laughed.

'The smell is enough for me,' she said.

The woman in the bed sat up.

The singing outside in the yard made her restless. And the moon.

The moon came up big in the sky. She could see it through the window. And the moonlight invaded the room. It filled it with light, and with shadows. And things crouched in the shadows and waited out of sight.

She picked at a frayed end of the sheet with quick, nervous fingers. Her eyes went roving round the room.

When she could not bear the suspense any longer, she got up and went across to the bolted window, stared through the misty glass at the big round moon.

She felt like fingers tugging at her nightdress. Fingers reaching out of the darkness where the shadows lay on the floor. She felt the clutch of fingers, little and tentative, against her flesh. She wanted to scream.

She rubbed the feel of fingers from one calf with the other foot, then the other, quickly swapping about. She pulled the night-dress up to her knees.

She wanted to put her head back and scream with laughter. She set her teeth against her lips to keep herself from laughing.

The moon looked like a great round mirror set in the middle sky. It could look through her, stare right through her, and out behind. She shuddered, feeling the moonlight going through her, mixing her thoughts up inside her head, turning the screaming terror inside her to a sterile laugh. She wanted to laugh, and laugh, and laugh, like that, staring up at the cold, impassive, mindless moon.

He could hear men snoring loudly inside the Bull Pen. A screech owl gave its eerie cry flying low over the hospital roof. He could hear the two guards laughing over a joke as they changed over inside the hospital; the sound of the double doors being barred and locked from out front.

Then: the crunching boots of the guard against the gravel, the man whistling a tune softly to himself, coming round the angle of the building, taking his own time.

Now.

He was ready to spring out on him, bear him down quickly, get him before he could utter a cry.

The guard stopped walking, whistling, all at once.

What the hell!

He was having a quiet leak against the wall.

Presently the soft whistling started up again. Boots scuffed in the gravel.

Now.

He got into his crouch, on his toes, close against the wall.

Zephyr saw Wilfie staggering across to her, a stupid, vacant grin on his face. She knew what it was caused it even before he bent down, breathed into her ear.

'Somebody at gate wan' see you.'

'Who is it?'

'You go see.'

She looked and saw it was Len.

She got up quickly and went toward the gate.

It made her happy clear through to see him. She didn't bother to hide it.

She caught him by the sleeve and said:

'Why Len, Len . . .'

He grinned at her, foolishly.

'Jus' passin', heard the noise . . .'

'Come on in, Len. Everybody'll be glad to see you. We're holdin' a nine-night. For Euphemia.'

She came down a step and stood beside him. She put one hand under his arm, close to the elbow, shut the other one about it, giving his arm a squeeze.

She laughed, said: 'Come on in then no? They'll be jus' crazy glad to see you.'

'Don't give a dam how glad they are. How about you?'

'Me? Course I'm glad to see you, Len.'

She was going to say, I missed you like anything, but checked herself in time.

He looked down into her face. Words choked him up. He wanted to blurt, 'Christ, it's good to see you!'

He said instead: 'My, you're lookin' swell!'

Oh God! Why couldn't they be friends for ever just like this? Oh God! Oh God!

She laughed, squeezing his arm.

'You jus' foolin'. What we standin' here holdin' up the gate for? Let's go on inside.'

275

He put his hand over hers, his fingers almost crushing hers.

'Look. Somep'n I want to ask you.'

She met his gaze squarely.

'Not now, Len.'

'Eh? Wha's matter?'

'Nothing. Don't ask me tonight.'

'Oh,' he said. The light went out of his eyes.

She said, quickly: 'Let's not stand here arguing. The folks'll be crazy to see you.'

'The folks, eh?' he said.

His lips made into a tight little smile. It hurt her deep down.

He let her drag him along with her inside.

The guard didn't have a chance.

His shadow passed over Surjue crouching against the wall. He passed without seeing his danger. Surjue leaped upon him from behind, his forearm thrown across the guard's neck, choking the cry in his throat. With the same spring he bore him to the ground.

The guard's helmet fell from his head, rolled on its rim a semi-circle. Surjue sandbagged him before he got over his first surprise.

He lay quite still, his face down against the sharp gravel. Surjue lost no time looking about him. He was in it up to his neck now. Assaulting a guard.

He turned the man over on his back. Took him under the arms and dragged him, like that, laid him out against the wall. Right up against it, under the shadow of the little projection front of the dispensary. He put the man's helmet on his chest, folded his arms about it. He lay on his back like one who had fallen asleep.

From where he was he couldn't see Cubano. He had to wait for Cubano.

That would be the beginning of the second act.

The screech owl went over the roof again. Or else it was another one. Inside one of the cells opposite a match flared up suddenly, dimmed, as hands were cupped around it, went out. One of the prisoners lighting up for a stealthy smoke.

He crouched down in the shadow of the wall, and waited. He could hear the sound of his own heart beating.

The big round moon stared down out of a naked sky. . . .

They were lurking in the shadows behind the bureau. And there was little oil left in the lamp. She went across to the table where the lamp was and took it up. She took off the shade and unscrewed the burner. There was some oil in the bottom, but the wick was too short.

She set the lamp down on the floor.

She raised her nightdress carefully above her knees and took a piece of cord that was around an old shoe box and tied it there.

She went down on her knees beside the bed. She was very quiet about all she did, as though she was afraid to disturb something that was huddled under the bed.

She groped under the bed with one hand, holding on to the edge of it with the other. Her groping hand found the old shoe box, she pulled it toward her.

She crouched down over the old shoe box with its accumulation of litter, in the centre of the floor.

She felt like there were tiny creatures climbing up her back. She knew what it was in an instant. They had come around behind from under the bed. She must have disturbed them getting out the box.

She put one hand up to her shoulder, the other around her back and up. She started picking them off as quickly as she could. They scrambled up faster than she could pull them down.

She fought hard to keep herself from screaming.

After a time she didn't bother do anything about them. There was only one thing to do. It was on account of the moonlight and the shadows it made. There was only one thing she could do about that.

She took the scraps of paper out of the box, made a little heap of them on the floor. She tore the box up into strips, laid those on top of the scraps of paper. Then she pulled the sheet off the bed and tore that too into strips. She laid these strips on top of the others.

She took up the lamp which was on the floor beside her, shook it around in her hand, sprinkled the remaining oil on the heap of scraps on the floor.

Then she went stealthily across on tip-toe to the table, where the box of matches was. She picked it up, and because of her trembling was a long time getting it open. It was as though it was

277

trying to resist her, to defeat her purpose. She struggled with it, shaking like a leaf, her terror growing within her every moment.

She got it open at last, and when she struck the first match she was so hurried and clumsy about it, what with the creatures leaping up her back, it broke off short and fell with a little hiss and splutter of flame at her feet. And went out in a puff of smoke.

And they chuckled and leaped on her the faster, and gathered around her feet, and pawed her shrinking flesh with their fingers.

Warder Nickoll took his helmet off his head and put it on again.

The nerve of his tooth wrenched at him, and he ground the rifle butt against the gravel, and stiffened a little, one hand to his jaw, his head jerked up, front teeth clenched and straining upper jaw against lower, looked up at the moon, swore inside him, the tears starting in his eyes, his body from his boots up all bunged-up with pain.

He ground his teeth together, clenching his jaw. The raw nerve tore and wrenched at him, and the only relief he could get, slight as that was, was to groan aloud, like a mule with colic.

Holding his face up against the night, lost to its still loveliness, his eyes picked out three stars, passed them over, his gaze coming to rest dully against the grim wall facing, a hundred yards distant, but without seeing it really, without anything registering in his mind but the pain from the decaying molar that made everything else null and of no account.

He took six paces one way, going toward the Assistant Superintendent's office, and came back the same six paces again. This was his beat, between this wall and that. He was stuck here until six o'clock in the morning.

It was just past midnight.

Jesus on the cross!

He thought of giving himself an anaesthetic by taking off his helmet and running his head against that brick wall.

Cubano reached the end of the building, without looking back once. Going toward the grilled opening of the last cell he took a quick glance to make sure no one was coming across the parade ground. All was clear. He covered the last few yards at a sprint.

He figured he would be comparatively safe close up against

278

the wall, because there was shadow there. Safe, that is, if Surjue had taken care of the guard who was detailed to this block of cells, if and when he should come around the corner from behind the Bull Pen.

If he didn't come around, if for instance he had stopped for a chat, it would be all right too. After he had done his job he would work around the other side of the building, get close up to the north wall where it made juncture with the west.

He pushed the bundle of rags he had soaked with methylated spirit through the bars. He could see the mattress and folded blanket on the floor. He threw the bundle so that it fell in the centre of the mattress.

Holding his hands inside the cell, through the bars, he struck a match. When it spurted into flame in his hand he lobbed it as lightly as he could toward the bundle. It went out in the air.

He tried another, holding it in his fingers until half the stick was ablaze. The same thing happened. The match went out in the air and fell, cold, against the bundle.

About ten matches later, he knew real panic.

Jesus God! The whole plan was going to fail because he had been fool enough to think he could toss a lighted match that way.

He broke out into a cool sweat.

He tried lighting a bunch of them together.

Nothing.

He tried striking and throwing the match at the same time. One of them fell on the floor beside the mattress. A pencil of flame licked around it an instant, went out in a tiny wisp of blue smoke.

He was breathing hard, like a man who has run a long way.

He tried again. The match fell on the mattress this time not near enough to the bundle.

The next one went out in the air.

The next landed beyond the mattress. It gave a nice flame that held for a little, long enough, before it finally went out harmlessly on the cold concrete floor.

Striking a match and throwing it at the same time was not so easy as it seemed. Not having regard to aim. The match fell almost anywhere, everywhere but the place he wanted it.

He withdrew his hands, wiped sweat off his face, counted his remaining matches. Found he had five left.

He was growing desperate.

Oh God . . . Lord Jesus . . .

He started to pray.

His panic lasted until he was left with one match only. Then he took a deep breath and tried to still the racing of his heart.

He heard the sound of boots crunching across the parade ground. He held himself flat against the wall.

The footsteps passed. He breathed again.

He thought about the single match. And thought, and thought. . . .

Sweat pricked all over his face again, and he didn't even know it.

Nanine sat bolt upright in the bed as Manny came in through the door. She had taken off most of her clothes. The night was warm.

She just stared at him and said, quietly enough.

'What you want?'

Manny said nothing. He came across to the bed and stood looking down at her.

She sensed something unusual in his attitude, and fear crept in.

'What you want?' she said again. Louder this time.

His hand came out and caught her about the throat. When he spoke his voice was thick.

'You make a noise, I kill you,' he said.

Her stare grew wider, looking at him, her breathing heavier, that was all.

He laughed.

'That's better,' he said.

He pressed her back against the bed, one hand still at her throat.

'Lissen,' he said, bending over her, his face close to hers, 'no woman goin' tell me no again, ever, when I want her that much.'

His laugh sounded in her ear again, thicker.

His hand at her throat pressed down hard, a moment, and then relaxed. His fingers came down her body, on a mission of discovery, across her breasts.

She lay unmoving, looking up at him with that wide stare.

Flame licked up from the heap of scraps on the floor. She was down on her knees beside it, and the first burst of the fire caused her to start back, throw a hand across her face.

Then everything in the room went bright, bright. And she was alone. They had gone out. Through the window? But the window was bolted. Under the door?

She set her hands, palms down, on the floor behind her. She put her head back, and laughed.

She leaped up. Laughed with the leaping flames. Something came free inside her — something to do with fire.

She tore the sheet off the mattress, ripped it, with a sudden access of strength, fed it to the flames.

They licked out at her. She leaped back. Shrank against the wall.

They crawled toward her across the floor.

The Chaplain reached up and pulled both sides of the window down. Looked out into the night.

It still wore the same mien of stillness and peace. Like a gentle madonna.

He said over to himself some lines that tumbled into his mind:

> Night, night set your feet
> Down softly upon earth —
> Night of our joy's and travail's end . . .
> All the journey and its worth.
>
> And all the gold we got of it,
> And all the dreams laid by;
> Gather, O Night, the lot of it
> And bless us where we lie.
>
> Come with your soft-stepping feet,
> Breathe lightly on our rest;
> O Darkness of the Night, let down,
> Let down — we trust.
>
> Shake out your sable tresses
> And cover the world of men;
> And bring us at the journey's end
> Unto our rest again.

He smiled a little, and turned away from the window, feeling deep down somewhat more at peace with himself.

He drew two fingers down the centre of his forehead to the tip of his nose. He opened his hand and looked at it, and shut it, and put it away in his pocket.

A poetic fancy?

Yes. Certainly.

Some people again came by it another way.

It had a lovely poetic name too . . . a triumph of the pharmacist's flair for word-finding . . . Luminol.

It was not until they were almost unable to stand on their feet that Bajun Man and the boisterous one started fighting. The fight started over something the boisterous one said which Bajun Man, who was by now past the stage of laughing at anything, regarded as a personal insult.

He said the other man was to take it back.

Take back what? the boisterous one wanted to know, because he had clean forgotten what it was he had said.

And Bajun Man didn't remember, either. But he insisted that he take it back, just the same.

So they got into an argument about whether or not he should take it back, and the boisterous one argued, holding on to the edge of the board and leaning heavily against it, that on principle he never took back anything he said.

And Bajun staggered over to him and hit him in the pit of the stomach, with his head. And it wasn't at all what Bajun had meant to do, but he had tripped and fallen before he could put his original plan into action, with the aforesaid result.

Before either of them could get up under his own steam Ras and Lennie, with the generous assistance of others, had pushed them through the gate.

Bajun, sitting in the gutter, concluded the argument by the adroit application of a single, unanswerable, unequivocal and explicit four letter word.

Lennie brushed his hands and came back to sit on the box beside Zephyr.

'Just a coupla bums,' he said.

282

'People like that always start a fight.'

'What'd he want to come here for, anyway?'

'Bajun Man? Ask me something easier.'

'I know the answer,' said Lennie. 'Free liquor.' And he laughed.

'That kind don't know anything that's too low.'

'You said it, honey.'

One of the Sisters was preaching and exhorting in a loud voice thick with emotion. But Lennie wasn't listening. He was holding one of Zephyr's hands.

He said: 'If I don't see you again, this is goodbye.'

'Eh?'

'I'm going to America.'

'You mean that?'

'Yeh. Farm worker. I got my ticket already.'

'Oh Len, I'm so glad.'

'I guessed you would be.'

'I don't like how you say that.'

He laughed.

'Just skip it, honey.'

'I'm goin' miss you,' she said, taking his hand in both of hers.

'Honest?'

'Course I will.'

A woman's crazy laughter went skirling through the night.

'Awe, honey —'

She snatched her hand away quickly.

There was a catch in her throat.

She pointed.

'Look!'

He looked and saw the orange glow of flames through Rema's window.

All around there was sudden confusion in the yard, with everybody shouting at once.

'*Fire!*'

Out of the blank confusion of his thoughts an inspiration came to him.

One match. And the match box.

The two together.

He carefully removed the single match, and crushed the match-box between his fist.

He shredded it out so that it would light easily.

He put his hands in through the bars again, held his breath, struck the match. He put the tiny flame to the shredded wood-chip matchbox. It caught.

He nursed the flame, turning the little bundle of shredded wood chips this way and that. He held it until it was blazing nicely, not daring to let himself get panicked.

Then with a twist and jerk of his wrist he lobbed it right up against the bundle in the centre of the mattress.

The cell burst into flame.

He dodged away from the window, and was round the other side of the building before you could say 'Rabbit!'

Christ, no! He couldn't stand this.

It was happening to him because he was too much of a dam coward to face the dentist's chair. Yet it was scarcely his fault, that, he just couldn't stand pain. The very thought of pain threw him into a panic.

He took a few steps toward the building that housed the Superintendent's office, trailing the .303 rifle on the ground.

He stopped. Turned. His gaze flickered across the opposite wall.

He saw a flame across a grille over by the western block of buildings.

Only a prisoner lighting up for a quiet smoke in his cell, he thought, but tonight he couldn't bother do anything about it.

He took off his helmet, feeling guilty of a breach of discipline at the bare thought of it. He was a stolid, conscientious man who knew the whole book of prison regulations from cover to cover.

He gazed up at the moon.

He thought, no prisoner who was smart enough to get out of his cell, could be fool enough to try to make a break on a night like this.

He went and sat down on the step leading up to the Superintendent's office, and took his head between his hands.

They formed a bucket-line from the standpipe, and broke

the window open, poured water on the flames, but already they had got out of control.

Ras tried to break down the door. It gave, but the flames leaped out with a roar, and he was unable to pass through them to get to the woman inside the room.

They could hear her inside, screaming.

Lennie tried to break in through the window at the back of the room that overlooked the gully, but it was the same. The flames seemed to have enveloped everything inside the room.

Smoke billowed out, and drove him back, choking.

The Sisters added to the confusion by standing around wailing professionally and wringing their hands. They said it was the judgment of God, and seemed to be enjoying the spectacle and endorsing God's wrath with their approval.

Zephyr and Wilfie had gone down the street to summon the fire brigade.

Manny stood like one dazed, looking on. At first he had helped with the buckets, but soon he saw it was little use, the fire had gained too much headway already. He joined the others who were trying to save their property from the burning building.

In a few minutes the yard was littered with household furniture and knick-knacks that had been hauled out of rooms and put out there.

Ras was wrapping himself in wet sacks, to make a last attempt to break into the room and save the poor demented woman whose screams seemed never to cease, when they heard the distant sirens of the fire engines coming up the street at full lick.

They reached the foot of the wall without incident. Neither spoke. They started immediately to put the second phase of their plan into action. The rope was uncoiled. Cubano tossed the end with the hook, high. It went over the edge of the wall with the second throw.

The third try it held.

He tested it again. It was all right.

They could hear the warders busy with the fire. Shouts, yells, commands, confusion.

Prisoners in their cells woke. Screamed. 'Fire! Fire!'

The shouts and screams went echoing around the walls.

The two men lost no time. Paid no heed to what was going on around them. To them just part of a well-organized plan.

Cubano went up first. He climbed up the rope like a cat. He was lighter, more agile than Surjue. Clutching the knots in the sheet with his hands and toes he got up to the top of the high wall so quickly it seemed impossible to the man on the ground.

Now it was his turn.

Cubano, lying flat on the top of the wall, held the hook in position with his hands. Surjue was heavier, his weight might dislodge it.

He took the rope between his hands, started to pull himself up. The hook held all right.

It was easy, he was filled with a wonderful sense of buoyancy and relief.

Behind him he could hear the shouts of the guards, the screams of the prisoners in their cells, the confusion.

Out of that feeling of sheer physical relief, he wanted to laugh.

The flames came creeping toward her across the floor.

They leaped up at her. She shrank against the wall.

She lifted one knee up, her foot out, palms of her hands pressed against the wall.

The fire leaped from the floor on to the bed. She choked with the smoke that had suddenly filled the room.

The crack under the door acted as a draught. It fed oxygen to the flames. She tried to get across to the back window, to break it open with her hands, but the fire cut her off.

She shrank back into the furthest recess from the flames, brought both hands up to her face.

The fire leaped at her, leaped her own height, higher. She pressed hard against the wall.

She laughed again. The last time.

It leaped, fell short by inches . . . leaped again, clutched at her nightdress.

She screamed, feeling its hot lick against her flesh . . . fought it with her bare hands . . . screamed . . .

It leaped up, higher still . . . caught and tangled in her hair.

She took a quick step forwards, tripped, and fell into the leaping heart of the flames. . . .

Zephyr came back into the yard, breathing hard.

She saw Len standing, looking on helplessly, a little sick. She ran straight to him, threw herself against him, her face buried in his shirt front.

Screams of the sirens down the street, way down, long and wailing and eerie.

The loud strident voice of a woman declaiming, shaking a tambourine before her, shouting the name of the Lord.

A woman's scream of agony. Loud and terrible and long.

The last.

Zephyr tried to take a good firm grip on herself.

'Oh Jesus! Jesus! I can't stand it.'

She turned, sobbing, and ran wildly across the yard.

A savage wrench of pain made him jerk his head up.

He alone of them all had not run to the fire. God's truth, he didn't care.

His face came up with a jerk like that, all twisted to one side with pain.

Saw like a shadow against the wall . . . an instant glimpse . . . a dim outline writhing up the smooth surface of the wall.

Without thinking he drew the rifle to him. His hand, of its own volition, jerked a cartridge into the chamber. The butt came up to his shoulder. Without even bothering to aim he pulled the trigger.

He was a dead shot.

He saw the thing against the wall stop writhing. For a split instant hang on, still. Then it toppled back and fell to the ground close up to the wall.

He scarcely knew what to do next, wondering if it was all a dream.

Halfway up already. More than halfway up. In a moment his fingers would clutch the edge of the wall. It was all so easy he wanted to laugh.

He could see Cubano's face above him. Cubano grinning down at him.

'Atta boy! You doin' fine.'

He pulled himself up another knot. Got his toes hitched

around the one below. This was easy. Reminded him of when he was a kid, climbing a coconut tree. He held the stout knot between his feet, pushed up, at the same time pulling with his hands.

He could hear the guards still shouting and yelling around the fool-bait they had built back yonder.

Above him the moon hung like a pendulum in the sky . . . a filmy cloud had just scudded across the face of the moon, made her come out big like that, and bright, so bright she put the stars from the sky.

His hand reached up and took firm hold of the knot above.

He was drawing himself up, and all, his eyes on Cubano's grinning face just ahead of him. . . .

He did not hear the sound of the single rifle shot.

For an instant that is too small to count or reckon he must have felt the steel-jacketed bullet tearing through his flesh, just under his right shoulder blade.

And that was all.

Darkness of night eternal and absolute shut upon him.

He hung suspended another instant, and then he seemed just to let go all he had won so desperately . . . fell back with a thud to the ground below.

He fell spread-eagled on his back, and lay still.

A scudding, shapeless mass of filmy clouds drew over the face of the moon. The stars put out again.

A dog howled in the darkness outside the wall.

He lay on his back, his arms flung wide, staring up at the silent unequivocal stars.